THE WILD ROSE OF MEATH

THE WILD ROSE OF MEATH

Carey Cleaver

HEADLINE

First published in Great Britain in 1995 by
HEADLINE BOOK PUBLISHING

10 9 8 7 6 5 4 3 2 1

British Library Cataloguing in Publication Data

Cleaver, Carey
Wild Rose of Meath
I. Title
823 [F]

ISBN 0-7472-1451-4

Typeset by
Letterpart Limited, Reigate, Surrey

Printed and bound in Great Britain by
Mackays of Chatham PLC, Chatham, Kent

HEADLINE BOOK PUBLISHING
A division of Hodder Headline PLC
338 Euston Road
London NW1 3BH

For my daughters Alison Burberry and Karen Wood
for their support throughout,
and Desmond . . . for all the burnt carrots

Acknowledgements

To my friends Florence Evans and June Tate
for having faith and spurring me on.

CHAPTER 1

Tullybra 1949

'I'm not happy about Theresa and the way she rackets around. I still think I should have a few words with her, Nuala.' Colin Brady looked towards his wife. This latest caper, when his daughter had been seen up on the bluff with some young man – as reported by Kathleen O'Rourke – was a matter for concern. He didn't mind when she went around in a group, but she was too young for such an intimate meeting.

Theresa Brady, on her way downstairs to get a drink of water, paused on the landing, her heart bounding in her chest at her father's words.

'Leave her be, Colin,' her mother's soft voice answered. 'She'll come to no harm. I keep telling you. She's a good Irish Catholic girl. There is more sense in her than you give her credit for. She has been well tutored by us and the church. She knows right from wrong.' She paused. 'I thought I heard something.'

A chair scraped and Theresa had time only to whip silently upstairs before her mother came into the hall. Entering her bedroom, she walked to the deep embrasured window and curled herself up to look out towards the sea. She didn't want to be a good Catholic girl; good Catholic girls never had any fun. She stirred and sighed heavily, curling over a bit more so that she could just see the waves crashing against the rocks by Lafferty's Cove.

Taking the exercise book she had previously been checking, she rolled it up to form a telescope and put it to her eyes. Now she could see the distant scene in better focus. With pleasure, she squinted down the roughly formed tube and feasted her eyes on the grey, turbulent sea.

The urge to go to it was strong but she curbed it, and a few minutes later she reluctantly unfolded the book and attempted to make some sense of the written word. She had exams coming up and she was only too aware that she was falling behind, except in Art, her favourite subject.

Theresa Brady was a tall, slim girl with a mane of wildly curling jet black hair which fell over her face as she bent her head to stare at the page, aware that her brain was not taking in a single word. She finally put it down in despair. She might as well have been reading from the Koran. She would have much preferred to be sketching than reading.

God! The futility of it. Here she was, approaching her seventeenth birthday, struggling with an essay, when life beckoned. She had earned a reputation for being a bit wild, but it was tame stuff when she considered the antics of girls of her age over the water in England, judging by the letters in the 'forbidden' magazines she read in secret.

It was a real bind being a good Catholic girl. Good Catholic girls had a hard time of it. With the parents acting like vigilantes and Father Corke ruling the community with a rod of iron there was little chance of tasting the forbidden fruits of life.

'I want to be Bad!' she cried aloud, and threw her exercise book at the wall in frustration. Bad girls had all the fun. Take Nora Adams: she flouted convention and went her own way. She was considered to be a sore trial by her brother Davey, and her parents tried to pretend she didn't exist, but she was the envy of all when she waltzed back from her job as a barmaid in Dublin, decked out to the nines in showy clothes and jewellery, declaiming that she didn't give a tuppenny fart for any of them. Theresa secretly envied Nora's courage and the resulting freedom. She was determined that she too would find a way out.

There was a knock on the door and her mother looked in. Nuala was an older version of her daughter, but slighter of build and shorter in stature.

'Supper's ready,' she said, smiling cheerfully.

Theresa followed her mother downstairs. She ate sparingly, her mind still dwelling on the awfulness of life in a small village. The knowledge that she was behind with her studies further compounded her dark mood.

Nuala, watching her daughter chase a carrot round her plate, said, 'What harm has that carrot done you? Will you take that vague look off your face and eat it up?'

Theresa glanced up, 'I'm fed up studying, Mam,' she said abruptly. 'I'm too depressed to eat.'

Nuala clicked her teeth with impatience. There were times when she wanted to clip her daughter round the ear, big as she was. 'It's just as well your father isn't here at this moment to hear you say that. You need to study for your exams. Is there anything worrying you?'

Theresa was silent.

2

'We'll wash the dishes and then have a chat,' said Nuala firmly.

The washing up completed, they returned to the big family room and Nuala pointed to her husband Colin's chair. 'Sit there.'

With a heavy sigh, Theresa folded herself into the large armchair. She had surprisingly small, dainty feet, which she curled under her body as she pushed the shock of black hair behind her neck.

Nuala's eyes softened. It wasn't like her normally bright and sparky daughter to be so miserable. She was usually haring around getting up to all sorts of tricks.

'Are you in trouble?' she asked gently.

'Of course not!' Theresa wasn't certain what kind of trouble her mother meant.

'Then tell me what's worrying you.'

'I don't know. If I was older I'd say I was goin' through the Change.'

'You wouldn't be far from the truth,' observed Nuala. 'You're passing from childhood into adulthood and your hormones are knocking seven bells out of your system. If there's something troubling you why don't you tell me? I'll bet it isn't as bad as you think.'

God! If her mother only knew the way her thoughts were running these days. There were so many things she wasn't sure about. For instance, she wanted to know about sex. She knew the mechanics of it all, but she didn't know how to cope with it. How far to let a boy go. How to kiss a boy. Were there degrees of kissing that separated the slut from the nice girl?

She wanted Jack Ross to kiss her, and to be filled with desire, but she feared the outcome. She wanted to wear clothes that would send the boys mad but wouldn't make her look tarty like Nora Adams. She wanted freedom to make up her own mind about things religious and things political and things sexual. She wanted . . .

'Well?' asked Nuala softly. 'Is there anything?'

'No, Mam.' Theresa sighed. 'Like you said, its probably my hormones. My mood will sort itself out.' Where was the use? Adults never understood. Her mam would be alarmed at the thoughts filling her mind.

'Why don't you go and see Eileen for a while? She might help.'

Amused at the idea of her friend, the shy Eileen, being able to sort out her thoughts on sex, Theresa rose and kissed her mother. Once outside the front door she turned on to the coast road and walked towards the sea and her own secret beach. She had a lot more thinking and sighing to do. It was up to her to mark out the lines along which she wanted her life to run. Of one thing she was certain. One day she was going to get away from Tullybra. One day she was going to meet the world on its own terms.

The school bus was late. Theresa was getting madder by the minute. She strode backwards and forwards, making tight turns and glancing at her watch impatiently. Her mood of the previous day was still upon her and she was showing it in her attitude.

Eileen, small and slightly plump with red hair and soft, gentle eyes, glanced nervously at her friend. Theresa had such a volatile nature Eileen was worried that she would say or do something to annoy Pat Maher, the driver. They didn't get on and that was the top end of it. Theresa was not Pat's favourite person nor he hers, though most days Eileen was able to divert Theresa away from trouble – but not this time. Today she was throwing a tantrum.

When the bus finally arrived there was a mad scramble to find the best seats. Pat Maher was whipping them on like he would his herd of cows.

'Come on! Heave up there. I'm in a hurry.'

Theresa shot him a lethal look. She had a range of them. This was the one that Eileen swore could cut flint.

'And you needn't glare at me like that, Theresa Brady,' said Pat Maher with a scowl even deeper than his habitual one. 'I have a cow in calf and I have no intention of losing it because you want extra time at the Tullybra bridge with your boyfriend. As it is I had to leave before the vet arrived.'

Pat was a dour man who had little time for the human race but would lay his life on the line for his animals. He drove the school bus to supplement the income from his small, uneconomically run farm, so that the few animals he possessed could have the best he could give them. It was common knowledge that the children – and teenagers in particular – gave him very little cause for joy.

For years Theresa and Eileen had been of the opinion that Pat ate children who annoyed him. As they got older they laughed about it, but Theresa had never forgiven Pat for the hours of fear he had instilled in her by his sour looks and his veiled threats.

There were loud cheers and hoots from the rowdy busload, and Theresa, fuming at the exposé, sat down in her seat with a defiant look.

'Take no notice,' said Eileen, pushing back a lock of her red hair.

'Is he a bloody farmer or is he a bus driver? He should make up his mind.'

Eileen hated it when Theresa swore.

Theresa continued. 'This country is the only one in Europe

4

where the bus service is secondary to the other commitments of the driver.'

'Now you don't know the truth of that—'

'Here today, gone tomorrow. God send Sunday. That's the philosophy,' Theresa interrupted.

Eileen sat back. When Theresa was like this there was no doing anything about it.

For a while there was peace. Eileen felt her tension lessen, until she realized that they were belting along at a rapid pace.

'We could have him for endangering the lives of children,' said Theresa loudly.

Eileen sank further into her seat as she caught sight of Pat Maher's furious glance in the rearview mirror.

'One more word out of you, Miss Brady, and you'll be walking the rest of the way,' said Pat, but it was noticeable that he slowed down and the pupils, disappointed that there was to be no further altercation between the two, started up with their noise again. When the bus reached the end of the road which led past the Tullybra bridge they tumbled out with whoops of delight and cries of 'See you on Sunday' and dispersed in all directions, scuffing the dirt and trampling the grass on the verges.

Theresa and Eileen were the only two who actually lived in the village. The others lived either in the outlying farms or in the small group of cottages further along the road on the way to Kilgaven. They had been built to house the farm workers' families.

The two friends walked towards the bridge to wait for the arrival of Jack Ross and Tandy Noonan as was their practice.

The bus, which ferried the boys from the school run by the Christian Brothers, hadn't arrived, so they threw their bags to the ground and hoisted themselves on to the broad parapet of the bridge.

Theresa idly swung her legs and crunched on the apple she had retrieved from her pocket, whilst Eileen stretched out along the top to enjoy the thin, but very welcome early spring sunshine, her eyes closed and her body relaxed.

Sometimes Theresa envied Eileen's serenity. Eileen accepted life as it unfolded, and was tolerant of the restrictions imposed upon her by the village and church – the greatest one being the control that Father Corke had over the lives of them all. Now, however, as Theresa looked towards the village with the April sun shining on the stonework, she suddenly felt a great affection for it. In many ways it had served her well. She felt safe here. She sighed. She was never satisfied.

Tullybra was a sprawly village, chiefly due to the lack of uniformity in the progression of houses, pubs and shops that lined the high street. Its pretty appearance had more to do with the style and antiquity of the buildings than the actual layout. Built of stone, they looked solid, weathered and dependable; able to withstand any storm.

Behind the main street, a profusion of tiny homes sheltered from the cold and sometimes fierce winds coming off the Irish sea. The rest of the village consisted of outlying farms, most of them small and uneconomically run in spite of the richness of the soil, for which the area was famous. Indeed, there were but three farms that could be said to be highly profitable, the richest belonging to Pat McGarry, who depended more on his dairy and beef herds for his wealth.

The church, the most imposing of the buildings and the one that the tourists came to see as part of their holiday package, resembled a mediaeval cathedral with its lacy spires and its enormous oak doors.

Theresa's father, the headmaster of the primary school, was heavily involved in church affairs and activities, which meant that she, as his daughter, was expected to set a good example.

Wherever she could, she escaped the demands made upon her, being of the opinion that good works were for when you got old and had to start storing up a few assets for entry into the Kingdom of Heaven. If it wasn't for Eileen she would go mad. Eileen, being of a more religious and gentle disposition, was only too willing to help her by taking over some of the more onerous chores.

Children were attracted to Eileen, and tended to cling to her like little barnacles. There was always a small group pulling at her skirt, clutching her hand, or holding their arms out to be swung up for a hug. They viewed Theresa, with her startling black curly hair and blue eyes, with awe. They sucked their small fingers and gazed at her as though she was a princess. They ran to get her things and shyly presented her with objects that they treasured, but it was to Eileen that they listened, and her word was law. Theresa felt guilty for the way she exploited Eileen's generous nature.

She harboured nasty thoughts about Eileen's mother, a gentle but weak woman who went through periods of being vaguely unwell. At such times Eileen had to run the shop and house, and this meant that Theresa had to help out with the children's functions.

Guilt about her feelings sent her to confession, but once there she became adept at parrying the probing of Father Corke. It had become a game of wits. There they would sit, the pair of them, each in their dark, dank little box, and after 'Bless me Father for I have sinned', the verbal game of chess would start. Theresa knew she had won when the old priest said, with a sigh, 'What the hell am I going to do with you?'

So much for the darkness and anonymity of the confessional, she thought. The old priest knew fine well who was behind the dividing wall; most of the eejuts that faced him hadn't sussed out that he could recognise every voice in the parish. Her heart went out to those who had worse to admit than a few uncharitable thoughts about Kathleen O'Rourke. She wondered if Maggie McCullough realised that every time she shared her bed with Jim Dolan and confessed it, the wily old priest knew who had warmed the sheets.

At last the bus arrived. Theresa nudged Eileen, who hurriedly sat up and adjusted her skirt. Jack Ross walked towards them, a tall, handsome youth of muscular build, with blue eyes and hair like polished coal. He was alone.

'Tandy is meeting his mother in Drogheda so he stayed on the bus,' he explained as he swung his large bag on to the parapet. He looked at Eileen, to see if the news of Tandy's absence had upset her.

Eileen hid her disappointment but she was sick that she wasn't going to see Tandy. She lay back on the bridge again and closed her eyes. Feeling drowsy in the sun, she let her mind drift.

She wondered if Jack was telling the truth. Was Tandy really with his mother? She knew that Tandy liked her as a friend but the depth of her own feelings had gone beyond that. She wasn't sure what it was that she did feel, but she was happy when he was near and her dreams were full of him. She was savouring the thought when she became aware that Jack was having an argument with Theresa.

'I am not going into O'Rourke's to buy you cigarettes,' he said firmly, holding out the money she'd given him.

Eileen looked at them in amazement. She had been so busy thinking about Tandy on his way to Drogheda she had missed the start of this.

'What are you two on about?' she enquired resignedly.

'Theresa wants me to go into your shop and buy her a packet of cigarettes.'

'Theresa! is there any limit to your madness?'

'Jack!' said Theresa, silkily, ignoring Eileen. 'I'm not taking it up seriously. I just want to know what it tastes like. Sure, where is the harm?'

'The harm would be to me. Your father would kill me stone dead if he knew. You know well his views on women who smoke.' He climbed down from the ledge and set off along the road towards the village. By the time they reached the shop he had calmed down and was able to smile at the girls, but Theresa was not to be put off.

'Go in Jack, and get me the cigarettes. I promise this will be the one time I'll do it. It's just one more of life's experiences to put under my belt.'

'Go in yourself.'

'Don't talk daft. Sure Eileen's mother and mine are like a pair of bookends. She would go straight to my mother and tell her.'

Jack sighed and regarded the lovely girl by his side. 'You'll try anything once. You must be a right worry to your parents. You are wild, Theresa Brady, you really are.'

Eileen added her opinion to his. 'One day you'll try something once too often, Theresa.'

Theresa turned her eyes to heaven as she gave Jack a push into the shop. 'A cigarette,' she said, to no one in particular, 'and my friends have me down as a candidate for hell.'

Eileen, shaking her head solemnly, went into the shop, passing Jack on the way out. 'Try talkin' to the moon. You'll get nowhere with that one,' she said to him.

When Theresa and Jack reached the bridge again, they were laughing with high spirits and breathless with running. Theresa swung herself on to the stonework of its wall.

Jack joined her, and for a time they sat in comfortable silence as they stared along the length of the narrow river, both deep in thought. Jack found Theresa's wayward nature endearing and she was an exciting person to be with, but there were times when she went a bit far – and it was at these times that he found himself puzzled by her actions. Perhaps he was over-reacting?

Jack's mother had been nearing forty when he was born, and his father even older. Living with two fairly sedate, elderly parents in an isolated farmhouse had coloured his view of life. He tended to weigh things up, just as his quiet, introspective father would when he dealt with matters to do with the farm. He was aware that sometimes the other lads saw him as being a bit of a killjoy, because when they were suggesting some outrageous scheme he would start to put the damper on it until they cried him down.

Tandy's friendship had been a godsend: his happy-go-lucky approach to life and all things passing was a foil for Jack's more serious outlook, and gradually Jack had learned to temper his attitude. Indeed, he had, over the years, taken on the role of leader, and was highly regarded.

'Poor Eileen,' said Theresa suddenly, jolting him out of his reverie. 'Why does she put up with us? We are a right awful pair.'

'Speak for yourself. You're the one with the crazy ideas. Which reminds me, what will you do if Eileen opens her mouth about the way you ran around the beach and into the water in your underwear the other day?'

'She'd cut her tongue out first.'

'I don't think she'd do it on purpose,' said Jack. 'Eileen is the sweetest and kindest person I know, but she's also the most naive. She may let it out unwittingly.'

Theresa frowned. She suspected that Jack would sooner she was more like Eileen. 'I don't see what the problem is,' she said airily. 'You would see more of me in a two piece costume.'

'You try telling your mam that,' said Jack, but his eyes softened as he remembered the sheer naturalness of that occasion.

Theresa held up the packet of cigarettes and sniffed it. She wrinkled her nose in distaste. 'I'm not keen on the smell. I hope the taste is an improvement. Do you want a cigarette?'

Jack shook his head. 'You wanted to try them, not me – and that's another thing. If you develop a taste for those things you will regret it.'

'Look! Give me a match and quit ramblin' on about it,' Theresa said impatiently.

'I haven't got a match. I don't smoke, remember?'

She looked ruefully at the packet in her hand and shrugged. 'Ach well! I probably wouldn't have enjoyed it anyway.' With a low, throaty chuckle which made Jack's spine tingle she threw the packet into the river where it sailed off like a tiny boat.

The sun was surprisingly warm for early spring. Deciding to make the most of it, Theresa jumped off the bridge and climbed down on to the bank. Jack followed her and sat down at her side, sinking into the long reedy grass. The sharp, spikey ends pricked his back, but he was content. He was sitting here with the most beautiful girl in Tullybra, and he knew that he was the envy of all his friends because of their close friendship.

He felt his blood stir, and realised that he didn't fully understand the feelings that were making holy mayhem of his senses. He was nearly eighteen years old and he was painfully aware of his lack of experience. Of course he'd had his moments of grappling and fumbling which had come to nothing, but this was his dearest friend; a girl whom he respected and admired, and for whom he would cut out his heart before offending her in any way. He sighed. All those bloody years of being an altar boy had done him no favours when it came to dealing with sex.

He was still dwelling on his thoughts when, with a sudden movement, Theresa hovered over him, the cloud of black hair blotting out the sun as she gently drew a blade of grass across his chin.

With eyes half closed she began to tickle him with it. He stared

9

at her, mesmerised, his body beginning to feel peculiar as she leaned close and he felt her warmth against him. He was not comfortable with this new Theresa who was driving his senses into a state of chaos.

'Jack, I'll knock your head off if you so much as whisper to your friends that you saw me in my knickers the other day.' Her voice caressed his mind with its soft and sensual tones as she slowly trickled the words out, all the time looking through those half-closed lids.

It was a few seconds before the content of her statement had sunk in. Suddenly his body stopped behaving oddly and he became aware that her elbow was, in fact, crushing the breath out of him.

'Let me up! That elbow of yours is crucifying me,' he said. 'And wash your mouth out. Talking dirty doesn't suit you.'

Theresa laughed her throaty laugh and he felt his body respond again. Jesus! What was happening here? They had been friends since childhood and she had never affected him like this. he couldn't count the number of times they had wrestled with each other in horseplay, and never once had he given any thought to her being any other than his friend Theresa. When, with a final smouldering look, she rolled on to her back and tucked her arms behind her head, Jack's breathing began to steady and slow.

'Jack,' she said dreamily, 'were you shocked when I took off my dress and ran into the water in my underwear? It was such a beautiful, warm day it just seemed to send all sense from me. I wouldn't want you to think badly of me.' She moved towards him and for a moment he was afraid that she was going to get too close again.

He sat up hastily. 'I'm used to you,' he said. 'I confess I was taken aback but I wasn't shocked.' As he spoke, he made a mental note to tread carefully around Theresa. His feelings on this beautiful warm spring day in April had changed, and he wasn't ready for it. His heart began to pound again as he rose from the grass and dusted himself down. 'Let's go!' he said, with a firmness that surprised him.

It surprised Theresa also. She followed him, puzzled by the shift of authority. Things had altered between them and she wasn't sure why.

'I'd better be gettin' off home,' Jack said gruffly as they reached her gate. He didn't look at her as he reached for his bike which he left just inside her gate each morning so he could cycle the rest of the way home.

Theresa frowned. 'Mam will be expecting you.'

He shrugged. 'Just tell your mam that I had to go home early. I'm sure she'll understand.'

Nuala Brady was surprised when Theresa came in without Jack. For years he had been coming in for a bite to eat and drink on his way home. Nuala had made the arrangement with his mother because of the distance to travel after getting off the school bus. Jack was a fine young man and dependable, with a strength of character that was impressive. Nuala had been astonished when he told her one day that he wanted to study medicine.

'I don't know why,' he had said. 'I suppose it's because I'm good at all the science subjects.' He had looked at her carefully to see her reaction. It hadn't seemed a very valid reason at first, yet when she thought about it she wondered if he'd chosen it quite subconsciously as a way of not having to take up farming – but there were other professions he could have considered.

'I'm sure you will make a very good doctor,' she had said, and meant it. Jack would be a success at anything he chose. He had the quiet, stoical personality for it.

'Why isn't Jack with you?' She asked Theresa now, as she kneaded the dough for the soda bread.

'He wanted to get home early today – something about his mother,' said Theresa evasively. 'Mam, I would like to have a bath; could you delay tea till later?'

Nuala looked thoughtfully after her daughter. There was some-thing amiss. It would be a pity if those two started having problems. Jack was now at the age when he might be getting more sexually interested in girls. She hoped that Theresa would cope with such an eventuality. She was a bit young yet to be thinking along those lines herself, but Jack would be eighteen very soon and she knew boys were quicker off the mark in this respect.

Theresa stood in front of her mirror. The bath water had been luke warm and she had not spent much time in it. Her da was obviously on one of his economy drives which nearly drove Mam to drink. How she wished she had one of those long mirrors that the film stars had. Life would be so much easier. As it was, she had to stand on a stool to see the bottom half of her body, so could only see herself in two sections. She couldn't be certain if the top half was in keeping with the bottom.

She was reasonably pleased with what she could see. Her breasts were on the small side – but better that than look like Molly Murphy with her swinging half-inflated balloons. Her bum stuck out a bit far, but her stomach was flat and firm. She had dancer's legs, long and shapely like Mam's. Wasn't it great that she hadn't inherited her da's knobbly knees and skinny ankles.

God! he looked a terror in a pair of shorts. Mam refused to be seen out with him if he wore them, remarking that he was a total embarrassment.

There was a knock on the door and Eileen's voice called out.

'It's me. Your da told me to come up.'

Theresa opened the door and Eileen shrieked. 'My God! You're naked.'

'So I am,' said Theresa in mock horror. 'What is more awful, I was born that way.' She dragged Eileen into the room and closed the door. 'Eileen O'Rourke. Will you get yourself in here before m'da comes up to see what is goin' on, with you squealin' like a demented Banshee. Why wouldn't I be naked? I've only just climbed out of the bath.'

'I couldn't walk around naked for all to see,' Eileen said, averting her eyes from Theresa's pubic area which was lushly carpeted and curly.

'Don't be daft. You don't mind displaying your arms and legs or your face, so why should the middle bit present problems?'

Eileen didn't answer, but sat on the bed and held one of the pillows across her knees, clinging to it defensively.

The action had not escaped Theresa's notice. 'You'll tell me next that you bathe with a shift on,' she remarked.

'Of course I don't – I just don't see the need to flaunt my nakedness.'

Theresa fiddled with her hairbrush. She wondered why was it that the sight of the naked body sent people into shock. Catholic girls in particular set great store in covering themselves from neck to knee. The few who didn't were regarded as mildly indecent and ran the risk of being treated in an offhand way by the boys.

'I can never understand why nuns do it,' she mused aloud.

'Do what?' asked Eileen, startled.

'Bathe with a shift on. After all, God made us in his own image, so they tell us – so why be ashamed to look at something he created?'

'I think it's to do with sex,' whispered Eileen, wriggling in embarrassment.

Theresa snorted. 'Rubbish! I've a strong belief that nakedness has little to do with sex. A woman can look more sensual half clothed than completely naked – look at Jane Russell. How you arrange your clothing and what you wear is the deciding factor.'

'You had better not let Father Corke know how you feel. You could be excommunicated.' Eileen sometimes wondered if Theresa was all there. She had some very odd views.

Theresa laughed and, putting on her dressing gown, she sat on the bed beside her friend. 'What are you doing here anyway. You

12

should be on the way to the catechism class.'

'It has been cancelled due to mumps.' Eileen paused. 'I – I wanted to tell you I won't say a word about Jack Ross seeing you in your knickers and bra the other day. That was a bad thing you did. You must promise me that you won't do it again. I know you meant no harm, but it isn't right to do—'

Theresa laughed. 'Don't be so prim and prissy, Eileen. You should hear yourself. No decent man worth his salt will look at you twice, and you will end up with somebody like Davey Adams.'

'Now that is a wicked and spiteful thing to say; Davey Adams is riddled with acne. Do you really think that?' There was a tremor in her voice.

Theresa showed no mercy. 'I do. Personally I have no objection to his acne – time and medication will cure that – but he is a bad article.'

'Well! I thought I'd let you know you could rely on me. I've been trying to pluck up courage to say it for days now.'

'I know you wouldn't tell a soul, just as I know that Jack won't be telling his friends either.' Theresa smiled at the somewhat chastened Eileen.

'Speaking of Jack,' Eileen said, 'why did you ask him to get you a packet of cigarettes? You don't smoke.'

'I still don't.' Theresa grinned. 'We didn't have a match between us so I threw the packet in the river. Don't I do the daftest things?'

'That's for sure. You have never improved on the sense you were born with.'

Eileen waited patiently while Theresa went to the bathroom to dress. Her thoughts turned to the dance which was to be held in the parish hall in two weeks' time. There wasn't a lot to do in Tullybra until the summer season began, when visitors from the nearby towns would descend on the village to see the church and visit the beach half a mile up the road. Until then the highlight was the fortnightly dance.

She hoped that Tandy Noonan would be there. He didn't always come, and for her those nights were a washout. She wanted Tandy to notice her for herself and not just as one of the group. Maybe, with her new dress, she stood a fair chance, it being blue and filmy – Tandy was very fond of blue.

'I'm looking forward to the dance next Saturday week, are you?' she called to Theresa.

Theresa put her head round the door. 'Only because there's nothing else to compete with it. Young Father Touhey will be prowling around as usual, trying to keep the lads in check and us off their knees. Mind you it will be fun keeping him busy and turning the poor man's brain trying to keep us from straying.'

'Better him than Father Corke,' remarked Eileen. 'He would be writin' a letter to the Pope sending us to hell and damnation for our sins.'

Theresa laughed, less at what her friend had said than at the fact that Eileen had the temerity to utter such a statement without crossing herself for the blasphemy of it.

'Do you want to do anything this evening?' Eileen asked.

'I thought we might go up to the club. There isn't a lot else to do.'

Eileen stood up. 'I'll be waiting for you then.' She went downstairs, called goodbye to Theresa's mother and made her way home. No doubt her own mother would be fussing round her da and she would have to get her own tea. Not that she minded doing that, but the contrast with Theresa's mother buttering hot soda bread to go with a green salad and cooked ham made her feel envious. May God forgive me for making such a comparison, she thought, and was determined to kneel longer at her prayers tonight to atone.

As Theresa passed the kitchen door that evening, Nuala said, 'Be good and bless yourself on the way out.' She stopped what she was doing and thought how much she'd miss her daughter when she went to university. If Sister Immaculata was to be believed there would be no reason why Theresa wouldn't go. Nuala would worry of course; she knew how headstrong Theresa could be – and naive. Those who saw the out-going madcap didn't always recognise the innocent girl beneath. She hoped the level-headed Eileen would be able to go with Theresa; they had been friends since pram days, for Eileen's mother and her had given birth within days of each other. Eileen had a restraining effect on her wilful girl, but she feared the chances of Eileen reaching university were slim. She was clever enough, but she didn't have the keen brain that Theresa had.

Nuala frowned. Lately she had been feeling annoyed with Eileen's mother. She hated the way Kathleen kowtowed to her husband who in turn spoiled her, to the detriment of their relationship with poor Eileen who was a saint. It was well known that most of the time Eileen had to fend for herself. Her parents were wrapped up in each other to the point where they forgot their daughter's emotional needs, although Nuala didn't think that Eileen even noticed. Materialistically she wanted for nothing, but the girl spent as much time with Nuala and her family as her own. It had always been so and had become a way of life, but she sometimes felt like hitting Kathleen for her total lack of insight. She made a mental note to invite Eileen to go to Kilgaven with them. She loved the big, bustling market town.

Colin walked in from the garden where he had gone to smoke his pipe, which was a bone of contention between them – Nuala didn't like him smoking indoors.

'Was that our Theresa on her way out?' Colin lowered himself into his favourite chair and gave a satisfied sigh. He liked nothing better than to be sitting here with the radio blaring out and his wife pottering around doing her chores.

Nuala looked at him. 'How many children do we have? You know it was Theresa, just as I know, Colin Brady, that you stayed out there till she had gone.'

Colin shifted uneasily. 'Why would I do that?'

Nuala smiled. 'Because you might let slip that you know about her being up on the bluff with some young man.'

'It was decided I wouldn't tackle her.'

'You are cross about it and you were afraid you'd say something all the same and start a war.'

Nuala sneaked a glance at him as he retreated behind his paper. She knew Colin Brady inside out. His conscience was bothering him. Never a man to shirk his duty under normal circumstances, when it came to his daughter he had a tough time acting the heavy father. Nuala knew he had gone into the garden to avoid a confrontation. He adored the girl.

Theresa felt dizzy after finishing her drink, unaware that Davey Adams had added gin to the orange squash. Eileen, with her delicate taste buds, had been the first to notice.

'I'm not keen on this juice,' she'd said, putting her glass down hurriedly.

The rest of them were gulping the iced liquid down at a rate of knots and noticed nothing. Theresa, having finished a jiving session with Seamus Brannigan, had a dire thirst, and the cold liquid hardly touched the sides of her throat on the way down. It was only when Eileen mentioned the odd taste that she realized the slight dizziness she felt was not due to the frenetic style of dance.

Davey denied it at first. 'I would be made to do that with Father Touhey keeping an eye on everyone. Anyway, where would I get the drink from?'

'Your sister is a barmaid. She could have got it for you,' suggested Theresa, now feeling very muzzy. She grabbed Eileen's arms.

Davey sidled away from the advancing youths. 'I'll have a word with Father Corke about this. You'd better keep your hands off me. I never touched the drinks.'

The lie of it was discovered when three of the group upended him and the empty bottle fell out of his jacket. Davey's face, reddened by the heat in the hall, looked more scarred than usual and someone mentioned the possibility of adding one more crater to it.

For Theresa and Eileen, the evening had ended there. It hadn't been a great one anyway, as Jack and Tandy had not turned up. Theresa had been surprised at this. Jack had not said he wouldn't be at the club that evening. She wondered unhappily if, in spite of what he had said that afternoon, he had been upset by her behaviour.

'Do you think Tandy is out with Nora Adams?' Eileen asked.

'Don't be daft,' gasped Theresa, hanging on to the wall as they hit the fresh air. She moaned. 'I'll kill that shite Davey Adams. I drank a gallon of that stuff.'

Eileen looked with concern at her chalk-white face, which showed up even whiter in the moonlight, framed as it was by the wealth of blue-black hair. Grabbing her arm she said, 'I'll come home with you and we will have a cup of strong, black tea.' Eileen thanked the good God that she had only taken a few sips of her drink.

'The parents are in bed. That's a bit of luck,' whispered Theresa wanly as they made their way to the kitchen.

'Sit there and don't move,' ordered Eileen. 'I'll put the kettle on.'

Theresa's voice was strained, but she managed to say fiercely, 'Will you keep your voice down? My parents are only asleep, not dead! If m'da finds me like this it's goodbye freedom.'

'Sure it wasn't your fault,' said Eileen, busy with mugs and tea. She glanced at Theresa who was cradling her face in her hands, her fingers gently massaging her temple. She really envied her those slim, tapered fingers; her own were like eight boiled chipolatas. In fact, she envied her friend's looks altogether. Theresa had the lot: a lean, elegant body, great legs, and hair you would kill for. Eileen handed her the mug of tea. 'You'll be all right after you drink this,' she said, and settled down to sip her own.

Theresa was grateful for the silence and the companionship. All their lives, when she had got herself into trouble with her thoughtless behaviour, Eileen had been there to smooth the path. There was a bond between them that she felt could never be broken. She was as close to Eileen as if she were her sister. Closer, in fact, because there was not the rivalry and jealousy between

16

them that was sometimes present between siblings.

When Eileen had gone, Theresa went up to bed. Still dizzy from the spiked drink she expected to fall asleep immediately, but it didn't happen. Her thoughts were whirling around. She recalled how disgusted Eileen had been the day she had run into the sea in her underwear. When she had emerged, dripping, Jack had given her his handkerchief. 'You'll have to make do with that,' he had grinned.

She had laughed as she took the small square of cotton from him. 'I'll need more than this. Turn your back; I'm going to strip. I'll put my underwear in my satchel and dry it off at home.'

Eileen had walked off, her face red with embarrassment, and Theresa had stepped out of her knickers and bra, facing Jack some minutes later, her hair wet and her uniform clinging to her damp body.

'You look like a drowned kitten,' he had remarked, and then he put his arm round her shoulders fondly as they walked towards the village and home.

CHAPTER 2

At mass, Theresa sat stiffly between her parents. Her headache was now just a mild throb and she felt more able to cope with whatever the day had in store. Her father was taking the collection this morning, which meant that he was even more conscious of his standing in the community than usual. Theresa knew that if she so much as turned her head she would get an elbow in her ribs and one of her father's more severe looks.

Colin was not a fanatically religious man – not like Eileen's father, who was so aware of his holiness he considered himself on a par with the angel Gabriel himself. Poor Eileen squirmed with embarrassment whenever Victor O'Rourke sounded off like an evangelist over one of their misdemeanours. No! Theresa's father was pretty decent about things, but he was nevertheless very strict about respect and general behaviour in God's house.

Her mother was kneeling with bowed head, frantically worrying her rosary beads and mouthing silently with eyes shut. There would be a few more souls in repose now. Risking a slow turn to see if Eileen was in the family's usual seat in the middle aisle, Theresa winced at the expected nudge from her father's elbow. He gave her a black frown which boded ill if she moved one more time.

'Have you no prayers to say?' he mouthed at her. She obediently knelt forward. Like many of her friends, she paid lip service to the offering of the Mass, rising with the congregation and genuflecting on cue. Not that she meant any disrespect. She said her prayers nightly and she never missed mass or devotion, but sometimes the temptation to let her glance roam was irresistible. Her mind had long ago become sated with the splendour of the interior of the church and its beautiful carvings.

The altar in particular was a dream of intricate design with its columns and carving of the Last Supper. The two smaller altars at the ends of the side aisles were separated by enormous marble pillars and were as elaborately designed as the main one. She preferred them for their shadowed intimacy. It was here that she

19

would try to come to terms with the person that she was and sometimes wished she was not.

The white satin cloth which draped the main altar bore the initials for I HAVE SUFFERED, embroidered large in gold thread; the words filled her with sadness for the man who died so long ago for mankind. She felt ashamed for her lack of fervour, when he had made the ultimate sacrifice.

She caught sight of white high-heeled shoes where Biddy Devlin was kneeling two seats ahead in the middle aisle. She was wearing a white hat and a pair of white gloves. The only relief was the pattern of red roses galloping across the white dress. Biddy was not known for her good taste. It was only April.

Theresa smothered a giggle as she saw Biddy swipe frantically at an unseen insect. If it was summer she'd risk being stung to death. Aware that her father was frowning disapprovingly at her she hurriedly bowed her head. At the appropriate moment she struck her breast with a lightly clenched fist and murmured in tune with the congregation: '*Mea Culpa, Mea Culpa, Mea Maxima Culpa.*' She had no great idea of its meaning. Sister Anunciata would kill her if she ever found out.

She was in two minds whether to receive holy communion, as she hadn't been to confession for over a month. She decided not to risk her father's displeasure so, stifling her feeling of unworthiness, she joined the long queue.

Seeing Mary McGrath in the opposite aisle dispersed her doubts. Theresa knew that Mary was having a whirl with Tom Nolan who worked for Pat McGarry. She had caught sight of them kissing when she had been walking on the hill.

There was a prod in her back and she realized she had reached Father Touhey, the younger priest.

'*Corpus Domini Nostra, Jesu Christi, Custodiat Animam Tuam . . .*'

'Amen,' she whispered, and put out her tongue to receive the Eucharist. One of these days he would knock her teeth down her throat with his heavy handedness. To atone for her impious thoughts she continued to kneel when the priest and the congregation, with a concerted, noisy shuffle, sat back on their seats for the moment of quiet contemplation.

The young people collected in their own group after mass to make the arrangements for the day, but no one seemed able to decide what to do. They argued like pixies at a fair until at last it was decided that, in spite of a fresh breeze, a picnic down by Lafferty's Cove was the best option.

'I still say it isn't warm enough yet for a picnic. The wind coming off the sea will be crucifyingly cold.' The speaker, a bespectacled youth called James Toomey, gave a theatrical shudder. It was well known that James wore a vest the whole of the summer – because as a baby he had croup very badly – so there was scant notice taken of his prognostications now, apart from someone remarking *sotto voce*: 'Once a sissy, always a sissy.'

'You could always cuddle up to one of the girls,' laughed Tandy Noonan. 'Is there any girl willin' to keep James warm?'

'I'll keep you warm, Tandy,' called out Nora Adams. It was common knowledge that Nora doted on Tandy and would have had her eye teeth extracted without an anaesthetic for a date with him. She was well in advance of the other girls in this respect, not having had much of an example set her by her older sister, who had been away with boys at an early age. Her brother Davey eyed her furiously. First Cassie and now Nora making an exhibition of herself over boys. He was sorely tried by his family, he really was.

Theresa didn't notice how Eileen had reacted to this blatant piece of flirting; she was watching Jack as he stood apart from the group. Since the scene by the bridge he had been behaving oddly. The intimacy they had shared in their friendship was suddenly missing. Not once had he looked in her direction since they had gathered outside the church, in spite of the smile she had treated him to on the way out.

'What about you, Jack?' she called to him. 'Have you any thoughts on what we should do?'

Startled from his reverie, Jack said, 'Ah, no – no! I'm not able to come. I'm going to visit the grandparents in Dublin.'

'You rarely go to see your grandparents. Why today?' asked a puzzled Tandy. 'You never mentioned it.'

Jack looked sheepish. 'I haven't been to see them for a long time. I couldn't say no to the parents. Look! I'll see you all tomorrow. Enjoy yourselves.'

As he walked away he heard Theresa say in a low voice, 'Well now, Tandy! Perhaps I could offer to keep you warm should the breeze prove too much for you.' There was laughter, and Jack winced as he heard Tandy's whoop of delight.

Sitting astride a stile a couple of fields away from home, Jack hooked his feet round the bottom bar. His heart was sore, and he put the blame fairly and squarely on Tandy for that. Tandy was the one who encouraged him to have his first 'golden explosion' with Bernadette Lynch.

Bernadette! Hah, that was a laugh. St Bernadette should know what her namesake got up to. Tandy's description of his own golden moment had not happened with him. In fact it was a bloody disaster, and as for setting him up as a confident man, the

21

occasion had rendered him an emotional mess. What chance did he have with a vital, beautiful girl like Theresa, when he had failed so miserably with Bernadette Lynch, who had had little to offer but her willingness to experiment? Thank God she had no idea where he lived. She was a girl Tandy had met in Drogheda when they had gone to a dance there. Tandy, in spite of his bumbling, good natured ways, was not a fool. 'Don't let on where you live,' he had warned him.

She had tried hard enough to find out. In spite of the fact that Jack had made a cod's ass of himself trying to perform, she had taken a notion for him and he'd had one hell of a time extricating himself from the situation. In the end he had told her that he lived over McGinty's pub in O'Connell Street in Dublin. Some poor bastard was going to get into trouble if she turned up. He just hoped it wasn't a married man. The thought gave him nightmares. He wished he hadn't told her that lie. He climbed heavily from the stile and set off home.

The day promised to be a long one. He was very fond of his granny, but an afternoon of family gossip and one of his granny's massive country teas was calculated to give him mental and physical indigestion. He'd give anything to be going to Lafferty's Cove with the others. He kicked the long meadow grass in his frustration. It wasn't that he didn't trust him, but he knew how Tandy felt about Theresa.

Jack would have felt less unhappy if he could have known Theresa's thoughts.

Theresa had been hurt by Jack's lame excuse to cry off going on the picnic. She was certain that it was a spur of the moment decision to go with his parents to Dublin. In all the years she had known and fought and loved Jack as a friend, he had never treated her like this.

She blanched at the thought that he might have lost all respect for her following the incident on the beach, although he had laughed heartily at the time, especially when Eileen had berated her for her 'badness' in stripping off. He had taken her side, and Eileen had been quite upset at his championship.

Only vaguely conscious of the noise and laughter behind her, she slowly walked along the beach, unaware that she was being followed. She stood by the water's edge to enjoy the sensation of the soft, wet sand squidging between her toes, revelling in the feel and texture against her skin, and the freedom from wearing stockings and shoes. Eventually she moved across to higher ground and sat down, hugging her knees and resting her chin on her arm. She started as she heard Tandy's voice.

22

'You jump easily. I saw you set off and wondered if you would like some company. That lot are getting a bit out of hand.' He nodded his head towards the group who were noisily chasing each other and chucking sand around.

Theresa smiled ruefully at Tandy's insensitivity. It wouldn't have occurred to him that she had walked away from the group because she wanted to be alone.

He sat down beside her, his cheery face split by a wide grin, soft brown eyes regarding her anxiously. Of all the boys she knew, he was undoubtedly the handsomest, but he lacked Jack's magnetic quality. He reminded her of a large St Bernard dog she'd seen once. Handsome, lovable, and totally devoid of guile, relying on charm and lolloping good nature to see him through. He was popular with everyone. She had a great fondness for him and was aware of his regard for her, but unlike Jack, he would never in this world understand her. He would be shocked at the ideas and thoughts that rumbled around in her head, for Tandy could be surprisingly prudish about a woman's behaviour.

She wondered what he would think if he knew that when things got too much for her she would dive, naked, into the surf, to feel that joyous satisfaction as the biting cold waves hit her body, buffeting her about as though she were a rag doll.

Tandy nudged her playfully. 'I have left my jacket behind. You said you would keep me warm.'

She laughed at his bumbling attempt at chatting her up. 'It's warm enough to paddle, Tandy. Get along with you.'

A voice hailed them. A distant figure was waving a cloth. It was Eileen.

'That's that then,' sighed Tandy with mock sorrow. 'If you're not going to keep me warm then sure we might as well go back and eat.' He held out his hand and pulled her to her feet.

Saturday was market day in Kilgaven. Nuala kept the promise she had made to herself and asked Eileen if she would like to come. Eileen was delighted.

'Wear your blue dress and those medium-heeled shoes – and bring some make-up,' Theresa whispered over the phone.

'Sure we're only goin' to Kilgaven market. What do we need to dress up for?'

'Do as I say,' hissed Theresa. 'The parents are going for the market, but we have other plans.'

Eileen bit her lip. One of these days Theresa would get the pair of them hanged. She didn't have the heart for the escapades that Theresa got her involved in. She spent more time on her knees asking for forgiveness than sitting on her backside. The trouble

23

with her was, she didn't have the courage to refuse. Theresa had a gift for making it seem just a bit of fun. It was true that she usually managed to extricate them with her silver tongue, but one day there was going to be retribution. Because of this, Eileen entered into all their antics with a dire feeling of trepidation.

'Mam is coming,' said Theresa quickly. 'Remember! Blue dress, medium-heeled shoes.'

When Theresa saw Eileen on the day, she nodded approval. Eileen usually looked pretty and virginal, but today, in her blue dress with its slightly low-cut front, she appeared sophisticated. With make-up on she would look even more so. It was a pity about the rosy cheeks and the innocent look in the soft eyes. Honest to God, there were times when Eileen looked like a nun in mufti.

She contemplated her own face in the half of the rearview mirror that didn't have her father's face in it. She knew just what to do to make herself look older. The hair would go up for a start. She was so busy planning the transformation she missed something her father said.

'Sorry?' She leaned forward and met his gaze in the mirror.

'I said: what are you two going to do while your mam and I are going round the market? I don't suppose you will want to be trailing us.'

'We'll do a bit of window shopping,' said Theresa innocently.

'Will we meet for lunch?' Colin wondered what his daughter was up to; but there – they had to be let off the leash sometimes.

Theresa hesitated slightly. 'Would you mind if we didn't? Eileen and I have arranged to meet Maureen McGarry and Shelagh Rooney.'

Her father nodded. 'That's fine. We'll meet up again later at the Gavin Hotel. Your mam and I will have a late lunch there. We'll start for home around 3 o'clock, so make sure you are at the Gavin just before then.'

He was satisfied with the arrangement. Shelagh Rooney was destined for the religious life, so he was reassured that Theresa and Eileen would be unlikely to get into trouble in her company. Unlike Nuala, he wasn't always easy in his mind about Theresa going off with Eileen. In spite of the other girl's more sober nature he felt she was too easily swayed by his strong-minded daughter! Shelagh Rooney, however, was a different packet of kippers altogether. It was no secret that Shelagh was going to enter the convent as a postulant when she left school, so his mind was at rest.

'You lied!' said Eileen, accusingly. 'I don't like it when you lie to your parents, or mine. Just what are you up to? I warn you, I

24

am not going to do anything stupid.'

'I didn't lie. We are meeting them for lunch.'

'That's next Saturday. You implied—'

'I implied nothing,' interrupted Theresa. 'No one asked which Saturday we were meeting them.'

'You gave the impression—'

'For heaven's sake Eileen will you whisht! I hate it when you go all saintly. We're not going to do anything terrible. I just want to have some fun today. We're going into the toilets to put on a bit of make-up before we go window shopping and then we'll lunch at the Ram's Horn pub. If you don't want to have a real drink you can have an orangeade with your lunch and your halo will be intact.'

Eileen hated it when Theresa made her out to be a saint without a grain of fun in her, and she usually gave in to her for this reason. Today was no exception. 'All right,' she said reluctantly. 'I don't think you'll get away with it anyway. We both look too young.'

Theresa smiled. By the time they had put the make-up on, even Eileen would look older. Just to be on the safe side she made a mental note that Eileen would seat herself in a dark corner while Theresa would get the drinks and order the food.

'How much money have we got between us?' she asked.

Eileen fumbled for her purse as they sat down on a bench to sort out their expenses.

'I have one pound that I saved for a trip, and m'da gave me another for what he called "incidentals".'

'Great stuff! With the money m'da gave us to buy lunch we have three pounds in all. More than enough for our needs. We'll use the money Da gave us and when we need more we'll go halves.'

'We could buy half of Kilgaven with that. Just what have you in mind?' Eileen looked dubiously at her.

Ignoring her, Theresa struck out for the shops. She loved fashion and although she couldn't afford to buy anything, she derived great pleasure studying colour co-ordination, and how accessories were matched. Eileen, on the other hand, saw clothes as a necessity; she wasn't bothered about high fashion so long as she was covered sufficiently to preserve her modesty and look decent.

Fashion had overdosed on bright and garish designs in the years following the austerity and drabness of the war, but the colours were now more muted and restrained, for which Theresa was thankful. With her ebony black hair and blue eyes, the sharp hues had tended to make her look overblown. This year's more sombre shades flattered her.

They spent the morning trying on clothes they couldn't afford and giggling helplessly at the sight of themselves in fancy, over-decorated

25

hats, stopping only to have an orangeade and – Eileen's idea of bliss – a lurid pink coloured milk shake.

By the time they reached the Ram's Horn they were exhausted, and Eileen was happy to fall in with Theresa's firm suggestion that she should sit in the dark corner by the family room. She was nervous about sitting in a public bar anyway. It wasn't the kind of thing that a nice girl should do, but she forebore to argue. It would do no good anyway, Theresa could be a right termagant when roused.

Theresa brought the drinks over. 'The waitress will bring the food,' she said, and ordered Eileen to sit well back so that the light didn't fall on her.

The table was big enough to seat six so there was plenty of room for Eileen to relax into the corner and await the food. She was starving.

They were half-way through a succulent dish of stewed steak and onions topped by creamy mash and carrots when a noisy group of four young men, seeing the empty chairs, dashed across.

'Can we sit with you girls?'

Theresa, looking very grand and grown-up with her hair in a velvet band, and her blouse collar sitting up stiffly in the Marilyn Monroe style of things, turned towards the speaker.

'Certainly, you are most welcome.'

Eileen cringed. Theresa was talking with a posh Dublin accent.

'What are you drinkin', ladies?' said one.

Theresa looked at her orangeade and smiled. 'Gin and orange.'

Before Eileen could so much as gasp, he'd gone to the bar and given the order for four pints of Guinness and two gins and orange for the ladies. She tried to blast Theresa with her eyes, but the wily Theresa avoided her; she was busy acting sophisticated, smiling cat-like at the gems being uttered by the young man beside her.

Eileen had to admit, though, half-way through her drink, that things were beginning to look rosy. When the lads had finished their meal they ordered brandy all round.

Theresa, her eyes flashing and tongue going nineteen to the dozen – as Eileen vaguely remembered later – was enjoying her precarious role, and when asked why her friend was so quiet, explained that Eileen had just lost her fiancé to another woman and was drowning her sorrows.

The lads nodded sympathetically and clicked their tongues at the injustice of it all. With complete understanding they left her alone with her brandy and continued to chat, noisily vying for Theresa's notice. Eileen, feeling positively glowing and relaxed, was past caring about the lies that were passing like demented butterflies from the mouth of her friend. Indeed, she was filled with admiration at the sharpness of her wit.

She was sick on the way home. Theresa was furious with her. She could see her father was suspicious, which was not surprising as there was a faint smell of drink hanging round Eileen as she climbed back into the car and laid her head carefully against the seat.

'What have you two been up to?'

'Nothing much,' Theresa said. She turned towards the hapless Eileen, whose eyes, in a white, anguished face, stared back at her.

'I told you not to stuff yourself with those liqueur chocolates,' she muttered, before turning and smiling vaguely at her father's face in the mirror.

Eileen felt too ill to protest at such injustice.

Colin looked at them. 'Hmmm,' he said, but kept his counsel.

Theresa opened the window to let some air get to the stricken Eileen. 'You bloody eejut,' she whispered. 'You should never have had that brandy with your coffee.'

'Oh God! I feel so ashamed. I will have to say a novena for this.'

'You did nothing wrong. You just aren't used to the drink.'

'And you are?' Eileen, with a momentary surge of strength, glared at her.

'What are you whispering about?' enquired Colin.

'Leave them be, Colin,' said Nuala. 'Whatever Eileen has been up to she is paying for it now.'

Eileen was destroyed at the unfairness of it all. There sat the perfidious Theresa whilst she was getting the blame.

At mass the following day it was noted that Eileen didn't receive holy communion. Her mother explained to anyone who enquired that the girl had been unwell. 'Something she ate the previous day when she was in Kilgaven with the Bradys,' she said.

God! thought Theresa. I'll be glad when I go to university if only for some privacy and anonymity. You couldn't scratch your ear in this village without being accused of setting off a flea epidemic. She had a strong word with Eileen. 'I suppose you'll be going to confession and admitting you drank alcohol?'

'I will indeed, if I can work up the courage.' Eileen held a hand to her still throbbing head.

'You do and I'll never go out with you again.'

'But, Theresa—'

'But nothing! You did nothing wrong except take a drink under age. It is not a mortal sin. It was illegal, not sinful. Even Father Corke has the odd tipple now and again – and in the pub, at that.'

There it was again, that silver tongue of Theresa's, making it

27

seem right. Nevertheless, Eileen's troubled mind stilled. She wanted to believe her. 'You're probably right,' she said, with a relieved sigh.

'Eileen, you're so naive, you really are. Now, give over and let's go over to the group.'

'I'm still feeling off colour,' said Eileen. 'I think I'll go home with Mam – and I won't be going to the dance tonight, either,' she added. She hurried away before Theresa could make her change her mind. She was in no fit state to stand up to her. God knows, she was no good at it at the best of times, she'd have even less chance feeling as she did now.

Theresa ignored Jack. She was still angry with him. She leaned against the church wall and chatted to Shelagh Rooney. They hadn't a lot in common at the best of times but Theresa considered that it would be a good thing to be seen talking to her, since her mother had her eye on her.

She hid her boredom as Shelagh ranted on about the wonderful words that young Father Touhey had used in the sermon. 'The man has the gift of wisdom,' she said dreamily.

Theresa was tempted to ask her if she would like her to arrange a date for her, but changed her mind in view of the fact that she would have shocked the silly girl into a state of rigidity. She also felt it would be unfair to talk like that to a future nun. Personally, she hadn't been aware of Father Touhey's apparent gift for rhetoric – she had been busy observing the fashion worn by the women in the congregation. The only one who had showed any sense of style was Eileen's aunt, who owned a dress shop in Dublin.

It was with relief that she saw Tandy coming towards them;

'Good morning, girls,' he grinned.

Shelagh Rooney frowned at him. 'Shouldn't you be helping the altar boys to tidy up?'

'I paid young Terry Dougan to do it for me.'

'That isn't the point of the exercise. You're supposed to take your turn. Father Touhey says it's good for the soul to help others, even when it goes against your own interests at times.'

'Well! That time is now. I'm afraid the flesh proved weak and the spirit didn't help by not showin' willin'. Anyway! What are you worrying about? You've already booked your place in heaven, Shelagh, so I'd not bother with a sinner like me.' Tandy grinned at Theresa. 'What wickedness have you been getting up to recently, Theresa?'

She started, taken aback by the relevance of the question. She recovered quickly, however, and said with a laugh, 'Aren't I past all hope, Tandy? There's no point in discussing my sins.'

Tandy, catching sight of Jack, touched her on the arm. 'There's Jack, are you coming to say hello?'

Without turning, she said shortly, 'No! I'm quite happy chatting away to Shelagh here. Besides, I'm waiting for my mother; she's gone to say a prayer or six at the shrine. I expect her back any minute. We're going to gran's for lunch.'

'If you're sure, then,' he said.

'I'm sure. Another time.'

'What's goin' on between you two?' Shelagh asked. 'Have you and Jack fallen out?'

'Goodness, no,' Theresa said. 'I meant what I said. I'm waiting for Mam. Why should I leave you to dash away to Jack? I have more manners than that.'

Shelagh looked unconvinced.

At last Nuala, having paid her respects to St Theresa, beckoned to Theresa. She was about to move when her mother called out to Shelagh: 'Did you enjoy your lunch in Kilgaven yesterday, Shelagh?'

'Take no notice, Shelagh. My mother is going senile. She's thinking of next week. Just smile. It will keep her happy.' Theresa hissed.

Shelagh, with a puzzled look, did so, and Nuala hid her amusement as she watched her daughter squirm with discomfort. Theresa had nothing on Nuala when it came to rebelling against the system. Only Colin and a stable marriage had made her behave responsibly. She was still able to recognize a cover-up when she saw one.

Grannie McClusky, Nuala's mother, was only sixty-two years old, but years of haymaking and stooping to lift the flax from its murky, wet bed had left her riddled with arthritis and looking much older.

The farm that she had helped McClusky run had long gone. It was now part of McGarry's farm, and Grannie McClusky lived alone, running her smallholding with the help of a lad from the village.

Theresa ran towards her and hugged the tiny figure gently, so that she didn't hurt the fragile bones. She adored her little grandmother. There was a feeling of trust between them that bound them closely.

Mona McClusky returned her grandaughter's hug. She is the image of Nuala when she was the same age, she thought. She has the same wild zest for life that Nuala had before she married Colin and became a pillar of family decency. She turned to her daughter, whose beauty still caught at her heart, although the wild and careless loveliness that she once had was now tempered by a certain carefulness of manner. Mona remembered how, when Nuala was born, she had looked at the tiny, puckered little face and knew that she had in her arms all she wanted from life. She had kissed every single finger and toe and thanked the good God for their normality.

Nuala had never given her any cause for worry, for all her wild ways, and Mona had revelled in her daughter's loveliness and her popularity. Nuala had been an exciting person – but now, that indefinable something that had made her so was gone.

Colin Brady came forward to greet Mona, and she punched him playfully as he lifted her for a kiss. He was a tall man and a good one, and she was grateful to him for making Nuala happy. If she felt a pang that Pat McGarry had not become her son-in-law, she hid it well. Anyway, Nuala might not have been happy living in the big farmhouse with servants and a husband too busy to keep her company.

Mona ushered them all into the cottage where Nuala made straight for the kitchen. She insisted that when they all came to lunch she would do the cooking. Her mother was no longer able to cope.

Nuala was amazed how well her mother did cope with everyday living in spite of her disabilities. She had fifty hens, a litter of piglets to fatten for market, and a couple of milkers and two calves to tend. John Kelly was a great help. He was a bit light on top, but he had enough sense to be able to take a great deal of the strain off Mona. He milked the cows for her every morning and evening, and tended the vegetable garden.

Nuala's mother managed to live fairly comfortably after paying John his wages out of the money she got from selling the milk, eggs, and produce. The money she got for the sale of the pigs and calves she put away for replacing the stock.

After lunch, Grannie McClusky took her granddaughter's arm. 'We'll go into the garden and talk. I want to hear what you have been up to. Let the parents take a nap.'

Like two urchins they went from the room and made their way to the seat by the duck pond. Grannie McClusky put her walking stick down by her side and patted the seat. 'We will pretend that this is a wonderful lake and not a murky old duck pond, and those perishing noisy ducks are swans.'

'Are you sad?' asked Theresa, laying a hand on her grandmother's arm.

'Take no notice,' Mona smiled. 'Your granda started all this. I was just thinking back for a moment.' She smiled again. 'Now! Tell me. How is that young man of yours?'

30

'He isn't my young man. He is just a special friend.'

'He is the one whose name is most often on your lips.'

'Only because I get along particularly well with him and we spend a lot of time together. Besides,' Theresa added dolefully, 'he isn't very friendly at the moment. Just lately he has been trying to avoid me.'

'Have you asked him why?'

'I think I know why.'

'You are a mind reader?' Mona leaned painfully back.

'No. It's – it's . . . Something happened that I think he disapproved of and I suspect he is showing me his disapproval.'

Grannie McClusky put her hand over her granddaughter's. 'If you believe that then you'll believe the devil is God's brother. What you tell me about that young man makes me certain that he would have more sense than to show his disapproval in such a way. He is more likely to give you a piece of his mind.'

Theresa stared at the dirty little ducks circling the pond and wondered what Jack was doing now. He was probably off clicking with some girl in Dublin. She had overheard him arranging something with Tandy and the name Dublin had come up.

'And you? Are you working for your exams?' Grannie McClusky enquired.

Theresa hesitated. She could work harder. She sometimes had nightmares thinking about the work she hadn't done, but life kept beckoning and there was always a reasonable excuse for not studying.

'I have another year before I sit mine.'

'A lot can happen in a year. You get your stock of learning by you in case of emergencies, my girl. tell me do you still hive off to your special place for a swim in the buff?'

Theresa laughed. Her Grandmother was an amazing woman. 'Yes, I do. For God's sake don't mention it in front of Mam and m'da. They wouldn't understand.'

'Never! I'm privileged to have your secret, even though I found out by accident. Be careful, though. There are those who would see harm in it.'

'Why are people so horrified at the sight of the naked body? Eileen came into my room and went paralytic at seeing me naked. We nearly had a row over it. I had only just got out of the bath so I had every right to be naked in my own room.'

'Of course you did, but Eileen would naturally have expected you to put something on. It would have been courtesy to do so. Nakedness, as you have realized, can sometimes cause offence. One day in the future – judging by the latest two piece costumes being worn on the beaches – nakedness in public will not cause a single lift of the eyebrow. In the meantime I wouldn't want Theresa Brady to be the one to lift the lid off convention.'

'You're right, of course,' said Theresa. 'I never gave thought to poor Eileen. She would be especially offended. I'll never be as kind and saintly as her.'

'Don't let Eileen hear you refer to her as being holy. She is probably trying to be as big a tearaway as you are, and not being very successful at it.'

'I won't be ashamed of my body,' said Theresa fiercely.

'I'd probably feel the same way if I had a body like yours,' laughed Grannie McClusky. 'I'd scare the devil out of his den with my misshapen joints and sagging flesh. Now, that *would* be flying in the face of modesty.'

'Nonsense,' said Theresa. 'There is no shame in an ageing body. I shall not feel any different when mine begins to show signs of wear and tear.'

'I wish I could be around to see the culmination of that resolve.' Grannie McClusky took Theresa's hand and smoothed it with her dry fingers. 'Don't fly in the face of convention, cusheen. The time is not right.' She rose stiffly. 'We had better get back to the house. Your mother will have the tea ready by now.'

During tea, Theresa was quiet. The unwelcome thought struck again that Jack had met some girl in Dublin. If he had met someone, did it mean the end of their relationship? She wasn't certain what the rules were.

The more she thought about it the more unhappy she felt. She found herself wishing that she was down by the sea so that she could think more clearly. Grannie's tiny kitchen seemed even smaller and hotter than usual.

When she had seen the family off, Mona McClusky sat down by the fire and stared into the hot centre till her eyes began to water. She pushed the kettle on the kleek over the flames and lifted the teapot and tea caddy from the side hob. I've all my orders here, she thought as she spooned tea leaves into the pot. She liked her tea like treacle. Her thoughts turned to her granddaughter: her innocent, headstrong girl, who had a risky disregard for the conventions. She worried for her; there were those who would not understand that what she did sprung from a deep-seated inno-cence, and Mona feared that the day might come when her actions would cause her grief.

As the darkness settled over the cottage and the flames from the fire died a death, Mona had a premonition which caused a pall to settle on her mind.

Only twice in her life had she seen something about to happen before it did. The first time had been when her great friend Annie Cooper had come to visit unexpectedly and she had seen a vague shape behind her. She had put it down to a trick of the light and thought nothing more about it until, three days later, she got news that Davey Cooper, Annie's husband, had died in a farming accident.

The last time had been two weeks before McClusky had died. She had been doing the washing at the time, staring into the big bungalow bath as she rinsed the sheets. Suddenly she saw his face mirrored in the water. She had turned quickly, thinking he had come up behind her, but he wasn't there, and when she had looked into the water again the image had gone. A coldness had filled her and she felt a sense of foreboding. The same feeling was with her now. There was a death about to occur just as it had then. But this time there was no image. She didn't know who it would be – but she knew it would be soon.

CHAPTER 3

Theresa closed her bedroom door behind her and held her breath as it clicked shut. She had good reason not to want her mother to see her going out. Fearfully she listened, then, holding her lightweight coat round her, she soft-treaded down the stairs towards the front door. She had nearly made it when her mother's voice called out, 'Is that you Theresa?'

'Yes, Mam.' She poked her head round the door. 'I'm off to the dance; don't wait up.'

Nuala settled back in her chair and smiled drowsily at her daughter. 'Bless yourself on the way out, and have a good time.'

'Yes, Mam.' Theresa let out a sigh of relief as she dutifully dipped her fingers into the little china font of holy water which hung by the door, and hastily blessed herself. Her mother needn't have bothered to remind her, but there! Parents were the great ones for giving out the orders; if it wasn't them it was Father Corke. Fat chance the young people of the village had of getting away with anything. The older generation, with their years of experience, managed it though.

She was thankful that her father was away at the St Vincent de Paul society meeting, working out how to prise some money from the poor to help the poor. She'd never have got away with this otherwise.

Wrapping her coat round her more closely, she glanced up at Eileen's window as she passed. Eileen hadn't lied about being unwell. The light was on. How could she even think that the sainted Eileen would lie? She felt vulnerable without her at her side, but the thought of what her friend would say to her if she knew what she was about to do sent a flicker of concern coursing through her body. With a shake of the head and a tilt of the chin she strode purposefully towards the church hall.

As she reached it, her heart pumped fast. She began to regret the moment of madness back in her room when she had made the decision to liven things up tonight. With her hand already on the door handle she hesitated – there was still time. A look of defiance settled on her face as she took a deep breath and pushed open the door. Oh God! Being without Eileen at her side was like having only one arm.

Resolutely, she crossed the barely furnished vestibule and entered the cloakroom. Mary Rice and that sneaky little fart Nora Smith were already there, dolling themselves up. They turned as one from the misty, cracked mirror that ran along the wall behind the basins and stared at Theresa in amazement.

Ignoring them, she walked to the other end and began to tuck in the few curls that had escaped the confinement of slides and clips which kept her hair in the style she had adopted for the evening. She added a touch of mascara to her eyelashes, removed her coat with a flourish, smiled sweetly at the open-mouthed pair, and walked from the room.

When she entered the hall where the dancing was taking place, she paused again. In accordance with the rules set up by Father Corke, the boys were ranged along one side, the girls along the other. She straightened her back till her spinal bones were in danger of becoming unhinged.

'Bloody hell!' Tandy Noonan gasped, and fell silent with his mouth open. His gaze followed Theresa's progress. What a stunner! She was wearing a figure-hugging little black number with a large, shiny belt which emphasized her tiny waist. Her long, slim legs caught his eye as she walked across in her high-heeled shoes. He had never seen her with her hair piled high before; it made her look older. He was definitely impressed.

Jack Ross also watched in silence. He saw the look on the faces as Theresa progressed down the room, and he wanted to go to her and pull her into his arms, but he felt rooted to the floor. He was suddenly afraid for her; that she had gone too far this time. She was wearing her mother's dress, and judging by the line of it she was wearing little else. If Father Corke or Father Touhey caught sight of her she was in dire trouble. His heart lurched. She looked so beautiful and, in a funny way, vulnerable. Was he the only one who saw the wavering lip and the faltering bravado? He smiled to himself. She was as unpredictable as mercury.

It was some time before he managed to grab her for a dance. 'What are you playing at?' he whispered.

'Having some fun; trying to liven the place up a bit.' Theresa laughed and whirled him round, happy to have him back with her again.

Jack grabbed her arm and marched her over to a quiet corner. 'Committing suicide would be easier if either of the fathers catch sight of you.'

36

Ignoring his words she did a twirl. 'Do you like my dress?'

His eyes softened. 'You look beautiful, but it's your mother's dress. The whole place will be buzzing with this tomorrow. What do you think your parents will say if they find out you were dressed up to the nines in your Mam's dress?'

'No one knows it is her dress; they probably think she knows I had my hair up and wore high-heeled shoes. Why not?' With a toss of her head Theresa brushed past him, and as she did so he realised, with a quickening of his pulse, that she wasn't wearing a bra.

With unfortunate timing, Father Corke walked in. Theresa, head down and eyes bright with unshed tears, didn't see the elderly priest who was watching her approach with a steady gaze.

As she passed him, he touched her on the shoulder. 'Come into the games room, Theresa. I would like a word with you.'

Aware that many of the dancers had seen the short exchange, she hastily did as she was told.

Father Corke watched the lovely young girl as she sat down on the hard bench ranged along the wall, and sighed. He was getting too old for this shepherd on earth bit. All he wanted in life was to say mass on Sunday, take confession, and spend a few days fishing in the many good trout streams around the area. He shook his grey head as he surveyed the young girl before him. She was so like Nuala McClusky. If genetic selection was to be believed there should be something of Colin there, but he could see no scrap of evidence of it. There was not a bit of the staid Colin Brady in her at all.

'Theresa,' he said at last, 'I'm worried about you. What happened to the pert, bright-eyed little child who used to strew rose petals in the Easter parade; the girl who never missed communion and came top of the class in catechism and religious instruction?'

'She is still here,' Theresa said defiantly.

'How long is it since you went to confession?'

'I can't see the point in going to confession. Why can't I ask direct for forgiveness anyway? God is supposed to be my father in heaven, isn't he? I don't go to someone else if I want to apologise to my own father.'

Father Corke folded his arms. 'He is not only your father,' he said gently, 'he is also the boss.'

'I still don't see why I need to go through a third party – no offence intended – to speak to God.'

'I've been called many things in my time,' smiled the old priest, 'but never have I been referred to as a third party.'

'I mean no disrespect,' said Theresa. 'You brought this up.'

37

'None taken. Best we know how you feel.' The old priest smiled, and leaning towards her he added, 'Look at it this way: if you go to see the boss in his office for whatever reason, wouldn't you first go to his secretary? Well! I'm the boss's secretary.'

Theresa knew he was poking gentle fun at her.

He looked at his watch. 'Theresa, I think that you and I need to talk, but now is not the time. You seem to have a confused notion as to what confession is all about. You know it is a sacrament and a blessing from God, but I fear you are trying to convince yourself that it isn't necessary because, like many another, you find it a tiresome chore.' He paused for a moment in thought. The girl was highly intelligent. He must respect that. 'Another time we will discuss your problem, but for now I'd like a word with you about your mode of dress.' He looked at her with a frown settling on his brow.

'I'm not going to discuss my manner of dressing. I see nothing wrong in making the best of myself. I'm sure my mother would agree with me on this.' Theresa rose from the bench, heart pounding at her temerity.

'I'd be surprised if your mother would consider the dress you are wearing now was suitable, lovely though it is in itself.' Father Corke ran his gaze critically over it. He sighed. The dress was sophisticated and charming, but he knew fine well that it belonged to her mother. He had noticed how smart Nuala had looked in it at the charity ball last year. On Nuala it had looked respectable. On Theresa, who was already taller and altogether a bigger girl, it was skimped and too short, showing off those long, shapely legs. He had seen the look on the lads' faces as she hurried towards the door.

'I suppose you'll feel it necessary to talk to Mam and m'da about this.' Theresa, still defiant, tried to keep the anxiety out of her voice.

'I'll give the matter some thought,' Father Corke said, but he had already made up his mind that a scare would be sufficient. 'Go home now and I expect to see you at confession more often.' His tone was friendly, but he hoped that Theresa would sense that the bargain he was making was a flick of the fingers short of a threat.

Theresa, as always when she was unhappy or worried, found herself walking towards her private beach to the north of Lafferty's Cove. Except for walks on a cool day, this part of the beach was not so well frequented. The sand petered out close to the south side of the cove and gradually gave way to pebbles and, further on, rocks and large boulders.

She loved this part of the coastline, with its rougher terrain and its resulting lack of popularity. No one ventured this far when there was a ten-mile stretch of beautiful sandy beach nearby, racing nearly all the way to Kilgaven. Dubliners who visited in their droves during the summer tended to stick to the sandy area.

The night was cool, but the sight of the moonlight shimmering on the surface of the sea weaved its enchantment. She made her way to the water's edge and stood there for a few minutes whilst the waves crept towards her bare feet and gently licked them before retreating again. The urge to strip off and cut strongly through the sea proved too tempting. She ran back towards the boulders, sheltered by the bluff from the road above, and pulled her dress over her head, letting it drop on to the pebbles. She wore nothing beneath it.

Being a strong swimmer, she had no fear of the sea. There had been times when she had swum in seas that were so rough her body had been slightly bruised by the buffeting strength of the waves, and times she had been forced under till her breath nearly gave out. She loved the exhilaration she derived from the exercise. Her parents, knowing that she was a good swimmer, had given up worrying about her.

She scored up and down, swimming with long, practised strokes till her body was tingling and her mind purged of worry. The sense of well-being that now ran through her felt great. This was how a martyr must feel following flagellation: exultant and replete.

At last, with reluctance, she swam back to shore and made her way up the beach towards the heap that was her dress, unaware that she was being observed by a shadowy figure to the right of the bluff that circled the modest little bay.

Richard Beck stood still, entranced by the sight of the lithe, long-limbed young woman as she walked from the sea. The light from the moon shone on her glistening body as she stooped towards the shadowy pile on the ground, and as he watched he let his breath out slowly. 'My lady of the baths,' he murmured.

At that moment his horse moved and the slight jingle of his harness sounded loud in the soft night. The young woman froze.

Richard spoke gently. 'Please! Don't be alarmed. I didn't realize there was anyone here.'

Theresa straightened as the man and his horse approached. There was something about his voice that instilled in her a feeling of trust.

'You startled me,' she gasped. 'I never see anyone this far up the coast – especially at night.'

'I came to walk my horse in the sea,' Richard explained. 'He became lame recently and there's no better treatment – I suppose I should take him to the vet.' He patted the horse's neck, saying quietly, 'Why don't you put your dress on?'

Theresa had just remembered as he spoke that she was still naked. She scooped the dress up and hurriedly pulled it over her head.

'I wouldn't want you to catch cold.' Regarding her in some amusement, he added, 'I don't often come upon a sea nymph whilst walking my horse.' It had not escaped his notice that the lovely girl been completely unaware of her nakedness until he mentioned it. It had further not escaped his notice that she wore no underwear.

She was stroking his horse now. 'She's beautiful. What's her name?'

'His name is Othello.' Richard laughed. 'It's a boy.'

Theresa smiled, her teeth showing even and white in the moonlight. 'It's so dark I couldn't tell.'

He held out his hand. 'I'm Richard Beck. I live up at Castle Donagh. I've been living there for the past six months.'

'I know,' said Theresa. 'I've seen your manservant in my friend's store.'

Richard laughed heartily. 'Good lord! If Bob knew he was considered to be my manservant he would be highly amused. He is my friend, my mentor, my dogsbody, my guide – he is just about everything – but a servant he would not consider himself to be.'

'I'm sorry. I didn't mean–'

'Don't be, there's no need,' interrupted Richard. 'How were you to know? You haven't told me your name.'

'Theresa Brady. My father is the headmaster at the local primary school.'

They shook hands formally.

'Do you ride?' asked Richard.

'I've ridden bareback on farm horses.'

He was suddenly aware that the girl before him was shivering slightly. 'You're cold. Have my coat.' Taking it off, he draped it over her shoulders. 'Do you often swim at night?'

'Not often.' She was grateful for the warmth of his jacket. It had a faint tweedy smell mixed with the spicy, lingering aroma of tobacco.

'I will stay away from this end of the beach in future,' promised Richard. 'I apologise again for the intrusion.'

'There isn't any need. I don't do it very often. Besides, this isn't my private beach.' She was sad all the same that she would now have to share it.

'We'll see. I'm sure there are other parts where I can walk Othello in the sea.' He looked towards the water and said, 'As I came to do just that I suppose I'd better do it. I hope we meet

40

again, Theresa. I'd like you to come and see the horses – that is, if you would like to.'

Theresa took his extended hand and shook it. She handed him his jacket. 'I'd like that. I really would.'

'I'll get in touch sometime and we can arrange it,' he said, and added, 'Are you sure you will be warm enough?'

'Quite sure. I'll run home. I'm late anyway – besides,' she grinned, 'I don't fancy explaining to my parents how I happen to have acquired a man's jacket.'

'Perhaps you're right.'

It wasn't till she reached home that she realized she had left her shoes on the beach. She was so used to running around barefoot she hadn't noticed, particularly as she had run along the soft turf on the side of the road. damn! If her mother found out she would kill her. Shoes were an expensive item, and Nuala hadn't been happy about Theresa's choice in the first place.

To her relief, the house was in darkness except for the light in the hallway. Her parents slept in the large bedroom at the back of the house overlooking the small garden; no lights meant that they were already in bed. She crossed herself, and offered up a small prayer that neither of them would need to use the bathroom. Quietly she eased herself up the stairs. If her mother happened to come out of her bedroom, Theresa was lost. Her mam was as quick eyed as a starling and would pounce on the fact not only that she was wearing her dress but that she wore nothing under it.

Please God! Keep her in bed and I'll be a saint at the Easter ceremonies. I'll walk down the aisle with the children and I'll carry the dreaded daffodils. I'll wear them in my hair if you like. Give me a sign, just don't let Mam see me.

She breathed a sigh of relief as she gently closed her bedroom door, then groaned as she realized she had committed herself to a day of purgatory on Easter Sunday. She knew she was going to have all the group falling about laughing at the grand sight of Theresa the wild one acting like a saint. She undressed and climbed into bed after stuffing the dress at the back of her wardrobe. She'd worry about consequences another time. She was too sleepy to care. Yawning, she pulled the bedclothes over her and drifted off.

Monday came and went with a slowness that drove her mad. Eileen was still feeling unwell and Theresa was only permitted to see her for a short time. Theresa was now concerned that she may have unwittingly poisoned her friend with alcohol. She had heard or read somewhere that you could die of alcohol poisoning even if you were a heavy drinker. She hadn't believed it at the time, her

41

own theory being that if it was true, then half of Tullybra would be wiped out already.

It was with some relief that she found Eileen sitting up in bed supping a bowl of broth, her mother waiting to see her finish it.

'I don't know what this girl of mine ate when she was in Kilgaven with you and yours,' said Mrs O'Rourke with a deep frown, 'I'll tell you this, though: it will be a while before she goes again. She has been sick all night.'

Thank God! Eileen has obviously said nothing about her visit to a pub, Theresa thought, with a rush of relief.

'Mam! I told you I'm fine. I think your broth has done the trick.' Eileen looked wanly at Theresa. 'I'm sorry I couldn't go to the dance last night. Did anything interesting happen?'

Aware of the hovering figure of the demented mother in the background, Theresa shook her head. 'I left early. It wasn't the same without you,' she said. 'I'll give you all the news at school tomorrow.'

'She'll not be going to school tomorrow,' said Mrs O'Rourke.

'I'll be well enough, Mam,' protested Eileen.

When she left the house, Theresa wondered whether she should go up to the hall and see if she could retrieve her coat, but changed her mind when she remembered that the ladies of the Council for Good Causes were holding a meeting and her mother would be there.

She went home and up to her room where, for once, she got out her books and settled down to do some studying, without trying every trick in the book to put off the evil moment as she normally did.

Eileen didn't turn up to school the next day, which worried Theresa. She was beset with worries. With even less enthusiasm than usual she worked her way through the school day, and it was with a feeling of relief that she packed her books into her holdall and set off to await the arrival of the bus. The mood she was in, she knew if Pat Maher said a word out of turn she'd go for the throat.

When she arrived at the Tullybra bridge, she settled on the parapet to await the arrival of Jack and Tandy. They weren't on the bus.

In fact, Jack and Tandy had taken the day off school to go to Dublin. At the moment Theresa was watching the school bus depart, they were leaning against the O'Connell bridge observing the droves of people.

'Everybody in this place seems to be on a bicycle,' observed Tandy.

'Ye'd wonder why God bothered to give us feet.' Jack laughed. 'When we start at university we'll probably be joining them.' He turned and leaned over the parapet, so failed to see the look on Tandy's face. 'Anyway! There are many walkers. We've just strolled up O'Connell Street and couldn't walk for feet.'

'I prefer the peace of the countryside,' Tandy grumbled.

Jack ignored his grumpiness. 'I can't wait to get here,' he said, his voice rising in excited anticipation. 'We'll have a great time, Tandy. There isn't a more exciting city in the world. Forget Paris and New York and all the others. We—'

'Stop!' said Tandy, his face creased in a frown. 'I've got something to tell you.' He swallowed hard. 'I'm not going to university.'

Jack stared. 'What are you talking about? Of course you are. If you're worried about getting your certificate then stop worrying. You have as much chance of getting your points as I have.'

'I'm not worried about my results. I know I can do it even if I don't get the high marks you'll get – I'm not going because it isn't what I want.'

There was a strained silence. Jack leaned over the bridge again and idly watched the swirling water below. 'Did you know that the Liffey is considered to be one of the cleanest rivers in Europe?' he said, inconsequentially.

Tandy didn't reply. He knew how disappointed Jack was feeling. For years, since they had approached their early teens, they had spoken often of the day they would get away from the claustrophobic society of Tullybra and spread their wings in Dublin. They would taste all the delights on offer and try and manage enough study to get them through their exams. It was what being a student was all about. Freedom, exploration, anticipation, study—

'Why?' Jack asked dully, turning to him.

Tandy shrugged. 'I don't know why. I just know that one day I realized that I wanted to go to college and learn all about farming.'

'Farming!' Jack's voice had a hollow ring to it. 'You've always said you wanted to get away from it. You've never put your heart into it when you've helped out on your parents' farm. Your main worry was that the farm wasn't able to maintain one more family member.'

'I know. I can't explain why I changed my mind,' said Tandy, feeling wretched. 'I want to try beef farming. That's where the money is.'

'What if everyone turns vegetarian?' The remark was partly facetious, but to Jack's surprise Tandy took it seriously.

43

'Things do change. That's why I want to go to college. After all, I could learn all I need to know about beef farming from Pat McGarry. But I want to go to an agricultural college to get an overall education.'

'Does your father know of this?'

'Not yet. I only made up my mind finally last week. I've been thinking about the pros and cons for months.'

'So you haven't sorted out a college yet?'

'Yes, I have. I've been told there is an excellent college in England – Sussex. It's in a village called Plumpton, situated just below the South Downs.' Tandy's brown eyes appealed to Jack for understanding. 'I've wanted to confide in you for a long time, but I had to be sure. You're the first to know. Will you wish me luck with my father? Whether I go to England or not depends on whether he feels that a college education in agriculture is money worth spending. I have to convince him that I need to go out on my own and gradually work round to owning my own farm. I'm hoping he will see the sense in not having to split the profits yet again.'

Jack, his grey mood beginning to lift, smiled at him. 'Why don't we go along to Mullen's bar and down a glass or two of the old black velvet? I'll get used to the idea quicker that way. Besides, they have a good ceili band there'.

They strode out on the long walk down the broad boulevard, saying very little. Both were busy with their own thoughts and were only vaguely aware of the people who parted to let them through.

Jack was looking forward to his university entry, but with some trepidation. Having to get through the initial process would be that much less enjoyable now that he wouldn't have Tandy by his side. He sighed. Life never went along smoothly.

He wanted Theresa to be a part of his life. His heart belonged to her – he knew that now – but he had years of study ahead of him and he could see no immediate future for them. Having chosen to study medicine he intended to dedicate himself to getting his degree.

Tandy was trying to work out a way of approaching his father about his change of heart. His father was a difficult man at times and might well look on his plan as a defection rather than a sensible appraisement of his future . . .

'We're here,' said Jack. 'You can wake up from your reverie now.'

'Sorry! I was thinking of a good way to break my news to m'da.'

'You go find a table as far away from the band as possible – it can get a bit loud, as you know. I'll get the first ones in.'

Mullen's bar was a very popular venue. Apart from the band,

44

which was the greatest draw, the place was well furnished and had retained its Victorian presence.

The large, curved bar had kept its original brasswork, which now reflected the soft lights, and the filigree work between the poles that separated the different areas where the patrons stood was exquisite.

For those who wished to drink in a more leisurely fashion, small tables dotted the centre of the large room, and there were alcoves set along the walls for families who wished to have a quiet drink together.

The band was drumming up its usual storm of excitement and Jack was having difficulty making his way towards the waving arm of Tandy over in a far corner, but eventually he arrived to find him sitting with a couple of girls.

'Wasn't it kind of Marie and Rosaleen to let us sit with them?' Tandy was now his old self again.

Jack groaned. Tandy never had any trouble getting into conversation with girls. They always fell for the charm he exuded with no real effort, and his soppy brown eyes didn't let him down either.

Jack set the glasses on the table and thanked the girls politely. They were both pretty, but then Tandy wouldn't bother if they weren't. To Jack's annoyance he was now forced to make conversation with Rosaleen, a girl whom he was not likely to see again and whom he had not the slightest desire to anyway.

Fortunately, Tandy had chosen well. He had chosen the quiet one who was quite happy to listen to the rogue at her side and laugh at his anecdotes. Rosaleen, on the other hand, prattled happily on and left Jack to his thoughts. Now and again, for politeness sake, he answered or ventured to make a small contribution to the conversation himself.

The band was good. The fiddler stamped away nineteen to the dozen and the patrons, having lost any inhibitions they might have had before the drink took effect, roared out the songs. 'The Rose of Tralee'. 'Paddy McGinty's Goat'. 'The Mountains of Mourne'.

Conversation was difficult, and by the end of the evening Jack was hoarse with shouting. God knows how Tandy was going to feel when he woke up the next morning, for he hadn't stopped to draw breath. At closing time Tandy offered to see the girls home.

'Are you sure you don't mind?' asked Rosaleen doubtfully. 'It's rather a long way to other end of the city.'

'That's all right, I've got the da's car.' Jack smiled at her.

He had intended to give Tandy a piece of his mind on the way home, but decided against it. They couldn't have done otherwise. Jack had been embarrassed, though, when they said goodbye to the girls. He suspected that they had been expecting to arrange another meeting, but he had no intention of getting involved, so while Tandy was making arrangements to meet Marie, he wandered back to the car. He knew he had banjaxed Rosaleen's expectations by the look of disappointment on her face as he walked away.

'Don't you feel a sense of loyalty to Eileen?' he asked Tandy on the journey home.

'Why should I?' There was genuine surprise in Tandy's voice. 'I'm fond of Eileen, but I'm not her boyfriend. Not like you and Theresa.'

'I'm not sure about Theresa and me,' Jack said slowly. 'She is only just touching seventeen; sure that's no age to be settling down into a stable relationship.' He stopped the car. 'To tell you the honest to God's truth, Tandy, I'm confused about how things are between us. Theresa is a mercurial creature who hasn't had a chance to test herself. How can I expect her to settle down into a relationship with me? And then there is the next few years of study I'm committed to.'

Tandy looked at him. 'Something has happened between you two. I had a suspicion that all was not right with you. I couldn't help noticing that just lately you've been a bit short with her, and you've been keeping out of her way more.'

'I needed time to work things out in my mind. It would be unfair to let things go too far . . . I think I'm in love with her,' he added ruefully.

All the while Jack was speaking, Tandy was staring at him in astonishment. 'I didn't realise you were in love with her – really in love. Of course we all knew within the group that she was special to you but I never guessed . . .'

'And you had better promise me that you won't say a word.'

'Not a single word. You have obviously given all this a great deal of thought and the decision is yours, but . . .'

'But what?'

'I think you are talking out of your arse. If you love her then tell her. Let her make up her own mind.'

But Jack shook his head. 'I'm going to leave things as they are and see what happens. we are all right as we are – and I wish to hell I hadn't started this conversation. Enough about me. What about you and Eileen? The girl is crazy about you. Surely you feel something?'

'Eileen is a sweet girl and I am very fond of her, but can you honestly think that Eileen and I would do well together? She's far too good for me.' Tandy shrugged.

'Hmmn,' said Jack. 'You're right there.'

After he had dropped Tandy at the farm, Jack drove home

slowly, his thoughts still on the idea of Theresa being in love with him. Somehow, he couldn't visualise it.

On Tuesday, Theresa was pleased to see Eileen at the bus stop. She had been seriously concerned about her.

Eileen was in fine form, however, and prattled on about the forthcoming Easter Sunday procession.

Theresa, remembering the promise she had recently made in haste, glared at her. 'I don't want to hear one more word out of you about the Easter services. I'm going to think of Easter eggs and Easter bunnies and dyeing hard-boiled eggs to roll down the hillside.'

Eileen looked at her in amazement. 'We haven't rolled eggs since we were small children.'

'I didn't say I was going to do it. I'm just going to think of it.'

Eileen shrugged. 'You're in one of your moods. I'll say nothing.'

Theresa sat back. How was she going to face Jack and Tandy when they came off the bus at the end of the day? She also didn't know how to tell Eileen about her stupid prank before she heard it from the lads.

During break, she found Eileen in the common room. 'I need to talk to you.'

Sister Anunciata came in at that moment. 'Haven't you got some study to do in the library?' she enquired, looking straight at Theresa.

'I'm on break, Sister. I was just meeting Eileen so that we could walk in the grounds for some fresh air.'

'You don't walk in the grounds during morning break. You know that well enough, Theresa.'

'Eileen has been ill over the weekend, Sister. I promised her mother, I would see she was all right. It was the only reason she let her come to school today.'

Theresa clamped her hand firmly over Eileen's wrist as she felt her move towards the nun.

'Is that so, Eileen?'

Eileen hesitated, and then nodded miserably.

'You do look pale . . . All right then, but when you hear the bell I want you back here immediately, so don't walk too far.'

Sister Anunciata swept out of the room without a backward glance. Eileen O'Rourke was an honest girl but she wouldn't trust the bold Theresa as far as she could throw an elephant. She stopped and smiled. She was very fond of Theresa. She saw a bit of herself in her. She wondered if the girl had ever given thought to taking the veil. She would make an excellent nun. She had a sense of fun, she was a born leader, and grave in the face of adversity. Take the way she had stared herself down just now. A nun of Theresa's calibre was of more use to the world than one who trotted along with hands folded in permanent prayer and fasted endlessly. She smiled. 'God has a weak spot for sinners, anyway.'

When Sister Anunciata had gone, Eileen turned to Theresa, her round, pale face looking cross.

'Why do I give in to you?' she wailed. 'I've just lied to that sainted woman's face and all because you have squeezed the life out of my wrist, and I have done your stupid bidding one more time.'

'Quit your blethering. I'm in trouble. I need to talk to you.'

'What do you mean, you're in trouble?' Eileen frowned. 'I've only been away from you one day and that was yesterday. How can you get into trouble so soon?'

Theresa took a deep breath and filled Eileen in on what had happened at the dance on Sunday night. Eileen gave a gasp half-way through the discourse, but Theresa ignored it and carried on with the tale of her stupidity. She omitted the meeting with the stranger and her swim in the sea; that would have been too much for the gentle girl to take in.

'How many times do I have to say that you are as mad as a buck goat, Theresa Brady?'

'I know all that. Do you think I haven't berated myself? How am I going to face Jack and Tandy? And what will I do if Father Corke tells my mother and father? I'm not concerned about anyone else. Only he and Jack knew I was wearing my mother's dress, so the others will put it down to Theresa Brady acting up as usual.'

'Father Corke is probably only putting the fear of God into you. He won't tell, and you'll have to face up to Jack and Tandy.' Eileen looked puzzled. 'Did you not meet them off the bus yesterday?'

'They didn't arrive. They must have taken the day off or got a lift from someone.'

'More likely they took a day off. They can do that now that they have their final exams coming up.'

The bell rang for the end of break and they made their way back to the classroom.

Theresa felt minimally better. Perhaps Eileen was right and Father Corke wouldn't tell her mother. Perhaps he just wanted to let her spend some time with the worry hanging over her head like the sword of bloody Damocles. God! She hoped he'd keep his mouth shut.

CHAPTER 4

It didn't go without notice during the Easter period that Theresa Brady was behaving like a model daughter of the church. The change was particularly observed by her friends.

Tandy remarked to Eileen: 'If Theresa carries on the way she's doing she'll be canonised. I preferred the old "hell bent for leather" Theresa. She's no fun any more.'

Eileen agreed with him. She found this new Theresa a bit hard to take, and having mentioned the fact to her she had got a sharp reply.

'There's no pleasing people,' Theresa had said with asperity. 'I'm prepared to admit that this isn't the mantle I'm easy with, but I am trying to reform.'

Eileen, biting hard into the apple she was munching, had replied, 'Give up then – you were all right before – and this holy Theresa act is overdone. In fact, it's laughable.'

'I'm trying to be humble.'

'Theresa Brady, you being humble is akin to the Pope jiving at a jamboree – it's completely out of character. It's sick-making, watching you shepherd the kids in the Easter procession.'

'You did it as well.'

'It's different for me. I love children, whereas you barely tolerate them. No one wants you to be different. We all like you as you are – were,' she corrected.

'I've decided to reform,' Theresa had said, firmly. 'Father Corke is right. I've got to settle down and take my religion more seriously – even if it kills me.'

'Don't worry! It'll kill the rest of us first – with boredom. I'm away home. There's more fun stroking the cat. I depended on you to add a bit of excitement to my life.'

At home, Nuala and Colin Brady were discussing their daughter. Of late, Colin had become concerned about a drop in the standard of her school work. Sister Mary Patricia, her form mistress, had expressed her concern to him.

'Theresa is an extremely bright girl. It would be a great pity if she became too complacent and did badly in her exams. She is university material. I'm certain of it.' She'd paused for a moment and looked straight at him and he'd been surprised at her next words. 'I did wonder if Theresa had ever mentioned to you that she might consider doing an Art course?'

Colin had shaken his head. He'd known of his daughter's skill, of course he had, but that it could be a major part of her professional career hadn't entered his mind. Now, however, Sister Mary Patricia's words had set him thinking. There was usually a sketch pad in Theresa's hands. It went everywhere with her. He'd seen the drawings and admired them, but hadn't noted their worth.

He spoke of the nun's concern to Nuala, but left out the bit about an Art course; time enough for that if Theresa brought it up. He would prefer her to go to university and get a degree which would help her to teach something like English or Maths.

Nuala leaned her elbows on the table and looked at him complacently. 'I have every faith in our girl,' she told him. 'She is just going through the stage of being bored with study. She'll pick up.'

'I don't know. She's a bit on the wild side is our Theresa – not that I don't trust her,' he added hastily. 'But the higher she grows, the wilder she seems to get. Take that trip to Kilgaven – now, it was obvious to me that Eileen was sick because she'd had a drink or two.'

'You noticed,' observed Nuala, with a smile.

'Aye! That nonsense about liqueurs saved her bacon. Only an innocent would think that a few chocolates would be strong enough to have the car reeking of alcohol. It worries me that Theresa might be trying too much, too soon.'

Nuala regarded her husband. Colin was a darling man, but it had to be said that he was just a teeny bit stuffy. She supposed it came of having to set a good example in the community.

'Colin, love, there's nothing to worry about. Our Theresa is like the wild rose which wanders where it will, climbing over any obstacle in its path. But it never really gets out of control because nature has a way of stopping it.' She paused. 'I don't want to see her lively mind and explorative nature warped by restriction. She has to grow and learn, and the best way is for her to mark out her own perimeters. We'll keep a wary eye on her. Anyway, I think she has enough common sense to know where to stop.' She smiled. 'She has our genes in her after all.'

Colin laughed. He loved his wife so much. He wondered sometimes how the lovely young girl he'd courted all those years ago could put with a dull old fart like himself. 'I know that. It's the uneven distribution that worries me – she may have ninety per cent of yours. I remember when I met you all those years ago you were pretty scatty yourself.'

'That just proves my point.' Nuala's eyes softened with memory. 'I had a good time goin' out with Pat McGarry. Then, as I recall, I was ridin' in the fast lane – but I reformed. After all, I chose you – solid, upright, sensible.'

'I certainly wasn't your mother's choice,' said Colin cheerfully. 'She would have preferred you to marry Pat. She thought he was God's gift. Sure I thought I never stood a chance.'

Nuala rose. 'You should be highly flattered that I chose you,' she teased. 'Pat McGarry had a lot to offer. He was handsome, rich, and had all that lovely land . . .'

'What did I have to offer?'

'You were good-looking, poor, and sexy.'

'Ah! It was my poverty that attracted you, was it?'

'No! It was your sex appeal.'

'Good Catholic girls don't mention such things. Wasn't Pat sexy?'

Nuala kissed him lightly. 'I suppose so. I just found something in you that he didn't have. Anyway! We were just a couple of youngsters – nothing much happened between us.'

'I know,' said Colin, but hid a frown.

Nuala went into the kitchen to prepare dinner, thinking her secret thoughts. No, my darling, you don't know. You don't know anything about my relationship with Pat. How I longed for him to ask me to marry him. How I lay awake at night thinking about him.

She envied Theresa her forthright manner and her occasional bucking of the conventions. In her day she had to stifle her wayward nature: her longing to do mad things, to run away from the restrictions imposed upon her by her parents and the church. She could remember lying in bed and crying with frustration.

She had married the quiet, introspective Colin on the rebound, but had never spent a day regretting it, even if there were times when, as she watched her daughter grow and develop, she hearkened back to the heady days when she and Pat racketed round the country in the sports car and she dreamed wild dreams.

If only Pat had cared more, had been less involved with the business of building up the beef herd with his father. If only he'd shown one ounce of jealousy when the quiet and gentle school master had started to show an interest, perhaps things would have worked out differently. But he hadn't – and the caring, thoughtful courtship of Colin Brady had won her. Her life with him had been

51

happy and secure, if a trifle dull for the girl who had once been Nuala McClusky.

She stopped what she was doing for a moment. In spite of what she had said to Colin, she did have some misgivings about her daughter. It was true that Theresa was more like her by nature, but although she had done a fair bit of haring about in her youth, she'd had her wits about her. Now, with Theresa, it was different; there was naivety partnered with a strong will, and it was this combination that worried her. Hopefully, the part of her daughter's nature that was influenced by Colin would temper the adventurous element that had been her own contribution.

Colin appeared in the doorway, pipe in mouth and hair tousled. He looked so endearing she felt her heart constrict. How could she be so disloyal in her thoughts?

'Will you get out of my kitchen with that noxious pipe?' She flapped the dish cloth at him. 'It's bad enough having to put up with it in the living room.'

Dutifully, he put the offending pipe in his pocket. 'I was thinkin' how well our Theresa behaved at the Easter services,' he remarked. 'She worked hard with the children.'

Nuala smiled. 'Yes, she did.' Secretly, she thought that the mantle of goodness had not sat well on her daughter's shoulders. She'd overheard Tandy Noonan's remark to Jack Ross that, given the choice, he'd swop the new Theresa for the old one any day. She knew just what he meant. Seeing her daughter walking demurely in the church procession with downcast eyes, carrying a bunch of daffodils for the altar, made her want to laugh. Still! Colin was pleased.

Theresa's burst of piety lasted only into May. There was little to sustain it now that the Easter period was over. Much to Eileen's relief she threw off the invisible, holy veil and said, 'To hell with it. Sure, who gives a tuppeny toss whether I'm being good or not? Let's take the bus into Kilgaven and have banana splits and coffee.'

It was the latest thing to visit the coffee houses. They were all the rage. Eileen said she'd heard that the fashion had started in America. Theresa said she didn't care if it had started in Coleraine; she liked the idea of drinking coffee served in glass cups. That was the great thing, and she was crazy about banana splits.

'Do we have to have coffee? It's a terrible taste – I hate it.'

'You'll drink it,' said Theresa sternly. 'Pretend you've been poisoned by the banana splits and you have to take the coffee as an antidote or die. I'm not that crazy about the taste myself, but there's no way we are sittin' there drinkin' fizzy orange and lookin' like a couple of social innocents.'

They dressed to kill. Theresa wore the new length skirt her mother, with some misgivings, had allowed her to buy, and the new clog-like shoes that were the current rage.

Eileen secretly envied Theresa her style, although she wouldn't have the nerve to be seen out in such an outfit herself. She wore her blue dress and a pair of pretty white sandals which flattered her tiny feet.

Half-way to Kilgaven, with the bus jerking over every rut in the road, they riskily applied the forbidden lipstick.

'I hate this stuff!' Eileen wailed. 'Do I have to wear it?'

Theresa gave her a look – it was enough.

'I refuse to wear mascara,' Eileen muttered, as they stooped behind the seats to escape Annie Lennox's beady eye. 'You look like Minnie Mouse.'

Theresa disregarded the slur and continued to apply the mascara in the short intervals between ruts. The operation was fairly hazardous, but was completed to her satisfaction.

Later, as they sat in the crowded coffee bar, she felt the buzz of excitement that surrounded her. 'Isn't this just great?' she said, and confided, 'Do you know, I've been so bored just lately I laughed when poor Dan McGonigle fell ass over tip down the pub steps, as drunk as a stoat. I know it was wicked of me.'

'That poor man is more to be pitied than laughed at. You should say a novena for him.' Eileen's tender heart was sore for the poor unfortunate. Theresa could be hard at times. She noticed Jack Ross and Tandy Noonan come through the door and was about to mention their arrival when the ice cream arrived.

Theresa picked up her spoon and dug into it with relish, then licked the rich, dark chocolate sauce eagerly from the spoon before digging it into the concoction again.

'You're a right pig,' Eileen remarked.

'I can afford to be. I'm built like a rake.'

'A rake with a bum,' said Eileen cruelly, and was instantly ashamed.

Theresa ignored the jibe and said dreamily, 'Do you suppose we would ever marry those two?' She had caught sight of Jack and Tandy at the counter.

Eileen secretly hoped that Tandy would find her so desirable he would ask her – perhaps she should try a new hairstyle, change her image.

'Only God knows what's ahead of us,' she sighed.

'Trust you to bring God into the conversation.'

'Theresa!'

'Well!' said Theresa, miffed. 'It's true. He seems to rule your life, that's for sure.'

'He rules—'

'I don't want a lecture, Eileen. Eat up your ice cream and stop cracking on about religion.' Theresa found Eileen's pre-occupation with the Church irritating at times, particularly her belief that everything they did was according to God's will. If so, thieves and murderers had a good case to put forward when they met St Peter at the golden gate. She smiled to herself. Next time she had to confess to one of the priests about some of her own wrongdoings, she could say, 'Don't blame me, it's God's will.'

Her thoughts turned to the night she met Richard Beck. She had forgotten about the meeting on the beach. She hoped his offer to visit him at Castle Donagh was still on. The way things were going she could do with a change in routine.

Eileen was toying with her dish of ice cream, guiltily aware of the extra pounds she would probably put on, when Theresa said idly, 'I wonder what will happen to us? Where will we all be in ten years time; will we have achieved our dreams?'

'If I achieve mine, I'll be married to a lovely man and have lots of children,' Eileen said, dreamily.

Jack and Tandy joined them. Theresa looked at Tandy, her eyes alight with devilment. 'Eileen wants to get married and have seven children,' she announced.

'Don't look at me,' he said. 'I'd kill myself first. What a sentence.'

Eileen, her face beetroot red, said, 'Take no notice. I never mentioned seven children.'

Jack was silent. He noticed that Theresa was wearing make-up. Whatever she had done to her eyes made them look dark and mysterious and her face, with its delicate contours, looked even more beautiful.

'You're very quiet, Jack,' observed Theresa. She found herself unusually shy in his presence. She was acutely aware that this was the first time she had seen him since the night of the dance.

'What? Oh yes. I'm just taking everything in. It's got a buzz, this place, hasn't it? Would you like some more coffee?'

'No thanks! One cup of antidote is enough,' said Eileen.

'Antidote?'

'Just a joke,' she said, adding hurriedly, 'Look! There's Davey Adams.'

'Let's go,' said Jack, just as hurriedly. 'Does anyone feel like going to the pictures?' No one did.

Jack had the use of his da's car. It had proved very useful since he had passed his test. 'Why don't we go for a drive?' he suggested. 'We can end the evening at my house for warm bannocks and buttermilk.'

'Won't your mother mind?' Theresa asked, knowing of Mrs Ross's pernickety ways. They had never been to Jack's house. He lived too far out of the village, and because of Mrs Ross's poor health Jack tended to limit the number of friends allowed to visit his home. Those who did were lads.

'Not at all. She knows Tandy was coming back and two more won't make any difference.'

Chrissie Ross was a little spider of a woman. Due to an unspecified illness she couldn't put on weight, and as a consequence she had painfully thin arms and legs and eyes that were too large for her face. Altogether she looked as though the breeze from a cantering horse would blow her over.

It was her manner, however, that people found irritating. She was forever straightening pictures, and when visiting other people's houses she would jump up to brush crumbs off a table. Once, when visiting Nora Connery, she'd licked her finger and cleared some dust off the mantelpiece when she thought she wasn't being observed; she then went on to smooth the fringing on the chenille table cloth. She was never asked there again.

Theresa had heard the story first-hand when the incident had been related to her mother by Nora herself. Now, as Jack lifted the latch, she could see his mother through the window, jumping up at the sound. Wiping her hands on her dress, she came forward with jerky, embarrassed little steps.

It was obvious that Jack adored his mother, by the way he protectively put his arm round her shoulders. 'Ma! I've brought some friends round. I hope you don't mind. I thought as m'da is out you wouldn't mind the company. Any chance of some of your bannocks and a mug of buttermilk?'

Her eyes lit up. 'Not at all, not at all. Come in. Come in.' She jumped round them excitedly. 'I'm pleased to have the company.' Having directed them all to chairs she disappeared into the kitchen.

Theresa was struck by the homely atmosphere of the place. Having heard the tales of Mrs Ross's eccentricities, she had expected neatness and strict cleanliness, but the feeling of comfort and warmth was overwhelming.

It was a good evening. Mrs Ross was in her element, dancing attendance on them, and the food was of the highest quality. The bannocks were lightly textured and the butter – 'Home churned,' said Jack proudly – was salted to the right degree. They played dominoes and ludo and Mrs Ross fidgeted and crocheted, quietly rising now and then to pull the curtains straight or twitch a cushion. She gave no trouble and smiled gently when anyone caught her eye.

To her own surprise, Theresa found herself feeling as protective towards the woman as Jack seemed to be. She quickly retrieved the skein of wool when Mrs Ross got up on one of her restless rambles, and once she stopped her from falling as Tandy, whooping with delight because he had won a game, nearly knocked her over as he half rose from his chair.

'Contain yourself, Tandy,' admonished Jack.

Tandy apologised.

'Think nothing more of it, son,' said Mrs Ross with a quick, nervous smile. She was used to Tandy. He was a regular visitor and she was very fond of him. She looked over at the two girls. She knew who they were, but this was the first time Jack had invited a girl home. She wondered which one he was interested in. She hoped it was Kathleen O'Rourke's daughter, with her plump rosy cheeks and sweet expression. She had seen her helping out at church and she seemed modest and kind. Not that she had anything against the Brady girl whose mother was so good to Jack. She had appreciated the kind actions with the wool and all, but there was something about the girl that twittered her.

Chrissie was well aware that everyone thought she had gone a bit 'odd' in her middle years, but she knew a thing or two about people, and this girl had a faint aura around her. Chrissie was sensitive to such things but she never let on to a soul that she had second sight.

As she covertly studied the girl she sensed unhappiness, and she felt vaguely sad as her eyes turned towards her son. Somehow he was involved.

The thick vibrant mane of dark hair hid the girl's face as she concentrated on the game, but Chrissie could feel the aura emanating from her. The slim young body held a tension like taut steel. She was a creature of nature. Chrissie closed her eyes and felt a strong surge of power. This girl was strongly associated with water – the sea, perhaps. Clouds were gathering. She felt that the future held many problems for the girl.

A feeling of unease filled the room, destroying the normality of the scene. She opened her eyes. The girl's eyes met hers, a startled awareness in their depths. Just as suddenly Theresa turned away, but not before Chrissie had seen her apprehension. The girl knew something had occurred between them.

The others were unaware of the tension and were still concentrating on the game. Chrissie struggled to her feet and, bidding them all goodnight and thanking them for coming, she made her way to her bedroom, aware of the dark, puzzled gaze boring into her back as she left the room.

Theresa was unusually quiet on the way home. When it was remarked upon, she made an excuse. 'I'm tired,' she apologised, leaning back and closing her eyes. The feeling of unease she had felt as she looked into Mrs Ross's eyes remained with her still. The look that had passed between them had left her trembling. It was as if the little woman had seen into her very soul. She started as she realised that Eileen was saying something.

'I'm sorry – I . . .'

'What's the matter?' Eileen said. 'You look pale. Perhaps you ate that banana split too quickly. Have you got stomach-ache?'

'I'm all right.' Theresa turned her head towards the window and stared out into the darkness.

'Well. I hope you aren't going down with anything. There's the dance tomorrow night.'

'I'll not be going. I forgot to tell you. Mam and I are going over to spend the evening with Gran. She isn't well and Mam is really worried.'

'I'll not be there either,' said Jack.

'That means I'll not go either,' said Tandy. 'I'll likely get stuck with someone like Davey Adams. Just as well I'm not bothered. What's your excuse?'

'I did tell you. I'm meeting Tom Drake in Dublin. We are going out to dinner and he's showing me round the university. He knows it well, as his brother Tommy is in his third year.'

Tandy was the first to be dropped off, followed by Theresa.

'I hope your gran will be feeling better,' Eileen said gently.

'I second that.' Jack had also noticed Theresa's pallor and her silence, which he now put down to worry about her gran. Probably she had started to think about it as she sat quietly on the way home.

Theresa warmed to the concern in his voice. 'I'm fine. Sure Eileen hit the nail on the head. I did attack the ice cream a bit hard.'

Jack turned the engine off when they reached Eileen's door. 'I've been thinking about this weekend,' he said thoughtfully. 'I don't suppose you will want to go to the dance, since none of the rest of us are going?'

'I certainly won't. Why?

'I have an idea. I'll get in touch with you when I have done some groundwork.'

'What kind of idea?' Eileen loved a mystery, but Jack would say no more.

★ ★ ★

Eileen didn't see Theresa after mass the next day. The family had rushed off before the last hymn, ignoring the heads that turned. She admired their nerve. She could never run the gauntlet of disapproving looks for leaving Mass before the priest said, 'Go! The Mass is finished.'

Jack wasn't among the crowd of young people deftly extracting themselves from family groups to form their own. She was disappointed. She had been looking forward to finding out what he meant last night. She sighed. This could be a dreary day.

She caught her mother's glance and forced a smile. Her mother was fine as mothers go, but Eileen never felt she could enjoy the luxury of being depressed or ill. She always felt guilty when her mother became harassed.

Later, just as the family had finished lunch, the phone rang. 'It's for you, Eileen,' her mother said; already a frown had appeared from nowhere. 'It's a man.'

'Oh!' Eileen tried to keep the excitement out of her voice. She ran to the phone. 'Hello?' she said, breathlessly. It was Jack. He wondered if she would like to come out to dinner with him that evening. John Drake was bringing his girlfriend and Jack thought if she would agree to making an evening of it, he wouldn't feel like a third arm with the other two.

'What about Theresa?'

'What about Theresa? She is with her gran. I'm only asking you to make up a foursome, seeing as you wouldn't be going to the dance. Theresa is hardly likely to cut your head off. You'll have to put up with a visit to the university first.'

Eileen hesitated. She couldn't be certain of Theresa's possible reaction, but as she was only going so that Jack wouldn't be embarrassed then that was all right. The thought of an evening out that was different wasn't one she wanted to turn down.

'I'll come! I'd enjoy a visit to the university. You never know. I might be going there myself one day.'

'Square it with your mam and da, then – I'll hold the phone – and you better mention that we might be a bit late getting back.'

Eileen ran into the large kitchen. Her father was elbow deep in newspapers and her mam was elbow deep in suds. 'Would you mind if I went out for a meal in Dublin with Jack Ross?' She waited with bated breath. Already her mam was looking flustered and glancing nervously at her husband.

'Certainly not! You're far too young to be going out with lads.'

'Please Da! He isn't going as my boyfriend. He just needs company as he is meeting a friend who is showing him round the university. Please! Jack's hanging on the phone.'

'Dinner, you say? Very grand. I'll have a word.'

It seemed an age before he came back, and Eileen tried to still the butterflies in her stomach. She would die if he said she couldn't go. Somehow, everything that was interesting happened to Theresa and now, for once, she was doing something different on her own, not hanging on Theresa's coat tails.

'The arrangements are that he brings you home no later than midnight – that's allowin' for the journey. So see you eat up sharply.'

Eileen hugged him. 'I'll gollop it down. Da. Don't worry. Jack will look after me.'

'Aye! Of them all he is the level-headed one. Anyway, he explained the situation. But remember that when you go out you are representing this family and I'll not tolerate anything that—' Seeing his wife's worried frown, he stopped. 'Anyway! Enjoy yourself.'

Theresa was shocked when she saw her gran. In sickness, she looked even tinier and more shrunken than Theresa remembered. Her breathing was laboured and her lips blue. Her eyes were closed, but it was obvious by the tension in the lids that the appearance of sleep was false. This was confirmed by the way the pale blue eyes shot open as they walked into the room.

'Mam! I'm going to fetch Doctor Owen. You look bad,' Nuala said gently.

'It's the breath. I'm finding it hard to breathe.'

'Don't try to talk, Mam.' Nuala looked worriedly at Colin. 'Will you go now, Colin?'

'I'm on my way.' He went quickly towards the door.

Nuala nodded at Theresa who sat down by the bed and took her gran's thin, blue-veined hand in her own.

Nuala followed her husband out of the room. 'I wouldn't bother to come back, Colin. I'm going to stay the night.'

'What about Theresa?' he whispered.

'I'll ask David to take her back with him. Let her have some time with her gran for now.'

She entered the room again to find Theresa stroking her gran's hand, with tears rolling down her cheeks.

Grannie McClusky looked beseechingly at her daughter. 'Tell–her–I'm going–to–be–all right,' she gasped.

'Of course you are – now stop being defeatist, Theresa, and go and make us all a cup of tea. Gran has a touch of flu and I'm sure she'll be better soon.' Nuala smiled at her mother and followed her daughter from the room.

'It doesn't do to make Gran feel unhappy by seeing your

59

distress,' she admonished gently. She'll be all right – old people look worse than they really are when they're ill.'

'She looks so bad,' Theresa whispered. 'I'm sorry for letting her see me cry; I just love her so much, Mam.'

Nuala took her into her arms. This was the first time Theresa had seen anything approaching a crisis of this sort in the family. She had never known her grandfather, and Nuala knew that the possibility that her dear gran might be dying had hit her hard.

'Will she really be all right?'

Nuala hesitated. She too had been shocked at her mother's appearance, but she knew that she had to be strong. She would be of no use to her family if she crumpled now.

'Let's wait till David Owen has a look at her; but I've seen your gran get over worse. She looks frail but she is a tough old bird.' She held her daughter gently from her. 'Go and make that tea. I'm dying for one and I bet Gran would manage a few sips.'

David Owen arrived an hour later. He had been visiting a farmer's wife at the other end of Tullybra.

Nuala showed him into the room and waited while he examined her mother. He placed the stethoscope on her chest and back several times before lowering her nightie.

'You'll do, Mrs McClusky,' he pronounced. 'You have the beginnings of a right lobar pneumonia, but I think we've caught it in time. You can stop saying your act of contrition. You'll live to sin another day. Lots of tender loving care, plenty of fluids and some antibiotics should do the trick.' He followed Nuala from the room.

Mona McClusky closed her eyes. She wasn't so certain. While she had lain there, waiting for her family to come, she had remembered the premonition she'd had recently. Now she knew why she hadn't seen a face as she had the other times. It was her own death she had seen, and she had a strong feeling that not a single pill or injection would do a bit of good. She was on her way to meet up with McClusky, and nothing on this earth was going to alter that. Even if she got out of this, she would be joining him soon – she was certain of it.

'She'll need round-the-clock care for the next few days at least,' David said to Nuala. 'Can you stay?'

'Of course I can. Colin and Theresa will manage without me, I'm sure – is she really so ill?'

'I didn't say that; but she is old and frail and will need a lot of nursing to help her pull out of this. With care I think we can do it.'

Nuala nodded. 'She'll get it. Could you persuade Theresa to go back with you?'

Theresa, having reluctantly agreed, was silent on the drive

home. David left her to her thoughts and concentrated on his driving. It didn't do the young any harm to see mortality staring them in the face; it brought life into perspective. He particularly didn't think it would be a bad thing for Theresa, who had a bit of a reputation. Nevertheless, he could feel sorry for the young girl; he knew how much she loved her gran. He hadn't been exactly truthful with Nuala. He was still worried about the old lady. He hoped to God she wouldn't have a relapse.

Theresa relayed the doctor's diagnosis to her father. 'He says she should be all right as he got there before her chest got too bad.'

'That's great news,' said Colin, putting his arm round her. 'David is a good man. If he says your gran is going to make it, then you can be sure she will.' He stroked her hair and pressed her head against him.

She smiled tremulously. 'She looked so little lying in that big bed, Da. Suddenly she looked old and tired. I've never thought of her as being old before.'

'I know just what you mean,' Colin laughed. 'She's like a pixie – always on the go, always making up stories for you, always ready with the comfort. I tell you, she will be all right. It would take more than a mild dose of lobar pneumonia to knock that one out.'

Theresa released herself from his arm. 'I'll go up and have a word with Eileen before I go to bed – it's only nine o'clock.' She had a sudden need to see Eileen, with her soft voice and her ability to make problems seem small. She could always make things seem better.

She looked anxiously up at Eileen's bedroom window. She usually went up to her room to read or study if she wasn't going out, but the window showed no light. She frowned, and then the frown lifted. Of course. It was Sunday – family night in the O'Rourke household.

She knocked on the shop door and waited. Mrs O'Rourke answered. 'Hello Theresa,' she said nervously. 'What can I do for you?'

'I've just come back from my gran—'

'Oh the poor soul,' interrupted Mrs O'Rourke. 'How is she? Your da mentioned she was ill.'

'She's pretty poorly, but Doctor Owen says she will be all right with a bit of nursing. Mam is staying up there for a few days to look after her.' She tried hard to keep the emotion from her voice, but her distress was noticed and Kathleen O'Rourke tugged her arm, pulling her inside.

'Come in. Don't stand on the doorstep. What am I thinking of? I have no sense of decency leaving you there.'

61

'Is Eileen about? I thought I'd have a word with her before I go to bed,' said Theresa, trying to regain her balance. Eileen's mother was enough to drive any sane person mad with her chattering.

Mrs O'Rourke looked at her vaguely. 'Eileen isn't here.'

God give me strength, thought Theresa, and said, 'I thought she wasn't going out tonight.'

'She has gone out to dinner.'

Theresa's eyes opened in surprise. 'Gone out to dinner?'

'Yes! She has gone out with – with—' Mrs O'Rourke flapped her hand.

'With Tandy Noonan?' Theresa prompted.

'No, no – the other one. The one with the odd mother who "sees" things.'

Theresa smiled weakly and nodded her thanks before walking away. She couldn't believe what she had just heard. Why hadn't Jack asked her? She hadn't known how ill her gran was then, and she would probably have put off the visit. A ball of indignation settled in her stomach. Eileen O'Rourke had some explaining to do.

CHAPTER 5

Once, when Theresa had told Eileen in strict confidence that when she left Tullybra she was going to explore alternative religions, Eileen had stared at her in horror.

'You needn't look at me like that,' Theresa had said. 'Wasn't it Father Corke himself who told us there was more than one road to heaven so we must be kind to Protestants?'

Eileen had retorted, 'In which case, you can rule out Buddhism, for you couldn't sit still long enough or stay quiet long enough to meditate.'

Theresa hadn't deigned to answer, but had thrown her one of her famous looks. Yet here she was now, sitting on the school bus, silent and pensive, when normally she would be hopping about like a Chinese firecracker.

With a tiny frown, Eileen leaned back into her seat and watched the scenery outside until she could stand the atmosphere no longer. 'Is there something wrong?' she asked tentatively.

'Nothing at all; in spite of the fact that my gran is seriously ill and my best friend has stabbed me in the back.'

Ignoring the attack on herself, Eileen said anxiously, 'Is your gran that bad? Oh Theresa, I'm so sorry. I'll pray for her this night. You'll see, she'll be fine – Doctor Owen is a brilliant man.'

'That's fine, then. I can rest easy. With your prayers and Doctor Owen's skill she'll make it.'

Eileen, hurt by the sourness of the rejoinder, decided that now was not the time to tell Theresa about the nice evening she had spent with Jack and his friends, so she settled back and immersed herself in reminiscence.

Things hadn't improved by lunchtime, but needing to clear the air, Eileen insisted that Theresa should listen to what she had to say.

'Jack asked me to go out to dinner with him so that he had company as Tom Drake was bringing his girlfriend. it was as simple as that.'

63

'He could have asked me.'

'How could he? You were going to see your gran.'

Theresa gave a slight scowl. 'I could have put it off.'

'Sure Jack didn't know you would be willing to. He asked me because I was free. It was a nice gesture on his part. He knew I was going to be alone.'

Theresa was quiet for a few minutes, and then she turned to Eileen. 'I'm sorry! You're right. Jack would have a kind thought like that.'

'Don't make me out to be a charity case,' said Eileen, but she said it with a smile, glad that her friend was being more reasonable.

'I was a bit miffed because Jack has never asked me out for a meal,' Theresa explained, and the matter was closed.

Several days later, a small, dapper man with a cheerful, smiling face and a shock of grey hair partially hidden beneath an incongruous bowler hat, emerged from O'Rourke's shop bearing a large box of groceries. Theresa recognised him as being the man who worked for Richard Beck. They had spoken of him when she'd met Richard at the cove.

Awkwardly, he doffed his hat and smiled fleetingly. 'Good afternoon – Miss Theresa Brady?'

Theresa nodded. 'Yes.'

'I have a letter for you.'

'A letter? And how did you know I was Theresa Brady?'

Handing her the letter, he resettled the large box of groceries more comfortably on his hip and walked towards a large black car. 'Description,' he called back. 'Very accurate – the letter will explain all.' Hoisting the groceries into the car, he said, 'Good day to you,' and climbed into the driver's seat.

She stared after the retreating vehicle before glancing down at the neat, flowing writing on the envelope. Hastily she stuffed it into her pocket. She had more pressing concerns.

Striding purposefully up the long hill towards the parochial house, she paused only to wipe the perspiration from her face. The day was warm and sunny, with only the faintest breeze to cool the skin.

Mrs Doughty, the priests' housekeeper, answered the door and remarked sourly, 'Ah! Theresa Brady – and what would you be wantin'?'

'I'd like a word with Father Corke, please,' said Theresa nervously. The 'please' nearly choked her, but Mrs Doughty was not the class of person she was used to and she wanted to keep her sweet.

Vera Doughty had a reputation for being unpredictable, due to the fact that she was fond of the drink. Father Corke had rescued her many years before from a life of dissipation and, having removed her from the hovel that was her cottage, had dressed her up and given her a job as housekeeper.

Whether he realised that she still had the odd lapse, no one knew. If he suspected, he kept his counsel. Vera did very well on the whole, but her temper was uncertain and many had complained about her attitude. Father Corke, with a small sigh, would murmur about being charitable and giving the devil his due, so the villagers put up with her vagaries out of respect for him.

Mrs Doughty continued to glare. 'Ye can't see him. He's away at a three-day seminar – you'll have to catch him at confession on Saturday.' She closed the door firmly.

'You mean, he's gone fishing on Lough Targ,' muttered Theresa, turning away.

Her father was at home when she arrived back. 'I'm taking some groceries up to Gran's. Do you want to come?'

Her eyes lit up. She hadn't seen her gran since the first day of her illness. Doctor Owen had insisted on a 'no visitors' regime. 'Does this mean she is really getting better?'

Her father smiled. 'Seeing as your mam has her sittin' by the duck pond, and declares she is eatin' herself out of house and home – yes! You could say that.'

'Isn't that great? I'd love to come with you.'

Colin glanced at his daughter briefly as he negotiated the sharp bends. There was a frown creasing her brow. He had noticed an air of distraction about her for the past week, but he had left well alone; teenage girls fazed him. He let Nuala sort things out when Theresa was having one of her turns. He continued to concentrate on his driving and left her to her thoughts.

They were heavy ones. Just lately she seemed to have lurched from one crisis to another, but by the grace of God had managed to extricate herself. This last one, however, was more serious. Too late she had realized that she had made a bit of a spectacle of herself at the dance. If the old priest had not seen her, everything might have passed over as one of her usual mad schemes – but he had, and therein lay the danger. He was the only one who might mention it to her mother, having recognized her dress. The others were hardly likely to bat an eyelid. She had to see him to find out if he would be giving her a second chance. She sighed heavily.

'What was the sigh for?' enquired Colin, forgetting his reluctance to get involved in his daughter's problems.

'Nothing!' Theresa gave a wavering smile. 'Just the usual irritations that beset us all sometimes.'

Colin merely nodded; he was thankful for the reprieve.

Kissing her mother quickly, Theresa ran into the garden to her gran. Colin waited till she had gone before turning to his wife. 'She's been worried about something for the past week,' he said. 'I've noticed her staring into space a lot, and she kept sighing as we drove along in the car.

'Don't give it a thought,' said Nuala, giving him an answering peck on the cheek. 'She has been having a few problems with Jack just lately – she'll recover.'

'I should have talked to her,' he said uneasily, 'but I'm not good at that sort of thing.'

'Don't worry,' Nuala insisted. 'We'll soon know if it's anything really serious. Theresa will ask our advice if it's important. We have always been here for her and she knows that – meanwhile, come and chop some logs.' She glanced towards the duck pond where Theresa was sitting with her arm around her gran.

Nuala was worried about the bond between those two, and how it might affect the future. Her mother was even more frail since the bout of pneumonia, and she hoped to God Theresa was aware that the situation was still fragile. David was concerned about the amount of hidden damage that may have been caused. He wanted to have her mother's chest X-rayed as soon as she was fit to travel to Dublin. God knows how Theresa would cope if – if . . . Her eyes filled with tears as she made her way to the kitchen. Occasionally she glanced out of the window at the sound of laughter.

Theresa and her gran were laughing at the antics of the dirty little ducks who were now, as gran observed with amusement, teenagers. There was a companionable silence for a moment until Grannie McClusky spoke.

'What's troubling you, cusheen?'

Theresa was startled by the question. 'Nothing!' she said hurriedly.

'There is something bothering you. If you don't tell me I'm likely to start worrying that it is something awful and then you will have my decline on your conscience.'

'That isn't fair, Gran. It's nothing awful anyway, and you aren't well enough for such discussions.'

'I'll be the judge. Tell me.'

Reluctantly, Theresa told her about borrowing her mother's dress and how Father Corke had threatened to tell her mam about the incident.

'Did you look good in the dress?' Mona laughed. 'Only if you did would it be worth it.'

Theresa gave a nervous smile. 'I'm told I did. The trouble is, the dress was too short and clingy on me because I'm bigger than Mam, and I'm afraid, with the high-heeled shoes I wore I shocked everyone. I only did it to liven things up a bit.'

'Well! It looks like you succeeded.' Mona took her granddaughters hand in hers. 'Why don't you get in before Father Corke and tell your mam?'

Theresa looked horrified. 'I couldn't, Gran. Never! Anyway, I'm hoping to catch Father Corke at confession on Saturday. He might go easy on me.'

'Please yourself, but I have a feeling your mam will be lenient with you. Did you know she was a right tearaway herself when she was young? She managed to give me a few heart attacks. Pat McGarry and her used to tear about in his sports car getting up to God knows what.'

'I heard she had a fling with Pat.' Theresa laughed. 'Was she really a tearaway? I just can't imagine it – my mam?'

'That's the trouble with each generation. They only see the person who has settled down into respectability and become responsible. They forget that what is now the "older generation" were once the "younger generation" who got up to all the same tricks in their day. There isn't much that you get up to that your mam hasn't done before, and I warn you – she probably knows exactly what you are about.'

When her mother called to say that the meal was on the table, Theresa helped her gran to rise from the bench and assisted her slowly to the house. During the meal, she looked at her mother with a new awareness and when her gran caught her eye and winked, she smiled.

She had been in bed an hour before she remembered the letter. Reaching into the pocket of her linen jacket, she drew it out and studied the writing. It looked artistic, with its gently sloping strokes and well-rounded appearance – like a woman's writing, she thought in surprise, remembering the tall man with his forceful, kind manner.

She had to read it twice before it sunk in that Richard Beck was inviting her to Castle Donagh to have tea and have a look at his horses. He wanted her to telephone to make arrangements. She could hardly get to sleep for excitement. No one had ever seen the inside of the castle; she would have a certain celebrity status. Here was something different to challenge the conformity of her days.

On Monday she broached the subject with her father. Pulling

the letter from her pocket she gave it to him.

'How did you come to meet this Mr Beck?' he asked.

'I met him just before Easter. He was riding up on the bluff beyond Lafferty's Cove.'

'What were you doing up there?'

Theresa hesitated before she told the lie. 'I went for a walk to do some thinking.'

'About what?'

She avoided the question and asked, 'What do you think, Da? Would you mind if I went up to Castle Donagh?'

'I can't see the harm,' Colin mused, stroking his nose in thought. 'But I think we had better discuss it with your mother. After all, we don't know a lot about the man.'

Colin was dubious, in spite of his earlier assurance. 'I've not heard anything bad about Mr Beck, but he is a stranger,' he said to Nuala. 'Theresa tells me he is very courteous and spoke pleasantly to her on the hill.'

'As Shakespeare says, "The devil can cite scripture for his purpose" – so I'd not set much store by that,' said Nuala.

Theresa and her father glanced at each other. 'Give me credit for being able to judge character, Mam,' said Theresa.

'And where did you get this expertise from?' enquired Colin, but he was smiling.

'Don't tease her,' Nuala said. 'What do you think?'

He hesitated. The ball had been neatly thrown into his court. 'All right! he said at last. 'He has to live here; he'll hardly run the risk of upsetting us—'

'By doing what?' Theresa interrupted sharply.

Nuala gave her a warning look. If there was one thing Colin couldn't abide, it was a lippy young girl. His sudden frown hadn't gone unnoticed.

'I'll make the telephone call,' Colin decided. 'We'll discuss the matter and take it from there.'

And so it was arranged. Richard insisted she should bring a riding hat, which meant a visit to Kilgaven. She rang Eileen to give her the news.

'Tell me all when you get back,' said Eileen. 'You're a terrible one for noticing detail, so look at every single thing this time.' It always amazed her that Theresa was so indifferent to her surroundings, in view of the fact that she had the artist's eye for colour and design. Her painting was the envy of every girl in the Art class and Mrs Nally, the Art mistress, had great hopes for her.

'I'm goin' to see the stables and the horses,' said Theresa. 'I'm not buyin' the castle. I don't suppose I'll see further than the kitchen.'

'He'll not entertain you in the kitchen,' Eileen scoffed. He'll want to show off his grand drawing room.'

Theresa resolved that she should keep her eyes open this time, if only to prove that she could be observant if she put her mind to it.

'I'll give you all the news,' she said huffily. Telling Eileen about her wonderful opportunity did no good at all. Eileen had not an envious bone in her body. It was a major fault which went some way towards taking the bloom off the whole trip. Why couldn't Eileen be as devious and marred as the rest of them?

On Saturday Theresa paid a visit to confession. She crept quietly towards a pew, well away from those still waiting to enter the confessional box – or sweat box, as Davey Adams called it. Someone coughed and the sound echoed around the walls and high-ceilinged vault, splitting the sepulchral quietness with startling clarity.

In response, there were more nervous coughs. The flickering candles wavering towards their own demise completed the feeling of mild unease Theresa always felt when sitting in the candlelit gloom, so different from the bright, colourful Sunday Mass.

She leaned back against the hard pew and waited for the last few penitents to enter the box. As ever, the mental clocks were ticking away, recording the length of time spent inside – the theory being that the longer the time inside, the bigger the sin.

Marian Rice emerged after a few minutes with a smile on her lips. Without a glance at those still waiting, she walked to the altar, a look of piety already settling on her coarse features. Tom Dougan took her place and Theresa watched the knowing looks that passed between the two women who were waiting their turn. It was common knowledge that Tom never left the widow woman Cassie Doran's house.

'What I'd do without Tom I don't know. He's the great one with the electrics. I'm always havin' to send for him,' Cassie would twitter.

If he's that good then how come her electrics break down with more regularity than the national grid? Theresa wondered idly.

Five minutes passed. Ten. When Tom emerged it was noticeable, even in the candlelit church, that he looked embarrassed as he quickly strode to the altar to say his penance. There was a rustle of movement as heads that had been bent in prayer lifted to follow his progress.

Theresa's sympathy was with him. The trick was not to give Father Corke any excuse to hold forth at length. Occasionally a

69

waiting penitent would sit tight, willing the others to go first. At these times Father Corke would open the door and call out: 'Next! Or can I go home to my dinner?'

When the last one had tripped towards the altar, Theresa went to the left-hand door of the confessional and entered. Her nose wrinkled in distaste. Judging by the musty odour and the strong smell of drink, old Sara McKenna had been an earlier occupant.

She was on the brink of losing her nerve when the small curtain covering the grille was pulled across and the vague outline of the priest's face appeared at the perforated screen.

'Bless me, Father, for I have sinned—'

'Oh! It's you.'

'I thought the confessional was supposed to be anonymous,' Theresa whispered fiercely.

'I have second sight,' growled Father Corke. 'Now make your confession.'

Hastily she did so.

'Is that all?'

'I've no more sins.'

'I'd commit more than that sittin' on the river bank, fishin'.'

She remained silent. She didn't want a lecture.

'Is there anything else before I give you absolution?'

'Can I talk to you after you've done?'

'Hold on a minute.' There was a click and a pause and then the priest spoke again. 'I've four more candidates tryin' to win their way into God's good books. Wait at the back of the church till I call for you.'

'Thank you, Father,' said Theresa, with a suspicious meekness of manner.

'Say three Hail Marys and pray for the holy souls while you are about it.' Father Corke smiled to himself. He'd wondered when she'd give in and come to see him.

Theresa rose as he emerged at last, remembered she hadn't prayed for the repose of the holy souls, and hurriedly knelt and blessed herself, muttering quickly, 'May the souls of the faithful departed through the mercy of God rest in peace. Amen.'

'I hope he heard you. You were goin' at a rate of knots there,' said Father Corke. 'Come into the Sanctuary.'

She followed him, trying to remember the line of conversation she had devised, and failing because of nerves. In such instances she usually became defiant, but this time she knew she had to keep control.

'Now! What can I do for you?'

She swallowed. The old devil knew fine well what this was all about. He was just making her sweat.

70

'It's about the business of the dance.'

'I see! You're worried that I will tell your parents.'

She remained silent.

'I'll let you off this time,' Father Corke said crisply. 'But one more caper like that one and I'll preach a sermon on it – anyway, if I'd been going to tell them about your escapade, I'd have done it sooner than this. I'm more concerned about your attitude to confession.'

'I was off my head. I was just saying those things for defiance's sake.'

'Is that so? Well, I'll tell you where that has got you.' Producing a small white book from his cassock, he looked sternly at her. 'Read! Absorb! And come back with the answers firmly in your mind.'

She took the book from him. 'A catechism? Sure I read this in junior infants.'

'And much good it has done you. You'll read it again, my girl – cover to cover – and in two weeks' time Sister Mary Patricia will discuss the text with you. It's back to basics with you. Now away off home and keep out of mischief for a while – and take this coat with you. I found it in the cloakroom. I believe it's yours.'

After she had gone, he settled himself in a chair to read his missal but found he couldn't concentrate. His arthritic hip was giving him gyp; it always did after he'd sat on the hard bench between the two confessional boxes, swivelling from one to another in turn. Tonight, half of Tullybra had seemed to require absolution.

The phone rang. It was Mrs Doughty asking disgruntledly if he was coming over for supper or did he think she was going to bring the rapidly congealing mess over there?'

'I'll be there in a few minutes,' he said. She was the most sour-faced, acid-tongued old biddy he had ever known, and he thought the world of her. He was still dwelling on the matter of Theresa Brady as he walked towards his supper. Somehow he had to get that girl into some sort of order before her wildness destroyed her.

Theresa ran down the hill, relief flooding through her. Having to read through the catechism presented no problems. The old devil had let her off lightly. She had to jump to the side as Davey Adams went flying past on his bike, his legs held out stiffly at an angle and the pedals flying wildly out of control. The daft eejut would come off one of these days. He was a menace on that bike. He stopped and waited at the bottom of the hill, a moony look on his face, his acne showing up redly because of the exertion.

71

'Been confessing your sins?' he asked cheekily.

Theresa bit back the retort she wanted to make; there was no point in crossing swords with Davey Adams.

'Were you wantin' to talk to me?'

'I hear I missed a great event at the dance.'

Her heart flipped. Davey could be a right bad article when he wanted to be. 'You did indeed, Davey. I sprung one of my little surprises. What a pity you missed it.' The laugh she gave sounded false to her own ears.

'I wish I'd been there.'

'My mother lent me her black dress so I could go looking like a cover girl.' Nerves were causing her to tremble. She stiffened. She had to make things seem as though it had all been a bit of a lark which her mother had been party to.

'Ah! I see.' Davey was disappointed. He had thought that he had something on the grand Theresa, but it was obviously all just a joke that his sisters, as usual, had over exaggerated. 'Well, I'll see you sometime,' he said lamely, and rode off.

Theresa drew in a deep breath of relief. She didn't think Davey would bother any more about spreading the tale. Her heart quailed at the thought that she may have gone too far by implicating her mother. God! she thought. Can you not stop me from doing things that get me into trouble? I know I said I wanted to be Bad, but I was feeling depressed when I said it.

By Saturday Theresa's mood had lightened. She felt more optimistic the further away the fateful dance night receded, and she hummed quietly as she cycled towards the castle to meet Richard Beck. The ride proved less arduous than she had expected. It was not a road she was familiar with as it led only to the castle, with a few farms scattered along the east side like beads on a rosary. To the west, on the other side of the forest which was part of the castle's lands, lay the large estate belonging to Lord Conliffe – or Lord Patrick as he was affectionately known.

Her first sight of the castle took her breath away with its grey turrets and its portcullis. Along the driveway there was evidence of some outer buildings long since gone. Large grass mounds with enormous stones protruding from them showed their position.

She stopped for a moment to look at a particularly large stone. It was as big as a small shed. She realised suddenly how little she knew of this historic place. Wasn't it always the way? They knew about the kings of England and their castles and battles and the great events that had shaped history, yet here on their own turf was the Castle Donagh, and she supposed there was not one pupil who knew a thing about the events that had shaped its destiny.

She set her bike carefully against the wall and rang the bell. It seemed an age before the heavy door opened and the man she had met in the village stood before her.

He smiled and beckoned her in. 'Mr Richard is waiting for you in the drawing room; he said.

Theresa's gaze darted from side to side as she followed him. He was going so fast she couldn't take it all in, but she did manage to take note of the beautiful tapestries hanging on the wall, and the real – at least she supposed they were real – suits of armour standing beneath two enormous flags.

Richard Beck came forward to welcome her and she felt a tension in her spine. She took his proffered hand and smiled nervously as he shook hers in greeting.

'I'm glad you could come,' he smiled. 'What do you think of my castle?'

'It's beautiful – and awesome. Is it as old as it looks?'

'Indeed! Of course, the rest of the castle, which included the outer and inner baileys, is gone. I expect you noticed the remains of the outer bailey on the way up the drive. Later, I'll show you the original plan and extent of the castle; meanwhile, would you like some tea or shall we go straight to the stables?'

'The stables. I'm dying to meet Othello again.'

Richard led her along the hall and out through a rear door. She couldn't see any sign of the stables.

'I'm afraid they are some way from the house. I hope you don't mind a walk.'

'Not a bit of it. Not bein' a member of the cushioned classes I have to do a fair bit of walking.' Theresa grinned up at him, her nervousness now gone. He was a man of easy manner and she was surprised to find that he looked years younger than she had imagined him to be when she had met him on the beach. Of course it had been dark, but his voice had sounded somehow older. His hair was grey but his face was firm and the few lines that creased his eyes and lined his mouth added power to his face. He was also a lot taller than she remembered – and slimmer. Altogether, he was very attractive. She loved his English accent and meant to try and copy it so that she could impress Eileen with the culture of the man.

One of the horses, sensing their coming, began to nicker and paw the ground and the movements set the others off. There was a mulchy odour of hay mixed with horse, and Theresa twitched her nostrils in delight at the farmy, country smell.

They spent half an hour at the stables. She met Night Star and stroked the shiny reddish brown coat as she murmured softly to her.

73

'Would you like to ride her for me after you have a few lessons?'

'I'd love to. Although I've only ridden the farm horses bareback. I'm told I have good balance.' The idea excited her.

'I'm certain if you can ride bareback and stay on you'll have no trouble with a saddle.' Richard smiled. 'Anyway! She's practically bomb-proof – a most gentle creature. Now meet Jupiter, the complete opposite.'

Jupiter was brought out. He was indeed the opposite. His arched neck and high step marked him down as an aristocrat. Like Othello, he was jet black, the only difference being the white flash between his eyes. He looked as though he might be hard to handle.

'What a magnificent animal,' Theresa breathed. 'Who rides him?'

'Certainly not me.' Richard laughed. 'I had arranged for a stable lad from the large stud over at Kilgaven to exercise him, but he has gone down with some obscure illness so I've had to find another rider.'

'He looks fast.'

'He is. He is being prepared to race in the Curragh. Once we get him into form he will be transferred over to the stables at Kilgaven for more concentrated training.'

'You must be very proud of him.'

'He belongs to my partner. George travels a lot on business, when he isn't at his gallery in London, so I've been saddled with arranging his future.'

They returned to the house, and after tea he showed her round the castle.

'Many of the rooms are not habitable now, but those that are have been overhauled and redecorated. Did you know that King Billy and his troops stayed here when he crossed the Boyne?'

'No! I'm ashamed to confess that I know very little of the castle's history.'

'The castle belonged to a descendent of one of the earls of Drogheda, who was hounded out so that it could be used as a billet for the King before he moved on to Mellifont Abbey. He used the abbey as his final headquarters during the battle of the Boyne in 1690.'

Richard crossed to the heavy bookcase and selected a book. 'This is a book that's been written about the area in which the castle and its part in the uprising is featured,' he said, adding, 'You may borrow it if you like, but please take great care of it.'

Later, as they were saying goodbye at the impressive front door, Richard paused for a moment, his eyes scanning the large wood in the distance.

'Can you see smoke coming from the woods?' He turned her round so that she could see where he was pointing. 'I know it isn't a bush fire because the smoke is spiralling upwards as though the fire is controlled. Do you know if anyone uses the woods for camping?'

'I think it might be a tinker and his family. They camp there every winter and travel around the country during the summer months, selling the stuff they have made during their stay.'

Richard's eyebrows rose. 'Is that so?'

'They've been doing it for years. However, it's the wrong time for them. They should be travelling the country by now.'

'No one mentioned that I was taking on a tinker family for the next twenty-five years when I leased this place. I'm not happy about this – not happy at all. I must do something,' Richard said irritably.

'Perhaps it's hikers on their way through.'

He continued as though he hadn't heard. 'Now I know why the woods are in such a disgraceful state. I rode over there a few weeks ago and I was appalled at the sight of areas where trees have been indiscriminately chopped down and litter piled up. I thought it was villagers who had chopped the trees and wondered what to do about it. Do you know this tinker chap's name?'

'But–But–Ben,' said Theresa, trying not to laugh.

'You're stuttering,' said Richard. 'It really isn't funny; those woods belong to me.'

'No! I'm not stuttering. His name really is But–But–Ben.' Unable to contain her mirth any longer, she laughed out loud.

'I can't believe that.'

'It's true. He's been called that all his life because he can't say Ben without stuttering.'

'Good God!'

'He has quite a temper,' Theresa warned. 'He will need careful handling. Why don't you have a word with Lord Patrick? He knows him well.'

'How can Lord Conliffe help?'

'He had some trouble with him a few years back – poaching – and he set his gamekeeper on to him. It was quite nasty for a time. The Garda were involved and threats were made. Anyway! In the end it was all sorted out and Lord Conliffe made his peace with But–But–Ben and his wife Shula. There has been no trouble since.'

When she related events to Eileen during the school break, Theresa made a point of repeating the history of the castle.

'Why did we not know about this from history lessons?' Eileen asked.

'I suppose it was too near home to be of great interest in the scheme of things,' Theresa surmised.

'What was it like inside?'

'I only saw the sitting room and the hall.'

'So?' Eileen's face was tense with anticipation.

Theresa told her about the beautiful tapestries and the great flags above the suits of armour and the fact that there was no rug on the enormous stone floor.

'I hope there are carpets or rugs upstairs. It would be cold for the feet to have to walk across stone floors without slippers.'

'I'm telling you about the objects – real true objects of a bygone age – and you are chuntering on about toilets and bare feet. I can't believe you're real sometimes, Eileen O'Rourke.'

'It would matter if you were the one with the urge to go and you had to plough across acres of freezing cold stonework,' said the practical Eileen. 'Anyway! What was the sitting room like?'

'It's called the drawing room. It was enormous, Eileen. There was a walk-in fireplace with great iron instruments for stoking the fire; I tell you, those things could inflict some damage. There was an enormous dark blue rug on the floor and the furniture was all shiny and very old-fashioned. The table was as large as the one at the Last Supper.' She paused to accept the apple that Eileen had shoved at her.

'Go on!' urged Eileen.

'There were chairs and tables and great high dressers everywhere. I tell you, there was too much to take in at the first visit without appearing nosy.'

Eileen closed her eyes. 'It's enough. Fancy living in a place like that. It sounds wonderful.'

'You could put both your shop and our house in there and they would be lost,' said Theresa, happily aware that she had fulfilled her promise to herself to be observant.

The bell rang. They reluctantly gathered their belongings and made their way back to the classroom.

'I'm having some riding lessons next week,' said Theresa as they walked. 'I'm meeting some stable lad from the stud farm at Kilgaven. He will be riding Jupiter.'

'I wonder what he'll be like,' Eileen mused.

'He'll be a dwarf of a man compared to me, that's for sure. Most stable lads and all jockeys are small.' Theresa moaned, unaware that a few miles away, a tall, pony-tailed youth with tawny eyes was polishing a pair of riding boots and whistling as he worked.

CHAPTER 6

Years later, Theresa was to remember the summer of 1949 as the year she changed from a naive young girl to a naive young woman. It was one of those hot and hazy summers without a hint of rain that were a rarity in Ireland; when the sand at the north side of Lafferty's Cove was as hot as the desert; when looking into the distance was done through a shimmering haze. A summer when a lot happened all at once and left her reeling.

And the wasps. She remembered the wasps. They were everywhere.

Minnie Doran, who owned the bakery at the lower end of the village, was fast running out of fly papers – those long, sticky tubes that hung from convenient areas to entrap any unwary creature that ventured near. This included the cat, who yowled with pain as chunks of fur got caught up. Mr Doran, with not a bit of sympathy, swung a dish cloth at the unfortunate animal and yelled, 'It serves you right, you mangy bugger. You shouldn't be near that top shelf.'

Those customers who plucked up courage to enter the sticky-bunned haven had cause to regret it when they found themselves leaving with chunks of their hair also trapped by the myriad glutinous streamers hanging from the low ceiling. The more prudent customers pointed to what they wanted and beat a retreat to the door whilst Minnie bagged their purchases.

That year, the beach was more crowded than ever. The shops prospered. Toby Adams – Davey's father – took advantage of the weather and the resulting influx of holidaymakers and day trippers by setting up his sandwich bar earlier than other years, and was delighted with the success of the business.

'I'll be able to retire early if this keeps up,' he said gleefully.

An enterprising Davey had suggested selling drinks as well and had done a deal with a store in Kilgaven, to everyone's satisfaction. He did a roaring trade, but was annoyed that he had to split the profits with his da, who insisted the drinks bar was part of the whole business.

School was over, and the joy of freedom was everywhere, together with an air of optimism which affected even the most pessimistic. Father Corke's step was lighter; he had finally managed to convince John Cahill, the Bishop, that being appointed Dean was not in his interests. With the promise of further fishing trips to ease his own pressures, Bishop Cahill agreed to drop the idea, and inform the Vatican that for health reasons Father Corke had regretfully declined the honour. Also, to add to his good humour, the church was raking it in. It was surprising how many visitors felt the need to light a candle for the repose of the soul of some relation when they entered the cool, dank peace of the church as a respite from the fierce heat outside.

Collection plates, propitiously placed at intervals around the church interior, were full. Holidaymakers were generous at the best of times, but their generosity more than doubled when the weather was good. He had not a bit of conscience about taking the money for the poor, who could not afford so much as a decent pair of shoes to walk to a beach.

Theresa, now a fairly competent horsewoman, divided her time between the stables and the beach. Richard Beck told her that he now felt happy about letting her take Night Star out for a canter on her own. Most of the time she was accompanied by Fergal, the young man who had replaced the injured stable lad who, it transpired, had fallen and broken his collarbone while out on a gallop. The first time she had met him she had been cleaning tack. The weather was cool but pleasant, the real heat of that particular summer no more than a whisper away.

Richard had introduced them, and having done so strode off to saddle Othello for his ride, leaving them to regard each other and mumble a few words in greeting.

Theresa had looked shyly at him. 'You look more the part than I do,' she observed. Dressed in jodhpurs and knee high riding boots, with a crisp white shirt, he had looked every inch the young Adonis.

His unwavering gaze had rested on her and she had dropped her own beneath the straight stare, acutely aware of the strange effect he was having on her. Normally, Theresa Brady would drop her glance for no one.

'You look fine,' he had said at last, eyeing her bottle-green cords and cream blouse. Having dispensed with the formalities, he had made his way towards Jupiter's stall.

Normally blessed with the 'gift of the gab', Theresa had found herself with nothing to say. His air of composure had silenced her. That he was already a very competent rider working for a prodigious training stable further made her feel at a disadvantage.

She remembered her gran's advice about going out into the world. 'Hold your head up high. You are as good as the next.' Her gran was a feisty, proud lady.

She had been frantically buffing the saddle on her knee when she looked up to find Fergal watching her as he stroked Jupiter. Jesus! Her gran hadn't covered everything, like how to deal with a young man with oval shaped, tawny eyes and a face of such dignity and beauty her heart caught in her throat.

'You are very beautiful,' he had remarked. It was a statement of fact, uttered in the same tone he would use to tell her there was a fly on her nose.

She had felt a blush rise from her neck to her eyebrows and was glad of the dim light of the stable. In a moment he was gone, and the day went suddenly flat.

When Richard had returned, she was clearing up, He had smiled at her. 'Has Fergal gone?'

'He didn't stay long,' she'd said.

'He only came to meet Jupiter. He had other things to do,' said Richard. 'Although,' he had added with a grin, 'I would have thought he'd have difficulty tearing himself away.'

'He's a young man of few words,' said Theresa ruefully.' But he did say I was beautiful.' Her voice lightened as she spoke.

'A very discerning young man.' Richard, by now having unsaddled Othello, had smiled. 'You will have plenty of time to get acquainted. You'll be out riding together, after all.'

'So we will,' Theresa had said, and added, 'I was a bit poleaxed by the unexpectedness of the meeting. I'll be prepared for him next time.'

'That's the ticket,' said Richard. 'From what I've seen of you in the short time we've known each other, you will have no problems.'

It hadn't been quite that easy, though. On her first ride out with Fergal she'd still found it difficult to converse. She was not helped by the fact that as he rode beside her he contributed little to her efforts; his keen eyes were looking around and his thoughts seemed elsewhere.

She'd had the line of conversation all set out and rehearsed to cover the opening moments of the ride, but she had quickly realised she might as well have been spouting *Ode to a Skylark* in a foreign language for all the notice he took. He'd just let her ramble on, occasionally turning to look straight into her eyes, an action that strangled the breath in her throat. Eventually she had fallen silent, until he startled her by grabbing her arm to halt their progress.

'Look! Two fox cubs', he'd whispered. 'Don't move!'

79

'Tell that to Night Star,' she had whispered back.

For answer he patted the horse soothingly, and Night Star had calmed. The two young foxes had darted and flashed in the sunlight until the parent fox, with a sharp nip, ferried them into the safety of the trees.

This was only the first of many such moments, and as time passed and the real heat of summer commenced, they began to relax in each other's company. Fergal, she was to discover, had a lot to teach her about nature. He knew the name of every bird, flower, and animal. of his private life he said little, other than to remark that he was the oldest of seven children.

Being an only child, she couldn't conceive the notion of what it would be like to be one of such a large brood. Four weeks into the friendship, she said so.

'Ach, it's all right; but being the eldest can be a bit dire. Mam keeps throwing the middle ones at me to get them from under her feet. It's easier now, though,' he added. 'Working for Mr Beck gets me away for a bit and the money is useful.'

'Your parents must love children a lot to want so many.' They had dismounted by the bank of a small lough that Theresa hadn't known existed, and as she spoke she looked longingly at the cool, silver water. They sat back against a lone tree.

'Not at all.' Fergal grinned. 'There isn't much can be done about such matters when the Church frowns on birth control.' He chewed on a piece of coarse grass and turned his eyes towards the sun, enjoying the warmth and the short respite from riding.

'I'm an only child,' Theresa mused. 'I've never asked why.'

'You're lucky. Our eighth is expected shortly.' He sat up, his eyes looking into hers. 'Perhaps your parents didn't want a large family.'

'I wonder – You don't suppose – I mean . . .' She stopped. 'They wouldn't be using birth control,' she said in disbelief.

'It's your parents' decision,' said Fergal. He sat back again. 'I don't mind the new baby. I do mind that I'm stuck here for a whole summer and a winter, though.'

Something stirred in Theresa's mind. 'You are from the stables at Kilgaven, aren't you?'

Fergal threw the now well-chewed reed away and hauled himself into a standing position. 'What are you on about? What stables? I'm But–But–Ben's son. Where did you get that idea from?'

'The lad who was hired had some kind of accident. I assumed when Richard said he was being replaced it would be someone else from the stables.' She rose and walked towards the edge of the small lough and sat down again, leaving her horse tethered in the shade of the tree. Jesus! He was the son of a tinker and here she was, thinking he was from McGarvie's stables. A tiny smile lifted her mouth.

Fergal joined her. 'Does it make a difference – me being a tinker?'

She laughed. 'Of course it does. It means I can stop being Lady Muck from Clobber Hill and be myself. I can stop trying to be Miss Prim and Proper.'

'Because I am a tinker's son you feel you owe me no social respect?'

'No, you eejut! It means we are alike – close to nature but restricted by society.'

'Whatever that means it sounds good,' he grinned.

Before his startled eyes, she tore off her blouse and cords, shouted 'Come on!', and ran into the cold, shimmering water in her underwear.

He watched her, stunned into immobility as she frolicked, her wild black hair tamed and sleek against her head by the weight of the water.

'Come on, Fergal!' she called again, her voice light with the joy of being there. 'It's wonderful.'

He needed no third bidding. A few minutes later he had joined her, his lean, brown body streaking along beside her as they swam together.

Later, they lay side by side on the soft bank to dry out under the hot sun, both busy with their own thoughts, all former restraint gone. Theresa was excitedly aware of Fergal's narrow waist and tight buttocks tapering to slim, muscular thighs, and arrows of pleasure went through her as she wondered what it would feel like to be held close to him.

Although she had no inhibitions about being naked, she would never embarrass friends by stripping everything off. With Fergal, though, she felt completely at ease lying by his side, and even considered taking off all her underwear. She relaxed, with eyes shut against the glare of the sun, and a tiny smile brushed her lips.

Fergal's thoughts were running along the same lines. He had seen many female forms, and naked ones at that, but he had not seen a body like Theresa's. Nor had he seen a woman use it so unconsciously to such effect. There was about her a sweet innocence which made him feel protective towards her – and also very happy.

'Have you ever done this before?' he asked drowsily.

'As often as I can. I usually swim completely naked at my secret cove – that's how I met Richard Beck.'

81

His drowsiness deserted him. 'You mean he has seen you without a stitch of clothing?'

'Well, yes,' she laughed. 'Nakedness doesn't worry me. I have no problem with my body. I am more concerned with my mind and my soul.'

'You are the most natural woman I have ever met.'

'How many women have you known?' She squinted at him, shading her eyes with her hand. She was pleased that he thought of her as a woman and not a young girl.

Fergal smiled. 'A few.' He remembered the few he did know and recalled the disappointment he had felt with those he had known intimately. He looked at her tenderly. 'You should be very careful,' he said softly. 'Not many of the older generation would understand.'

'I know it.' She rose. 'We had better get back. I've got to be home for tea and then I have some church work to do.' She grimaced. 'It's my turn to take the children for catechism.'

He laughed, a hearty, joyous laugh. All awkwardness between them had melted. Being a traveller, he had little time to make friends and he felt happy that in Tullybra, he now had one.

'Why don't you come along to the club tonight and meet my friends? I have never seen you in the village, although I understand your father frequents the pub occasionally.'

He shook his head. 'It isn't for me.' There was a faintest trace of bitterness in his voice. 'I don't think your friends would accept me.'

She couldn't persuade him, and when later she bade him goodbye, she felt instinctively that he would prefer she didn't mention their developing friendship.

Jack and Tandy were at the club. Tandy was in a bad mood. He had just that day broken the news to his father that he wanted to go to England to study agriculture. He had suspected that his father might prove difficult, but he was unprepared for the war of words that erupted.

'Are you bloody mad?' Rory Noonan had glared at his youngest son. 'I can teach you all you need to know about farming – and what I don't know about beef rearing, you can learn from Pat McGarry.'

'I know that, Da; but agriculture is changing fast. The world of technology and farming husbandry has moved closer. I want to discover the latest techniques, work with the latest equipment.'

'For what?' Rory had ranted. 'This farm isn't big enough to warrant all that tarradiddle. We've done very well working by the old methods.'

'I know! I know!' Tandy had said placatingly. 'But the farm isn't big enough to take on one more son. Don't forget I'll marry one day and there will be yet more mouths to feed. This way I'll not be a drain on the profits.'

'You're sayin' you won't be working here, even after you finish with this college business – is that it?'

'I don't know, Da. I just know that this is the way for me to go.'

Rory Noonan did not have a head for business. He was a bull of a man with the strength of ten, and his farm had prospered as far as it would go because he worked like a Trojan all the hours that God made so that his sons could inherit a bit of land.

His weathered face had creased in anger. It hadn't worked out the way he had planned. Of his ten children, only three were working on the farm. Four of his sons had become priests. The only two daughters he had were nuns, and now his youngest son wanted to go over the bloody water to England to learn how to farm in Ireland. Sure where was the sense of it? What had English methods of farming got to do with the way things were done in Ireland, which was a different kettle of fish altogether? The weather was different; the soil was different; the size of the fields was different – there was little bloody comparison at all, at all. 'I'll not listen to another word, so,' he had said finally.

Tandy had joined his mother in the kitchen. She never interfered, but he knew his quiet, soft-spoken mother, who had a fine head on her shoulders, had been listening keenly to the row between him and his da. She would have more idea of what he wanted and why.

'Can you see the sense of what I've been saying, Mam?'

She had nodded. 'I can, son. Say no more for now. Leave it to the pillow talk. Many battles have been won when two heads share the same bolster.'

Reena had given him a pat on the shoulder. Rory was not a stupid man, but neither could he see further than his nose. He generally listened to her. 'I'll do my best, son.' She was not a demonstrative woman, but she had a deep love for every one of her children – even 'Bad Tad', as her seventh son was nicknamed because of his drinking and his womanizing.

'Thanks, Mam.' Tandy had held the hand on his shoulder for a moment or two before making his way to his room to get ready to go to the club.

Jack tried to convince him that it would all work out, but Tandy stared morosely around, uncaring that Eileen, her soft eyes glancing at him with concern, had been drafted on to the floor by Pat O'Neill – a lecherous bastard by anyone's standards, who was not one of the group.

Theresa and Jack wandered off to the games room when Tandy took a girl on to the floor. 'How did your exams go?' Theresa enquired.

'They were a bit stiff, especially Chemistry,' he said ruefully. 'It isn't my best subject but I think I managed. I hope so.'

'You'll pass,' she said. 'How did Tandy do?'

'I think he is fairly happy.'

'I did wonder, as he seems to be in a bad mood.'

Jack glanced towards Tandy. He wasn't sure how much he should tell Theresa. 'He had a row with his da, that's all,' he said. 'He'll be fine. Tandy never holds a grudge for long.' He handed her a glass of orangeade. 'How is the riding going? Will we be seeing you riding in the Curragh?'

'Wrong style of riding,' she laughed. She and Jack were getting along just lately. Whatever had ailed him had been sorted out. 'I've got a new partner now – his name's Fergal and he is a grand horseman. What he doesn't know about wildlife could be written on a sixpenny piece. It has been fun as well as educational, listening to him,' she said, unaware of the thoughts she was engendering in Jack's mind.

He felt a surge of jealousy at her words. This situation with Theresa was driving him mad. Christ! He loved the girl. Why did he not come out with it and tell her so? He groaned inwardly. He knew why. She was just seventeen years old. One day he would tell her, but not yet. It wasn't fair to saddle her with such a responsibility when life called and she was wanting to go all out to meet it.

'Is he handsome?' He tried to put a teasing note in his voice but was aware that it sounded false.

Theresa, with almost brutal honestly, said, 'Evenly tanned, slim body, oval shaped light brown eyes, dark hair worn long and in a pony tail, and teeth like a toothpaste advert? Oh yes! He's handsome.'

'So you're not too taken with him, then?' This time he spoke with heavy sarcasm, and thought, 'I'm going to university soon; I don't need the commitment.'

'He's all right,' Theresa said, with studied casualness. She wondered if Jack felt jealous.

Tandy, now on his third drink, joined them. He had cheered up. It was Jack now who had gone quiet.

'If it wasn't the best evening we've had – it wasn't the worst,' Theresa remarked to Eileen on the way home.

By Wednesday everyone's spirits had lifted. On that day they were holding a beach party. It had been planned some time ago to

84

celebrate the start of the school holidays and the end of exams. It had been Theresa's idea, so she took on the bulk of the preparations. Having the party on Wednesday meant they could avoid the weekend trippers.

They had chosen the area toward Lafferty's Cove as it was less popular. Colin Brady had opted to transport the baskets of donated food and drink. The weather was perfect, and there was enough sandy beach left, before the rocks around the cove began, to play beach games. Those who wanted to, swam, and all were glad of the breeze blowing in from the sea to cool them down following their exertions.

It was Theresa who first noticed the two girls. One was tall, the other much shorter in stature. They were coming along the beach in the direction of the group, and as they approached some of the group sat up to stare. The reason became obvious to the others as they came closer. They wore very brief costumes, exposing large areas of midriff and generous portions of bosom and thigh.

'Now you see what I meant when I said that how you dressed had a greater effect than being naked,' Theresa whispered to Eileen. 'Those strips of material draw the eye very nicely to the parts which, if they were uncovered, wouldn't cause the lift of an eyebrow if seen more than once.'

Eileen's face reddened with embarrassment as they neared and she noticed that every boy in their party was staring with glee.

The two girls, now aware of the sensation they were causing among the group of young people, smiled hugely and began to lengthen their stride.

'Jesus Christ!' said Jack, in Tandy's ear. 'Do you recognise them?'

Tandy burrowed into the rug he had been lying on, his face puce. 'Get your head down, you eejut,' he whispered fiercely, but it was too late.

'Jack! Jack Ross!' The taller of the two called excitedly.

Jack groaned. White faced, he gave Tandy a poke with his elbow. He wasn't going to go through this alone. Tandy had been the instigator of the whole thing. He was bloody well going to share his embarrassment. He was the one who had introduced Jack to she of the 'golden explosion' that had fizzled out like a damp squib.

Gathering his courage, he stood up. 'Goodness, Tandy, it's Bernadette Lynch!' He prodded Tandy into life and, to the astonishment of the others, sauntered towards the girls.

Theresa and Eileen exchanged glances. Theresa looked towards the group of four now talking nineteen to the dozen, and her glance hardened. She shifted her gaze seaward and watched the sun-capped waves. The sight of their gentle, onward progress helped to still the tumult of her mind. She was aware that her companions were waiting with curiosity to see what was going to happen. Was Jack going to leave with these girls? As soon as she saw the look on his face as he walked towards them, she knew that he was.

He put his hand on her arm. 'I've got to go, Theresa,' he said, his eyes begging her to understand. 'We foolishly promised these two girls that when they came to Tullybra they should look us up and we would show them around. I've asked if they would like to join us but they say they would like to go on a tour of the place.'

Theresa, her head held at an angle so that the others could see that it didn't matter, said, 'For goodness' sake Jack, sure it's no big thing. We are your friends; we will understand. You go off with these girls and have a good day. I'll see you soon, I've no doubt.'

He had to be content with that, but in his heart he knew that he had dealt the proud Theresa a cruel blow. Eileen, her soft eyes staring towards Tandy, looked devastated.

'Tandy asked me to apologise to you, Eileen,' Jack said, although the devious Tandy had said no such thing. I'll kill him stone dead when I get him alone, Jack thought as he walked back to the trio. He had lied to Theresa; he had never done that before and he hated himself.

CHAPTER 7

Theresa had just finished mucking out when she saw Richard approach the stables.

'Good morning, Theresa.'

'Good morning.' She smiled doubtfully at him. 'Is anything wrong?'

'No! Why should you think that?'

'I thought you sounded a bit – well – stern.'

Richard chuckled. 'I'm not a stern sort of person,' he said lightly. 'I've been watching you work. You enjoy working with the horses, don't you?'

'I love it. I find that the time seems to race along when I'm with them.' She laughed. 'My father says I spend too much time here and not enough doing my home chores, and my friend Eileen gets mad at me because she says she hardly sees me nowadays.'

'You do tend to spend more time than we arranged.' He looked at her keenly. 'You don't have to spend extra time here, you know – not unless it is your wish. Our arrangement was that you spend four hours every day grooming and riding – except Saturday – yet I understand from Bob that you are often to be seen up here on Saturday afternoons. I'm not surprised your family and your friends are concerned.'

'I do it because I want to. I've never spent such a fulfilling time during the school holidays.'

'Are you going away this year?'

She frowned. 'Away?'

'On holiday,' Richard prodded.

'We never go away on holiday. My father says that we have it all here – the sea, the lovely countryside, the market in Kilgaven. He doesn't see the need.'

'But there are so many other lovely places and things to see . . .'

'Oh! We go off on day trips. We go to Dublin, to the theatre, and we travel up north for the whole day. Once, now I remember, we stayed overnight in Newcastle because m'da fell in love with the Mountains of Mourne. He thought we might spend a week up there sometime, but that was years ago now and the idea sort of got lost.'

He looked thoughtfully at her. 'You get along well with young Fergal, I understand.'

'I do indeed.' She was surprised at the sudden switch of subject. 'I didn't realise he was But–But–Ben's son, though. I somehow got it into my head he was from the McGarvie stables.'

'My fault. It didn't occur to me that you didn't know him.' Richard walked over to the bench by Othello's stall and motioned her to sit beside him.

'The family keep very much to themselves,' Theresa said. 'Only the father comes into the village a lot. Fergal's mother comes in for groceries once in a while, but for the most part Fergal says they do their shopping in Kilgaven when they do business there. All that is known of them is that Fergal's mother is called Shula and there are lots of children.'

'Do you mind riding out with a tinker?'

She looked at him in amazement. 'Why should I?'

'Some might,' he said evenly.

'I like him. He's great fun. He has taught me a lot about horses and about the countryside.' She frowned. 'He should be here by now. It isn't like Fergal to be late.'

'That was the reason for this visit. It was to tell you that he wouldn't be coming today.'

'He isn't ill is he?'

'No! He's helping his father to sort things out at the camp.'

Theresa smiled. 'You've obviously had a word about the smoke we saw.'

Richard nodded. 'It took a while, but I had lunch with Patrick Conliffe and he arranged for his head keeper to come over to see me. He had some very good suggestions as to what I could do to solve the problem. It wasn't just the fire, you see. The fact is, the family were chopping down the trees indiscriminately to make ornaments and clothes pegs and other things, for sale. The forest was being devastated. Something had to be done.'

'What did Lord Patrick's gamekeeper suggest?'

'He suggested that I invite But–But–Ben to the castle and discuss the situation over a glass of his favourite Irish whiskey – as he put it, "in a civilized manner".' Richard laughed. 'It worked very well. After the third glass, he was in a more amiable mood and we were able to set down a few ground rules.'

'You'll never get him to stick to them.' Theresa smiled.

'He does so or I'll have him chased off my land. I think he

realizes that he is on to a good thing here. Not many would allow a tinker family to winter on their land every year, so the lesser of two evils will be for him to conform and stick to the arrangement.'

'Which is?'

'I've told the old devil – and this was John, the gamekeeper's suggestion – that I want to cull the trees as the wood is becoming too dense for light and sun to get through for the flora and fauna to survive. John, with the help of someone from the forestry commission, will select certain trees for chopping. That way we are both well served, as But–But–Ben can use those he chops down for any purpose he likes. I have also elected to build a latrine and a storage hut in a large glade nearby.'

'And he agreed to it?'

'The canny old devil asked for time to think things over, but in the end he knew he had a good deal.' Richard laughed. 'I quite like the man.' He glanced at his watch. 'I must go. I have a meeting to attend and I will have to give the other two horses some exercise.'

Theresa went back to her task. As she worked, her thoughts were of Fergal. She would miss him on her ride today, and their bathe in the lough. She had wanted to discuss Jack and Tandy's defection and consult him on how she should treat the matter. Fergal had a simple way of looking at a problem and getting to the heart of it.

In a way she was glad she hadn't seen Jack since the incident, for she knew that she would have torn a right strip off him and possibly ruined things between them. Of course there was no reason why Jack should not have a girlfriend. God knows, there was nothing like that between them – theirs was a deep, caring friendship that had been established since they had started school all those years ago, and in spite of the fact that within the group they were lumped together as a couple, it was not in the romantic sense.

She frowned. It was the way he'd done it. She and Eileen had felt let down in front of the others. She stopped what she was doing. Who was she kidding? If Jack found himself a girlfriend she'd want to tear the eyes out of her. For too long he had been part of her life, and even though they had never got to the romantic stage she nevertheless had, over the years, regarded him as hers.

She persuaded Eileen that it would be unwise to go to the Sunday dance, although it was Eileen's opinion that they might be doing the wrong thing. 'Can you not see that we are going to look like a pair of sulky eejuts if we don't turn up? Everyone will be convinced we got our comeuppance.'

'I don't care,' Theresa said defiantly, but she knew in her heart that she did. The proud Theresa had been spurned for a gum-chewing tart. They'd all be bursting not to laugh.

Eileen reported next day that the two boyos hadn't turned up to the dance, either.

'Afraid to meet us,' Theresa crowed.

'I wish you would make up your mind what you are about,' said Eileen. 'We didn't turn up either.'

'Your loyalty is slipping, Eileen,' said Theresa. 'What else did you hear with your little ear?'

Eileen hesitated. 'They were seen by Davey Adams. He was visiting his Aunt Bessie – it was her wedding anniversary – and he strolled down to the pub for a breath of fresh air and to get away from all the gabbing – and there they were, bold as brass, laughing and talking together.'

Theresa's eyes darkened. 'That is the end,' she fumed. 'The two of them have made us look a right pair of fools.'

Eileen's soft mouth trembled. 'Don't do anything rash. I know you – you'll end up regretting it. Sure we don't know what the true circumstances are.'

'That's true,' Theresa said, her voice heavy with sarcasm. 'I wonder which one of the girls had the gun in Jack's ribs. Come on! I want to go up and see Night Star – are you coming?'

'Oh! Can I? Mr Beck won't mind?'

'I have him in the palm of my hand.' She omitted to mention that she had already asked Richard if her friend Eileen could come and see the stables.

Eileen was nervous of Othello and Jupiter, but she timidly stroked Night Star's soft nose.

'You'd never think you were country born and bred,' Theresa laughed. 'The horses won't hurt you – at least, not while you are on the ground.'

Eileen helped clean the tack while Theresa tidied out the stalls and, as the afternoon passed, her annoyance gradually cooled.

They had almost finished when Fergal walked round the corner of the stable and stopped at the sight of a stranger. Eileen looked up and promptly dropped the girth she was working on, her round face reddening as her gentle eyes gave an unspoken apology. She guessed that this young man was Fergal whom Theresa had mentioned many times.

'Who are you?' Fergal enquired, looking around for Theresa.

'She's Eileen – Hi, Fergal.' Theresa poked her head out and shook the large pitchfork at him. 'Where have you been for the last few days?'

90

'I expect you know already. Mr Beck would have told you.' He grinned. 'Why don't you introduce me to your friend Eileen?'

'Eileen, meet Fergal. Fergal, meet Eileen.'

Fergal sat down beside the slightly flustered girl. He smiled at her. 'Do you also ride horses badly?' he asked, and ducked as Theresa threw a forkful of hot, smelly straw at him. His oval eyes raked her and it was some seconds before he realised that Eileen was answering his question.

'I could ride a rocking horse, but anything that moves under me causes my muscles to tense and my brain to go to pieces.' She looked over to Theresa who was leaning on the long-handled fork. 'I've finished the tack,' she said. 'Is there anything else?'

'Everything is done now,' Theresa replied, looking at Fergal with a tinge of regret. 'See you tomorrow, Fergal.' She and Eileen gathered up their bags and set off.

'You didn't tell me that Fergal was so handsome and tall,' said Eileen as they cycled slowly home.

'Perhaps because I don't see him as being handsome and tall.'

'You are not blind, Theresa Brady, nor are you daft. I think Jack Ross had competition here.'

'You could be right,' said Theresa thoughtfully. Fergal was an experienced lad. She could learn a lot from him. She stopped and got off her bike. Eileen did the same. They walked along in silence for a while before Theresa said, 'Have you ever considered the possibility that we are the forgotten ones?'

'What?'

'Think about it. We are not children. We left that state when we entered senior school and our periods started, but at the same time we are not considered old enough to be adults. There we are, in the middle without a designated role. Neither one thing nor the other. No one ever talks to us about boys, and feelings, and sexual matters—'

'Theresa!'

'For God's sake, Eileen, think about it. I'm right. Who can we ask? The sisters at the convent would go into a decline if we asked them. Our parents still see us as "older" children and have no notion of the feelings and the turmoil that's in us at times. Our hormones are knocking seven bells out of us when we are around the boys we like, and we don't know how to deal with the situation. Our parents, having been brought up in the same social system, assume that we will make our way along the path in the same confused way they did. They would be rocked back on their heels if we sat down on our backsides and asked them about sex.'

'God almighty,' Eileen gasped. 'What has got into you?'

Theresa knew fine well what had got into her. She was sick to death of stumbling through a sexual minefield, not knowing how far to go and how to cope with the feelings she had towards Jack and the even stranger feelings she had when Fergal had looked at her with those eyes as she lay beside him by the lough.

Eileen stopped, her face white with shock. 'I don't really get these feelings you speak about,' she said, almost in a whisper.

'Don't you ever wonder what it would be like to make love? With Tandy, for instance?'

Eileen reddened. 'I think the world of Tandy – although I realize that he sees me only as his special friend – but I never . . . I never . . .'

Theresa sighed. 'Considering that you were chuntering on about having lots of children when we were in Kilgaven the other week, I'm surprised that you didn't give thought to the mechanics necessary to get them.'

'I know a bit about that – I just don't think about it. Anyway, I only know what I was told by you. How do you know you have it right?'

'That's just what I mean,' Theresa exploded. 'I *don't* know. We learn about it from people like Nora Adams who have done some experimenting. We play games, Eileen. we chant things like "Theresa Brady loves Jack Ross, Ya ya yaya ya." It isn't a game. Someone should come out with it and tell us.'

'Have you never asked your mam?' Eileen enquired.

'Mam went around with Pat McGarry when she was young and had a great time. You'd think she would be willing to let me into the big secret, but she is as bad as all the other mothers; I would be too embarrassed to ask.' Theresa got on her bike. 'Anyway, Jack will be off to university soon. I'll see very little of him. He'll make new friends and will find a girl to fall in love with . . .' Her voice trailed off.

Eileen hadn't realized how deep was the regard Theresa held for Jack. She had always seemed to use him, as she did everyone, as a vehicle for learning about life. She was as wild as the wind and attracted a following of those wishing to ride on the tail of her passion for life, but Eileen suddenly saw clearly that none of it mattered without Jack's regard.

Nuala, engrossed in setting the table for supper, glanced up as her daughter passed the door on her way to her room. Theresa gave her a vague smile and carried on.

'If you're going to have a bath I'll delay supper,' she called after her. 'Don't spend too long, though.'

'Yes, Mam.' Theresa answered.

Nuala stopped what she was doing for a moment. Just lately she had noticed Theresa's mood swings and had wondered if she should have a word with her. She had changed her mind, putting it down to the fact that she was 'at that age'. Just lately it was feast or famine with her daughter. Either she was talking the hind leg off a donkey or she was as close as a clam. Nuala wondered if there had been a rift in her friendship with Jack. He too had been a bit subdued when he had come asking for her.

She filled the kettle and put it on the hob. Colin peered through the window and made motions towards his mouth. That man could eat a horse, raw and without garnish. She smiled and waved him away.

During supper, Theresa began to recover. She told her parents how Eileen had reacted to the horses. 'You'd never believe she was reared in the country, with horses and cows at the stretch of the hand,' she said.

Nuala, buttering a soda farl, remarked, 'Eileen was born timid and she'll probably be that way till the say she dies.'

'I can't see that girl marrying and having children,' volunteered Colin.

'Don't say such a thing. Eileen adores children. I think she'd die if she wasn't around them.'

'I know that. I think she'll always be *around* children,' explained Colin. 'I don't think she could cope with producing them, though.'

'You mean you don't think she could cope with having sex.' Theresa held her breath. She never thought she'd have the temerity to make such a statement. It must have something to do with her earlier thoughts and feelings of resentment.

'Mind that tongue of yours!' Colin gave his daughter a hard look.

'Da!' said Theresa, her heart thumping at what she was about to say. 'You are an educated man – a headmaster – and you can't talk about the subject of sex without cringing.'

'I said mind your tongue, Theresa. I'm not having such a discussion over the supper table. There are ways of saying things that doesn't border on the vulgar.'

'You mean we can waltz around the subject just so long as we don't use the proper terminology. Jesus! No wonder Irish girls are considered to be naive.'

'Go up to your room, and when you feel like apologising you can come down.' Colin was shocked. Never had Theresa spoken to him in such a manner.

When she had gone from the room he turned to Nuala. 'What is the matter with that girl?'

Nuala put down her knife and looked straight at her husband, her mind seething with the thoughts that had been going round while she listened to him and watched him squirm as he spoke to Theresa. What chance did the young girls of Ireland have, going out into the world, when such discussions were taboo between them and their parents? What chance did a young marriage have when a young wife knew little about the art of seduction, and less still about eroticism and sex? Small wonder that some husbands got their kicks elsewhere, leaving the wife to rear the increasing number of children with little expectation of any demonstration of love and affection.

'Theresa is right, Colin. There should be no stigma attached to sex and the discussion of it. It is a perfectly normal part of life and I'm afraid we Catholics are not doing our children any favours by telling them that children are sent down by the grace of God, and forgetting that he also instigated the means by which they are begot. We should be educating our children to the facts of life, but I fear we are sadly wanting in that area.'

She smiled to take the sting out of the implied criticism. Colin was a proud man. She laid a hand on his arm. 'Theresa was a bit careless in her choice of words, but she is a sensible girl. Give her credit for speaking her mind. She'll come to less harm if she isn't afraid to meet things head on.'

Colin nodded. 'You're right. I'll go up and make my peace with her.' He sighed. 'It's a different generation. They speak their mind but, as you say, it is probably a good thing. I haven't kept up with the pace of modern thinking, have I? I don't want change.' He rose slowly.

Her gaze followed him. He was only forty-two, and he was talking and thinking like an old man.

Nuala mentioned Jack's visit when Theresa came down to breakfast next morning.

'Did he say what he wanted?' Theresa asked, her pulse racing.

'No. Just that I was to tell you he had called and he'll catch up with you another time. If he calls again what do you want me to say?'

'Nothing! I'm sure we'll run into each other soon.' Theresa grabbed her lunch box and stuffed it into her bag. 'I'm off now. I'll see you mid-afternoon.'

'Will you be seeing Eileen?'

'We're meeting after tea to go for a swim down by Lafferty's Cove.'

Fetching her bike from the tiny shed, Theresa set off for the stables. She felt an odd kind of excitement because she was going to see Fergal again. seeing him so unexpectedly yesterday had made her realize how much he had become a part of her life.

He was already waiting when she arrived. He had saddled Jupiter, who was tethered nearby.

'You could have prepared Night Star for me,' she complained.

'Pigs might fly. I've no intention of spoiling you by doing the work you are being paid to do.' Fergal grinned, then got up and trotted the little mare out so that she could saddle her.

The day was hot, with a haze settling in the distance. Already Theresa could feel the heat permeate her thin blouse. 'Are we going for a swim?' she asked, longing in her voice.

'If the way is clear, but first we have to give the horses their exercise.' He was now busy untying the reins and Theresa was able to study him secretly. Even through the shirt she could see his lean form and she felt a flutter of excitement go through her as she watched him leap nimbly astride the big horse.

Catching her eye, Fergal grinned. 'Stop admiring my fine physique and let's get started. I can smell that cool water from here.'

'Don't kid yourself, Fergal,' Theresa said coolly. 'I have other fish to fry.'

'So I hear. I understand Jack Ross is high in the running.'

'How do you know about Jack Ross?' she asked.

'I have my contacts; my lines of communication.' Fergal grinned.

The ride was a good one. The gallop across open country cooled them down, but it was with relief that Theresa dived into the cool water of the little lough. The nape of her neck was stinging from the heat of the strong sun and the soft ripple of wavelets caused by the faint breeze was soothing. She trod water for a while and watched Fergal scoring along with strong, even strokes, his lithe body twisting and turning as he changed direction. It was at this moment that she realized she had, without thinking, stripped completely. Until today, she had kept her underwear on. Either Fergal hadn't noticed or he accepted it. She gave a mental shrug. If he didn't mind, she didn't.

Later, as they lay side by side under the subtle shade of the tree, she broke the silence. 'Fergal?'

'Hmmn?'

'Have you been making enquiries about me?'

'Why? Are you worried that your friends might find out that you are associating with a tinker?' he asked smoothly.

She whirled over him, her blanket of hair blotting out the sun. 'No, I'm not. You're the one with the fixation about your worth. I couldn't give a damn about who you are, but I do resent having you probe into my life out of curiosity.'

Fergal, who all the while she had been speaking had kept his eyes closed, now opened them and looked at the furious face above him. 'If you had spent a lifetime – indeed, many lifetimes if you consider the generations that have gone before – being the butt end of jokes and having people point you out as "one of those bloody Tinkers", then you too would have a complex.' His tone was soft and smooth, belying the look in his eyes.

Theresa rolled back on to her side.

Fergal explained. 'I discovered about you and Jack Ross from my father, who has been helping Mr Ross senior with the hay. Your name was mentioned – I shouldn't have teased you.'

She was cross with herself. Could she go ahead and discuss her problems with him now? 'I'd like an apology from you for your remark about me being ashamed of knowing a tinker.'

'You have it. I should have known better.'

They lay for a long time without speaking. The horses were gently cropping the grass with a pleasant crunchy sound.

'Have you ever made love to a girl, Fergal?'

Fergal's eyes opened and he looked at her, startled. 'What kind of question is that?'

'An honest one. I want to discuss sex with you. I have a bit of a problem in that area.'

'Christ almighty! Will I ever meet a girl like you again?' He let out a loud burst of laughter. 'You aren't the usual product of a small village, that's for sure.'

'I just have this thing about going out into the world unprepared. There is so much to learn. When I go to England I don't want to behave like a culshie. They are very sophisticated over there, you know. I understand that no one turns a hair if two young people sleep together without being married.'

'It happens here too,' Fergal said in amusement. 'And I think there are many parents over in England who would frown on the idea just the same.'

'I know that, but it isn't looked on as being as dreadful a crime as it is here.'

'What makes you think that?'

'I read the agony columns in the magazines in my friend Eileen's shop when she is in charge behind the counter.'

'What has all this got to do with my sex life?'

'Will you answer the question? Have you ever made love to a girl?'

'The answer is no! I have never made love to a girl.' He laughed. 'I've disappointed you.'

'I thought you were quite the lad,' she said. 'You are nineteen years old. I was certain you would have had experience.'

'I haven't made love to a girl,' he said, 'but I have had sex with one or two.'

'What's the difference?'

'The difference for me is that I would make love to a girl because I love her and the moment will be tender and fulfilling, but I would have sex for quite a different reason.'

'You mean – having sex is purely functional?'

Fergal looked at the sun. 'I think we had better be getting back. Fascinating though this conversation is, the horses have to be fed and watered.'

'You sound like a very intelligent man.'

Fergal frowned. 'You are close to making an insulting remark, but I'll take it that it wasn't meant that way. I admit my schooling wasn't up to the level of yours, due to lack of continuity, but I read a lot and I study human nature and I learn as I go.'

Theresa apologised. 'Just answer one more question.' She looked pleadingly at him. 'Would you have sex with me?'

His heart missed a beat. 'No! I would not,' he said gently. 'You aren't ready.'

'I'm not a half-cooked bannock,' she replied stiffly.

'There is another reason. I respect you too much. With us it would have to be love.' He raised her to her feet. 'You shouldn't ask such questions. Someone could take advantage of an invitation like that.'

'Of course I wouldn't ask just anyone. I trust you. I just thought you could teach me about sex; no one tells us anything.'

He drew her towards him. 'When the right person comes along, you will know what to do – like having a baby – sure nobody knows what it's like till they get down to doing the job for themselves.'

'I have never kissed a boy properly. I've only played at it when we've been codding about.'

'I can certainly remedy that. When we have settled the horses for the day, I'll see you to the main gate and I'll kiss you goodbye.'

A thrill of satisfaction ran through her. She was nervous at the thought of a real kiss, but she was sure Fergal would be patient with her. The great thing was that if she ever got to kiss Jack she would be able to do it with the right degree of skill, for she was a quick learner.

CHAPTER 8

Jack Ross felt optimistic. He had gone to bed the previous evening feeling dire because he hadn't been able to contact Theresa and it was imperative that he do so. He had much explaining to do thanks to that turd of a friend of his. Would he never have the sense to keep out of Tandy's schemes?

He glanced at his watch. It was mid-afternoon. He would try another visit to Theresa's house. Having made the decision, he pedalled his bike furiously along the high road and down the hill to the schoolhouse. He knocked on the door. Theresa's mother answered it yet again.

'I'm sorry, Jack. Theresa hasn't come home yet. I'm sure she must be on the way because she and Eileen are going for a swim after tea.' Nuala glanced at the hall clock. 'I expect she has already set out from Castle Donagh – you could cycle along to meet her.'

He thanked her and turned his bike towards the road. 'I'll do that. Will you tell her I called – just in case I miss her again?'

'I will, indeed,' Nuala said with a smile.

He turned and waved before riding up the hill. Half-way up he dismounted and strode along, head down, his mind still working on his explanation. So engrossed was he in his thoughts, he didn't see Davey Adams till he was at his side.

'Hello there, Jack.' Davey measured his step with his.

'Hello Davey.'

'Have you seen Theresa Brady lately?'

Jack stopped suddenly, causing Davey to stumble. 'Is that any of your business?' Jack was well aware of Davey's devious mind.

'I'm just being friendly. I wondered if everything was all right between you, in view of your going off with that girl the other day.'

'I repeat: it is none of your business.'

Davey's face reddened. 'I was going to tell you something that would be helpful to you, but I won't bother now. You can work out your own salvation. Theresa Brady is a proud one – you could do with all the help you can get.'

'Just how can you help?' Jack eyed the red faced Davey curiously.

Davey, with a shrug of his shoulders, walked away, calling back, 'You'll never know in time, that's for sure, my fine bucko. Let's see how you get on.'

Davey strode along, smiling at the knowledge that he had set Jack Ross's mind astir. Serve the cod right. He thought he was God's gift. If he knew what his wonderful Theresa had been getting up to by the lough with a bloody tinker, he might feel less like treating others with disdain.

He grinned as he visualised the scene he had witnessed a couple of hours ago. The bold Theresa and that tinker, lying side by side, mother naked, with all their bits on view of the sky. Maybe he could get some action there. He knew enough to be able to get it without begging. He was fed up with being called Crater Face because of his acne, and fed up with his bloody sisters and their shameful ways, causing him embarrassment. It would make a change for Theresa Brady to be on the cross.

Jack's gaze followed Davey as he veered off the main street and disappeared between McGinn's pub and the solicitor's office. He really was a devious blirt. He was only allowed to be in the group on sufferance because they all felt sorry for him because of his horrific family. Jack frowned. What had Davey meant by his offer of help? He could twist anything round, that one. With a shrug, he pushed on until he reached the top of the hill, where he turned right at the church. he rode swiftly along the road to Castle Donagh half expecting to meet Theresa, but she still hadn't appeared by the time he had reached the large iron gates.

Propping his bike against the tall hedge, he settled down on the soft grass in a shaded spot to wait. The afternoon sun was hot and he felt drowsy. The ground where he was half lying, half sitting was soft, and the song of the birds was pleasantly causing his mind and body to feel relaxed. His lids drooped; he knew that if he slept he ran the risk of missing Theresa, so he moved towards the cool shade of the high hedge and as he did so he heard the sound of laughter.

He leaned forward and looked towards the sound. His heart constricted. Theresa was being held in the arms of a tall, tanned youth. She was giggling softly as the youth bent his head and murmured something to her. She stopped giggling and put her arms round his neck as he bent his dark head and brought his lips down on hers for what seemed like a lifetime to Jack. His mind felt numb as he watched, undecided whether to make his presence known or remain hidden. He remained hidden.

At last they drew apart. He lay back and waited for them to go. Theresa's voice had a lilt in it as she said something to her companion before laughing again and riding off. She called out, 'I'll see you tomorrow, Fergal.' Jack crouched back into the hollow his weight had made in the hedge and watched the slim, muscular youth make his way back through the tall gate. So this was what Davey Adams has been trying to tell me, he thought as he mounted his bike for the journey home. Thank God he was going to university soon. He would immerse himself in study and get to know a new set of people to help him get over a girl who blew his mind and for whom he was not ready.

As she rode home, Theresa had an uneasy feeling that something was not quite right. This had happened before – the most recent time being when she had looked into Mrs Ross's eyes on that memorable visit to Jack's home. Later, when she met Eileen to go for a swim, the feeling persisted. Not even the joy of swimming in the sea helped.

Eileen, watching Theresa, noticed her preoccupation and her langour as she swam around – quite unlike her usual fierce, thrusting strokes. 'Is anything the matter?' she asked, as they dressed later.

'Not a thing.' Theresa rubbed her hair vigorously.

'You didn't attack the water with your usual energy, that's all.'

'Eileen. Can I not have a lazy swim once in a while without you thinking that I am in a state of terminal depression?'

Eileen didn't answer. She wasn't satisfied with the reply but she knew better than to argue when Theresa's face had that belligerent look.

Theresa retired early that evening, and with a cup of cocoa in her hand she settled down to read, but although her eyes scanned the pages, her brain refused to make sense of a single word. She put down the book and crossed to her favourite place in the window, and easing herself into the small space she gazed out towards the sea, her mind drifting. Just lately, life had jazzed up for her, but she had paid the price by finding herself in trouble on more than one occasion. She didn't know why she needed to find excitement. Eileen was content with her life – why couldn't she be content with hers?

Her thoughts turned to Jack. Somehow their relationship had shifted slightly. Sometimes he seemed to be almost uneasy in her company. She thought she could trace the change back to that day they had lain on the bank of the Tullybra river. Curse adolescence. It was a minefield of uncertainty.

101

Her sleep that night was a troubled one. She tossed and turned and woke up twice, her mind vaguely curling itself round some problem that, in her half sleep, she couldn't quite focus on. Her mother remarked on her appearance at breakfast.

'I had a bad night, Mam.'

'Your gran was saying just yesterday that you haven't been up to see her.'

Theresa stared at her plate, idly shoving the now greasy egg around. 'I would like to see her,' she said. 'I'll ask Fergal if he would see to Night Star for me one day next week.'

'Shall I tell your gran you'll be paying a visit?'

'It will depend on Fergal.' She bit into her toast. 'Tell Gran I'll be up soon – if Fergal can't do Night Star then I'll go one evening.' She was about to rise when her mother spoke again.

'Did you meet Jack yesterday? I forgot to mention that he'd called again.' Nuala, busy pouring tea, failed to notice the look of alarm on her daughter's face.

'Jack?' said Theresa weakly.

'Yes! Jack. I told him you were up at Castle Donagh, but you were due to arrive home shortly and I suggested that he cycle towards you and meet you on the way home. Obviously you didn't meet him. He must have changed his mind.'

'I didn't see him.' She was puzzled. If Jack said he would come to meet her, he would do so, but there had been no sign of him when she had come out of the gate. She recalled Fergal's kiss and how pleasant it was, although she had been surprised at how little excitement she had felt. Her pulse hadn't raced and she hadn't felt like swooning with desire like the heroines in books.

Later, during their morning ride, Fergal noticed Theresa's moodiness. He remained silent. She obviously had some weighty problem on her mind. If she wanted to tell him what was bothering her, she would. It wasn't till they reached the lough, and she dropped down from Night Star's back and walked towards their favourite spot, that she spoke.

'Fergal, did you notice anyone around when we were at the gate yesterday?'

He hesitated. With his hunting instincts and the experience he had for catching the faintest sound, he had been fully aware that there had been an onlooker. He had, as a result, cast a quick glance around and noticed the bike lying on the verge. Once inside the gates he had quietly waited until he saw the figure of a young man riding away. He was surprised that Theresa had also sensed another presence. 'No,' he said, looking away over the lough, 'I think you must have been imagining things.'

'You're probably right,' she agreed, and was relieved. Determined

102

to throw off her mood, she leaned on her elbows and looked into his eyes. 'So how did I do yesterday?' she grinned.

'You did all right. Mind you, I'm not going to repeat the lesson. I don't want to become addicted.' He turned to look at the girl by his side and smiled, his tawny eyes alight with fun.

'Good as that, was I?' she said wickedly, feeling secretly pleased. She had been surprised at the intensity of Fergal's kiss. If she had known better she would have thought he had put more into it than was necessary. It was pleasant to know that he had enjoyed the experience.

'Are we going to swim today?' Fergal sat up.

Her face reddened slightly. She had the 'curse', accompanied by the usual terrible cramping pains; the cold water would have her doubled up. Why was it that women who had to put up with this monthly agony? Probably because God was a man, she thought sourly.

'Ah, no!' she said aloud. 'I'll give it a miss today.' She watched as he stripped off and ran into the water before she lay back on the soft turf.

When they arrived back at the stables, Richard Beck was waiting. He glanced at Fergal. 'Would you unsaddle both horses? I want to have a word with Theresa. It won't take long.'

Fergal nodded. 'Certainly, Mr Beck.'

'Good lad.' Richard took Theresa's arm and led her over to the gate leading to the paddock. He let go and leaned over the top bar. He was silent for a moment and she shot a quick glance at him.

'I'd like you to come up to the castle on Sunday,' he said. 'I have something to show you, and I also have a proposition to make to you.' He turned towards her. 'Will Sunday be convenient? Perhaps you could lunch with me?' His tone seemed rather peremptory.

Theresa's mind seized up. 'I – I – yes, I suppose so. I have to go to mass, but I'm sure my parents won't mind. I'll ask them. Shall I telephone you to confirm that I'll be coming?'

'Only ring if you are unable to come,' Richard said. 'It will be simpler that way.' He opened the gate and passed through.

By the time she arrived home lunch had finished, but her mother had left a note telling her that there was a cold meat salad for her, and would she please wash up after her? She looked quickly at her watch. The group had arranged to meet by Lafferty's Cove for a swim. She hastily ate the food and ran upstairs to change.

There was a knock on the door. It was Eileen. 'Good!' she said, with relief. 'I hoped you wouldn't get caught up at the stables.'

'I nearly did. We were late getting back from our ride and Richard Beck was waiting to have a word with me.'

'What did he want?'

'Nothing much, but it meant I was held back from grooming and watering Night Star.'

They walked quickly along the top road – it was easier than ploughing along the sandy beach. There was a rough and slightly dangerous track down from the road but it was manageable. To Theresa's surprise, Tandy and Jack were there. She looked at Eileen. 'This should be interesting,' she remarked.

'Haven't you seen Jack since they went off with those girls?' Eileen stopped.

'He has been trying to contact me,' Theresa replied. 'Mam says he has been to the house twice, but each time he came I was at the stables. Obviously you have spoken to Tandy.' They were standing on the bluff above the group below. 'Sit down here for a minute.' She pulled Eileen by the arm, causing her to slide.

'Theresa! Have a care. I could have fallen just then.'

'Sit down and quit your blethering. Tell me what excuse Tandy gave for their actions the other day.'

'I don't see it as an excuse,' Eileen said, keeping her voice low. 'He explained that everything happened so quickly they didn't have time to do much about it. Apparently they had met the girls at a party they went to in Dublin. The girls were holidaying up here that week and caught sight of them—'

'What has that got to do with Jack and Tandy going off with them?'

'They couldn't get out of going with them because Tandy had foolishly told them that if ever they were up this way, they were to look them up and they'd show them round.' She had just seen Tandy rise from his position, dressed for a swim. Anxious to get down before he went towards the sea, she continued hurriedly, 'It was all Tandy's fault. Jack gave him a good roasting for getting him involved.'

Before Theresa could answer, Eileen was up and away, sliding down the last, hazardous piece of slope till she reached the group below. Theresa followed more leisurely. She was only half convinced that the story Tandy had set out was the true one, but she was pleased that Jack had less part in the caper than she had at first thought.

She couldn't go for a swim now, any more than she could have earlier, so she settled down next to Davey Adams. Jack and Tandy were already in the water and Eileen joined them. Soon, the others had gone in and she found herself alone with Davey, who was eyeing her intently.

104

Her gaze turned flinty. 'Why are you staring at me, Davey?'

'Aren't you going in for a swim?' he enquired, with a smirk on his face so suggestive it made her skin crawl. He really was a bad article.

'I'm not going in today. Is there a reason for your smirk, Davey?'

'I just wondered if you had already been swimming and were too tired to bother again.'

'What are you on about?' She felt a sharp tingle in her mouth. Before his next words were out she had guessed what they were going to be, and the sharp tingle turned to a surplus of saliva as she realized the danger if she was right.

'I was walking over the fields a mile from Castle Donagh the other day, and who did I see cutting through the lough, stark naked, but the bold Theresa Brady?' Davey gave another smirk and Theresa had to swallow hard to hold back the panic that was raiding her insides.

'I've no doubt you saw more than that, judging by the look on your face.' To her surprise, her voice sounded steady and as cold as ice.

'I also saw you lying buck naked beside a tinker,' said Davey, but now his eyes were shifting away and he was lifting sand and letting it drift through his fingers, not daring to look at her.

'I thought you might have done. It never occurred to you to wonder if there was any badness in it? You immediately decided that I was up to no good?'

'It isn't the kind of thing a nice girl would get up to.'

'Why not? There isn't anything wrong with the naked body. Not everyone who strips down does so to have sex. Only a bad-minded person would think that.'

Davey gave a gasp. This one is a right tearaway, he thought. His sisters were getting themselves a bad name and Theresa Brady could sit calmly beside him, talk dirty and get away with it. Was there any justice? 'I'll not say a word to a soul, of course,' he said, 'but I wouldn't mind having a swim with you at the lough sometime. If a tinker can swim with you, surely you wouldn't mind swimming with a friend.'

'Let me give the matter some thought, Davey,' said Theresa slowly. A plan was forming in her mind. She was a match for the likes of Davey Adams any day of the week. She lay back with a casualness she wasn't feeling. 'Anyway, what were you doing on Mr Beck's land?' She became more confident as she watched Davey wriggle. 'You wouldn't have been poaching by any chance, would you?'

'I was not!'

105

'If you say so, Davey. I wonder where they got the pheasants for the game pie they were serving at the hotel last night?'

Davey blanched and she realized she had struck home. It had been a wild guess, but she knew that Davey did a bit of poaching on the side, and she also knew that a lot of his catch went to the hotel. 'You know, of course, that the pheasants are not ready for the gun for at least another four weeks? You could get into trouble – serious trouble – if you were caught.' Her voice was silken.

'I don't know what you're talkin' about. You are just tryin' to get yourself off the hook, Theresa Brady, but it won't work.'

'You may be right,' Theresa said, to Davey's relief.

The others were coming back. Davey quickly said, 'What about it, then?'

'Oh, yes! You want to swim naked with me to buy your silence. All right then, Davey. You've not got much going for you. I might as well allow you a bit of excitement. God knows you don't get much of that. I'll meet you up at the lough on Monday at the same time.'

'You'll be alone?' His eyes held a trace of alarm.

'I'm sure as certain not going to invite an audience,' said Theresa.

'You'll not bring . . .' Tandy and Jack arrived at that moment and Davey moved away an inch or two. He'd wanted to warn her that he wouldn't put up with any nonsense like her bringing along the tinker, but when he thought about it, he realized he wouldn't need to show himself if she did the dirty on him. She would regret it if she did. He would see that the news spread round the village in double-quick time.

Jack sat down beside Theresa. There was an awkward silence for a moment before he said, quietly, 'Do you fancy a walk along the beach?'

'Why not!' Theresa rose. 'I believe in clearing the air.'

She set the pace as they walked along, until they reached the low groyne some way from the others.

'We can sit here for a while. I know you have an explanation to give, Jack, so we might as well get straight down to the matter.'

He joined her, his heart rate accelerating. He'd known that he was going to find their first meeting difficult, but he hadn't bargained for Theresa's forthright approach. He should have remembered it was her way.

Theresa listened, scuffing the damp sand with her foot and staring straight ahead. Jack's explanation echoed Tandy's as she knew it would, but she heard him out before she spoke.

'As a form of apology it goes a fair way to redressing things,

106

Jack,' she said, 'but I think that there is no excuse for the way you and Tandy conducted yourselves that day. I know we have no claim on either of you, but you made us look a right pair of has-beens.'

'I know. Panic set in as they approached us and before we knew it we were in deep. We didn't want to go with them. You must believe that.'

'I do. I saw the look on your faces at the time. Are you seeing them again?'

'Of course not! She was a girl I met in Dublin. Nothing more than that.'

'And what does our friendship mean to you, Jack?' She looked straight into his eyes for the first time since they sat down. She felt she had to know that she still had his regard.

'I've know you since we were tots. You are very special to me.' He meant every word in spite of her deceit with the lad, Fergal. After all, he had no claim to her.

With his words, Theresa had to be content. She didn't want to rock the already unstable truce that had been formed between them, and from which she hoped they would rebuild their old relationship. What he said next startled her.

'What does Fergal mean to you?' he asked, his eyes boring into hers.

She sighed. 'You were there, weren't you? I sensed it. I always sense when you are near. I tried to convince myself that I was imagining it, but I knew.'

'You were kissing him pretty expertly, and judging by your giggling, you were enjoying the experience.' Jack's voice was heavy with hurt.

'I didn't think – as usual,' she said softly. 'It all started because I confessed to Fergal that I had never had a real kiss. He was amused and I asked him to show me how to kiss properly. There was nothing in it, Jack. I was giggling because I was making a right hash of it.'

'You could have asked me,' he said.

'No I couldn't. You are Jack. I think the world of you, you know that. I could no more beg you to kiss me than fly. You are too near to me. Fergal was different. We didn't mean anything to each other – it was a bit of a laugh.'

Jack knew how she felt. Didn't he feel the same way? He wanted to kiss her, many times, but the fact that they had been together since they were tiny tots strangled the whole thing. He wanted to protect her. 'Just another experience to add to your list?' he suggested.

'That's all it was.'

He was silent. When he spoke again, he held her hand. 'Next time, try me. I'm not experienced either but we could learn together. We both acted daft. If you forgive me. I'll forgive you.'

'Done!' Theresa said. She felt heady because the whole business had been sorted out and a delicious feeling of warmth stole through her. She closed her eyes against the sun and leaned back against the groyne, so failed to see the look of uncertainty in Jack's eyes.

On Sunday she kept her lunch appointment with Richard. Her parents had been quite happy about the arrangement as they were going to see her gran and were lunching at the cottage.

Richard met her at the door. He was alone in the castle. He had given Bob time off so that they could be free to discuss his plan.

'I'm afraid it will be a cold collation. Bob set it out before he left.'

She was amazed at what she saw set before them. There was fresh salmon, various salads, crusty bread, chicken in a creamy sauce; and to follow, fresh fruit salad or trifle. All to be washed down with a fine white wine.

'Bob has done you proud,' she remarked.

'Let's fill a couple of plates and retire to the garden. It seems a shame to miss out on the sun.' Richard smiled, crinkling his eyes in amusement at her obvious delight in what was to him a perfectly ordinary repast.

Although it was now the end of August, the sun still retained its heat and they sat in comfortable chairs to enjoy both the food and the warmth.

When they had finished, he turned from the light conversation they had been enjoying to the more serious matter he had brought Theresa along to discuss.

'You told me you were interested in art,' he started. 'Are you interested in a serious way, or just as an onlooker?'

Theresa was surprised at the question. 'I'm very serious. I hope to study art if I can persuade my parents. My father wants me to teach. He is hoping I get to university. Why do you ask?'

'Have you ever wondered what I do for a living?'

'I suppose I assumed you had lots of money and were interested in running this estate and liked horses.'

He laughed. 'I'm not interested in either to any great extent. Both were thrust upon me. The horses belong to my partner, who spends most of his time at his London gallery when he isn't doing business abroad. I came here because I needed somewhere to live that was quiet and beautiful so that I could look after the horses and carry on with my work – I am an artist.'

Theresa had been studying him all the time he had been speaking. He had an interesting face. Deeply tanned by the sun, with dark brown eyes that contrasted oddly with his thick, light grey hair. His hands were slim and tapering with – dare she believe it – beautifully manicured nails. When she considered it, he was definitely not the kind of man who would be interested in manual work.

She nodded and he continued. 'I would like to show you some of my work, and then I would like to put a proposition to you. Knowing that you too are interested in art makes what I am about to discuss with you that much easier.'

She was intrigued.

'Come with me.' He rose and held out his hand to assist her.

She followed as he led the way up the stone steps which turned in a broad spiral from the great hall. At the top they reached a gallery from which she peered down into the hall below. Her excitement mounted. The upper landing was ringed by many doors, and the stone walls were decorated with medieval flags and pennants. It was the most colourful, most fascinating place she had ever seen. She would try to imprint on her memory all that she saw, so that she could regale Eileen with this latest tour of the upper rooms.

'In here,' said Richard, and opened a door which led into a large, empty room.

'It's empty!' she said, and could have bitten her tongue for the stupidity of the observation.

He nodded absently, and strode towards the far wall. Once there, he opened what looked like a cupboard door, which she discovered led into a smaller room with a flight of steps leading upwards.

'This is it,' he said, and they emerged from the gloom of the stairway into bright sunlight.

Shading her eyes against the glare, she saw that they were on the roof of the castle, most of which was taken up by a chalet-style construction set in the middle. It looked incongruous in its mediaeval setting, and was fortunately hidden from view from the grounds by the high, crenellated wall with its four turrets, one at each corner – a wall built high enough to withstand arrows and protect the archers crouching on the ledge beneath as they shot their arrows through the slits.

The chalet was set out as a studio, with one wall almost entirely composed of glass. There were paintings and canvasses strewn everywhere, some leaning sedately against the wall, but the majority rubbing shoulders with frames and materials and props of all sorts.

'This is wonderful,' Theresa breathed. 'I can see why you find it irksome to have to deal with the horses and the running of the estate.'

Richard didn't reply. He walked towards the easel on which stood a covered canvas. 'I would value your opinion on this,' he said.

Theresa faltered in her step. She wondered if he was having fun with her. What opinion could she offer a man of such artistic talent, judging by the work – some unfinished – hugging the walls?

He pulled the cover off the easel with a flourish, and she drew in her breath. The painting was obviously Richard's current project. It depicted a bath house containing a large pool. Sitting at the poolside was a beautiful young nude girl combing her hair. In the background a large wolfhound lay sleeping at the foot of one of a row of ivy-clad pillars bordering the pool.

'It is beautiful – but . . .'

'But?'

Theresa reddened. 'I – I'm sorry. I have no right to comment. What do I know?'

'Tell me. Tell me! What do you see that is missing?' Richard spoke with urgency. 'I want you to tell me. You know what is missing, don't you?'

'I'm not sure,' she said slowly. She had been startled by the sudden change in him.

'For heaven's sake, Theresa, stop pussyfooting around. What do you think is missing?' His voice had now risen with excitement; his hand was making encouraging circular movements in the air.

'Another bather; another woman. The balance is not quite right – look, I'm sorry. I have no right to criticize. I am a rank amateur.'

To her surprise, Richard's taut shoulders relaxed and his eyes darted fire as the sunlight caught them. 'I want you to be that other figure,' he said. 'When I saw you on the beach that evening I knew I had found my Lady of the Baths. I suddenly saw you in the painting, having climbed from the pool, stooping to lift your towel, just as you did that evening.'

'You mean you want me to pose nude?'

'No! No! I wouldn't ask you to do that. I don't think your parents would be at all happy about that; but they might agree to allow you to pose with a bathing costume on.'

'I'd certainly have to ask my parents, that's for sure.' Theresa felt excitement rise at the idea of being on canvas.

'I don't want anyone to know about this. It could cause all sorts of problems for you. First, I must have a word with your parents.'

In a way, Theresa was disappointed that she wouldn't be able to tell Eileen about it, but then again it was an exciting secret to keep

110

to herself. She could revel in it on those days when things were getting her down. At least she could tell Eileen all about the wonderful furnishings and the wall hung with pennons and flags of old.

Richard escorted Theresa down to the ground floor with only half his mind attending to the courtesies of seeing her out. He knew what he must do. He would send a letter asking Colin and Nuala Brady to lunch with him on an arranged day in the near future. He was certain that he could persuade them to consent to Theresa posing for him.

On Monday morning, when Theresa met Fergal at the stables, she told him of the conversation she'd had with Davey Adams. 'The little blirt told me that he would spread it all round the village that I'd romped around naked with you if I didn't give him a taste as well.' Her face was pink with annoyance.

'And?' Fergal stopped half-way to the saddling enclosure, his almond eyes searching Theresa's face.

'I have a plan,' she said. 'I'm to meet him today.'

'Oh?'

'Fergal! You are lookin' at me like a cow lookin' over a gate. Have you nothing more to say to me than two words leavin' your mouth like bullets?'

'I want to hear your plan,' said Fergal evenly.

Theresa outlined it for him. 'I'll be waiting for him, and when he comes to me, you'll come out from behind our tree and threaten him with annihilation if he so much as breathes my name in that respect.'

Fergal continued his walk and Theresa followed. When at last he spoke, he had saddled his horse and tightened the girth. He gave her a severe look. 'You'll keep out of this. I'll deal with the matter.'

'I don't want Davey killed – just frightened!'

'I'll handle it. If we do it your way this Davey Adams will still have a hold over you in that you would be a party to anything that might happen to him. My way will be to creep up on him and frighten the sauce out of him. I think he'll see reason.'

'He'll not show himself unless he sees me – alone,' said Theresa.

'He'll be hiding within sight of the lough and our tree well before the time you are expected. I've done a fair bit of poaching and animal watching; not even the sensitive badger knows when I creep up on it to observe it. I'll find him before you are expected. When I've done, you can rest easy in your bed.'

'You – you won't harm him?'

'I promise you I won't lay a finger on him,' said Fergal grimly.

111

'Now! You take off in the opposite direction today. I'll meet you back at the stables in two hours.' He looked down at her from his horse. 'I don't want you to question me about what happens. The matter will be sorted out and needs no more discussion.'

She paled, but mounted Night Star and set off on her ride, her heart in her mouth with the fear of what might happen to Davey, even though Fergal had promised he wouldn't lay a finger on him.

Fergal hadn't returned from his ride when she reached the stables later. To keep her mind off the matter she fed and watered the little mare and led her into the paddock, leaning on the rail as she watched her circle the field, delighted with her freedom. Theresa had grown to love Night Star, and dreaded the day she would have to say goodbye.

Taking the saddle to the tack room she set about cleaning it, her mind searching for a reprieve from her present worry. With more force than usual she buffed the leather until a sound outside set her feet moving for the door.

Fergal was dismounting; she searched his face for some evidence of a fight, and seeing none, she sighed with relief. 'Everything all right?' she enquired tentatively.

He nodded. 'To my satisfaction,' he said, and concentrated on loosening the girth.

'You didn't—'

'I didn't lay a finger on him.' He busied himself with removing the saddle, his rigid back telling her not to question further.

She had to be content, but she watched him from the tack room as he watered the big horse, and bit her lip nervously. A tearaway she was, and she sometimes regretted her impulsive nature, but she had never harmed anyone and she certainly didn't want any harm to befall Davey, even if he did deserve it.

Eileen was waiting for her when she arrived home.

'I thought you were going to be earlier than this,' she grumbled.

Theresa gave her a killing look. 'I can't always stick to the exact time, Eileen. I am dealing with animals; they don't always play the game the way you want them to and their power of reasoning is non–existent – however, I'll mention next time that my friend Eileen is waiting and could you hurry your feed? You never know – miracles can happen.'

'You're being very sarcastic,' observed Eileen mildly. 'What put you in a bad mood?'

'Oh, don't mind me! A cup of tea and I'll be fine – I could drink the Liffey dry.'

'I'll make it. Your mam has gone up to our shop to get some foodstuff.'

'God! I didn't even notice she wasn't here.' Theresa flopped into her father's armchair whilst the willing Eileen brewed the tea.

When she had drunk it she felt better. They had arranged to go into Kilgaven to see a film and Eileen immediately started fussing over time, so Theresa hurried upstairs to change. They only just made it to the other side of the Tullybra bridge when the bus came bowling round the corner. 'This film better be worth the rush,' she grumbled, trying to catch her breath.

It was, as was the light meal they had afterwards at McCoy's café just up the road.

'Have you seen anything of Davey Adams today?' Theresa realised as soon as she spoke that she had done the wrong thing.

'Davey?' Eileen looked at her in surprise. 'Have you taken a sudden notion for him or something?'

'Forget I mentioned him.'

'Well! I did see him, now you mention it. He was coming out of Hughie Green's.'

The chemist. Theresa groaned inwardly.

'Why are you so interested in Davey? Most of the time you wouldn't bid him the time of day.'

'He was cheeky to me on the beach the other day. I just wondered if he'd said anything about the slanching I gave him.'

'I didn't speak to him, but I noticed his face was all scratched.'

Fortunately, Eileen was still romancing over the film they'd just watched and her curiosity waned quickly. The subject of Davey didn't come up again.

Colin and Nuala enjoyed their lunch with Richard Beck. They had found him to be a man of culture, and Colin, having a great interest in music, was pleased to have found someone who shared his passion. He hadn't been so happy about the reason for the invitation, and was annoyed with Theresa for not letting them know beforehand. Of course he was flattered that Richard Beck should consider his daughter to be worthy of painting, but he didn't want it going to her head. Lord knows, she was high and mighty enough, now.

Later, having digested an excellent lunch and smoked an equally excellent cigar, much to Nuala's astonishment, Colin relaxed into his chair; he was in a receptive frame of mind.

'I have some reservations about this, Richard,' he said. 'It's a bit out of the ordinary for people like us. This is a small village and we have to live here.'

'I can assure you, Colin, I have the very best intentions. Perhaps you would care to look at some of my work?'

Richard left the room, having filled his guest's glasses once more. He had no intention of presenting the actual canvas on which he was working; instead, he had prepared two that had been commissioned privately.

He retrieved the canvasses and took them along to the drawing room. The Bradys – as he had guessed they would be – were impressed. One picture was of Lady Maria Valentine-Coutts. It had been commissioned by the lady's husband for her thirtieth birthday. The other one was a family portrait of a wealthy businessman and his wife and four children.

Satisfied, Colin agreed that his daughter could pose for Richard.

Nuala, however, was not entirely happy; she said so on the way home. 'I'm surprised at you,' she admonished. 'I said nothing at the time as I wouldn't belittle you in front of Richard Beck, but I'm not certain you should have so readily agreed to his suggestion.'

'I can read the man. I have no concerns about him.' Colin patted her hand and was surprised when she pulled it away forcefully.

'Don't patronise me, Colin.' She remained silent for the rest of the journey home. She was uneasy. Artists were a different breed altogether. What an artist saw as being acceptable didn't necessarily fall in line with what the ordinary class of person considered moral. She chided herself for being disloyal to her daughter. A tearabout she might be, but she'd had a good Catholic upbringing. She wouldn't pose for anything that might cause offence.

CHAPTER 9

The exam results were out. Theresa was ecstatic. She had passed with top marks and had won the coveted Art shield. Eileen, with typical understatement, was fairly pleased with her results. She mentioned with the merest hint of pride that she had been awarded the Catechism and Bible History prize.

'If you hadn't got it I'd have considered the possibility of a "fix",' Theresa laughed, adding, 'I wonder how the lads got on. Their results are the important ones; ours are just the end-of-term exams.'

In fact, Jack did extremely well. He was on his way to university. Tandy, although pleased that he had passed with high enough marks to get into the agricultural college he had applied to, was miffed that he hadn't done so well in Chemistry.

'Do you *need* chemistry?' asked Eileen. They had all assembled at Lafferty's Cove for an analysis, and they were huddled together behind a huge rock as the day was overcast and slightly cold.

'No! but in modern farming, a good knowledge of chemistry can prove very useful.'

'You know enough about the subject whether you got top marks or not, so quit going on,' said Jack amiably. Nothing could dampen his joy. Not even the fact that he got fired up with jealousy on occasion, ever since he'd caught Theresa kissing Fergal – though to be fair, he hadn't behaved well either.

Theresa was unusually quiet. She was contemplating the fact that their lives had taken another turn. Jack and Tandy would be gone in a few weeks' time, and there would be no one to wait for at the Tullybra bridge. She would miss the arguments and laughter with Jack, and the precarious excitement when he was near. Who would keep her in check now? She looked towards Eileen, whose rosy-cheeked face was creased in laughter at something Tandy had just said. Hadn't they realised that things would never be the same again; that a major part of their childhood had gone?

Jack shook her out of her reverie. 'You look unhappy. What's the matter?'

She wanted to scream at them all for their insensitivity, but smiled instead. 'I'm sorry. I was miles away. Why don't we go into Kilgaven this evening and have some fun? Celebrate properly.' She tried to inject some colour into her voice as she spoke.

'To hell with Kilgaven. Let's go to Drogheda. There's more life there.' Tandy pulled Eileen to her feet. 'We'll go for a meal and then sort something out from there. What do you say, Jack?'

Jack had been looking at Theresa and hadn't heard a word.

Tandy poked him in the back. 'What do you say? How about going to Drogheda for a meal and a bottle of wine?'

'Fine idea, Tandy. Just how do you think we are going to get anyone to serve us with a bottle of wine for two underage girls?'

'You leave that to us,' said Theresa. 'It's been done before; right Eileen?'

For once, Eileen didn't put forward an argument, merely smiled nervously and nodded.

Later, when Jack and Tandy met them, they were astounded at the transformation.

'How did you two get past the parents looking like that?' Tandy eyed them appreciatively. 'You certainly look older with the make-up on.'

'It's wonderful what you can do with a hand mirror behind a stone wall,' Theresa laughed.

Jack was silent, although he nodded at Tandy's observation. He had never seen them look lovelier. 'Here comes our transport,' he said at last, as the bus came round the bend in the road. 'I'm only too sorry we couldn't have the car this evening. Going by bus seems dull for two such lovely ladies.' He swept his arm down in a courtly gesture and smiled at them.

As she had promised, Theresa paid a visit to her gran. She had been warned that Mona was still a long way from recovery, but she was shocked to see how much her little gran had shrunk. There is nothing of her, she thought, trying to hide her concern as she stooped to kiss the tiny figure.

Granny McClusky returned her granddaughter's kiss and hugged her. 'It's so good to see you, cusheen,' she said softly. 'I've missed our talks by the duck pond.'

'I'm not to tax you too much, so I've been told to stay for one hour only,' smiled Theresa, realizing that she too had missed their chats.

'Nonsense. This is as good as a tonic. I'll not let you go till you've had a bite to eat with me.'

'I'll prepare it,' Theresa insisted.

'I've got it heating on the kleek.' Mona pulled the kleek with the large pot hanging on it towards her. She lifted the lid and the lovely, wholesome smell of Irish stew filled the room as she gave it a stir.

'How are you managing, Gran?'

'I do very little. What needs doing outside is dealt with by John Kelly. He is a real treasure. And Pat calls in every evening for a chat and to see I'm all right.'

This surprised Theresa. She'd known Pat McGarry all her life. He never missed her birthday. There was always a card and a lovely present. A simple string of pearls – a handbag that she giggled about because it was completely wrong for her – a beautiful scarf – always something that was exciting, if inappropriate for a young girl. he was a big man with shoulders like a bull; Theresa recalled how he used to swing her up on them, when she was younger, and hold her up so that she could pick apples from his trees. She knew how fond he was of her gran, but she was surprised to learn of the many small kindnesses he had done for her since her illness.

'Pat is like a son to me.' Gran smiled. 'I lie easy at night, knowing that he is living nearby.'

'I've always liked Pat,' Theresa said, still lost in her thoughts. 'It seems that I've lost touch with him lately, though. I often run into him, but it isn't the same as when I was younger. He seems shy of me.'

'You are growing into a beautiful young lady. Pat is more at ease with children – but he'll always be there if you are in trouble. Remember that.'

'Why won't you come and live with us like Mam asked you to?' Theresa asked.

'I'll live my days out here, cusheen. This is where I've been happy and where all my memories are. Your granda's spirit is here and I feel his presence in every corner. I'd not be happy away from him.' She sighed. 'I wish you could convince your mam that it is best this way. She can have me carted away if there are signs that I'm not coping, but until that day comes – and with John's and God's help – I'll manage. Besides, as I said, Pat McGarry calls in daily to make sure I have all my needs.'

They continued to chat as they ate the succulent stew. Grannie McClusky wanted to hear all about the latest happenings in her granddaughter's life.

'Jack passed all his exams with very high marks,' Theresa told her.

'So I hear! He'll be off to university soon.' Granny McClusky

117

looked shrewdly at her granddaughter. 'You'll miss him a lot.'

'Yes!' said Theresa wistfully.

'I'm told that you did very well. I hear you got the Art prize.'

Theresa laughed. 'How do you know all this?'

'It's all round the village. John brings me the news. I know that Eileen got the Catechism and Bible History prize.'

'Then you know that Tandy is going to England to study agriculture?'

'I do! And I know that Davey Adams has run off to England and left a note for his mam and his da.'

Theresa's voice was a whisper. 'I – I didn't know that. How did you find that out?'

'John told me. He only lives two doors away. Davey's mam knocked on their door at six o'clock this morning with the letter in her hand, crying buckets.'

Theresa remembered Eileen's remark that she'd seen Davey come out of the chemist shop with his face a mass of scratchmarks. She had to control her hand as she gave her gran her mug of milky tea.

Mona grew tired, and Theresa suggested that she should have a rest. She helped her into the tiny bedroom and settled her in the large bed. Later, as she cycled home, her face was creased with worry.

Her mam was ironing in the kitchen when she arrived back. She joined her and stood with her back against the large dresser, her face grave.

'Is Gran going to be all right? She looks so ill.'

Nuala, seeing her daughter's face crumple, put down the iron and folded her in her arms. She had been anxious for Theresa to see her gran and to know that she was still very ill. It was a form of preparation for her; but it hurt to see her distress.

'It will be a long haul back to health for her,' she said quietly. 'David says the X-rays are better, but her whole system has taken a hammering. Anyone else would have licked it by now, but Gran, being a bit fragile anyway, is taking longer.' She pressed Theresa to her. How could she tell her she had doubts that Gran would ever get better? She just didn't seem to be pulling her weight to help things along. it was as though she had given up.

'I think Gran has given up.'

Nuala drew a sharp breath. 'What makes you think that?'

'The way she was talking about Granda. She says she feels closer to him now than she has done since he died.'

'I hope you're wrong,' said Nuala. 'But even if you are not – then we must be glad that Gran has this comfort. Dry your eyes. It could be that we are reading the signs wrongly.' In her heart she

118

didn't think so, but it was something for Theresa to cling to. At least, now, she was prepared for the worst.

Theresa couldn't wait to see Fergal next morning. She had hardly slept all night for worry; consequently, her temper was close to the surface. She was leading Night Star from the stable when he arrived, whistling tunefully, his ponytail flicking about as he strode across the cobblestones of the yard. He looked as though he hadn't a care in the world, and for some reason this irritated her still further.

She tied the little mare to the hitching rail and turned to look at him. His tawny eyes looked back. 'Good morning, Fergal,' she said.

Fergal, sensitive to the coolness in her manner, said shortly, 'What's up with you? You sound as though your teeth were made of icicles.'

'I'd like to talk to you.'

'Certainly! Just let me get Jupiter out and we can saddle up and talk at the same time.'

'This is important. It won't take long.'

He looked coolly at the girl facing him. Her lovely face looked grim, her large eyes as cold as charity. 'Have I done something to upset you?'

'Did you not promise me that you wouldn't lay a finger on Davey Adams?'

'I did! And I kept my promise,' Fergal said, a trace of impatience in his voice. 'And didn't you, in turn, promise me that you wouldn't talk about it – or question me?'

'That was before I heard that Davey had run away to England. That was before I discovered that he was seen leaving Hughie Green's chemist shop with scratchmarks all over his face. I want to know if you had anything to do with it.'

'I told you I wouldn't lay a finger on the devious, whey-faced blirt, and I didn't. Consider the matter closed.' Fergal turned and walked towards the stables, a tiny smile settling on his lips. He reminded himself to pick up the large, thorny briar on his way home. It would burn very nicely.

When they reached the lough, they led the horses to the shelter of the tree before stripping off for their swim. Fergal broke the silence that had lasted for the whole of the ride. 'I have no time for rows,' he said quietly, looking into her eyes.

Theresa smiled. 'It would be a shame if we let Davey Adams come between us.'

'Then let's get into the cool water quickly, before I roast.' Fergal ran for the water and Theresa, her heart flipping at the sight of his tensile young body arching in a perfect dive, followed.

Later, as they lay in the shadowed coolness of the tree, listening to the muted munching of the two horses, their bodies became saturated by the heat of the day. Theresa felt her lids droop, and gradually the sounds receded as she subsided into sleep.

Fergal, leaning on one elbow, gently eased her blouse across her body to keep off the hot rays of the sun. He was trying to control his feelings, his muscles tensing with the effort. Why now? They had done this many times before, but suddenly he had become aware of the woman rather than the young girl he had met just a few weeks ago. Jesus! he wasn't made of stone. He moved away abruptly and she woke.

'What's wrong?' Her voice was still drowsy with sleep.

'It's time we went.'

'We haven't been here more than half an hour. We usually stay an hour before going back.'

'Christ! I know that! Just get dressed.'

'Must we?' she pleaded. 'We—'

Taking her by the shoulders, he pulled her roughly towards him, bringing his mouth down on hers, crushing her to him with an urgency he could no longer control.

Theresa felt herself responding. It was as though a million moths were running up and down inside her body, tickling the life out of her, particularly in the area that the older generation referred to as 'down below'. It was a delicious feeling, which became so overpowering it was almost painful. She gave a gasp and shot up into a standing position. 'What?' Fergal yelled.

'This is not right!' she gasped, wondering if she would be mad at herself later for the missed opportunity.

Fergal glared at her, not just because she had ruined the moment, but because he had let it happen in the first place. Desire for her had overtaken his common sense, and a feeling of shame now ran through him, quickly replaced by cold anger. Needing to appease his conscience, he directed the anger towards Theresa, letting his frustration dissipate as he railed at her.

'What do you expect? You lie beside me with not a clout on, looking so beautiful – it's more than flesh and blood can stand.' He began to pull on his clothes and became silent. Her and her bloody search for knowledge – tormenting him with a body like that – unaware of the power she had. He was furious at his lack of control, his lack of respect and understanding. he looked away from her fumbling attempt at dressing, her hands nervously trying to control their shaking. Thoughts were warring in his mind. He should have taught her a lesson. She had been asking for it. But his shame at his lack of respect and his denial of the trust she had in him tortured him. He strode towards Jupiter and yanked angrily at the reins, causing the big horse to nap and shy, eyes rolling.

He swung himself up and, without a glance at the half-clad girl, set off up the field at a gallop.

Theresa watched him go as she struggled with her riding boots. Her heart felt like lead. Jupiter was really gathering speed now, and she froze as she watched horse and rider approach the tall hedge. There was nowhere to go. He had to jump. She watched as Fergal, his elbows pointing out from his body, spurred the big horse on. She drew in a sharp breath as they rose as one, etched against the blue sky momentarily, before both disappeared over the hedge.

She shaded her eyes against the sun and strained to see into the distance. They should have been galloping across the next field by now – but there was no sign of them. She grabbed Night Star's reins, her eyes still scanning the fields. By now her heart was pumping rapidly. She let out a cry as she saw the riderless horse galloping towards home. She mounted Night Star and rode fast towards the place where Fergal had jumped the hedge.

'Please, God, let him be safe,' she cried aloud. Tears were blinding her. It was true. It was all her fault. Yet again, her disregard for convention and her desire for excitement had driven her to excess, but this time it had come back at her. This time the situation was serious.

Frantically, she rode along the hedge, looking for a gate. At last, she found it. It was locked. Leaving Night Star tied to it, she climbed over and ran down the hill towards the spot where she thought he might be. 'Oh God!' she cried again.

When she reached him he was lying in a hollow at the bottom, his body still, his right leg bent at an angle. 'Fergal,' she cried. 'Oh, Fergal!'

He moaned. His eyes opened slowly as she cradled him. 'Get help. I've broken my leg.'

'I can't leave—'

'Go!' His eyes were dull with pain.

'Can't I make you more comfortable?'

'It might make things worse.' His face contorted. 'Go quickly.'

By the time she reached Castle Donagh, she couldn't see for the tears. She ran up the few steps to the front door and knocked frantically. Bob opened the door and caught her as she swayed. 'What has happened?' he said, briskly shaking her out of her momentary lapse.

'Fergal has had an accident,' she cried. 'Where is Richard?'

'He's over at Lord Conliffe's place.'

121

'We've got to get him back. Don't you understand? Fergal has broken his leg. Has Jupiter arrived back? He ran off – oh, please do something.'

'You go into the drawing room. I'll contact Mr Richard at once . . .'

'I'm going back. I left him there, badly hurt.'

Bob took the girl by the arm and led her into the drawing room. 'You wait here!' he said firmly. 'You have done your bit. I shall ring Mr Richard and tell him what has happened. He will know exactly what to do.' Crossing to a small table, he poured a small amount of brandy into a glass. 'Drink this.' Aware that she was going to argue, he placed it into her hands and, with his own cupped round hers, he raised the glass to her lips and made her sip, ignoring the look of distaste on her face.

'Now! Exactly where is Fergal lying?'

Theresa took a shuddering breath and gave him the exact position and, under pressure, drained the glass. Already she felt a little more in control.

Bob squeezed her shoulder. 'We'll get him sorted out. No one dies of a broken leg.' He made his way to the telephone in the hall.

When he came back into the room, he found Theresa sitting there, staring into space. There was a glazed look in her eyes. He knelt in front of her. 'It's all right. Mr Richard, Lord Conliffe, and Bill, his assistant gamekeeper are on their way. They are going to use the big tractor to move him. The doctor in Tullybra has been informed and will meet them there.'

'Can I stay here till I know that all is well? Please!'

'I'll ring your parents and let them know.'

'What about Fergal's family?'

'Bill will go along and give them the news.'

When he returned some time later, Theresa was asleep in the large armchair. Her face was still white with shock but the look of panic had gone. He closed the door softly. Mr Richard could deal with her when he came back.

Theresa woke to the gentle shaking of her shoulder. She opened her eyes and looked at Richard. Slowly it all came to her – the reason for her being here. 'I've been asleep!' she cried, grasping his arm. 'How could I?'

'Best thing for you. Bob tells me you were pretty shocked . . .'

'How is Fergal?'

Richard drew a footstool over and sat down. 'Fergal is in casualty at this moment having his leg seen to. He will probably have to have a day or two in hospital and then, if all is well, he will come home with it in plaster.'

'It's all my fault!'

Richard frowned slightly. 'I don't know why you think that. Fergal told us he was doing a bit of showing off to you and misjudged the height of the hedge.'

Theresa faltered. 'I'd like to see him.'

'Wait till he goes back to the clearing. The doctors seem to think that he will be hobbling round soon with a crutch.'

'How will he cope? He won't be able to ride – and there is the culling, and – and . . .'

'Allow me to worry about that. I employ the lad.' Richard smiled at her. 'Stop worrying. Everything will be all right now. You have played your part. If you hadn't acted so promptly things might have been worse.'

That night she tossed around, longing for sleep to come, but it wasn't till the early hours that she managed to fall into a light doze. Her mam brought her up some tea and toast. She was to stay in bed for a while. There was no hurry to get up.

Theresa looked anxiously at her mother. 'Have you heard any news of Fergal?'

'Richard rang earlier . . .'

'Earlier? What time is it now?'

'It's mid morning. You had a bad night. I heard you tossing about, so I let you sleep on.' Nuala pushed her daughter's hair back with her hand. 'I hear you acted very promptly.'

'Only because I was in a panic. Don't give me any credit. I blame myself for the whole thing . . .' She didn't enlarge on it, and Nuala didn't press her.

The last two weeks of the holiday seemed to pass with greater speed than usual. The new term was about to start and the end of freedom had arrived. Theresa was being as volatile as ever. To Eileen's despair, within minutes of entering the bus she had managed once again to antagonise Pat Maher.

'Did you deliberately arrive early so that we would have to race for the bus leaving ourselves out of breath and on the verge of a heart attack?' she demanded of Pat.

'You've breath enough to go spoutin' on as usual, Theresa Brady. Your friend Eileen hasn't complained.'

'My friend Eileen is a saint. I'm not. Nor am I intimidated by you.'

'I'll have you out of this bus within the next few minutes if you don't shut that gob of yours.' Pat Maher shot the gears so roughly they made an excruciating noise and turned a furious face to Theresa. 'I'll swing for you yet,' he yelled. 'I'm tired of your lip. Just remember that two can play at that game, my girl.'

Theresa opened her mouth to answer but, seeing the pleading look thrown at her by Eileen, closed it again and sank into her seat, contenting herself with throwing one of her lethal looks at Pat's back.

Later that morning she was called to Sister Anunciata's office and admonished. A complaint had been made by the driver of the school bus. Had she got an explanation?

'He doesn't like me. I only have to make a small complaint and he goes off at a tangent.'

'And what was your complaint, pray?' Sister Anunciata folded her arms into her wide sleeves and regarded the girl before her.

'He arrived too early. I told him so. Eileen and I were out of breath and I had a stitch in my side from running.'

'You are an intelligent girl. You got high marks in your exam results. You have great potential. Don't tell me that you couldn't reason that Pat Maher would wait for you.'

'You don't know Pat Maher, Sister. He'd say we were well over time and leave without us.' Theresa knew she was being foolish. Pat Maher brought out the worst in her.

'I'll not listen to another word, Theresa. I would ask you to curb that temper of yours. Now get back to your classroom and don't let me hear one more complaint about you.' Sister Anunciata rose and opened the door to allow the girl through.

Theresa knew why she had locked horns yet again with Pat. Things had happened so fast lately she needed to tear into something or someone, and Pat had been the chosen one. Of course she had known that Pat wouldn't go without them. The whole thing had been silly, but it had let out some of the tension that was deep inside her.

She felt battered by recent events. The business with Fergal had frightened her. She really hadn't meant for things to go as far as they did; because of her careless attitude to life and the feelings of others, she had come as near as dammit to destroying his livelihood. If it hadn't been for the kindness of Richard, Fergal would have fared badly. As it was, he was now of little use in helping his father with chopping down the trees, and he wouldn't be able to ride for months.

At least he still had money coming in. Richard had treated him as an employee and continued to pay him stable fees. Jupiter was now at McGarvie's stables as intended – albeit a bit sooner. Fergal could only help his father by carving the figurines and animals from the wood they culled; Theresa consoled herself with the fact that Lord Patrick had sent someone over to help with the trees.

She had plucked up courage to go and visit Fergal, and was

surprised that he saw the whole sorry business as his fault. They had argued about it, but she had come away feeling less unhappy. However, she still wasn't able to view life with her usual easygoing attitude. It didn't help that her gran's health was still poor. If she lost her little gran she didn't know what she would do.

She was so busy with her thoughts that she wasn't aware the Art mistress was standing by her shoulder till she spoke.

'Theresa, you have been staring at that piece of paper for the last ten minutes. Do you intend to reproduce the exercise I have set the class or not?'

'I'm sorry,' Theresa said, her eyes focusing again. She hated this particular lesson. They were doing exercises involving line and perspective, and she found it confining and boring. Nevertheless, she applied herself to the task, and for an hour at least her mind gave her peace.

She told Eileen during the lunch break about Pat Maher's complaint. She got little sympathy.

'I don't know what came over you,' said Eileen. 'You lit on the poor man like a locust. You knew he wouldn't have gone without us. It would be more than his job is worth.'

'I know. I am my own worst enemy. You keep telling me that, so I should take more heed.'

'Have you heard any more about Fergal? It was a terrible thing to happen.' Eileen was busily peeling an orange and didn't see the look on her friend's face.

'He's all right. I went over to see him a couple of days ago.'

By Friday Theresa felt less troubled. She was helped by the news that her gran seemed a lot better, and was actually pottering around the vegetable patch under John's supervision.

They were going dancing with Jack and Tandy; as usual, Eileen arrived early. She was wearing a pretty apple-green dress which toned well with the red hair.

Theresa smiled. 'You're looking great tonight. Tandy might well decide to stay in Ireland when he sees you looking like that.' Eileen blushed.

Theresa was wearing a shell-pink blouse with a tiny ruffle collar, and the new length navy blue skirt. She picked up her matching half coat and moved towards the door.

'When did you get that outfit?' Eileen asked. 'It's lovely.'

'I bought it with my birthday money. Mam and I went into Kilgaven this afternoon and got it.'

'It looks good on you – but then, everything does. I've said before that you could put a sack over your head and tie it at the waist and you would still look stylish.'

125

Jack hadn't been able to borrow his da's car, so they were meeting them at the Tullybra bridge to catch the bus. The boys were already there. Jack was leaning against the parapet, whilst Tandy sat atop it, swinging his legs.

Tandy was the first to catch sight of the two girls and, quickly jumping down, he nudged Jack in the ribs and came to meet them.

'Well! Would you look at this pair of fashion plates, Jack.'

'You look – superior,' Jack grinned, eyeing them both in appreciation.

'Don't we just?' laughed Theresa. Tonight she felt more lighthearted than she had done for many a day. She was determined to enjoy herself and shelve her worries.

There was no ceili dancing at the Curran ballroom. This was a real ballroom, and English dancing was the order. The hall sported a glittering mirror-ball in the middle of the high ceiling, and around the floor were dotted many small tables which were already full.

'We'll have to go up to the balcony,' said Jack. 'There's always more room up there – it takes longer to get down to dance. Everyone gets here as soon as the door is open so as to get one of the tables round the floor.'

'Have you two been here before?'

'I haven't,' said Tandy. 'I'm as surprised as you are.'

'I came here with John Drake some weeks ago,' Jack said. 'He's the boyo who was supposed to be joining me at the Uni – but he won't be going now. He didn't do well in his exams.'

'The Uni?' repeated Theresa. 'Already you are into the jargon, Jack.' She said it laughingly, pleased that he hadn't been here before with a girl.

'I'm dying for a dance,' said Eileen excitedly. 'I love English dancing.'

They began to enjoy themselves. The best bit – and one that caused the most amusement – was when the lights, already low, were turned down to the point where the dancers were but moving shadows down on the dance floor.

'Father Corke would go mad if he saw this,' said Tandy.

'It's a bit decadent,' Theresa laughed. She could hardly make out any of the others' features, and was excitedly aware that the close proximity of Jack took on a new meaning when the lights were this low.

'Watch the confusion when the lights suddenly come on again,' Jack whispered. 'There will be a few red faces. I think the management do it on purpose.' As he spoke, the lights came up again.

Theresa and Eileen giggled helplessly as couples sprang apart, the boys hastily adjusting ties and the girls quickly smoothing their hair.

'I wish I'd known this place existed,' said Theresa.

'It only opened three months ago. It was in the Dublin press,' Jack said.

They all went down on to the floor for the next dance, and afterwards, Jack and Theresa returned to the balcony leaving Tandy and Eileen to wait for the next one to start up.

'I'll never cease to be amazed that Eileen has learned to enjoy dancing as much as she does,' said Theresa. Now that she and Jack were alone she was feeling nervous.

'You aren't keen?'

'Not madly. I prefer riding and swimming.'

'Speaking of riding, how is your friend Fergal doing? I understand he had rather a bad accident when you were both out riding – m'da mentioned that he'd heard it from But–But–Ben. Wasn't he schooling a horse to be raced in the Curragh?'

'Not quite. He was riding him to keep him exercised and teach him control, so that when he goes to the stables he'll not behave like a carthorse. Fergal is well in himself, but his leg is badly broken and will need a while to heal.' Her tone had turned cool.

Jack, sensing that the subject was a sore point for some reason, hastily spoke of other things. 'It will seem odd not meeting you at the bridge after school,' he said, his voice low and intimate. 'I'm going to miss you, Theresa Brady. I'll miss your wild ideas and your short bursts of temper. I'll miss the fun we had together – all of us – down at Lafferty's Cove.' He took her hand in his. 'You have been a part of my life for so long; part of my childhood and part of my life. Wherever you are and whatever you do in the future, I hope you won't forget me.'

Theresa swallowed hard. 'Of course I won't forget you. You're the one likely to do that. Wait till you meet all those girls at university, and go to all the parties. I'll be lucky if you can still remember my name.' Her voice sank to a whisper as she realised the truth of what she had just said.

'I could never forget you. You'd kill me if I did – anyway, what are we on about? Sure I'm only in Dublin, and in a year's time you'll be joining the rest of us.'

Theresa smiled weakly. Now was not the time to tell him that she had other plans.

Jack smiled back. 'What I want to know is, who is going to stop you doing all the mad things you would like to do? Poor Eileen has no chance.'

Theresa sighed. 'I'm awful. Mam says I was cut out to be a lady but the devil ran away with the pattern.'

Jack laughed. 'She is right there.' He took her hand in his again and dropped a light kiss on it, quickly releasing it as the others joined them.

'That was great. Are you two not going to dance tonight? Tandy and I have done three in a row – I'm dying for a lemonade.'

Theresa listened fondly as Eileen rattled on and settled herself into the seat.

'Anything for you two?' Tandy asked.

'No, we are all right,' said Jack.

And they were, Theresa thought. Even if it was only temporary, she was resolved to cherish every moment with him.

Jack was staying overnight with Tandy, so they had to be certain to catch the last bus. Eileen was sad that the evening was at an end, but Theresa had a very early start in the morning as she had to exercise Night Star before going to school, so she was quite happy to go.

When they arrived back at the bridge, Tandy and Eileen wandered on towards the village while Jack and Theresa hung back.

'Do you remember the day you tried to smoke a cigarette and had to throw the packet away?' Jack's voice was soft and quiet in the darkness. 'It seems so long ago and yet it was only in the spring.'

'Indeed! I remember, also, how we lay side by side on the bank, and I threatened you with annihilation if you told a soul that you had seen me bathing in my underwear.' The darkness hid her smile. 'Why do I do these things, Jack?'

'Because you are you; the one and only Theresa Brady, who is not meant to settle down in Tullybra and marry some local man. Life calls to you. Go out and meet it.' As he spoke the words, Jack felt his heart constrict. He was right, though. She was too exciting, had too great a lust for life, to settle down anonymously with someone like himself.

Theresa stared through the gloom. There was no moon tonight. She said breathlessly, 'You are being very profound, Jack – already sounding like the important young doctor you will be.' Her heart was beating seven bells out of her rib cage. She put a hand there to still the throbbing. She realised that she loved him. No other man would do. What she had experienced with Fergal was nothing like the comfortable, constant feeling she had when she was with Jack. There was no rush of passion, no fast stirring anywhere – just a feeling that her destiny should lie with him.

He turned to her as they reached her gate. 'I'm going to kiss you,' he said tentatively. 'Will you mind?'

'Of course not,' she replied softly.

128

'I ask because knowing you as I do, I run the risk of getting a clout round the ear. It has taken me some time to work up to this, and I don't want to court a rebuff from which I might never recover.'

Before she had time to reply, he had taken her in his arms and brought his mouth down on hers.

'Hold on to that, Theresa Brady, until I see you again,' he said, and was gone, swallowed up in the darkness of the moonless night.

It had been a kiss made in heaven, she thought later, as she sat in her window and looked beyond the darkness towards her beloved Lafferty's Cove and her secret beach.

Fergal was right. He said she'd know what to do when it was the real thing. Jack's kiss, awkward and sweet, had taken the breath from her body with its intensity.

CHAPTER 10

On the day Tandy sailed to England, Jack felt as though a bit of himself had gone with him. Tandy and he had rarely been parted the whole of their lives, so when the little group of friends who had come to wish him safe journey had disbanded, he and Theresa and Eileen trailed disconsolately to the car. There was silence on the journey home.

Jack felt sorry for Eileen, knowing how she felt about Tandy. He wanted to say something comforting, but what? He couldn't say anything that might give her hope – that would be cruel – so he silently cursed his friend for his cavalier attitude and remained quiet.

A week later, as he looked round the crowded hall of the university, his mind vaguely taking in the noise and the bustle, the toing and froing and the occasional shout of joy as friend met friend, he wished for the umpteenth time that Tandy was here, beside him. He could only remember one other occasion when he had felt as bereft as this. It was when he had been persuaded to go on retreat by the Christian Brothers, who were great ones for encouraging the older boys to spend at least one week away during their senior years – to 'set them up for life.'

They had arranged for Tandy to go to a different area, knowing full well that the idea of the two of them getting any gain from the experience would be banjaxed from the start if they were together.

Jack had become an unwilling guest at the small abbey of St Augustus at the foot of the Wicklow mountains – he'd forgotten where Tandy had gone. What did he remember was that Tandy had come back with glowing accounts of his nightly escapades, whereas he had calluses on his knees from constant kneeling at prayer, and a backache that had lasted for weeks from the hard cot he had slept on in a sparsely furnished cell. He had a permanent headache from the set hours of contemplation, which had consisted of silently cursing and bemoaning his lot, and getting more depressed as the time passed.

The self-awareness sessions had done little more than compound his feeling that life could be an absolute shit at times, and that at that moment his own was up the Swanee on several counts. He'd since wondered how many certified nutcases could be found to have been away on a retreat in their early years – quite a few, he suspected. It didn't help that John Drake had failed to make the grade in his exams, leaving Jack not only without Tandy's support, but without his.

He brought his mind back to the present. He was growing restless; the registration lines seemed to be static. There were six lines and many of the students were queue-hopping frantically. He was considering wearily whether it was worth waiting when there was a tap on his shoulder. Turning, he looked into a pair of hazel eyes set in a cheeky pixie face.

'Hello!' said the pixie. 'I'm Pat Armstrong. I joined this queue for two purposes. One, to cheer you up because you look so miserable; and two, to convince you that we would be better served going for a cup of something and coming back later.'

The pixie tipped her head on one side, and for a moment it seemed that the bright red beret that clung precariously to the side of her head would fall off, but teeter though it did for a moment, the large hat-pin did its job.

Jack, although unused to being approached by attractive young girls who put propositions to him, smiled and nodded. 'Why not?' he said. 'To hell with losing out on the best options.' Suddenly, life at university was beginning to show promise.

By the end of October he had settled into the routine that was to be his for the next year. He enjoyed the anatomy sessions, for which he was paired up with a lad called Declan Morris. He didn't think he'd have a lot in common with him; a decision he had come to when Declan had blinked at him over his large specs and said, 'My great ambition is to be a surgeon.' He was stroking a leg bone lovingly at the time and Jack found himself wondering if he would swap partners. This fella was too intense for him. Learning should be fun.

As days passed, however, he found him very useful. When he became confused about the whereabouts and the names of bone cavities and nerve passages, Declan was there with the answers. The bloody body had more routes going through it than an Ordnance Survey map.

He received his first letter from Tandy in mid-November, and pushed it into his pocket on the way to a lecture. This was a letter he wanted to read at leisure, to savour every word.

Declan had held a seat for him. 'What kept you? I nearly had that fink O'Connor sitting beside me,' he whispered fiercely.

Jack grinned. 'I told you. He fancies you.'

Declan had time only to glare at him before the prof was at the lectern, bashing the gavel for silence.

It wasn't till coffee break that Jack was able to find a quiet corner to read his letter. He smiled as he read:

Dear Jack,

I'm writing this sitting on a bucket in the middle of a pigsty. What better place, I ask myself, to write to an old friend – especially as it's the only place I can find to get away from all the girls who are chasing me and plaguing the life out of me.

Jack laughed as he read on. He'd forgotten how wicked Tandy's humour could be.

The buggers have fallen for my Irish accent and not the charm and the good looks for which I am famous. I find this vaguely insulting. Mind you, my lad, I'm not complaining too much. I'm never short of company, although I have to say that the class of girl you get studying agriculture tends to have ankles like a Mullingar heifer and arms that could crush a tree trunk.

There is one girl who shows a bit of promise. I don't know what the hell she is doing here, seeing as she has the build of a dancer and eyes that only dreams can conjure up. She also has a boyfriend built like a wrestler – I've seen him lift a young bull up on his shoulder and throw it down again. I have no wish to emulate the bull, so I'm practising my new religion – cowardice.

This is a grand place. The college is at the foot of the South Downs – which, believe it or not, is a range of high hills straddling some of the southern counties. You'd never believe the language problem I have at the moment. I can't understand the English spoken and no one can understand a cotton-picking word I say.

In spite of aforementioned difficulties, I'm enjoying it here. It would be a charitable thought if you would consider writing in answer, to

Your old, but hopefully not yet forgotten, friend,

Tandy

P.S. Actually, I'm sitting on the bucket in the aforementioned place because I'm skiving off.

Jack folded the letter and returned it to his pocket, a smile still playing around his lips. Trust Tandy to fall on his feet. He

133

wondered idly if what he had read between the lines meant the death knell for poor Eileen's dreams. Tandy was a charmer, with coaxing eyes and a big lolloping frame which sent the girls wild, but what they didn't realize, and Jack had known for all the time they had been friends, was that Tandy had a streak of ruthlessness in him and would have no hesitation in dropping a girl like a hot brick if a venture didn't take off.

As he strolled off towards yet another lecture, he wondered if Eileen and Theresa would cast a second glance at the Tullybra bridge on their way home, now that they had no reason to wait there for the bus that had deposited Tandy and him on the grass verge, every day of the week.

A feeling of melancholy hit him. There were times when he wished to God he hadn't decided to study medicine. He could have stayed on the small farm with his father and worked to make it bigger. Had he been a fool to himself for choosing the option? Certainly his parents, although proud of his achievements, had wondered where the hell the idea had come from. He sighed. The truth of the matter was, he missed Theresa.

Theresa was no happier than Jack. She spent hours hunched up in the window embrasure, staring out to the strip of sea that could be seen through the glass.

She was moody and uncommunicative at times, and had been ticked off on several occasions by Eileen, who said she was sorely tried by her, and if love made you behave like this she wanted none of it.

And it was true, thought Theresa. Love should be roses and moonlight and soft-centred chocolates; not tentative hope one minute and hard-edged despair the next.

On their way back from school one day, they made their way towards the bridge and flung their bags on the ground. They sat astride the parapet like a pair of wayward eejuts before Theresa remarked, 'What in God's name are we doing here?'

Eileen giggled. 'Old habits die hard.'

Theresa looked at her. 'Do you miss Tandy?'

'Of course I do, but there's no point in being miserable. He'll come back, or he won't . . .'

'If you say it's all in God's hands I'll strangle you,' Theresa threatened.

Eileen said, 'It's true, though. If Tandy meets some other girl over in England, there isn't a lot I can do about it.'

'Well! I'm not suffering from the "whatever will be will be" syndrome. I shall apply myself to the problem if it should arise.'

'Just as you did when Jack went off with those girls,' Eileen said.

'That was different. I would have leathered into him if he hadn't given me a good explanation.' Theresa's tone was firm to the point of belligerence.

They jumped off the bridge and Eileen linked her arm through her friend's. 'You have nothing to worry about where Jack is concerned. He holds you in the highest regard.'

'I hope so. But I tell you this, Eileen: I'll not take any nonsense. If I find that he is seeing another girl I'll let him know in no uncertain terms how he stands in my estimation.'

'I still say you have nothing to worry about.' Eileen's placid smile was comforting in a strange way.

Theresa laughed affectionately. 'Honest to God, Eileen, if a thunderbolt landed in that field, you'd turn calmly to me and ask what it was, but I'd be half-way home with my reflexes goin' like a fiddler's elbow. That's the difference between us.'

It didn't help Theresa's mood when she got home and her mother observed, 'I'll never get used to seeing you come in without Jack following behind.'

Theresa received a letter from Jack to say that the first term had finished and he would be coming home for the Christmas break. She met Eileen next morning and mentioned it.

'I've had one from Tandy,' said Eileen. 'Unfortunately he won't be home for Christmas. As he has only been in England for a few weeks he thinks it would be foolish to spend the money when he needs every penny. He says he will miss us and the great gas we'll have at the party on Christmas Eve. We're not to forget to offer a toast to absent friends and mention him in particular.'

Eileen's face was pink with pleasure. This was her first letter from a boy, and the fact that it was from Tandy went a long way to temper the disappointment she had felt that he would not be with her for Christmas.

Theresa was relieved that she was taking it so well. Thinking about it, there was no guarantee that they would see much of Jack. His mother would have first call on his time, anyway. She frowned slightly as she re-read the letter later that evening.

He had mentioned someone called Pat, whom he had met on the first evening, and remarked how helpful Pat had been.

'I met the sister as well,' he wrote. 'She is a third-year med student. Very grand and very clever. I only met her once and don't suppose I'll have a lot to do with her as she is with a different set whom we don't see much of professionally or socially.

'My mother hasn't been very well lately so I'll be able to give her a bit of attention when I'm home.'

On Saturday Theresa and Eileen went into Kilgaven to finish

135

their Christmas shopping. The arrangement was made with the parents that they would be picked up at the usual place and time.

'You'd better get the feet moving,' warned Colin and, remembering a previous occasion, added, 'And see you stick to lemonade this time.'

Her da needn't have worried. Neither of them felt like stepping over the line. Eileen was anxious to find a bargain as she'd used up most of her savings, and Theresa, equally short of money, was salving her conscience for having spent too much money on a new blouse for herself by trying to find a decent present for her da with what money she still had.

'Have we enough left for a banana split?' she wondered aloud.

'Don't be silly,' said Eileen, her brow puckered as she tried to decide between a pretty glass paperweight to control her father's riot of papers and bills, or a tie.

'Don't even think about the tie,' advised Theresa. 'A man considers a tie a personal choice – anyway, the paperweight will be more useful.'

'Since when have you become so knowledgeable about men and their ideas on fashion?' Eileen scoffed.

'I heard m'da saying so a long time ago. Mind you, he was discussing a new pair of drawers. I think Mam wanted him to go more modern.'

'A paperweight seems so impersonal,' Eileen mused.

'I'm dying for something to eat and drink, so make up your mind. I don't suppose your da will care one way or the other, so long as he has a present to open.'

Reluctantly, Eileen decided on the paperweight, 'I know I'll regret this.'

'Food!' said Theresa. She had no time for the way Eileen dithered.

'I'm having something a bit more substantial than a banana split,' said Eileen. 'I think I'll go for a bowl of soup and a chunk of bread and butter.'

'You're mad. I'll eat when I go home. I don't get banana splits too often.'

Theresa was sick on the way home. Eileen sat in the car and watched as she ran for the bush by the side of the road.

'What have you two been up to again?' Colin asked suspiciously.

'Theresa insisted on eating a banana split with oodles of cream on an empty stomach,' Eileen said, trying vainly to hide her glee. God would forgive her just this one time. Last time when she was sick on the way home Theresa had been rotten to her. After all, the bible did say 'an eye for an eye and a tooth for a tooth.'

136

'Take that smirk off you face,' Theresa said on her return.

'You two will be eighteen in eight months' time,' said Colin, shaking his head in amazement. 'You behave more like twelve year olds at times.'

'It's our restrictive upbringing.' Theresa regretted the words as soon as they had been uttered. Her father chuntered on for the next few miles about cheeky upstarts and thankless children.

Nuala held her tongue. Least said the better, she thought; besides, she had other worries. She was concerned about her mother. As the days passed Mona looked more frail and the heart and soul seemed to have gone out of her. Nuala had made excuses as to why Theresa shouldn't go to see her gran just lately, and she wondered if she would regret having done so. If anything did happen to her gran, Theresa would not easily forgive Nuala for not letting her visit.

'Would you like to come with me to see your gran?' she asked on impulse.

'Of course I would, Mam. Is she feeling better? Only two days ago you felt that she couldn't cope with visitors.' Theresa glanced at the side of her Mam's face, which was facing rigidly to the front as though she wanted to devour every inch of the frozen scenery. 'She is all right, isn't she?' she asked.

'Yes! She is all right, but – but – you must understand that she hasn't recovered from her bout of pneumonia as well or as fast as we had hoped.

To the end of her days, Nuala would never forget the moment she walked into her mother's bedroom followed by Theresa.

She crossed to the bed and bent over to look at the sleeping form, and felt the blood run from her face. She reached out for the tiny hand with its veins showing through the skin. It was like looking at an autumn leaf with the sun behind it, the tracery was as delicately marked. The hands were deathly cold.

Theresa was silent, her face marble-white and her lips blue with shock. Her lovely little gran was dead. There would be no more chats by the pond with the dirty little ducks. Her mother crossed to her and held out her arms. With a loud sob Theresa lay her head on her mother's shoulder as Nuala stroked the wild curls back from her forehead.

'She loved you so much,' Nuala said softly. 'Hang on to your memories – they will help you through.'

Theresa lifted her head and gave a wan smile. 'She loved you too. She told me once that there wasn't room to put a piece of thread between us, we are so alike. She told me that there was no use me trying to put one over on you with my capers, because whatever I do now you have done it before me. She said you were a bigger tearaway than me.'

Nuala, pleased that Theresa was able to talk of her moments with her gran, smiled back. 'She's right. There is more of me in you than there is of your father – more's the pity. He's the one with the sense.' She pushed her daughter gently from her. 'I'll have to run up to Pat's place and ask him to go for help,' she said gently. 'Will you be all right here, or would you rather go for Pat?'

'I'll sit here with Gran,' Theresa said, after a moment's hesitation. 'You go.'

Nuala, her eyes misty with tears, said, 'I hate to leave you here alone.'

'I'll be fine. Besides, I want to be alone with her.' She pushed her mother towards the doorway.

'Oh, Jesus Mary and Joseph,' Nuala cried, 'I didn't know she was so near the end, Theresa. I'm so sorry. I am so very sorry.'

Theresa said dully, 'Go, Mam. How were you to know?' She ushered her mother from the room and settled down to wait, holding her gran's hand in hers.

The crying and the regrets could wait. This moment was too precious to waste.

She refused to attend the wake. Nuala and Colin listened in horror as she defiantly faced them. 'I'll not sit there while everyone goes on about her past life and sings songs they think were her favourites. I'll not watch everybody drinkin' till they become maudlin.'

'It's the Irish way,' Nuala protested. 'Everyone will want to pay their respects to a woman who has lived among them all her life.'

'And where were these people when she needed help during her illness?'

'That's enough, Theresa,' Colin said. 'Had they been asked, I have no doubt they would have answered the call.'

Theresa clenched her arms and crossed the room to stand by the window. Her da was right. The truth was, she didn't want to see her little gran lying in a coffin with a shroud up to her neck, her eyes closed for eternity, her face unnaturally youthful and her tiny hands folded in prayer with her rosary beads wound round them.

When she'd sat by her bed on that last visit, her gran had looked as though she was asleep. Her face had been peaceful and the skin still warm to the touch – except for her hands. They had been so cold. Theresa turned. 'I'll not be there!' She ran from the room.

Nuala looked at Colin, her eyes misted with tears. 'She loved her. What's got into her?'

Colin took his pipe from his pocket and moved towards his

138

chair, motioning his wife to the chair opposite.

There was silence as he puffed on his briar, savouring the mellowness of the smoke drawn slowly through the seasoned wood. At last he leaned forward and looked at his wife sitting there, waiting for solace.

'I understand now,' he said. 'This is her way of coping. Have you noticed she hasn't shed one tear?'

Nuala nodded.

Colin continued. 'You see! If she doesn't see her gran laid out, she can remember her the way she was. Everyone has their own way of coping. This is Theresa's. It is right that we should allow her the privilege of conducting her own grief.'

'But people—'

'I don't care what people think. My daughter is more important.' Colin took Nuala's hand in his. 'You are dealing with it your way. Let Theresa deal with it hers.'

The church was crowded for the funeral service. There were people there whom Theresa had never seen in her life before. She hadn't realised how well respected her gran had been. This was reflected in the amount of money collected. It was generally considered that the total amount indicated the popularity of the deceased. There were gasps of astonishment when Father Corke disclosed the exact figure from the pulpit. Theresa felt quietly proud.

She went through the routine of the day with what dignity she could muster; her little gran deserved no less. When her mam broke down in near hysterics as they lowered the coffin, she supported her on one side, her da on the other. They glanced at each other over Nuala's bowed head and Theresa, looking into his eyes, knew he understood what she was about. One day she might cry. Today was not that time.

Jack came over to offer his condolences. 'It won't be much of a Christmas for you,' he said, putting his arm round her shoulder.

'I haven't given it much thought,' she answered. 'Are you enjoying university?' She was anxious to move away from the sadness of the day. She craved normality. She felt she was acting a part in a play – a tragedy.

Jack was surprised at first by the sudden shift away from the day's events. The question had no relevance to the occasion. But when he looked into the lovely eyes and saw the pleading look, he knew that Theresa was trying to stop the terrible sorrow she felt from overwhelming her. He played the game.

'I'm coming to grips with it now. I was very nervous at the start, but Pat and a few others have become friends and I'm feeling more at home.'

139

He has changed, she thought. He seems taller and slimmer. There was about him that certain air of confidence that a man has when he is happy with himself and how he is. The slight diffidence of youth had gone. She felt she didn't know this Jack.

She smiled wanly. 'I can't wait to get away. Now more than ever,' she said. 'I spend a lot of time up at Castle Donagh. I feel free there, and riding Night Star gives me a lot of pleasure.'

'Have you seen the tinker lately? That was a bad fall he had.'

'His name is Fergal.' She tried to keep the censure from her voice, but she was annoyed at the way he spoke of her friend.

Sensing her hostility, Jack said, 'I'm sorry. I didn't mean—'

'I know you didn't,' she interrupted. 'Take no notice. I'm taking my grief out on anybody who happens to be around. In answer to your question – yes! I've been over to the camp. He is making the best of things. He does all the carving and Shula, his mother, says he is great at keeping the younger ones out of her hair.' She smiled a little at this. Fergal found this the biggest chore of all.

To veer out of trouble, Jack said, 'I hear there's a new family living in the dower house on Lord Conliffe's estate.'

Theresa nodded. 'The father is in charge of the new road scheme over at Ballybridge.'

'Oh! It's got under way, has it?'

'Have you not heard the racket? You'd never think that it was being built four miles away. I think they are trying to shift the half of the hill that divides us.'

'Are there any children?'

'There is a daughter. Her name is Moira Kennedy. I've seen her at the dance at the Gavin Hotel. She's pretty.' She had no idea why she added that last bit; it was irrelevant.

Jack bade her an uneasy goodbye. His heart ached as he looked into the lovely eyes again and saw the pain there.

'Come and visit me in Dublin when you have the time,' he said gently.

She promised she would and watched him walk away.

Pat McGarry took her aside while those who had come back for a bite and a sup were making noisy conversation. 'Come outside. We'll get away from this for a while.' He took her hand and led her out, dragging a warm coat off the peg as they passed. It was frosty and cold, but Theresa was glad of the fresh air and the calm.

'We'll go for a long walk. It will help to clear your mind,' Pat said as they stepped out towards the hill above the cove.

Theresa felt a calm settle on her as they walked in silence. She had known Pat since she was a tiny tot and he used to dandle her on his knee when her mam took her over to Gran's cottage for a visit. He was often there, keeping an eye on the little woman. It was well known he adored her gran, and for all the years she could remember, this big, gangly farmer had been part of her life. His quiet sense of humour had been a godsend when she had confessed her misdeeds to him and asked for advice at those times when she had felt it imprudent to speak to her parents. He had been loyal to her and had never cracked on that he had been her confessor. He said not a word now, but left her to her thoughts, and when they arrived back at the house to find most of the mourners had gone, he gave a secret wink and left her to hang her coat up and enter the room alone.

Christmas for Theresa was a non-event, and she was glad when it was over. On the day after Boxing Day she slipped out of the house and made her way to her secret beach. The need to get away by herself was overwhelming. Huddling in the lee of an enormous boulder with her coat wrapped around her and her arms cuddling her knees, she stared for a long time at the now grey, tempestuous sea. Spume was dashing against the walls of the cove with such force it was rapidly filling up. Some of it sprayed against her face, but she was safe enough where she was. No one ever came to this side of the cove where all the rocks lay, and where seaweed made the going slippery.

Here was where she felt at home. Here was where she needed to be to come to terms with the deep sadness inside her. She hadn't yet shed tears. They wouldn't come; not even at the graveside, when she had watched her gran being lowered into the pit which seemed so ridiculously deep for such a little person. Now, as she watched the wild waves and felt the spray, she realized that the tears had started to flow at last, and she allowed herself the luxury of sobbing her heart out.

Somehow she managed to get through the winter. Being at Castle Donagh helped. When she wasn't riding and looking after the horses, she was posing for Richard.

She liked this best. She was happy to pose for long periods, her body bent in the position he wanted, stooping to pick up an imaginary towel, apparently having just come out of the water.

The painting was nearly finished. She eased the support under her left armpit, which Richard had concocted so that she could rest her arm and take the brunt of the pressure from her back.

Richard was never happy with what he had done. Today was no exception. He threw down his palette in disgust. 'I can't get it right!' he cried. 'The breasts are wrong. They look stiff and unnatural.' He crossed the room and helped himself to a cup of coffee from a flask. 'Have a rest. Help yourself to a cup.'

Theresa threw a wrap over her shoulders. She was wearing a

bathing costume. The day was chilly for early spring, but Richard had supplied some heating.

He was silent, staring moodily at his work. It wasn't going how he wanted it. The inspiration he'd had when he saw Theresa coming out of the water, when transferred on to the canvas, bore no resemblance to the vibrant, spray-soaked young body of that night.

'What the hell am I doing wrong? Why can't I get it?' he asked peevishly.

Theresa smiled. She had got to know Richard well over the past few months, and she was now aware that there were two Richards. The painter was a permanently dissatisfied artist who drank gallons of coffee, swore like a trooper and threw things across the room. In no way did this resemble his other self – the confident, charming owner of the castle, who spoke quietly and dealt with all areas pertaining to his home, his social life and his business with humour and tolerance.

She studied the painting as she sipped her coffee. Richard was still having his mini-breakdown, striding backwards and forwards in front of the canvas, ruffling his hair and spilling coffee as he switched his cup from hand to hand.

Theresa spoke. 'It's wrong because I'm posing in a bathing costume.'

He stopped and crossed to her side to study the canvas again. He looked at her. 'By God, you have it. I'm not getting the contour of the natural breast because of the tight costume. Now, why didn't I realize that?'

Theresa smiled. 'You were probably concerned about the idea of me posing naked – I'll strip off.'

Richard hesitated. He rubbed his chin. 'I don't feel I could ask you to pose naked,' he said. 'I'm not certain it would be ethical.'

'Why not? You've already seen me naked.'

'By accident, on a dark night.' He looked doubtful. 'It might be misconstrued. Your parents – I promised . . .'

'I'm surprised at you. You use models all the time.'

'That's different. They are older and they do it for a living. I've never painted a young Irish lass from a small village which has been caught in a time warp – besides, you're only seventeen.'

'Sure who will know? You can't even see my face in the painting. My hair is hanging over it as I stoop.'

She lowered the straps and gently pulled the bathing costume from her body. 'I told you once, I have no problem with my body,' she said and, crossing over to the dais, took up her position.

CHAPTER 11

Theresa disliked Moira Kennedy. Moira, she complained to Eileen, was one of the 'More' people. 'She has more nerve, more money, more clothes, more boys – more everything. She's even got more piety than a scatter of saints.'

Eileen sucked on the sweet grass stem she held in her hand and swung on Pat McGarry's five-barred gate.

'I forgot to add,' said Theresa, 'she is also more over the top.'

'How so?'

'For God's sake! You saw her on Ash Wednesday, Eileen. Everybody else is content to walk to the altar to receive their ashes – not so Moira. It's bare feet and a crawl to the altar on bended knees. Mind you,' she added, with a degree of spite, 'it was noticeable that she was only three rows away from the front.'

Eileen frowned. 'Are we going to the dance at the hotel on Saturday night?' she asked.

'I don't know.' Theresa climbed on to the gate beside her, having first taken a quick look round to make sure Pat McGarry wasn't in sight, for he'd scalp the pair of them if he found them using his gate to sit on. 'Half the boys will be hanging round Moira and the other half will be propping up the bar. Sure where would be the point? I don't think we'd get a look in.'

'Don't exaggerate,' said Eileen, but she knew there was more than a grain of truth in it. Moira did seem to attract the boys with her golden hair and slinky dresses. 'Do you think she wears any knickers under those dresses?'

'Sure where's the room?' Theresa was envious of Moira's dresses. There was money there. She gave voice to her thoughts. 'I'm surprised that for someone who takes Holy Communion every Sunday with head bowed and collar up to her nostrils, she manages to look like a *femme fatale* at the dances. That one has double standards.'

They went to the dance. As expected, Moira Kennedy was there, surrounded by a group of brawny studs eyeing her hungrily as she tossed her head and flicked her hair like a filly at a race meeting.

'What did I tell you?' shouted Theresa over the din, nodding towards Moira.

Eileen didn't have time to answer as she was already being towed on to the floor by Sean Riordan. It was no great achievement in Theresa's opinion that she, herself, was grabbed by Dan Herlihy junior, for he had a glass eye – compliments of his father's prize bull. Still! It was better than nothing.

Eileen joined her after the dance, her face glowing with the exertion. 'Guess what Sean told me.'

'How should I know? If I could read minds I'd know what makes Moira Kennedy tick.'

Eileen, her face alight with her recent acquisition of gossip, was not to be put off. 'We'll go into the cloakroom, it's quieter there.'

Once there, Eileen leaned against the basin and said breathlessly, 'I have it on good authority that Moira Kennedy is going to be the Virgin Mary in the "Queen of the May" procession.'

Theresa was unmoved. She suspected that in spite of her tarty dressing and wayward looks at the lads, Moira Kennedy was virginal enough for the part. There would be more chance of a sinner gettin' past St Peter at the gates than a boy gettin' past Moira's determination to hang on to her assets. The bold Moira was too shrewd to waste her talents on any of the underfunded lads that hung around her.

'Good luck to her. I'd rather dance on my own grave than make a cod's ass of myself decked out with a tiara and flowing robes.'

'Well! That's me squashed,' said Eileen, heading for the door.

When they entered the hall again there was a quickstep already in progress. They stood by a big pillar trying to look nonchalant but painfully aware that they resembled two wallflowers.

'It's times like this I wish I smoked,' said Theresa through gritted teeth and fixed smile. 'What are you doin' with your hands? I feel as though I have six of them.'

'Don't ask,' wailed Eileen. 'I can't make up my mind whether to bite my nails, fold my arms, or try to disappear.'

'If that Moira Kennedy smirks over at us once more I'll go straight outside and let her tyres down and she'll have to walk the eight miles home.'

The dance ended, the floor emptied and the band leader hastily wiped his sweating face before starting up for the next dance.

Eileen shoved her elbow into Theresa's waist, causing her to gasp. 'Look who's walking this way,' she said excitedly.

Theresa looked. Her heart beat wildly with the joy that flooded her. Jack was making his way towards them with a tall, serious looking young man in tow.

'What are you doing here?' were his first words. 'I'm surprised the parents let you come this far.'

'They've become more relaxed with their restrictions now that we are older – but what are you doing up this way?'

'Declan has an old banger. We thought we'd come along and see what this new dance venue is all about.'

Introductions were effected and Eileen and Declan took the floor.

'You're a long way from Dublin.'

'It's not that far for the odd occasion. We won't get home till the early hours but we can miss the first lecture. You're looking well, Theresa.'

'Thank you.' She smiled brightly. He wasn't going to know about the times she wasn't all right. Life had to go on and she knew that she couldn't inflict her inner sadness on others. The bright face sometimes hid her still deep sorrow.

Eileen and Declan returned. 'It's too crowded on the floor now,' Eileen explained.

'Let's all have a drink,' said Jack. 'You girls stay here and Declan and I will fetch them.'

When they had gone, Eileen turned to Theresa. 'Is this the same Jack we have known and loved? He has changed a lot.'

Theresa had also noticed how much broader he was since their last meeting, and there was a new air of sophistication about him. She also noticed when there was a break in the mass of bodies in front of them, that Moira Kennedy was standing next to him at the bar.

During the next half-hour she observed that Moira couldn't take her eyes off him. Theresa's eyes narrowed. Let her dare, she thought.

A short time later, Moira made her way towards them. Theresa knew fine well that she was going to ask Jack for the ladies' excuse me.

She waited till Moira, with flirty eyes said to him, 'May I have this dance?'

'No you may not. I've already asked,' Theresa answered.

Jack looked at her in surprise. She had done no such thing, but his blood raced as she smiled into his eyes and drew him towards the floor where she deliberately put her arms round his neck and held him close. Jack wasn't the only one who had changed, she thought with glee.

Sunday, God forgive her, was to Theresa the most boring of days.

She was glad when Monday came and she was able to go up to Castle Donagh after she had done her chores – unlike Moira Kennedy, who was able to swan around where she wanted and didn't have to do a stroke of work except groom her horse till his very ass shone.

Eileen popped in to see her on Wednesday. Theresa unburdened her uncharitable thoughts on her. 'That Moira Kennedy is in for a right lashing. Did you see her trying her wiles on Jack?'

Eileen, easygoing as she was, thought Theresa was getting a bit uptight over the other girl.

To her surprise, Theresa sighed and agreed. 'You're right, of course. I'll have to go to confession. Mind you. It'll be more of a bloody penance being forced to confess because of that girl than saying an act of contrition and three Hail Marys.'

They discussed the weekend. Theresa thought it would be nice to have a meal out in Kilgaven for a change, hard though it would be on their pockets. 'I don't think I could stand Dan Herlihy this weekend,' she said huffily. 'He gets more like one of his father's bulls the older he gets and I never know which eye to look at when he's talkin' to me. I don't mean that nastily,' she hastened to add, but they both burst out laughing all the same.

Theresa tried to restrain herself. It was no good. She felt the laughter driving up from the depths again like a gas bubble. She punched Eileen in the back and started them both off again.

Nuala, busy in the kitchen, stopped what she was doing to listen. She was pleased that Theresa was now beginning to enjoy life again. She had been desperately worried.

For the first weeks after her gran's death, Theresa had gone around like a zombie. No one could get through to her. Then there was the stage she went through when she was being deliberately and falsely bright and gay. It was patently obvious that she had been putting on an act. For the first time, the laughter upstairs had the joyous ring of sincerity about it.

Colin came in. 'Isn't it great to hear that?' He took his pipe from his mouth and pointed upwards. 'It'll soon be time to tell her about her inheritance.'

Nuala frowned. 'Not yet, Colin. Let's leave it a bit longer.'

'Well, you know that Paddy Moore thinks she should have been there when he read out gran's will. He was saying to me only the other day that she should know soon. There are papers to sign, decisions to make.'

Nuala was troubled. Pat McGarry was anxious to buy her mother's bit of land, and when she had met him the other day he'd tackled her about it. He wanted to build a swimming pool near his house and extend his garden, and he wanted to replace the lost

146

ground with her mother's two acres.

He'd already given a good price for the livestock, and Nuala knew that he'd done it out of love and loyalty, for Pat didn't go in for pigs and milking cows, and God knows he had enough chickens to feed the five thousand if he wanted. He'd also taken on John, who would never be bright enough to work anywhere else.

'Give it another few weeks,' she pleaded. 'I don't want to upset the applecart. I think it would be in order to tell Pat McGarry that he'll be able to go ahead with his plans, though, don't you?'

'I suppose so. I'll be seeing Pat at the meeting this week. I'll have a word.'

The dreaded exams were finished. The sense of escape was making them all lightheaded.

'Do you realize that when we break up for the summer we won't have to go back?' Theresa whirled Eileen round till she was dizzy.

Eileen slowed down, her head reeling. 'For heaven's sake, stop it.' She sat down heavily on the grassy bank. 'We'll be going somewhere else, that's all.'

Theresa was not to be put down. 'That's different. Now we will be doing something of our own choice.'

'Are you really set on going over to England to study Art and Design?'

'I haven't discussed it with the parents yet – but yes, I am.'

'What about Jack?'

'What about him? If Jack and I are ever going to mean anything to each other then time will tell. Meanwhile, I too have to make my way and it might as well be in London as Dublin, seeing as that is where I feel I want to go – that is where life can be exciting.'

'Don't you think you should get it sorted out?' Eileen suggested.

'I'm going to discuss it soon. The parents will go mad, seeing as I've already got a place at the Uni.' Theresa groaned.

'I'd like to be hidden somewhere near when you tell them. Why didn't you sort it out when you applied for your place?'

'I was going to, but I lost my nerve. Richard Beck has offered to back me up. He knows I am determined to go over the water. He says I am talented and could study at a college in a place called Camberwell Green in South London.' She cast a look at Eileen and fidgeted with her hair. 'He also says I could stay at a house he owns nearby in Dulwich Village. His housekeeper would chaperone me and, as he goes over two or three times a year on business, he would check that everything was all right.'

'Well! I hope he can swing it. You seem to have it all planned. I

147

shouldn't let your parents know that you have already arranged things with Mr Beck, though. It might go against you.'

Theresa had already thought along those lines. She intended to discuss the best way of breaking the news to her parents with Richard at their next session. The painting was nearly finished. Her part was done, but Richard liked to have her there as usual, and paid her the compliment of asking for an opinion on occasions.

'What will you do if you don't get your grades?' Theresa asked.

Eileen smiled. 'I'll help out in the shop. I'm not bothered about going to university, and knowing you won't be there has made me more certain that it might not be for me.'

Later that evening, as she undressed for bed, Theresa mulled over the whole business. She hoped she was doing the right thing. Jack seemed to be loving every minute of university. Perhaps she too would have enjoyed it. She hadn't seen him again since the night they met at the Gavin, but she'd had two letters from him – the last one extending an invitation for her to visit him. Last summer, when they had been together, seemed a long time ago. Yet it was less than ten months since they had lain on the sand by Lafferty's Cove and discussed their futures.

When Colin and Nuala broke the news to Theresa about the money her gran had left her, she looked at them in shock. In her wildest dreams she had never imagined that her little gran had anything worth leaving.

'How come?' she asked weakly.

'Your gran had a nice little business going there, and her needs were few,' said Colin. He tapped out his pipe and placed it in the rack, pausing awhile before he turned to speak again. He coughed. 'There is also the matter of the land—'

'That too?' Theresa gasped. She looked at her mother. 'She was your mam; why did Gran not leave all this to you?'

'She left me enough.' Nuala smiled. 'Your gran idolised you. She told me a long time ago that she would be doing this.'

Colin made a noise in his throat. 'Do you mind? I'd like to get this sorted. Now! Pat McGarry wants to buy back the land. He will be giving a good and fair price for it and, subject to your consent, your mam and I think that negotiations could begin.'

Nuala glanced back to Theresa. 'What do you think?'

Theresa shrugged. 'I don't care what we do. My gran is gone. There is nothing there now.' Her eyes clouded. Nuala crossed to her.

Colin spoke again. 'That's that, then. We can make an appointment with Paddy Moore tomorrow.'

148

'There is something I have to say,' said Theresa, drawing a deep breath to bolster her courage.

Both her parents sat down again.

'I don't want to go to university!' She screwed one hand round the other, waiting for the blast from her da. It didn't come. Instead, he rose and walked towards his pipe rack, studiously regarded them before making his choice. The dark briar. His thinking pipe.

'Why not?' he said quietly, drawing the air through with tutting, puffy little noises. When it caught he shook the match and carefully placed it in the large ashtray before turning again to his daughter.

'I would make a lousy teacher,' she said simply.

'How do you know? You've never been one.'

'You know how I dislike working with children, Da. I get Eileen to do my turn at the children's group as often as I can.'

'You don't have to do primary school teaching. Get the right degree and the right experience and—'

'No!' Theresa interrupted. 'I would hate it. Richard agrees that it would be wrong to go into something like teaching if my heart wasn't in it.'

As soon as the words were out she realized the big mistake she had just made. She held her breath.

'So! You have discussed this matter with a perfect stranger before consulting with your parents.'

'It wasn't like that. It was during a sitting for the painting. He asked me what I was going to study at university and I told him that what I really wanted to do was study Art and Design – that was when he passed the remark that it seemed silly to do something I didn't want to do. He suggested I should discuss the matter with you. Here I am – doing just that.'

'And how long ago was this?'

'Some weeks ago.'

'Why did you wait so long?'

'I knew you were keen on me becoming a teacher. I – I didn't want to disappoint you, Da.'

'It is your future we are talking about here,' said Colin. 'I'm sorry that you didn't think I would be sympathetic. Of course I wanted you to teach. That didn't mean that I wouldn't have listened to you. Am I such an ogre?' Pulling the ashtray towards him, he tapped his pipe against it. The damned thing had let him down at the wrong moment.

Theresa crossed the room and squatted by his knee. 'Of course you are not. It was silly of me – as I said, I didn't want to disappoint you, that's all. I kept putting things off.'

'So! All that tedious form filling was for nothing. How do we go about this new development? Has Richard made any plans, seeing as he has been involved?' Theresa drew in her breath gently. If she went carefully, things would work out. She rose and sat on the arm of his chair.

Her mother started towards the kitchen. 'I'll leave you to it,' she said. She and Theresa glanced quickly at each other, relief showing in both their faces.

Theresa said, 'I asked Richard if he knew how I should go about the matter, but he said that he would discuss it with you if you were agreeable. He felt that he shouldn't interfere unless invited.'

'I'll ring him tomorrow,' said Colin. The matter was closed.

After supper, Theresa stole out and rang Richard from the telephone box outside the post office.

A week later, she and her parents paid a visit to Paddy Moore to sign over the deeds to Pat McGarry. Theresa was now a lady of means. Not that she could get her hands on it yet, it was held in trust till she was twenty-one.

'I'll be able to meet Moira Kennedy on the same level now,' Theresa gloated to Eileen.

'Theresa, I don't suppose Moira would give a tinker's curse for the knowledge of your new-found wealth. We hardly know the girl. She came here five months ago and she goes to a private convent school in Kilgaven so, apart from the odd sighting at mass and the occasional hooley when we see her through a curtain of lovesick swains, we have very little contact.'

Theresa smiled secretly. In spite of what Eileen had said, she knew that there was a great buzz in knowing that she could meet Moira eyeball to eyeball without feeling that the other girl had it all.

She was still feeling grand at the end of the day when she had finished the dreaded mucking out. This was the time when she missed Fergal most. He had been gone two weeks now, on his travels round Ireland with his family, selling the things they had made during the winter months. His leg was strong again and gave no more trouble.

Jupiter had been given a new name in keeping with his new role. He was now being ridden daily along the gallops in preparation for his first race at the Curragh. She missed the big horse almost as much as she missed Fergal, but she managed to push the emptiness away by keeping herself busy.

Her thoughts were interrupted by the sound of the gate opening. She turned as Richard passed through and walked towards her.

'Hi!' she said. 'I've got everything ready for your ride. Othello is champing at the bit in there.'

'You've taken to this very well; like a true professional,' he observed. 'I did wonder if . . . Oh, never mind.'

Theresa grinned. 'You wondered if, when Fergal went on his travels, I would be able to cope.'

'Something like that.' Richard laughed. 'However, you are a very determined young woman. I noticed the quality when I first met you.' He paused. 'I am meeting your parents for dinner on Saturday. Will you be there?'

'I didn't even know a meeting was arranged. I don't think my da would consider my attendance a major necessity – pity though, I would have enjoyed the dinner.' She grinned.

Later, as she freewheeled down the road towards home, she had a sudden urge to visit her gran's cottage. She surprised herself by the thought. She had vowed she would never go there again: there were too many memories – lovely ones, but memories that she was afraid would be too evocative and would unsettle the major plan she had formed to get her life kickstarted again.

When she reached the church, the point where she would normally turn left down the main street to home, she kept straight on and continued along the rough road that led to Pat McGarry's farm and the cottage.

She dismounted a short distance away and leaned the bike against the hedge. She wanted to walk slowly into the yard lest she miss anything, because, now that she was here, the knowledge that she had signed it over to Pat made her realize that this might well be the very last time she set foot where her gran had lived for most of her life, and where they had laughed together like a pair of urchins.

The windows of the cottage looked like empty sockets, curtain-less and soulless. She shaded her eyes to keep out the glare of the sun and stared through. It was too shadowy to see much, but she could just make out the kleek jutting out from the big open grate with gran's kettle still hanging on it.

She wandered through the garden. The sods of earth which had been turned over on the vegetable plots had sprouted coarse couch grass, and small clumps of shamrock, clover and thistle carpeted the beds. It looked like a lumpy lawn. The neatness it once had was gone.

The duck pond looked sad. The surface was covered in slime and water weeds, and the lily pads had grown so much they were covering a large area. There was no sign of the little ducks. Theresa curled up on the seat she had shared so often with her gran, and stared at the neglect, her eyes filling with tears.

151

The sound of a voice startled her. She turned. Pat McGarry was by her side.

'Are you all right?'

'No! I'm not,' she said, truthfully. 'I shouldn't have come. The heart and soul has gone from here. Coming has only served to remind me how much I miss my gran.'

Pat sat by her side. 'That makes two of us,' he said softly.

Theresa turned to him in surprise. 'You miss her?'

'Like a piece of my heart has been torn from my body,' he said, looking away.

Theresa leaned against him. He lifted his arm and put it round her shoulder and held her close.

'Mona McClusky was more of a mother to me than my own,' he explained. 'She skelped my ass more times than I can count and hugged me to her and dried my tears when I was unhappy. If it hadn't been for your gran I might well have ended up a right bad article. In fact, I might even have ended up in jail.'

Theresa leaned back and looked up into the still handsome face. 'Is that right?'

He nodded. 'My parents loved me – I didn't doubt that – but they were busy working up the beef herd to the point that it is now considered the best in the whole of Ireland. They had little time for a small lad, and I ran a bit wild – got into trouble. Your gran took me over. She soon sorted me out. I have her in my heart forever.'

Pat gazed, unseeing, towards the far field where some young bullocks were grazing. 'You have to get on with your life now – we both have, if we are to keep faith with your gran. She was the spunkiest woman I know and she would be horrified to think that we sank under the weight of her passing.'

'Do you think she knew she was going to die?' Theresa whispered.

'It wouldn't surprise me. Mona McClusky never let anything creep up on her. She was always ready for whatever life chucked at her.'

'What happened to the little ducks?'

'John has them safe.'

'It was kind of you to take him on.'

'No it wasn't. John may be light on top but he is a good worker and he'll be a real asset to me.' Pat removed his arm. 'It's time you were getting back,' he said. 'Your mam will be worried.'

She looked at him, those straight, honest eyes boring into his. His heart leapt. The look was a familiar one. He'd seen it, and loved it in her mother many years ago.

'I'm going to England soon.'

'Why?'

'I'm going to study Art and Design.'

'Why England? Is there nowhere in Ireland?' They had started the walk towards the gate.

Theresa stopped. 'I want to get away from here. I feel that I am restricted on all sides: The Church; the parents; Father Corke. I just feel that I can't function here. I'll come back, I know I will, but I need to escape to see what I'm all about. Can you understand that?' She looked at him imploringly.

'Indeed I can. I am the original wild one, as you may have heard. I've often wished I'd done the same, but in my day it wasn't possible. There was the beef herd and the farm . . .' Pat smiled. 'I wish you well.'

Nuala looked at the clock for the umpteenth time. Theresa was never this late. She wandered into the little study that Colin had set up for himself. He was poring over some exercise books, his unruly hair hanging over his forehead.

'What's keeping Theresa?'

Colin took another book from the pile and said, without looking up, 'Now what kind of a question is that? Sure how would I know, any more than you? She's probably got caught up at the stables.'

Nuala tutted and walked from the room. He was too bloody complacent by half. But there, that was Colin. There'd be two moons in the sky and one in the dung heap before Colin ever got in a real stew over anything.

The sound of the door opening heralded Theresa's return. She poked her head round the door.

'I'm sorry I'm late, Mam. Have I time for a wash?'

'Certainly! Another while won't make a blind bit of difference to the congealed mess waitin'.'

Theresa tore up the stairs without answering. The meal would be the usual delicious offering. Her mam was just cracking on a bit because she was late. The truth was she hadn't wanted her mam to see her swollen eyes.

During the meal, Colin brought up the subject of the meeting they were going to have with Richard Beck.

'And why am I not invited? Seeing as it's my future that is being discussed.' Theresa was golloping down her food as she spoke.

Colin admonished her for her manners and then said, 'Don't get lippy, my girl. I've had occasion to tell you this before: there isn't any need for you to worry. You can go out with Eileen that night, though you'll have to take the bus. I'd give you a lift in, but Richard is picking us up in his car.'

'Posh!' Theresa grinned. 'You'll never be content with yours after riding behind a chauffeur in that limousine.'

Colin smiled back. 'You're asking for trouble, my girl. Get off with you.'

Eileen turned down the idea of going into Kilgaven. She'd recently taken to working in the church, doing some cleaning, and at these times she came away feeling that some of the tricks she and Theresa got up to had very little worth in the scheme of things. She didn't say so. Theresa would scoff and roll her eyes in that way she had that made Eileen feel silly. 'I'm a bit tired tonight,' she excused herself.

Theresa shrugged. 'It was just an idea.'

Eileen looked at her suspiciously. 'You mean you don't mind not going out on a Saturday evening? Have you seen the light or what?'

'No! I'll make my own arrangements. After all, when I go across the water I'll not have company till I make friends and I'm certainly not going to sit indoors waiting for the world to call me out.'

In spite of her assertion, Theresa did feel apprehensive about going alone to Kilgaven. She toyed with the idea of walking to her secret beach, but the weather was not all that warm and the idea didn't catch. At least she'd be able to have a bun and a drink in Kilgaven.

The phone rang as she let herself in. She lifted the receiver, assuming it would be for her da as she got precious few calls herself. The voice at the end of the line caused her to stiffen.

'Theresa?'

'Jack!' She tried to hide the tremor in her voice.

'I know it's short notice, but I rang to ask if you would like to meet me in Kilgaven in an hour. I'm at the bus station in Dublin and I reckon if you get the bus from Tullybra in half an hour from now we should hit it about right.'

'I'll be there.'

'Great girl – I've got to go now. The bus is due to set off any minute.' The line went dead.

She fairly flew upstairs, mentally assessing time scales. The walk to the bridge would take five minutes if she went at a fast trot; which meant she had about twenty minutes to get ready. She wrenched the wardrobe door open and had yanked out several outfits before she saw sense. What was she on about? She was meeting Jack, not the King of England. He'd seen her in her knickers, so he was hardly going to care if she arrived looking casual. There wasn't time to change.

Rushing to the bathroom, she hurriedly washed and put on a

little make-up – not too much – Jack didn't like her face plastered with the stuff. She pulled a brush through her hair, but gave up the ghost as it did nothing but spring back to its former position. Hurriedly grabbing her bag, she gave a shrug at the pile of clothes on the bed and ran from the room.

Jack's bus hadn't arrived so she went into the waiting room; she'd have time to control her emotions.

When he entered the stuffy room ten minutes later, Theresa rose to greet him, and the thought occurred to her that every time she did so he seemed different. A tiny trickle of concern ran through her. He mustn't be a stranger. He mustn't!

He was wearing baggy trousers, a light tan shirt and a tweed jacket with leather patches on the elbows. He looked like a typical university student. The Jack she knew always dressed in a navy blazer and dark grey trousers. Here was a man, not a youth. His hair was longer and shaggier; all he needed was a pipe or a cigarette and he was there.

He hugged her. 'It's grand to see you,' he said. 'You're like a breath of fresh air to me. We'll go for a meal at the Gavin – if that's all right with you.' He folded her arm in his as they walked.

'Can we afford this?' she whispered, once seated in the restaurant.

'No, but who cares? I haven't seen much of you lately. Let's make this an evening to remember.'

'You've only been home twice. I wondered if you'd got a girlfriend.' She made her voice sound casual and unconcerned, but she was watching carefully to see if her words evoked a reaction.

'I'm a popular lad,' he grinned.

Theresa bent her head over the soup the waiter had placed in front of her and took a sip. She didn't like the slickness of the reply. She had asked for it, though. His face had registered only good-natured tolerance at the question.

'Have you sorted out your options yet?' Jack asked.

'I've filled in the forms, but I might as well not have bothered—'

'Ach Theresa, you're not going to go all coy on me and say you might not pass your exams. I know your worth and I'll not respect you for saying you have any doubts.'

'I have no doubts.' Her tone was faintly admonishing.

'Sorry. Go on.'

'I've decided I'm not going to university.'

'Why not?'

'I don't want to teach. I want to go to art college.'

'Does your father know?'

'Of course he does. We had it out and he was quite good about

155

it. As a matter of fact my parents are being wined and dined by Richard Beck at the Abbey Hotel at this very moment, to discuss the idea of my going to England.'

Jack was silent as the waiter removed the soup bowls and began to serve the main course. He was shocked at Theresa's revelation. He had been worried that if she came to Dublin to study she might not understand the relationship that he had with Pat, but he couldn't bear the thought of her going so far away. He had once mentioned Pat's existence but, to his surprise, she hadn't reacted. Perhaps it meant nothing to her.

When the waiter had gone Theresa continued revealing her plans for the future, and Jack toyed with his food as the full scale of what she was saying hit him. She was beautiful and innocent, and there wasn't a man over in that bloody country who wouldn't see her and desire her. His blood ran cold at the thought that she might be misused.

'Are you listening to me, Jack?'

'Of course I am. I'm in a state of shock, that's the height of it.'

'I asked you what you thought of it all.'

'I have no say in the matter. If you've made up your mind and your parents have agreed, what more can I add?'

'You could wish me luck,' Theresa said wistfully. She knew she was going to be heartbroken at being so far from him, but she had to be strong. She had a career to map out, and if she and Jack meant one day to make a go of life together, then a couple of years apart wouldn't make a difference – and she would see him from time to time when she was home for holidays. She was suddenly aware that he was speaking.

'Just take care, and don't rush things. You will be dealing with a different race of people. They won't always understand you, or you them. You will have to learn as you go along – just as Tandy did.'

They had finished their meal. 'What now?' Theresa asked lightly.

'Would you like to go for a walk along the Mile?'

The Mile was a stretch of road leading from the edge of the market town into the hills, which gave panoramic views of the outlying countryside. In the distance, one could see the waters of the little lough which was popular with anglers. Tonight, though, only the exhilaration of the walk itself was of benefit, as it was too dark to enjoy the other advantages. At night it was left to the lovers.

Jack took Theresa's hand in his. Once he would have been too unsure of himself to do so, but such was the change in him he did it now with complete confidence.

156

Theresa was in a state of silent panic. She wasn't certain of the significance of the action. She tried to appear cool, as though it had happened many times before, but her mind was racing. Jack was silent as she tried to give rein to her own thoughts. What would she do if he kissed her? Jesus! Why couldn't she have been born somewhere else, where girls knew about these things?'

The moon sailed from behind a cloud, looking like egg yolk escaping. Will you get back behind that cloud, she screamed silently. That's all she needed to wind her up – a lover's moon. Her heart was pounding with fright, and when they passed a couple trying to climb down each other's throats, she threw in the towel.

'I'd better get back now,' she said more loudly than was necessary. 'The bus will be coming soon.'

'Don't talk daft. You have half an hour.'

'But we have the walk back yet.' She was panicking now; they had just passed another couple of grunting kissers who were making a meal of each other's lips. Wrenching her hand from Jack's, she turned on her heel and set off down the road in the direction of the town.

Jack set off after her and caught her up. He held her firmly and turned her face towards his. 'Is this what you're afraid of?' He pulled her close and brought his mouth down on hers. He softly kneaded her lips till they opened slightly, then he pressed gently. He didn't want to scare her, but he had a job to control the sudden rush of passion as he held her firm, slim body to his and felt her soft round breasts against him.

The kiss was making Theresa feel weak. She had never known such bliss. Suddenly she found herself returning it, and her lips opened up under his persistence. The warmth of him and his male scent enfolded her. She didn't want the moment to end.

She was about to climb on to the bus, tears beginning to form behind her eyelids because she knew now that she would miss him more than she thought possible, when Jack pulled her back.

'Are you crying?' he asked softly.

'I'm not crying. Theresa Brady doesn't cry that easily. I've got something in my eye.'

He folded back the thick hair that was obscuring his view of her face. 'Will you come and visit me at the university sometime?'

'Do you really want me to?'

'I've asked you several times. You have never shown a lot of interest in taking me up on it.'

157

'We'll arrange something then. It's just – well – with my work up at the stables and – and everything . . .'

'Just give me a ring – I don't mind if you just turn up, but the problem with that is that I may be at a lecture. I wouldn't want you to make the journey for nothing.' He kissed her lightly again. 'The driver is getting impatient,' he grinned. 'You'd better get into your seat.'

She turned to wave goodbye as the bus set off, but Jack hadn't waited.

CHAPTER 12

For days after her trip to Kilgaven, Theresa's state of confusion continued; not even Pat Maher could get a rise out of her. He certainly tried hard enough.

'Are you sickening for something, Theresa Brady?' he called out. 'I've been travelling at sixty miles an hour and you haven't opened that gob of yours.'

She didn't answer. Pat, disappointed, slammed on the brakes as he narrowly missed a wandering sheep, and climbed from the bus to herd it safely into the nearest field.

'I think Pat will actually miss you when we finish at the end of term,' said Eileen. Theresa, staring blindly out of the window, made no reply.

Pat Maher called Eileen back as she was about to get off the bus at the bridge.

'Is she all right?'

'I think so. Shall I tell her you asked after her health?' She smiled at him. He wasn't a bad old thing. She would miss him.

'Tell her nothing. She has ruined my day whichever way you look at it. I never thought I'd see the day when I couldn't get a rise out of that one, with her temper being what it is.' Pat slammed the bus noisily into gear and tore off along the road, the now empty vehicle swaying from side to side.

Eileen caught up with Theresa. 'What did you get up to on Saturday evening?' she asked.

'What?'

'Theresa, will you return to the real world? If you don't, I'll leave you be until you do. I don't like talking to myself.' Eileen forged ahead, her shoulders set in a high huff.

Theresa hurried after her. 'I'm sorry. I've been getting into trouble at home about it. I'll concentrate; really I will. What did you say?'

'I asked you what you did on Saturday evening.'

'I went out with Jack.'

159

'You did what?'

'Close your mouth, Eileen. He rang just as I got home after seeing you. He asked me if I would like to meet him in Kilgaven – so I did.'

'Is that it? You aren't going to tell me any more?'

'We had a great evening. Jack wants me to visit him sometime at the university. I said that I would – that's all.'

'All! No wonder you've been going round looking dazed.'

To take Eileen's mind off her evening with Jack, Theresa volunteered information that she knew would startle her. 'Richard has arranged for my parents and me to spend a week at his house in London so that they can inspect the college and the area where I'll be living.'

'You lucky thing. When are you going?'

'There is no set date. His housekeeper has only to be given warning and she will have all ready. She's in permanent residence.'

'You've fallen on your feet, haven't you? I'll miss you when you go over for good.'

'I might not go. You never know,' said Theresa mysteriously. Eileen took not a bit of notice. Theresa said things like that with no notion of enlarging further.

Eileen was having a few problems of her own. She had a major decision to make, the outcome of which would have an effect on others as well as herself. She would need the help of prayer and the grace of God to help her find the answer. She had toyed with the idea of consulting Father Corke, but had dropped it. She hadn't the confidence in his ability to be neutral. Instead, she had made an appointment to see Sister Anunciata, who had always been there for her when she had a problem.

Things had changed drastically in her life since Tandy went across to England and Jack to Dublin. The desire to go dancing and partying had waned, and although she let Theresa drag her into her little schemes she now followed with even more reluctance than before.

More and more she had turned to her duties for the church. She particularly enjoyed it when she was assigned to the altar for cleaning. It was here she felt a calmness and a quiet joy as she polished the bench seats, put the freshly washed and starched linen strip along the altar, and Silvoed the candle sconces and communion salvers.

For a long time now she had become aware that she felt happiest in the presence of God, and she cleaned his house and worked with his little children with a feeling of contentment.

160

She arrived home that afternoon to find her mother, as usual, faffing around her father, who sat in his armchair reading the paper during his afternoon break. It was Eileen's duty, when she came home from school, to look after the shop for an hour so that her mam could get the evening meal ready and her da could catch up on the news – generally found on the sports page.

'You're late,' said her father, eyeing her over the half-moon glasses that gave him a Dickensian look. 'The bell has just gone in the shop. You'd better go and see to it.' He adjusted his spectacles on his nose, rustled his paper, and waved her from the room.

For the next hour she opened packs and stocked shelves between serving customers. She was dying for a drink of something, but she'd have to wait. It was not considered a priority that she should have a cup of tea when her parents did. She felt a small prickle of resentment, quickly squashed.

The telephone rang. It was Theresa.

'Can you come over this evening? I have something to show you.' She sounded excited.

'Can you not tell me what it is about? I hate it when you leave me in suspense.'

'I'll see you later,' said Theresa, and the phone went dead.

Theresa went upstairs to her room as soon as she had helped her mam do the dishes. While she waited for Eileen to arrive she fidgeted about her room, lifting this and settling that. Jesus! She was behaving like Jack's mother.

Eventually she crossed to the window to watch the spume dash against the rocks, lose impetus, retreat, gather force and make a new attempt.

It was here Eileen found her. 'Well then! What is this all about?'

Theresa uncurled herself and went to her dressing table. 'Read that,' she said.

When Eileen had finished reading the card she had been given, she looked at Theresa. 'Why should Moira Kennedy invite you to her eighteenth birthday party?'

'You didn't get one, then?'

'Of course not, otherwise I'd have known what your phone call was all about.'

'I thought not.' Theresa tapped her chin with the card. 'Don't you see? I only got one because she thinks I'll bring Jack along. I knew she had taken a notion for him at the dance that time.'

'She could have asked him herself, then she needn't have

161

included you, seeing as there's no love lost between you.'

'I wondered about that,' mused Theresa, 'but then I realized she didn't know where he was, and the possibility was present that he might not have gone without me – you had noticed that it is worded "and friend"?'

'Will you go?'

'Will the Pope say mass? Of course I'll go. I won't be taking Jack, though. I have no intentions of letting that madam get her hands on him.'

'Sure you can't go alone. You'd never have the nerve.'

'Certainly not. Remember the "and friend"? I'll ask—' She hesitated. 'I'll ask Richard.'

Eileen let out a deep sigh of relief. 'For one dreadful, awful, stultifying moment, I thought you were going to ask me.'

'Not at all. There would be no game in that.' Theresa waltzed round the room. 'I have plans forming. Indeed I have.' Her eyes were alight with devilment.

'You're not going to ruin that girl's party. I'll never speak to you again if you do that.'

'Of course not! I'd not do that to anyone. I just intend to play her at her own game. She wouldn't give me the time of day – never mind include me at her birthday party – if it wasn't for her own ends. I am just going to make sure they are not met – that's all.'

'It's going to be a very grand "do". I notice it's being held in the ballroom of Lord Patrick's mansion, and the dress is formal, Eileen remarked.

Theresa shrugged. 'So what? I'll not feel out of place. My old gran told me once that when I went out into the world I was to remember that no one was better than me. They could be richer or poorer, fatter or thinner, prettier or uglier, but they are no better, seeing as we all came into the world without a stitch on us.' She smiled gleefully. 'If I do start to feel inferior I'll look at Madam Moira and visualise her as a banshee.'

'What will you wear? You haven't an evening dress to your name.'

'I don't know yet. I haven't told Mam and m'da yet.'

When Eileen had gone, Theresa went down to the big, warm kitchen. There was an untidy, homely feel about it. The chairs and sofa didn't match, and the furniture was a hodge-podge of old and new, but it had that lived-in family feeling that did the heart good to be in it.

'Mam! Da! I've something to show you.' Theresa handed the invitation to her father, who read it before passing it over to Nuala. She waited with bated breath.

162

'I don't know what to say.' Nuala looked over at her husband. 'What do you think, Colin, love?'

'I suppose it is a compliment in its way that our Theresa has been asked.' He turned towards his daughter. 'You didn't tell me you knew these people.'

'I don't! Not well, that is. I meet Moira at the odd dance, and we've spoken, but it's a surprise to me as well.'

'You'll be going, will you?'

'I would like to.'

Theresa's attitude was so demure and timid that Nuala looked at her suspiciously. 'Do you like the girl?'

'Would she have asked me if there was any problem?'

'Hmmn,' Nuala glanced at Colin, who was re-reading the invitation.

He drew his pipe from his mouth and tapped the card with its stem. 'It says formal dress.'

'Yes! I'll need a long evening dress.'

'I don't think that will be a problem,' said Nuala. 'Do you, Colin?'

'I suppose if it has to be, then we will manage.'

There was no mention of accessories. Nuala, as though she guessed what Theresa was thinking, lowered her eyebrows and shook her head ever so slightly. 'Send your acceptance,' she said.

'Who will you be taking with you?' asked Colin.

'I don't know. I'll have to think about that.'

'Jack, surely.' Nuala looked at her daughter. 'He can come from Dublin, can't he? It isn't all that far.'

'I'll give it some thought,' said Theresa. 'Jack isn't the only man around.' She rose and hurried from the room before her words could sink in. There weren't many lads her parents trusted, and Jack was the one they would want her to invite. She had three weeks to get things together before the big night.

When she saw Richard on Saturday, she spoke of the invitation.

'I got one as well.'

Her heart quailed. 'Does that mean you will be taking a partner?'

'I doubt it. In fact, I wasn't thinking of going at all. It isn't the kind of evening I enjoy, I'm afraid.'

Theresa took a deep breath. She hung Night Star's saddle on the block before speaking.

'I need a partner,' she said simply. 'Could you not change your mind?'

'What on earth would a lovely girl like you want with me as a partner?'

163

Theresa watched his eyes crinkle. He really was attractive. She wondered why there were never any lady visitors to Castle Donagh.

'I wish you would partner me. If you don't, I can't go.'

Richard threw back his head and laughed. 'It's not much of a compliment to know that one is being asked only because there is no one else – although I can't believe that.'

'Oh! No! I didn't mean . . . It's just that there isn't anyone I wish to ask.'

'What about your friend Jack?'

'He – he can't make it. He has a lot of work on.'

Richard looked at her. He suspected she wasn't telling the truth. 'All right. You win. I'll be your partner – but I warn you: I do not dance. There is no way you are getting me on to the floor. I'm strictly a drink-in-one-hand – cigar-in-the-other man. If someone talks to me that's fine. If not, I take myself into a quiet, dark corner and watch the fun from there.'

'You're great, so you are. I'll not forget this.' Theresa started polishing the saddle enthusiastically.

Richard went to the stables and walked Othello out. 'One day we must ride together. I heard from Fergal that you had become quite an expert horsewoman.'

'I'd like that,' said Theresa. She watched him saddle up and ride off, his back straight, his hands loose on the reins.

The matter of the dress was settled by a remarkable stroke of fate. It all began when Eileen's aunt Margaret came up from Dublin for the weekend. During the course of her stay she remarked that Eileen was walking around as though she had the worries of the world on her shoulders and looked decidedly peaky.

Eileen had a great deal of time for her aunt. She and Mam were very different. Aunt Margaret dressed in colourful, modern clothes and had her shoes hand made at McCafferty's leather goods shop in Dublin. Her eyes were always twinkling and she wore her wide smile like a badge. She was game for anything. Her mother considered her aunt a bad influence because her views were liberal.

'Why don't you let Eileen come to me for a few days soon?' Margaret asked her sister.

'She has school for another few weeks,' said Kathleen O'Rourke.

'She has finished her exams; what would a few days away matter? I bet the school is well depleted now.'

Eileen, her chest rising and falling rapidly with breathless excitement, said, 'Please, Mam. Theresa could come with me. You wouldn't mind if Theresa came, would you Aunt Margaret?'

'Not at all. I like Theresa. She's a good gas and she'll be company for you when I'm working in the shop.'

'I don't know,' said Kathleen. 'I'll have a word with the sisters at the convent. If they don't mind, then you can go.'

Eileen tore down to Theresa to impart the good news.

'That would be great.' Theresa waltzed her round. 'We'll have a great time. The parents won't be round and your aunt Margaret won't give a tuppeny toss what we get up to so long as we don't burn the shop down.'

Eileen stopped. 'You needn't think we can take advantage of Aunt Margaret. She's more understanding than our parents on many counts, but she'll not stand for any nonsense.'

'Did I say we were going to do anything drastic? I meant that she wouldn't start saying novenas if we were out a bit late. Maybe she would take us to the theatre one evening?'

Nuala was all for it. 'Margaret has some lovely clothes in that shop of hers; you might find something you like for the dance. Whatever else can be said for Margaret, she has good dress sense – she's certainly colourful.'

Later, Nuala took a stroll up to Kathleen O'Rourke's house to see Margaret. She wanted to have a word with her about the style and colour of the dress.

'You leave it to me,' said Margaret. 'I will take her youth, her colouring, and yourself into account when I help her choose. I would like her to be a credit to me as well – which brings me to a point.' She closed the sitting room door. 'Would you object if we worked out a bit of business regarding the dress?'

'How so?'

'This is quite a big event. There will be money around at the party. If Theresa could let it be known where she got the dress, you and I could do a very good deal. I'd let you have it for half price.'

'Oh! I don't know. I wouldn't want Theresa to be embarrassed.'

'She won't be. Look, if no one comments on the dress, well and good; however, if someone remarks that it is lovely, then all I ask is that Theresa mentions where she got it. Fifty per cent off is not to be sneezed at.'

'W-e-ell. I leave it to you and Theresa; if she has a mind to do it, then I'll not object – but it must be done tastefully.'

'You're on!'

By the time Colin came in from his meeting Nuala was filled with doubt.

165

'Are you not well?' asked Colin, noting the nervous twisting of the hands.

'I may have done a tasteless thing, Colin.'

'Never! Not you.'

She told him about the deal with Margaret. 'It isn't in the best of taste, is it?'

'I suppose not,' he laughed. 'But it's done all the time. I suspect that many members of the aristocracy do it – even if it's only wearing the dress with the label hanging out so that someone has to help shove it back in and thereby just happen to read the name on it. I wouldn't give it another thought.'

When Theresa looked round the shop after it had closed, she was enthralled. She had never seen so many beautiful dresses. She ran excitedly from one rail to the other, lifting out dress after dress and holding it against her.

Eileen looked on. She'd never understand Theresa's great love for clothes. For herself, she was content to be neatly covered and clean.

Margaret came in from the store room. 'I've been studying you since you came,' she said. 'I have put six dresses on a rack in the store room; one of those is the dress for you.'

'But there are some beautiful ones here, Margaret. What's so special about the others?'

'They are for your age, type and colouring, so let's see what we can do.'

They were a disappointment. Margaret realized that she had been selecting dresses for a young girl. What she hadn't observed was that Theresa had the sensuous, lithe body of a woman. She threw the dresses down in a heap. 'I've got the very thing. Your mother will kill me. This dress is worth double the others, but what the hell – I need the business. Get into this.'

The dress was of a soft, creamy woollen material, so fine it looked as though only a whisper could pass through the delicate weave.

'It's got long sleeves, and there isn't a flounce to be seen,' cried Theresa.

'Exactly! This – ' Margaret gave a dramatic swish of her arm – 'is a dress for a sophisticated woman with carnal desires.'

'I wish!' But Theresa's excitement mounted as Margaret put the dress against herself and whirled round the room, causing the beautiful cut of the cloth to catch the light, giving the dress a life of its own.

'Try it on,' Margaret commanded. Eileen blushed at the

sensation she too had experienced at the movement of the dress.

Theresa put on the dress and stood on tiptoe to stop it trailing.

Margaret shook off her high-heeled shoes. 'Put these on. They'll pinch, but we'll get the effect.'

'It's beautiful! I want it, I want it,' Theresa cried, adding, 'Eileen, close your mouth.'

'You can't wear that dress, Theresa Brady,' Eileen gasped.

Margaret bit her lip. The change in this young girl was nothing short of miraculous. The dress hugged the slim young body, showing every slight, delicate curve. She would drive the young men to madness.

'The outline of your knickers spoils the shape,' she said in a matter-of-fact voice.

'No problem,' laughed Theresa. 'I'll not wear any.' She glanced at Eileen. 'That's the secret of Moira Kennedy's style for sure.'

'You wouldn't!'

'She won't,' said Margaret. 'Have you heard of the G-string?'

They hadn't, so she explained. 'It will cover your modesty and there will be nothing showing to spoil the line.'

It was settled. There was now the matter of the accessories. Margaret sent them to a store with a note for the owner, and there Theresa was fitted out with a pair of cream satin shoes and a matching clutch bag.

'I'm a bit worried about everything being one colour,' she said to Margaret that evening.

'Trust me! That dress needs no colour. With that skin of yours and that mass of black hair . . . The dramatic effect will be stunning – and you must wear pearls.'

When, next day, Eileen and Margaret visited some relatives, Theresa, left to her own devices, boarded a bus to the university. The place was teeming with students who strode along, some with head bent, some in pairs and groups, arguing the toss as they walked.

'Excuse me! Could you direct me to the Medical section?'

The young woman she had accosted pointed to a large building. 'I should enquire there. The hall porter will set you right.'

Theresa thanked her and walked away. She was feeling more nervous with every step she took. The porter, a fat little lard of a man, stared at her through a window.

'I'm looking for one of the medical students,' she said. 'I have no idea where he might be.'

'No more do I,' the porter said, giving her a look that said he thought she was off her head to think she had a chance in Hades of finding said student. 'Have you any idea, young miss, just how

167

many medical students we have here, and how many lecture halls? He could be anywhere.'

'Is there not a call system?' The pompous kitter was getting on her nerves. Theresa Brady took no guff from anyone.

'I'll not put out a call. That is done only for lecturers or for a dire emergency – and this is not one.'

She changed tack. 'Please?' She looked up at him with wide blue eyes and trembling lip; all the while thinking that Sister Mary Theresa was right the day she said in exasperation, 'Theresa Brady, have you ever thought of taking up acting? I can't believe even you could come up with all these excuses and lies without you thinking you are playing a part in a great drama.'

'Give me his name,' said the porter gruffly.

'Jack Ross. He is a first-year student.' She waited while he studied a clip-board on the wall.

'You were born under a lucky sign, young lady. The student you mention just happens to be attending a lecture in this very building. Lucky for you they have to sign in – fire regulations.'

'Oh! You're great. How long will the lecture take?'

'Ah, well! That's the bad news. It started ten minutes ago and generally takes at least an hour – more, if there are a lot of questions at the end.'

'Is there anywhere I could get a cup of tea?'

'Not in this building, but there's a tearoom just down the road.' He looked at his watch. 'I'd be back by midday if I were you.'

When she returned, she waited, refreshed by the cup of tea and the buttered farl she'd eaten. She scanned the wide stairways to the balcony above from where, she had been assured, the mass would descend.

The nearer the time got to midday, the more nervous Theresa became. She convinced herself there was no reason why Jack should mind her being here; after their last meeting, when he'd kissed her tenderly, he'd asked her to visit.

It was well past midday when she heard the doors crash open on the floor above, which heralded the stampede. She rose from the wooden bench in the shadow of the porter's wooden office and rapidly scanned the faces, so many of them, as they tore down the steps.

Then she saw him. Jack was head and shoulders above the group he was in. His eyes were creased in laughter and her heart swelled with pride at the handsomeness of him. She moved towards the open hall to accost him, but stopped suddenly as the masses in front of him parted and she saw that his arm was across the shoulders of a small red-haired girl who was smiling in

168

response to something he had just said. Her breath caught as he bent his head and kissed the girl full on the lips, cuddling her to him as he did so.

Moving back into the shadows, Theresa leaned helplessly against the wall of the cabin and watched them leave. She just knew the girl's name was Pat. She had assumed Pat was a man. With her eyes closed and her lips clenched between her teeth, she felt a deep anger fill her at Jack's betrayal. Two could play at that game, she thought. Next time she saw Jack she wouldn't be quite so vulnerable.

On the night of the birthday party, Theresa, regarding herself in the mirror, was pleased with what she saw. Margaret was right. The whole ensemble – against the background of her black hair and clear skin – looked elegant. Her mam had lent her the beautiful cream shawl with the gold thread through it that had been her gran's. She threw it lightly over her shoulders and went downstairs.

Colin caught his breath at the beauty of his daughter. Nuala looked anxious as she realized, with a woman's intuition, that her daughter had taken on another role under the influence of the dress. She suspected that Theresa felt a power tonight that she had never felt before.

'Mind how you go,' she whispered. 'Remember who you are. Bless yourself on the way out.' There was a swish of tyres outside, heralding Richard's arrival. Theresa noticed that neither of her parents had said she was to enjoy herself.

In the car she began to tremble. She was going into the unknown. 'Will Lord Patrick be here tonight?' she asked, breaking the silence.

'No! He's in England at the moment. He let the Kennedys use part of the ballroom because the dower house is too small for dancing,' Richard explained.

The place was teeming with cars when they arrived. Richard told Bob to go home, saying he would ring when he needed him to return.

Theresa was disappointed when they walked the few yards to the front door from the shadows. She had been looking forward to a grand entrance. But she felt like a great lady all the same as she was directed to a cloakroom where she tidied her hair and deposited her shawl, before joining Richard again.

'I'm shaking with nerves,' she whispered.

Richard, having watched her cross the wide hall towards him, thought she was the most stunning woman there. The Theresa he knew was gone for tonight. Here in her place was a beautiful woman with a body that would fill any man with desire.

'You'll do. You look wonderful. There isn't a man here tonight who will not want to dance with you. Those who can't will be biting their fingernails in frustration.' He squeezed her arm as he whispered the words in her ear. 'Remember, though, I will not be one of them.'

Theresa held her head up and walked into the beautiful room where the dance was being held.

Moira Kennedy greeted her. 'I thought you would be bringing your friend Jack,' she said, her green eyes showing annoyance.

'Afraid not. He had another engagement; but I'm fine. I came with Richard here, a man of the world. I am well served.'

She moved on, happily aware that Moira was seething. She had seen the way Moira's eyes had raked her from top to bottom, and when her mother commented on her beautiful dress, Moira's mouth had closed up like a purse-string.

Several times that evening Theresa was complimented on her dress, and she made certain, on polite insistence, that each time she mentioned where she had bought it. Bad taste or not, she owed Margaret a favour.

Richard retreated to a large sofa and sat down. He was confident that Theresa was well on the way to being the belle of this ball. He had seen several young men waiting to pounce.

He looked towards the receiving line. Moira's glance was following the swirling cream dress and its beautiful wearer. Looking at Moira with an artist's eyes he felt that, pretty though she was, she lacked the class of Theresa. Her dress was smart and the colour chosen wisely, but it was a young girl's dress; whereas Theresa's dress was not only elegant but sensual in line as well. He wondered who had helped her make the choice. Not Nuala – of that he was certain. No mother would have dared choose such a dress for her daughter.

All thoughts of Jack and his perfidy had gone from Theresa's mind. She was breathless with exertion and glowing with the triumph of her success. She gave as good as she got in the conversational skills, and was delighted when she overheard someone refer to her wit. Three of her new friends escorted her to the buffet and helped her choose from a large selection of delicacies. She thanked them, then asked if they minded her looking for her escort, as she had been neglecting him.

She found Richard exactly as he said she would, with a cigar in one hand and a drink in the other. She joined him.

'Do I have to ask if you are enjoying yourself?' he smiled.

'I'm having the time of my life. Have you eaten?'

'I had a mouthful. I rarely eat at these functions. I loathe balancing a plate on my knee.'

170

They chatted whilst she ate, and then Richard whispered, 'You'd better finish eating. There are two young men waiting for your last mouthful to go down so they can grab you again.'

Theresa handed the plate to a passing waitress and rose. Richard was right. As soon as she stood up, Ross Carling – a friend of Moira's who had come over from England for the birthday party – hurried across, leaving a very disgruntled Michael Cummings at the starting line. His eyes had strayed for a moment.

Moira Kennedy strolled over later in the evening. 'I hope you are having a good time, Theresa. It's a shame your boyfriend couldn't make it.'

You're not hoping I'm enjoying myself, you poisonous banshee, thought Theresa. She knew Moira had dropped her little bit of information in the hope that the lads with her would be warned off.

'I'm so glad you invited me. It's a pity about Jack, as you say. However, I'm not missing him too much with all the attention I'm getting from these lovely men.'

Moira's look was lethal. 'Don't forget our dance, Ross,' she said, smiling up at him. She moved away, her retreating shoulders stiff with anger.

Next morning, Eileen lay on Theresa's bed with her chin on her hands, listening wide-eyed to Theresa's account of the evening. She was as thrilled as Theresa by her success.

'Did Moira like your present?'

'Don't be so naive, Eileen – sure what do I care? I expect she is opening them on her bed at this very moment, and I don't suppose mine will register more than two on a scale of ten.'

'Did she ask why Jack wasn't with you?'

'She made a sliding remark about it. You should have seen her face when she realized he hadn't come.'

'You can be quite spiteful at times. Isn't it something that the girl asked you to her party? You might be a bit more charitable towards her.'

'Eileen, the only reason I was there was because she hoped Jack would come. I don't like her and I'm not going to pretend I do. She is a class one chancer, that one. If she could get Jack, I'd be consigned to the social dungheap and you know fine well that I'm right.'

'I'm not going to argue.' Eileen puckered her brows. 'Is it right that Pat McGarry is building a swimming pool? M'da says he was talking to him about contractors coming in shortly to dig a hole in front of his house.'

171

'Yes!' said Theresa. 'He wants it done quickly. I don't know why.'

'I do!' Nuala had come into the room with a pile of sheets. 'Get off the bed, the pair of you,' she fussed. 'The ball is over for Cinderella here, and the slipper is lost. There is no prince. The story was a made-up lie. The ugly sister got the butler in the long run.'

Theresa rolled off, grinning. 'That's what you think.'

'So! You're boasting of your great social success.' Nuala threw the sheets down and folded her arms. 'I had a phone call from Richard this morning. He tells me that you went down a treat.'

'You would have been proud of me, Mam. I had the boys all goin'.'

'That's my girl!' Nuala hauled the bedclothes off. 'Don't let it go to your head. That dress had a lot to do with it. For one night you were a desirable woman; today you are a dirty scut who hasn't had a wash and brush up.' She gave her a hug.

'You said you know why Pat McGarry wants the pool put in urgently,' Eileen broke in.

'I said it without thinking.'

'Come on, Mam. You can't leave us guessing.'

'Will you keep it to yourselves?'

The girls nodded.

'Brace yourselves.' Nuala paused for effect. Theresa threw a pillow at her.

'Well! As you know you both have your eighteenth birthday coming up.'

'Yes?'

'That's the reason, you pair of eejuts. He is going to throw a barn dance and a swimming party for you.'

The two girls looked at her in astonishment. 'Why should he bother?' Theresa gasped.

'It was something I said. I was talking about you going to Moira Kennedy's party and I said, jokingly, that Kathleen and I would have to come up with something good to beat that – and he thought I was serious and came up with the plan. Remember! Not a word to anyone. We'll all look a right lot of prawns if nothing comes to pass.'

They crossed their hearts.

Theresa saw Eileen to the door. 'I'll be up to your house as soon as I've had a bath,' she said. 'We'll decide what we want to do; meanwhile you can put on your thinking cap.'

'The beach?' suggested Eileen.

'Think about it.' Theresa shut the door and went into the

172

kitchen. There were two letters addressed to her on the table. She recognized Jack's bold hand, but she looked in puzzlement at the other. She opened that one first.

Dear Theresa, I miss you. we are in wicklow as you will see by the stamp we are doing the coastal countys this year. We are cuttin across at wexford and movin back towards home. There was a bit of trouble on the border we heard and that is why we are pushing south. they say the IRA are becoming active there. we dont want any trouble. we are only a family of tinkers. will I see you again or are you off to dublin soon. I hope I see you again as I enjoy your company.

Your very good friend
Fergal

She hugged the letter to her. Lovely, kind Fergal, who had become very dear to her. He might not know where to put his capital letters, but he had more common sense and sensitivity than many a graduate.

She went to the kitchen and made herself a cup of strong tea before sitting down to read Jack's letter.

Dear Theresa,

I have now finished my first year at the Uni. I've taken a job for four weeks at the hospital – as a porter-cum-dogsbody. I need the money. I did fairly well with my pre-med subjects. We had a go at anatomy but it was only a taster. The hard work starts next year.

You never got around to visiting me at the Uni, did you? I was disappointed but then, you will soon be here on your own account, I'm certain. I enjoyed our evening together recently. I'd like to move on from where we left off. I hope you feel the same way. Meantime, I'll earn some money and I'll see you when I get back to Tullybra in four week's time.

Love,
Jack.

Her mother returned, cuddling a cup of tea in her hand. 'From Jack?' She nodded towards the letters as she curled up in the big armchair.

Theresa nodded. 'The other one was from Fergal.'

'That's nice. I only met the boy briefly but I liked him.'

Theresa wondered wryly if her mother would change her mind about Fergal if she knew what had taken place by the lough. Even now she could recall the sensations running through her body as he had kissed her. She would always blame herself for what had occurred, and she was glad that she and Fergal had remained firm friends. It had taken some time to convince him that he hadn't lost her respect. She was pleased that he had written to her.

'And how is Jack?' her mother enquired.

'He's well enough. He is staying in Dublin for another four weeks to earn some money.'

'I hope he'll be home in time for your party.'

Theresa didn't reply, but rose from her seat and went into the kitchen to rinse her cup.

She looked again at the two letters in her hand and then, with a sigh, she tucked one into her pocket and tore the other one into small shreds and pushed it into the bin.

CHAPTER 13

The trip to England was fairly straightforward. There was only one slight mishap on the English side, when Colin mislaid one of the cases. It was quickly found and they made their way down the gangplank to the quayside.

In spite of the bright sunshine the quay was draughty, and Theresa gave a slight shiver. The fishy smell that pervaded the air was making her feel squeamish, so she was glad when they had settled in a compartment on the Liverpool-to-London train. She hadn't been able to sleep on the ferry for excitement, and now she was exhausted.

Richard had suggested they take a taxi to the south-east side of the city. 'London can be a nightmare for anyone not used to the chaotic traffic,' he warned them.

His house, in Dulwich Village, was just a twenty minute bus ride from the Art college in Camberwell Green where Theresa would be studying. Her interview was scheduled for ten o'clock the following morning. They were all nervous.

When Richard had put the idea forward that they should stay at his home and inspect the area, Colin's anxieties had been partially relieved. Dulwich Village sounded a safe and fairly respectable place for their daughter.

From the moment they met Richard's housekeeper they liked her. Mrs Beatty was a surprisingly slim woman in her middle years – surprising in that Richard had extolled the virtues of her cooking skills, and assured them that his weight problem was entirely her fault. He'd smiled as he had said it.

Mrs Beatty showed them to their respective rooms and told them she had some food prepared when they'd had a wash. Theresa had bucked up considerably, Nuala noticed.

The meal was 'as tasty a meal as they'd had in a long time', Colin assured Mrs Beatty.

Nuala, feeling miffed at his effusive compliment, said, 'He does eat well at home, Mrs Beatty. He'd soon kick up a fuss if it wasn't to his satisfaction.'

'I'm sure he does, Mrs Brady.' Mrs Beatty cleared the dishes and suggested that they go into the drawing room, where she would bring them coffee.

Colin took out his pipe. 'Drawing room, eh?'

'Do you think you ought to smoke, Colin?' asked Nuala anxiously.

'In view of the fact that Richard smokes cigars, I don't think there would be a ban. In any case, I'm sure Mrs Beatty will soon tell us if there is an embargo on it. And don't you go offering to help with the dishes; the woman would be embarrassed.'

'I had no intention,' Nuala said. 'I may come from a backender of a village in Ireland, but I do have some idea of the social graces.'

'Sorry, my dear. No offence meant, but you have a heart of gold and would maybe feel the need to pull your weight.'

Nuala forgave him. He was a bit of a dear, in his way.

Theresa moved over to the window and looked out over the seemingly endless rear garden. Lord knows, she had been impressed by the grandness of the front entrance – with its wide driveway and avenue of rhododendrons, not to mention the big double garage and the turning bay – but the rear garden was like a park.

Mrs Beatty arrived with the coffee. Colin took his and looked suspiciously into the dark, murky brew. He'd never tasted the stuff. Still, there was a first time for everything. He took a sip. Only the presence of the housekeeper held him from making a rude comment. The stuff was poisonous.

Theresa hid a smile. She had felt the same at her first sip, all those months ago when she and Eileen had first tried it. Nuala valiantly persevered. She was, and always would be, a tea lover.

Armed with a map of the area – which included Peckham Rye, should they want to stroll round the park, and Brixton, should they want to visit the market – they set off next day to find the art college.

'Get off near the cinema, and make your way a few hundred yards in the same direction towards the Oval,' Mrs. Beatty had instructed them. 'The college is on your right.'

They had a long way to walk to the nearest bus stop. Mrs Beatty had warned them that there were no buses nearer than Dulwich Grove, which was at least half a mile away. 'Go past the hospital and first left into Lordship Lane.'

Theresa and Nuala walked together with Colin taking up the rear. 'Just think, Mam. I'll be part of all this soon,' said Theresa excitedly.

'Well, if you take ill, you *are* near the hospital.'

Theresa read the name as they passed. 'Dulwich Hospital. It looks a bit grim.'

'Many of the hospitals in London were once poor-houses – I read it somewhere – anyway, so long as the care is good, you needn't worry about the look of the place.'

Colin sat behind them on the bus, studying the map. Women! he thought. The main operation was to see what kind of college his daughter would be attending and here they were chuntering on about hospitals.

He was impressed by the look of the college, a large red-brick building fronting the pavement. He'd have liked to see inside the Theresa insisted that she went into her interview alone. They were to collect her in an hour.

Later, as they walked along the main thoroughfare, Colin pointed out landmarks so that Theresa wouldn't lose herself when she was over on her own. Little mention was made of the interview and how it had gone. Colin enquired only if things went well.

'I think so. I'll tell you all later, over lunch.' Theresa made a face. 'Can we not go shopping, Da? I'll manage to find my own way around when I come over in October – if I'm accepted.'

'I wonder where the church is?' said Colin, ignoring the plea. 'You may have to travel some way to hear mass. Mrs Beatty thinks there isn't a Catholic church in the village.'

They asked a passerby for directions. The church was, in fact, on the bus route. Colin was happy that he'd located it.

'What would you like to do now?'

'Tour round the dress shops,' they said.

'Not me! I'll have some tea with you and then I'm going to do some more exploring. I'll meet you for lunch.'

During lunch Theresa told them how the interview went. 'They were quick to point out that I had made a late application,' she said.

'Did you mention that you have a university place in Dublin if you get your points?'

'No! I thought it better not to.' Theresa hesitated. 'I'll only get a place if there is a cancellation.' She toyed with her food. She didn't want to see the look of relief that she was certain would be in her father's eyes. She knew that he had been persuaded against his own judgement.

'You'll have to get a bike; that walk to the bus stop is too far,' he remarked.

They arrived back at the house in time for dinner. Colin, having discovered that Dulwich Village had a beautiful park, insisted that they spend some time there. They had to drag him away. The small oasis of green in a built-up area had eased the stress he was feeling.

He wouldn't have said so to his family, but the hustle and bustle and the noise and speed of the traffic were already making him yearn for the quiet and peace of Tullybra. He didn't know how he was going to last the week out. It had not escaped his notice that his family were enjoying themselves, and he had no wish to spoil things for them.

He marvelled at how Theresa could contemplate living and studying here. Indeed, if it wasn't for the fact that he had already made the arrangements with Richard and was aware that she would be safely and comfortably housed, he would have insisted on her staying in Ireland. This place, to him, was a hell hole.

By Wednesday he'd had enough, and said so. They had travelled by bus and tube to recommended places and buildings of interest and his enthusiasm had held, but the crushing number of people striding the pavements and shoving him around in the tube stations had done for him.

He gave Nuala a sum of money and said, 'I'm going to spend the next few days in the peace of the park, or reading in the relative quiet of Richard's garden. You two can go where you want. Do you think you could find your way around?'

Nuala and Theresa looked at each other, trying to hide their excitement. Colin had been a real drag. The idea of setting off on their own held no fears.

'It seems to me that a number twelve bus is the answer to it all,' said Nuala. 'Once it deposits us at the other side of the river, we will be fine. Don't worry about us. Are you sure you don't want to come?'

They held their breath as he hesitated for a moment. 'No! I can't stand the thought of it. You two go off tomorrow and enjoy yourselves.'

Next day they set off on the most memorable day of the whole holiday. Nothing, they decided, was going to daunt them. This was a great adventure. If they didn't know where to find something, they would ask – and they did, many times, and laughed like eejuts at the way their helpers treated them as though they had come from another planet, articulating pointedly when they heard the Irish accents, and repeating every instruction twice.

They visited Harrods, and marvelled at the array of goods and the structure of the building. They tore up and down the escalators for the sheer hell of it, and rode up in the luxurious lifts and got totally lost on the top floors. The food hall filled them with awe, and Nuala remarked that Colin would have loved it.

They had lunch in a posh restaurant, and stared with horror at the bill before bursting into laughter. Afterwards, they made their way to oxford Street and the glossy shops. They didn't buy a stitch of clothing but had fun trying everything on.

'Could you see me wearing this to mass?' Nuala asked, *sotto voce*, and whirled round in a flouncy grogram dress with an off-the-shoulder style.

Theresa, trying on a pair of green slacks and a beige and green striped blouse, laughed and shook her head.

They made their way back after tea to find Colin ensconced in a deep armchair, reading a book on the history of the Plantagenets.

'A fascinating book,' he said, putting it down and regarding the two women in his life. 'Did you enjoy yourselves?'

'Wonderful!' they said, in unison.

'Have you two been drinking? You seem a bit high.'

'What a good idea,' said Nuala. 'There is a very nice looking pub just down the road. Why don't we go for a dram after dinner?'

'We can't take Theresa into a pub.'

'Don't show your ignorance, Colin. This is England. Sure no one will take a blind bit of notice. She'll drink orange juice.' Nuala was surprised at herself. She had thrown off all the inhibitions that had developed over the years she had been with Colin. England was fun.

It was a good evening. Colin got talking to an Irishman from County Clare and they couldn't drag him home. He laughed at the other man's anecdotes and asked for more.

On the last day, Colin had a surprise in store. 'We are all going to the theatre,' he announced. 'Mrs Beatty will be joining us.'

'Great!' said Theresa. 'A lovely way to end the holiday. Where are we going?'

Mrs Beatty, who had joined them, smiled. 'We're going to the Victoria Palace to see the Crazy Gang – you'll love them.'

'I'm glad you are coming with us,' Nuala smiled. 'You've been so very kind.'

'I've grown to like you all,' Mrs Beatty said quietly. 'I am truly sorry that you are going back. The time seems to have flown.'

'You may live to change your mind when our Theresa comes over in October. She will plague the life out of you.'

'I'm sure we'll get on very well together. I'll keep an eye on her for you.'

On the Saturday following their return, the Brady family joined the whole of the village of Tullybra – and indeed anyone who happened to stray in on the proceedings – at the marriage between John Owen and Kate Brannigan. It was a marriage that had been

179

hastily arranged following the death of John's mother three months previously.

Tommy Herlihy, the best man, had been the instigator of the whole thing some weeks before.

'Jesus Christ, man, you've been engaged to that poor girl for the past sixteen bloody years. It's time you put her out of her misery. I have bulls that are quicker off the mark than you.'

'A man has to know his mind. This is a serious step, Tommy.' John Owen had eyed the froth on his stout and shifted his elbow on the bar. 'I'll not be rushed.'

Will ye not? We'll see about that, Tommy had thought. He ordered a double whiskey for his companion and excused himself. 'I'll only be a minute, John. I want a word with Pat McGarry. drink this up; McGinn will do you a refill.' He had nodded to McGinn, who was grinning at him, and made a drinking motion with his hands, signalling three times more. McGinn winked.

'A word with you Pat?'

Pat McGarry turned. 'Hello Tommy. What's the word then?'

Before ten more minutes elapsed, the wedding had been planned. Pat McGarry, with a hoot of laughter, had promised to let the village hold the reception in the open air in his bottom field. The idea of railroading the reluctant bridegroom to the altar had appealed to him.

'He'll have to know,' he laughed. 'I heard tell that when he got engaged to Kate, he told her that he wouldn't be able to marry her until his mother died for he couldn't keep two women. Now a man that could take that view will not be rushing down the red carpet.'

'One more whiskey says he will. You mark my words,' Tommy had said, and patted his nose.

No one actually knew how he did it, but Tommy was observed, later, bundling the now totally relaxed John into his car and driving off towards Kate Brannigan's cottage.

On the big day, Colin Brady, sitting in the sixth row of the opposite aisle to the bridegroom, couldn't help noticing that the poor man, straitlaced into an unfamiliar black suit and starched white shirt, was sweating like a stuck pig. Every so often he would turn his head to look up the aisle towards the entrance, and as he turned, Colin observed that the highly starched collar of his shirt didn't move with him, but pointed resolutely forward.

Your man will cut his own throat if he turns once more, he thought. His own collar was a bit tight, so he knew how John was feeling at that moment.

'Is he drunk?' whispered Nuala. 'He can hardly stand straight.'

'He's here! That's what matters,' whispered Colin. He knew, for Tommy Herlihy had told him, that there were two double whiskeys floating around in John's bloodstream that accounted for the slight waver. It also accounted for his presence. The man was a bundle of nerves. Without the whiskey he would have been on a boat to England by now.

The opening bars of the Wedding March signalled the bride's arrival. Nuala turned to look towards the little tub of a woman who was beginning the slow walk to the altar. She smiled. Kate looked grand. It had taken some doing for herself and the others in the sewing group to convince Kate that she shouldn't wear a 'lovely white dress with a train'.

Margaret Ryan had duly been consulted, and had persuaded Kate that a pretty dress with a shower o' hail pattern, a cream hat and shoes, was more suitable.

Nuala thought that the dress, with its white dots on a navy blue background, had been the right choice.

Everyone who could had contributed to the feast that had been laid out on the big trestle tables lent by Father Corke, and those without transport were ferried to the reception on a decorated trailer pulled by the bright blue farm tractor, cleaned up for the occasion. It looked as though the whole county had joined the party.

'Will we have enough food?' Nuala said worriedly to Pat, as she eyed the hordes entering the field, laughing and calling out jubilantly to the bride and groom standing sheepishly side by side.

'Sure what does it matter? If we run out we can raid the orchard, and when that's done we'll start on the leaves.' The man who spoke shook Pat by the hand. He was an old friend whom Pat hadn't seen in years. Nuala left them to it.

Theresa, who was standing with Eileen by the laden tables, was amazed to see Moira Kennedy and Ross Carling drive through the gate.

'Look who's here.' She dug Eileen in the ribs. 'Surely she wasn't invited?'

'Nor were half the others. It seems Pat McGarry and Dan Herlihy's da put up notices saying that everyone was welcome at the bash.' Eileen was enjoying herself. She loved weddings. Her eyes always grew misty on such occasions, and a lump had filled her throat when the bride looked lovingly into the groom's eyes. The world should always be like this. Gallons of happiness and a sunshiny dollop of laughter and good-natured banter.

The party was great. That was the general pronouncement. Every dog and child seemed to have accompanied their owner. Tommy Herlihy twice tripped over Pat McGarry's Irish wolf-hound. 'In the name o' God,' he said tipsily. 'I don't remember sendin' that bloody donkey an invitation!' He grabbed John Owen by the arm and the two of them staggered towards the still laden tables.

Pat McGarry and Colin viewed the proceedings with satisfaction. 'Tommy's in for trouble when he gets home,' remarked Pat. 'Did you see the look on Maggie's face when he tripped over Cormac?'

'I did,' said Colin, pulling on his pipe. 'The drink is flowing down willing gullets like a drought was coming.'

Hugh McGrath and his ceili band supplied the music. McGinn had done a good deal by supplying the drink, and he was sorry when he had to leave. He hadn't had a day like this for years. He was usually dry eyed and dry throated behind his bar.

Theresa, mortified by the sight of Tommy Herlihy, apologised to Ross Carling. 'The Irish love a hooley. I'm afraid we tend to overdo it a bit.' She realised as she spoke that she sounded priggish.

'I'm enjoying myself enormously. Please don't apologise. I wish we overdid things a bit more.' He looked round. 'Where's Moira?'

'Don't worry about Moira. She's talking to Jack. I don't think she is missing us.'

'Good!' said Ross. 'If she's happy then I am.'

Theresa was not happy. She had watched Jack arrive with Tandy. When Eileen ran over to see them she had remained where she was. Jack had looked towards her as Eileen pointed.

Realizing that he was about to walk towards her, she had deliberately turned her back on him and joined Ross Carling; such was her feeling about Jack, even a chat to Moira Kennedy seemed preferable.

Some time later, Tandy came across to her. The band was having a break and the general air of hilarity was more subdued. Now and then a burst of laughter would rise again to stir the guests, and those who wanted to rested for a while before the start of the next session of dancing. Jack was nowhere to be seen. Eileen and Moira had also disappeared somewhere. Ross was now in conversation with Theresa's father.

'Hello, Tandy. It's lovely to see you again.' Theresa smiled.

'Then why didn't you rush over and sweep me into your arms? The brave Eileen did.' Tandy's smiling face hadn't changed a bit, but his figure was leaner and the muscles tighter.

'You've lost weight,' she said approvingly. 'You look tough and hard-muscled.' The soft eyes were still like a St Bernard's, though.

'It's all the hard work I've been doing. Don't forget, I didn't do a tap of work – well not really hard work – for m'da.' Tandy laughed. 'I could write a book on the best excuses.' His eyes searched the lovely face. 'Is it true you are going to England?'

'It is.'

'But you have a place at university.'

'So has Eileen; she isn't going either. She is convinced she won't make the grades.'

Tandy looked at her, puzzled. 'That's not what she's just told me. Fast on the heels of the information about you, she mentioned that she was going to take up her place doing a teaching degree.'

Theresa frowned. Her first reaction was annoyance that Eileen had told Tandy – who had only been home a few hours – and hadn't mentioned it to her. Her second reaction was curiosity. Why had she changed her mind? She had been adamant at one stage that she wasn't going to take up her option. 'I didn't know. Last time we spoke of it – and that was only a matter of weeks ago – she was certain she didn't want to go to university.'

'Well! She has changed her mind.' Tandy, realizing that he had put his size nines in it already, didn't tell Theresa the other piece of news Eileen had imparted, which had left him stunned but had also, for reasons he was keeping to himself, left him with an overwhelming sense of relief. He had no doubt that Eileen would tell Theresa in her own time. 'Would you like a drink?'

'I would, yes, if my parents weren't around. If they saw me I'd be in dire trouble.'

'Sure how would they know?' Tandy lifted an eyebrow. 'How about a gin and orange?'

She laughed. 'You'll not find that kind of drink here.'

'God! I forgot I was home. We'll go over and see what there is.'

His father was at the drinks table. 'Are you going to have a drink with your da, Tandy?'

'Hello, Da. I've invited Theresa over for one.'

'The soft drinks are on the other table,' he admonished, eyeing Tandy severely. 'You aren't teaching Colin's girl any of your newly acquired bad habits?'

As ever, thought Tandy, his da had said the wrong thing. He had only been home a day and already his da was gettin' on his wick with his snide remarks about his accent and his 'new' habits. He steered Theresa away. 'I'll get you a gin and tonic in a minute,' he whispered. 'They'll all think it's lemonade.'

'Will I like it?'

'You will not, but it will make you feel great. Meanwhile, tell me, what is going on between you and Jack? He was looking forward to seeing you and you gave him the frozen shoulder.'

'It doesn't seem to be bothering him too much,' Theresa observed. 'I notice he has gone off somewhere with Moira Kennedy.'

'He was shanghaied. The girl has him by the ears. You know how polite Jack is when he is around women. How long has she been around? She's quite a stylish piece.'

'She has the money to be stylish,' said Theresa, unable to keep the resentment from her voice.

Tandy looked at her. No love lost between those two. Had Theresa, who had been queen bee for so long, now found a rival? 'You don't like her.' It was more a statement than a question.

Theresa shrugged. 'I hardly know her, but I have to say that I am not dying about her, no! Enough about Moira Kennedy. I think she was put on this earth to plague me; where's that drink you promised me?'

Next day, when mass was over, Theresa leaned against the wall and waited for Eileen to arrive. Eileen nearly drove her mad with her lingering prayers. An hour of worship was enough for normal people, but Eileen had to bow the head and flatten the knees for longer than everyone else.

As Theresa waited she thought of those other times she had walked out of the church to join her friends. The group no longer existed, yet it seemed such a short time ago that they had gathered each Sunday to plot their activities for the day. Now they were all scattered: Tandy to England; Jack to Dublin; James Toomey, with his new modern-style glasses that made him look owlish, had gone to live in Belfast where he was studying at the university.

Davey Adams was God knows where; she'd heard that Nora Adams had gone to join her sister in Dublin. If it was true that Eileen was going to take up her place at the Uni after all, then that was the end. They'd all have drifted off like snow under a sudden sun.

Eileen appeared from the dark recesses of the church and made her way towards her. 'Have you seen anything of Tandy and Jack?'

'I haven't seen hide nor hair of them. Were they at mass?'

Eileen nodded. 'I saw the pair of them at the back of the aisle. They may have gone out by the rear door.' As she spoke, Jack and Tandy walked round the corner of the building and came towards them. Theresa found her heart thumping. She was suddenly anxious about this meeting; she hadn't been friendly at the wedding reception. Her chin tilted and her back straightened in an effort to hide her feelings.

Tandy eased the moment by hugging both girls and saying, 'Isn't it great to be together again, even if only for a short time.'

Jack and Theresa looked at each other. 'I second that,' Jack said softly, and smiled gently at her.

184

'Now then,' Tandy continued. 'What are the plans for the day?'

'I fancy a picnic on the beach,' said Theresa, willing to enter into things. She had no intention of letting Jack know how he'd hurt her.

'It will be rather crowded. It's the height of the summer, remember,' Eileen said doubtfully.

'I know a strip of sandy beach on the other side of Lafferty's Cove,' said Theresa. Now that she was going to England it no longer mattered that she should share her secret place.

'Why do we not know of this magical place?' It was Tandy who asked the question.

'I found it by accident,' said Theresa. 'It's partially hidden from the top road by a bluff. People never see beyond Lafferty's Cove where the beach starts to get very rocky.'

'You mean all these years we have lived here we didn't know of this strip of sand? How long have you known?' Jack eyed her curiously.

'Look!' said Theresa with defiance. 'Do you want to picnic or not? I'm not going to be the subject of an inquisition, for goodness' sake.'

'We're on,' said Tandy hastily. He could see the famous Theresa Brady eyes begin to look stormy. He dragged on Jack's arm. 'We'll see you there at three o'clock. Jack's coming home with me for lunch.' He grinned. 'I take it that you two lovely girls are going to supply the food?' It was thus arranged.

Later, as Theresa and Eileen lay on their towels and the two men swam, Theresa brought up the question of Eileen's plans to go to university after all.

Eileen looked embarrassed. 'I was going to tell you. I wish Tandy hadn't mentioned it. You would have been the first to know had not Tandy brought up the subject at the reception.'

'What changed your mind?'

Eileen hesitated. She had also another plan for the future, but she was still so uncertain about it she felt reluctant to discuss it; anyway, her parents had the right to know before anyone else.

'I love children . . .'

'I know that,' Theresa interrupted. 'You always have. That can't have done it.'

'It was part of it,' Eileen continued. 'The idea of teaching them began to appeal to me, and the more I thought about it the more the idea grew that I would enjoy primary school work.'

'Eileen! I've known you all my life. I know when you are keeping something back. Let's hear the other part that you've missed out.'

Eileen looked uncomfortable. 'I don't know what you mean. I—'

'Eileen!'

'Theresa Brady, why is it I can't keep anything from you? You always seem to worm things out of me.'

'So there is something.' Theresa frowned. 'What would you want to keep from me?'

'It's something that I feel I should discuss with my parents first.'

Eileen's eyes looked pleadingly at her friend, but Theresa persisted. 'What is your big secret – and for that matter, why are you suddenly not concerned that Tandy lives over the water? Not long ago you were having visions of having his babies.'

'I was not. That was your interpretation. If you must know,' she burst out, 'I'm going to take the veil.'

Theresa looked at her in shock. 'What!'

Eileen folded her arms, her gentle face looking worried. 'I did want my parents to know first; but as you've got it out of me I'll explain. The fact is, I began to realize that I was happiest when I was helping out in church. I feel a peace there that fills me with contentment, and one day, after hours of prayer, I suddenly knew what I was going to do with my life.'

'Was this brought on by Tandy's departure?'

'It had to do with a lot of things. There has been change all round. Tandy and Jack went away; you spend a lot of time at the stables; the group broke up . . . But mostly it was because I did more work in the church as you were no longer around. I found I really enjoyed the quiet solitude which gave me time to pray, and time to think.'

Theresa laid her hand on Eileen's. 'God! Eileen. I'm sorry.'

'Because I want to serve God?' Eileen asked, shocked.

'No, you eejut! Because I forced this out of you.' She should have guessed Eileen would become a nun, she reflected. 'You were never really happy with the things I got up to. When I think of the things I made you do . . .'

'I don't think Himself up there will hold it against either of us,' Eileen laughed. She felt great relief now that Theresa knew of her intentions. 'You mustn't breathe a word, Theresa.'

'I promise.'

Jack and Tandy arrived back, dripping with sea water, and began to towel themselves dry before delving into the thickly buttered barnbracks and currant scones and jam donated by Eileen's mother. Theresa's contribution was the fat seed cake and fruit followed by home-made lemonade.

'This is the life,' laughed Tandy. 'I keep telling them over in

186

England that they don't know they're living if they haven't tasted Irish baking.'

'What do you do over in Sussex in the evenings?' asked Theresa.

It was Eileen who dropped the bombshell. 'He has a girlfriend called Fliss,' she said, 'and they spend a lot of time in the local pub.'

Tandy caught her glance and they both broke into a peal of laughter at the look on the other's face.

'I told Eileen about Fliss yesterday. She didn't mind a bit,' said Tandy.

'Not a bit,' Eileen agreed, but failed to admit to the relief that had flooded her when he'd made the confession the day before. It was then that she had told him her own news, and today they felt more relaxed in each other's company than they had ever done before.

'Is that her real name?' asked Theresa.

'She's called Felicity Tate, but as it's a bit of a mouthful I call her Fliss – I'm pretty serious about her,' Tandy added sheepishly.

Jack watched Eileen as she handed over another scone to Tandy. She really doesn't mind, he thought.

When the others had gone for a stroll along the beach, Jack turned towards Theresa. 'Have you any startling pronouncements to make?'

She shook her head. 'I'm going over to England, as you all know, and I am going to study Art and Design. That's it. What about you?'

'Nothing new,' he said. 'You know all about me.' He leaned back on to the sand and closed his eyes against the sun. He hoped that whatever had been ailing Theresa was now resolved.

Theresa looked down at the young man she loved, and her heart ached. He had a girlfriend whom he didn't see fit to tell her about, and yet he could lie with such ease and tell her there was nothing new.

She was glad she was going away soon. It would hurt less when she started her new life; meantime she would behave as though nothing was wrong. He would not know that she had visited him and seen him laughing and kissing a pretty girl.

Later, she asked casually if Eileen had mentioned that Pat McGarry had offered to host their joint birthdays at a swimming party and dance at his place. She hadn't.

'I heard he was having a swimming pool built – the daft kitter,' remarked Tandy. 'Sure, what does he want with a swimming pool when his farm is only a matter of two or three miles from the sea?'

'He never had room before, and he hates the crowds we get

187

during the summer. He says it's been a dream of his for years that he could come in from a day on the farm and just plunge into the pool to relax.'

'Why did he wait this long, then? He has the money,' insisted Tandy.

'But not the land near the house,' Theresa explained. 'Now that he has bought Gran's place he is able to move things round a bit. Anyway! When he was talking to my da a short while ago, he suggested hosting the party. Are you both able to come?'

'Certainly, if we are invited.'

'We haven't sent the invitations out yet,' said Theresa, 'but you two would have been first on the list.'

'I don't suppose the snooty girl with the style will be invited,' Tandy said teasingly.

'He means Moira Kennedy,' Theresa explained to Eileen.

'I recognise the description.' Eileen laughed, and went on to answer Tandy. 'We have no option. She invited Theresa to hers which was held at Lord Conliffe's place.'

'What about the boyo who was with her at the wedding?' Tandy had noticed his interest in Theresa.

'The invitation will say "and friend", and I don't care who she brings.'

'Who did you go with when you went to her birthday party?'

'Richard Beck.'

'The artist fella? Sure he's old enough to be your grandfather,' Tandy said, raising his eyebrows.

'But he's safe,' Theresa said, a note of caution in her voice. Tandy was going too far.

Jack rose and extended his hand to her. 'Will you walk along the beach with me?'

When they had gone a fair distance, he casually draped his arm round her shoulder. 'I've missed you,' he said.

Theresa tried to control the feelings that were running through her at the touch of his arm on her skin. 'And I've missed you, Jack. I expected you would be too busy to give a thought to me though, with all that goes on at the university.'

He was puzzled by her tone. 'What do you mean?'

'All the girls and the dancing, with a bit of study thrown in. Your life must be one grand round of parties and meetings these days.'

'It's true I find the days passing pleasantly – when I'm not studying.' He grinned. 'But I still have Theresa Brady in my thoughts most of the time.'

Do you? she thought bitterly. I wonder when. Aloud, she said, 'Well that's nice.'

188

'Nice! Is that all you can say?'

'How about this for a reaction then, Jack?' She turned in his arm and put both hers round his neck, pulling his head slowly towards her. She kissed him with a gentle but insistent ardour that caused him to tighten his hold and return it, but she forced her mind to block off the moment so that she didn't expose her true feelings. The kiss was expertly executed – she knew by his reaction. Fergal's lesson had been well learned. With a smile, she unfolded herself and said, quietly, 'So hold on to that, Jack, till we meet again.' She wondered if he would remember saying much the same thing to her some time ago.

CHAPTER 14

Colin and Nuala were sitting in the tiny garden at the back of the house. The drone of bees was such that the sound almost drowned out what Nuala had just said.

Colin leaned nearer. 'I didn't hear that remark,' he said. 'You'll have to speak above the noise of those bees.' He swiped at one that was trying to settle on his upturned face. 'I'm going to dig up that sedum bush,' he said crossly. 'They regard it as home.'

The noise wasn't that bad, thought Nuala. She had noticed just lately that Colin seemed to be saying 'pardon?' a lot. She raised her voice a little. 'I wondered if you thought our Theresa was going around in a daze. She looks unhappy at times.'

'I hadn't noticed. I think you're imagining it; sure she's got what she wanted – thanks to you and Richard Beck. She's off to England shortly and no doubt she has plans to have the time of her life. Why should she feel unhappy?'

'I just wondered – I expect you're right. I worry too much.' Nuala didn't pursue the matter further. The subject of Theresa going to England was a touchy one. Colin still felt he had been railroaded into the agreement – and that it was costing him too much money. She had been surprised at his capitulation, especially since the trip across the water seemed to have put his mind at rest.

Settling back into her deck chair she turned her face to the sun. It wasn't often she got the chance to do this; she must make the most of it. She made a mental note to have a chat with Theresa.

There was silence for a time, till Colin said, 'How are the arrangements for the party going on your side of things?'

'My side of things?' Nuala gave a derisive laugh. 'There is *only* my side of things, Colin Brady. You aren't doing a tap about the arrangements.'

'I've had a word with McGrath about his ceili band, and I've arranged for some of the bigger lads to set up the tables and blow up a few balloons – and don't forget the fairy lights: I've arranged for them to be strung up the night before.'

'All verbal! But who has the bulk to do? Kathleen and I have all the invitations to write out, the baking and the cooking to do, the tables to pile up with food . . . need I go on?'

'You're a martyr to the cause.' Colin grinned. 'You love it all. I've done my bit, though. The rest is up to the women.'

It was always the way; the men got away with murder while the women made life easier for them. We women should have changed things years ago Nuala thought. The trouble was that things took longer to catch on in this dozy, pleasant country, and somehow they had missed the boat – at least her generation had. She noticed that the young were becoming more influenced by what was happening abroad, and were beginning to stand up for themselves. Good luck to them. Theresa might be considered to be a bit of a handful at times, but by God there was enough spark in her to stand up to any man.

'I'm dying of druth,' said Colin, smacking his lips. 'How about a nice mug of tea?'

Nuala rose immediately. 'So much for progress – old habits die hard.' She watched Colin lie back in his chair waiting for her to quench his thirst. With a sigh of exasperation she laid her hand on the door latch and pressed it down.

The exam results had come. Theresa and Eileen had gained the requisite grades to enable them to take up their places at university. Eileen was relieved.

'I told you that you'd pass with flying colours,' said Theresa.

'I wouldn't say that. You're the one with the grand marks,' Eileen replied, but she was pleased with her results all the same.

Theresa, watching Eileen's glowing face, wondered for a moment if she had done the right thing by passing up the chance of going to university with her. She could have studied Art in Dublin just as well as England; in fact, it would have been easier all round. The thought came and went quickly. She needed to get away from Tullybra, to meet life head on and cope with her mistakes and successes her own way. She craved freedom, even at the expense of being lonely.

Jack and Tandy took them out for a celebratory meal in Kilgaven. They went to the same restaurant that Jack had taken Eileen to some months before, and she glowed with importance as she pointed out the decor and showed Theresa where the toilets were.

'Is your middle name Moira, by any chance?' laughed Theresa.

192

Eileen blushed at her attempt at oneupmanship. 'I am showing off a bit,' she giggled.

It was a wonderful meal. Afterwards, as there was little to do in Kilgaven, they got into the car and drove back to Tullybra for a walk along the sand.

It was a warm and sultry evening. The sun had long ago dipped below the horizon and the moon, having taken its place, was casting mysterious shadows along the rocks, tipping the lightly crested waves with silver.

As they walked, Jack put Theresa's arm in his and she held her breath for a moment, feeling a pulse beating in her throat. She tried to pull away. He stopped and looked at her. The others had forged ahead and were but two wavering, moonlit shapes in the distance.

'Why did you try to withdraw your arm? Don't you feel comfortable about it being there?'

What could she tell him? I saw you with that girl? Has her arm been where mine is now? Could she say that if things had been different there would be nothing she wanted more, and perhaps, later, let him take her in his arms and kiss her as he had done before, till her mouth softened under his and her heart burst out of her chest? She had had a taste of what it was like to be held and kissed by him, and she wanted more. What she did not want was to be used for a while because his Pat was not around.

'I'm quite content,' she said.

They walked along in silence. Jack was puzzled by the change in her attitude. He had been certain that the last time he had kissed her she had returned it with fervour. The spectre of Fergal rose. He was obviously not measuring up to the tinker, with his lean, virile body that was honed by the wild life he led roaming the country.

'Let's catch up with the other two.' He removed her arm and took her hand instead, pulling her along at speed and giving himself no time to conjure up any more unwelcome pictures in his mind.

Later that week Theresa and Eileen were in Dublin, togging themselves up for the birthday party. They had raced round the shops looking at accessories and now felt exhausted and in need of sustenance. It was Theresa's intention to go into the nearest pub for lunch. In Dublin not a soul would lift an eyebrow, so she was surprised that the usually malleable Eileen should so forcibly refuse to follow her plan.

'A café will do me well,' said Eileen firmly.

'Come on! What is the matter with you?'

193

'I'm not going into a pub and that's that. I don't feel comfortable in them. If you want to have a drink you can order a glass of wine with the meal.'

'In a café?'

'We'll go to a restaurant then, I don't mind; but I am not going into a pub!'

'You've not taken the veil yet!' Theresa had mixed feelings about Eileen's stand. It was irritating that she wasn't getting her own way, yet it was an impressive sight to see the rosy cheeks getting rosier as Eileen firmly held her resolve.

'Oh all right! A restaurant it is. I haven't the time to argue. I still have a pair of shoes to buy.'

Eileen's aunt Margaret had come up trumps again. She had kitted them out in dresses that were suited to their personality and colouring.

'You should always consider your personality when buying clothes,' she instructed. 'For instance, could you see our Eileen in a low-cut, sexy dress? it would be like dressing a nun in floating voile.' Aunt Margaret laughed.

Eileen was miffed at the idea that she was not seen as being able to carry off a risqué style, nevertheless she could see the sense of it and smiled.

For her, the choice was a mint green shirt blouse with a white skirt. For Theresa, with her dark hair and creamy skin, Margaret had suggested a deep blue dress with short sleeves and a full skirt.

'You both look beautiful,' she observed.

The girls looked critically at each other.

'It's a pity Aunt Margaret can't come to our party,' said Eileen on the way home. 'Surely she could have managed one day off?'

Theresa nodded but remained silent. She had a feeling that Eileen's aunt was in trouble. She'd heard her on the telephone having a rather frantic conversation with someone. The one sentence that stuck in her mind was: 'I'm one hundred per cent certain that there will be an upturn. It's just a cash-flow problem.' Margaret had hastily held the receiver in the palm of her hand as she caught sight of Theresa, and said, 'Go into the sitting room; I shan't be a moment.' Her smile had been distracted.

Theresa wasn't entirely certain how cash flow affected profits, but she thought the business might be in trouble.

Nuala liked the dress. 'I knew we could rely on Margaret's good taste. The woman always makes me feel dowdy, she wears such lovely clothes when she visits Kathleen.'

Theresa said, 'I've always thought you had very good taste, Mam. You always look good.'

'You wouldn't be prejudiced, would you?'

194

'Certainly not! I'd die the death if you went round looking like Biddy Devlin. I'd soon tell you if you were makin' a cod of me. You always look nice. Even Father Corke remarked on it.' Theresa's heart nearly stopped as she realized her mistake. Unfortunately her mother caught her up on what she'd said.

'What are you on about? Why would Father Corke discuss my mode of dress with you?'

'He was complimenting me at the time,' said Theresa, trying to keep the panic from her voice. 'It was at one of the dances. He said he liked the dress I was wearing and remarked that I took after you for good taste.'

'That was nice of him – unusual, but nice. I must thank him some time.'

'Oh! I wouldn't, Mam, really. The poor man was mortified that he had spoken in such a personal manner. I think he would be embarrassed.'

'I suppose you're right,' said Nuala thoughtfully. 'Still! It was a nice compliment. It has quite set me up for the day. Now, away with you and get yourself sorted out for the party tomorrow.'

Theresa made her escape. God! She had a mouth on her as big as a carp.

Theresa and Eileen had been holding combined birthday parties the whole of their lives, but never on a scale such as this.

When they had been told that Pat McGarry had offered to stage it at the side of his new swimming pool they had been completely knocked back by the idea, and looking round now they were ecstatic.

The invitations had included the instruction to bring a bathing costume, so now they were praying that the weather wouldn't change. It didn't. The day was hot and sunny. The kind of sunny that made things shimmer.

They stood on the large, newly built patio and awaited the arrival of the first guests. Theresa wished that Richard could have come, but he had an exhibition in London. He had sent her a handsome cheque with his apologies.

The pool looked cool and inviting, and the chairs and deck-chairs dotted around colourfully matched the umbrellas which shaded the white tables along the edge.

Larger tables lined the patio, white-robed with linen cloths and heaped with food covered by muslins and shaded by the house from the hot sun. The bar was set up by the large patio windows, and was framed by fairy lights, as was the side of the house, so that the evening dancing would be well lit for those who wished to stay.

'Isn't this grand?' breathed Eileen. 'I'll be able to store this memory forever when I'm – when I'm . . .' She faltered.

'When you're what?'

Eileen swallowed. She had nearly said 'when I'm a nun'. She laughed shakily. 'When I'm an old lady.' Theresa's mother was standing close by. It was essential that no one else should know of her plans. She was still at the crossroads herself. Anything could happen – she could change her mind, and then where would she be? She would look a right fool.

Theresa gave her friend a look of exasperation. There were times when Eileen's dithery nature tried her patience. She was diverted by the arrival of a car.

Eileen's mind was still on the problem of telling her parents about her decision, and she continued to stare into space. Her mam was always on about how she was looking forward to having grandchildren, and telling her friends how Eileen, with her way with children, would make a wonderful mother. Parents could be a drag at times. Eileen came to with a start as Theresa, seeing her vacant gaze, dug her in the ribs.

Guests were now beginning to arrive by the carload, and within the next hour the place became alive with noise and laughter as many of the young people splashed about in the pool. Theresa was still greeting latecomers. Finally, she was able to change into her costume and join the other bathers. Eileen preferred not to swim, and watched from the terrace.

Jack and Tandy had arrived early and were already the centre of attention. The young trainee doctor was a great catch; Tandy qualified for equal attention because of his good looks and charm.

Theresa, hair flattened and saturated, took a breather and sat next to Eileen just as a large black car was parking in the field. Moira Kennedy and Ross Carling had arrived.

'Trust the fair Moira to make an entrance,' remarked Theresa, conscious of her own soaked appearance as she went forward to greet them.

Her smile broadened as she greeted Ross Carling, and she left Eileen to direct Moira to the house to change while she showed Ross to the bar.

'Happy birthday,' he grinned. 'I see you both have a heap of presents. Mine will be lost in that lot.'

'We are going to open them later. There are too many to manage before the sun goes down.' Theresa grinned. 'I thought you weren't coming – you were so late.'

'Moira's father had the car and he got delayed. His own is out of order.'

At that moment Moira came out of the house wearing a stunning white and gold trimmed two-piece which showed off her tan. Theresa could have killed her. I don't care if I am being unreasonable, she thought. The girl has everything. She caught Eileen's eyes and made a face.

Eileen looked away. She had guessed, when she saw Moira coming from the bedroom looking as she did, that Theresa would be irritated. If only Moira could be nice with it, she thought. That was what made Theresa mad. Moira's attitude was always one of haughty awareness of her wealth and her worth.

It was noticeable that many of those in the pool had momentarily stopped their jauntering to look in Moira's direction. Fully aware of the interest she was creating, she sauntered down to the pool like a model going down the catwalk, greeting those she knew with a cool smile and a regal wave.

Theresa, hoping the girl would trip over her upturned nose, watched as she reached the pool to be met by Jack. She turned to Ross Carling.

'Well! That was safely negotiated,' she said with a touch of malice, which was not lost on him.

'She loves making an entrance, does Moira.' Ross was amused by Theresa's overt dislike. 'She really isn't too bad, you know,' he added.

'Well, she obviously hasn't read Dale Carnegie's book on *How to Win Friends and Influence People*, that's for sure.' Theresa took his arm. 'Why don't you get changed and we'll join them in the pool?'

By late afternoon all animosity was forgotten. Everyone was having too much of a good time. Ross Carling was paying flattering close attention to Theresa, who was opening out under the warmth of his regard. She laughed and splashed and, when the pool emptied and the guests made their way to the laden tables, she swam up and down with her strong strokes and excellent technique, completely unaware that she was being watched in admiration.

'Where did you learn to swim like that?' asked Ross, when she eventually joined him with a plateful of food.

'Self taught,' she mumbled, her mouth full of delicious chicken.

'You are competition standard. Surely someone has noticed.'

'The sisters have, but they aren't heavily into competition swimming. Do you really think I'm that good?'

'First class.'

They were joined by Jack, Tandy and Eileen.

'Where's Moira?' asked Theresa.

'She's joining us shortly. She's getting dressed.'

'That means the game is up for me,' sighed Ross.

'Are you coming back for the dance this evening?'

'Certainly.'

Jack and Tandy were staying. Everyone else except family and close friends left for home; most would be returning later. Those in the village who hadn't been there in the afternoon were invited to the dance in the evening.

'It went very well,' remarked Pat McGarry.

'Couldn't have been better,' agreed Colin. 'Mind you, that pool of yours is what made it a success. Fancy having that all to yourself – the sheer luxury of it makes the mind boggle.'

They were relaxing on the patio, where the heat of the sun was less intense. Eileen's parents were leaving because they had to take over from the friend who had been looking after the shop for them.

'Do you mind if we don't attend this evening?' Kathleen said. 'It isn't really our kind of thing, and there's a lot to do to get the stock sorted out for Monday.'

Eileen already knew that her parents wouldn't be staying. 'I'm sure everyone understands, Mam,' she said.

There was a chorus of assent.

Pat McGarry simply waved his hand. He was studying Theresa. His eyes began to comb every inch of her, under cover of the leave-taking. His mind was a mess of uncertainty and tension. His head ached.

Seeing her in the pool when everyone else had left, he had noticed the large birthmark on her left shoulder blade, the sight of which had left him stunned. The significance of it didn't bear thinking about. He hoped he was mistaken. At some time during the evening he had to speak to Nuala, whatever the cost.

To take his mind off his thoughts he turned to Colin. 'What you were saying just now about me having the pool to myself . . .'

'Yes?'

'You're right. It's a terrible waste. I've been thinking about it while you were all chatting. I'll open it to the villagers on certain days of the week. Do you think the young ones at least would make the two-mile trip?'

'Not in the summer, man,' said Colin mildly, 'and in the spring and autumn it would be too cold.'

'I'll have it heated.'

'That'll cost you something, Pat.'

'Man, I can well afford it. Sure what do I have to spend my money on? I rattle around in this great house on my own. It would be nice to hear a bit of life and laughter around the place.'

'What do you fellas think?' Colin, taking his pipe from his mouth, addressed the two lads.

'Great idea!' said Tandy. 'I wish you'd thought of it before Jack and I left for the great world outside.'

'You, Jack?'

'Like Tandy says, great idea.'

'That's it, then. I'll get Father Corke to announce it from the pulpit at the mass.'

'I think the world and his wife are here tonight,' Colin remarked to Nuala. 'Have we enough drink? You know what the lads are like if their throats aren't slaked.'

'Pat has been very generous. He threw in enough Guinness to turn the Liffey black,' Nuala replied. To make certain, they toured the tables and counted the remaining crates in the barn.

Huge boards had been hired, and they were now bouncing with the tramp of feet performing reels and jigs.

McGrath's ceili band had been hired again. He travelled the width and breadth of Ireland, and they were lucky to have him.

Theresa watched as Jack and Moira partnered each other for the Haymakers' Jig, and her heart felt dead at the sight.

During the afternoon she and Jack had spoken civilly to each other, but they were both aware of the tension between them.

Jack was bewildered. He could think of nothing that he had done to change her from the girl who had kissed him willingly the night they'd done the Mile walk to the girl who was now being so coldly polite. He had tried to break the tension but was only partially successful. Just for a moment he had seen her soften, but then just as suddenly the coolness descended again and he was shut out. He gave up trying. He could see no purpose in cutting his own throat.

Theresa was staring moodily at the dancers. She jumped as Ross Carling spoke. 'That looks easy. Next time it comes up how about us having a go?'

'I'll get a two-step going,' she smiled. 'You'll be able to cope with that.'

'Would you like to bet? I tried Irish dancing at Moira's ball if you remember. I had two left feet.'

'You were not too bad!' Theresa lied. 'Anyway, a two-step is easy.'

'I still have two left feet,' he grinned.

'In that case, come round the back of the big barn and we'll have a practice. I'm not making a cod of myself if you can't dance.'

Jack saw them go and felt hurt. It hadn't taken long for Theresa to find a replacement. He swung Moira round, laughing with forced glee, and was rewarded by one of her special looks. Moira was a good-looking girl. It was obvious she liked him. He would be mad not to respond.

Eileen, watching from the sidelines with Tandy by her side, felt uneasy. There was something brewing between Jack and Theresa. She knew how much Jack meant to Theresa, and she was at a loss to understand why her friend had disappeared behind the barn with Ross Carling. God help her if her father caught her.

Later, during the two-step, Theresa and Ross had a grand time. He had been a quick learner and his body followed the music on time, his feet surprising light.

'You had better have some time with Moira,' Theresa said, gasping for breath. She had noticed the black looks she had been getting.

'Moira is doing very well with your friend,' replied Ross. 'I'm only here to chauffeur her. She has designs on that young man.'

'I've just heard that Moira Kennedy has designs on Jack,' said Theresa furiously to Eileen when Ross had begun to circulate.

'I didn't think you cared. I've been feeling sorry for Jack for the way you've been treating him. You'll get no sympathy from me.' Eileen walked away, leaving Theresa standing alone.

Furious at the turn of events, Theresa strode towards the barn. She suddenly felt the need to sit somewhere quiet and sort out her thoughts.

She walked silently through the door into the aromatic, shadowy darkness. Most of the hay had been gathered in and the bales were stacked high, forming sinister looking shapes in the gloom.

She shivered and was about to walk out again when she heard the unmistakable voice of Pat McGarry cry out: 'Jesus! How could you have done this to me, Nuala?'

She froze. There was a short silence and then her mother spoke, her voice low but agonized.

'I didn't know when I married Colin that I was pregnant. I swear. Once I was married there seemed no point in anyone knowing.'

'Surely I had a right to know. Jesus! Theresa is my daughter. You have denied me.'

'I have denied you nothing. You had every chance to marry me, Pat. I longed for it. I waited and waited, but all you wanted of me was a companion to racket around the country with you.'

'I loved you. You know I did.' Pat's voice was wild with hurt.

200

'We made love together. Would we have done that if we hadn't loved each other?'

'One time!' said Nuala bitterly. 'Just one time, and then, if you remember, you met a girl from Dublin and I was left.'

'She meant nothing to me.'

'Am I a mind reader? You didn't even seem to care that I'd met Colin and had started going out with him. Were you so sure of me that you didn't let your feelings show?'

'I was devastated when you chose Colin. How was I to know that you were pregnant and needed a father for our child? Why didn't you tell me? I would have married you. I loved you.'

'You stupid man! I keep telling you: I chose Colin Brady because I was falling in love with him – maybe on the rebound, I don't know – but I did not, and I repeat, did *not* marry him for any other reason. I didn't know I was pregnant. I loved him then and I love him now, and if you ever say a word about this I will kill myself. I couldn't bear the hurt he would have – and my Theresa would never forgive me, either.

'I won't do anything about it now.' Pat's voice sounded bitter and tired. 'Sure where is the point of ruining everyone's life? But I have spent all these lonely years without a wife and child, for no one could take your place.'

'I'm sorry you had to find out. I didn't realize the significance of the birthmark. I wouldn't have hurt you for the world. You must understand that I love Colin Brady and I will till the day I die. I'm sorry.'

There was heavy silence till Pat spoke again. 'All's been said. We must get back to the party before we are missed.' His voice sounded dull and resigned.

Theresa crouched back into the corner as they passed. She was so close she could have touched her mother's dress. One sound and all was lost.

As soon as they had gone she sat down on the floor, uncaring that her lovely dress was getting dirty. Tears rolled as she sobbed. Her world had fallen to pieces. The wild, proud Theresa Brady had been toppled.

Suddenly she felt herself being lifted, and a pair of arms held her close. The dearest voice in the world spoke. 'Don't! Don't! It breaks my heart to know that you heard this and must be suffering. I hoped you would never know.'

Theresa put her arms round her father's waist – only he wasn't her father – and sobbed uncontrollably. This didn't seem real. It was like a play on the radio. She had lost all sense of where she was. Her life was ruined. The sounds from outside drifted round her and she wanted none of it. Music and laughter had no place here.

Colin drew her further into the shadows and held her till she'd cried herself out. His heart bled for her pain. There was nothing he could do until she had finished and was able to listen. For years he'd had nightmares that such a scenario would happen, but still he was unprepared.

'How long have you been here?' she asked at last, her voice thick with tears. 'It must have been just as big a shock for you.'

'No. You see, I've known for years that you were not mine. I had no proof, but I suspected you were Pat's child.'

Theresa's body stiffened against his. 'How did you know?'

Colin stroked her hair and explained, his voice gentle. 'I assumed that you had been conceived on our honeymoon, and when you arrived I fell madly in love with you. When that little hand of yours clutched my fingers you wound yourself round my heart. I adored you.' He paused, remembering the moment.

'So when and how did you find out?'

'It was some time later. I enjoyed you so much I wanted more children. When, after four years, nothing happened, I decided to have a test. I knew it couldn't be your mother's fault as she had already conceived, so I had to assume that something had happened that stopped me producing.'

He kissed her hair. 'When the results came back, I was told I could never father a child. I probed further and discovered that – according to the experts – I had never been able to do so. That was when I realized that you couldn't be mine.'

'And you never had it out with Mam?'

'There seemed little point in ruining all our lives. I loved you and I knew that, although I had not been your biological father, I was more than that. I was the one who had changed your nappy and skelped your bum when you were naughty, and it was I who had helped influence your character.' Colin held her from him. 'You do understand that she must never know we overheard all this.'

'How can you love her, knowing what she did?'

'When you love someone as deeply as I do, you forgive all. You heard your mother. She didn't know she was pregnant. She married me for love and she loves me still. I will not lose that, not for all the world. She had already finished with Pat because of his philandering, and we had already decided to marry. I think that the one time she and Pat made love was shortly before our wedding. I can't blame her. She loved Pat – in a way, she still does. I have to live with that.' He hugged her close. 'I don't want to lose you. I love you both to death.'

Theresa sighed heavily. 'I'll try not to let it make any difference. I won't ever let on I know – I promise.'

'That's my girl. Now let's go out. No one will notice that you have been crying. It's dark now and the lights aren't too bright.'

Theresa spoke, her voice laden with sorrow. 'I'm glad I'm going over to England soon. I'll be less likely to let anything slip. If I had to stay here I think I couldn't keep up the pretence. I hope I can find it in me to forgive mam for what I am feeling at this moment. My birthday has been ruined!'

Father and daughter walked out of the barn. One feeling bitter, the other feeling gut sad at the outcome of a day which had started with such optimism and joy.

CHAPTER 15

At last! She was here, making her own way – in charge of her own life. Theresa could hardly believe it. A feeling of exhilaration ran through her.

Things had become very strained at home after the scene she had witnessed in Pat McGarry's barn. It was only the pleading in her father's eyes that stopped her from confronting her mother on at least two occasions when Nuala had complained of her attitude. The fact that she had only a few short weeks to spend with them before she set sail for England helped, and when she became tense she headed for Lafferty's Cove to lie behind the rocks and try to calm her own riotous thoughts.

The strain had eventually told, and on the night before she left her mother had come to her room, concerned, she said, by Theresa's obvious unhappiness. Theresa had wanted to laugh hysterically as her mother counselled her in the belief that she was frightened of going over to England, away from all she had grown up with. Jesus! She couldn't wait to get away.

There was a shift in the lines awaiting registration and Theresa brought her thoughts back to bear on the job in hand. She lifted the handsome case, filled with all the artist materials she would need, and moved forward with the line. The case had been bought with Richard's present to her for her eighteenth birthday.

She looked carelessly around. The only art students she had known had been those at the convent, with their neat uniforms covered by green linen aprons worn to protect their clothes. Suddenly she was aware that she stood out in her slacks and her woollen jumper with its matching spencer, and her face reddened when two young men passed by and one said with a grin, 'Like it! Like it!' She guessed they were referring to her style of dress.

The others were wearing clothes that, though rather old, had a certain style to them – baggy jumpers, well-worn skirts or trousers; shoes that were heavy but comfortable and strictly functional. Some of the girls wore bandannas to hold back their long hair and all had the look of belonging. She felt embarrassed by her own neatness, and regretted the beautiful case at her feet as the other students in line swung capacious bags over their shoulders to move along.

At last, as she stood by the wall wondering what to do next, she noticed a tall blonde girl weaving towards her. She watched her approach in fascination. She walked as though her hips were on special hinges; the long legs crossing, one in front of the other over an imaginary central line. Just like a model on the catwalk.

'Hello!' said the vision. 'You look lost.'

Relieved at hearing a friendly voice, Theresa laughed, her natural honesty coming to the fore. 'I'm not only feeling lost. I'm also embarrassed by my clothes.'

The girl held out her hand. 'I'm Polly Armstrong. I come from Southampton.'

Theresa shook it gratefully. 'Theresa Brady – from Tullybra.'

'I take it that Tullybra is in Ireland, judging by your accent.'

Theresa nodded.

'Let's go for a cup of something in the canteen,' said Polly. 'Nothing much will be happening today except for a rather boring introduction to the course and the tutors. All we need to know is in the timetable we've been given.'

'But won't we be expected to—'

'We aren't at school any more,' smiled Polly. We are considered to be adult enough to make our own decisions. It's up to us how much we put into it. If absenteeism gets too bad, of course, then there would be reprisal because it could reflect on the college if the exam results are bad, but providing we act within reason, the extent of our commitment is our responsibility.'

They had reached the canteen and Polly fetched tea and a sticky bun each. Theresa fumbled in her purse but Polly stopped her. 'Don't worry; it will be your turn tomorrow. After that, it's everyone for themselves. Funds are short. Nice case, by the way.'

'A present from a friend.'

'Full of artist's materials?'

'Yes!'

'Get rid,' Polly advised, and smiled to soften the effect of her words.

'Too pretentious?'

'Much – most of us can only afford the basic colours.'

'I think I shall need a canvas bag,' Theresa grinned.

'And a couple of baggy jumpers and a couple of men's shirts to use as smocks – would you like me to come with you?'

'I'd appreciate it.'

Polly, Theresa discovered, lived in a rented room near the

Oval. Her parents helped to pay the rent and Polly had to take whatever small jobs she could find to cover the rest. She helped out in the canteen, and also had a job in a pub in Peckham, which she cycled to most evenings on an ancient old bike.

Theresa often invited her over to The Grange. Mrs Beatty had no objection. She was glad to see that Theresa had a friend, and usually spoiled them both by making a special supper. Polly loved these visits, she told Theresa. 'What with the food I cadge at the pub and the suppers I get from Mrs Beatty, I'll have less chance of starving in my garret.' She laughed as she said it, but Theresa knew she meant every word. She realized how fortunate she was having a friend like Richard and parents who could afford to send her some decent pocket money.

Polly loved to hear about Theresa's life in Tullybra. She told her of her friend Fergal the tinker, of the restraints set upon the young people, who had to conform to Father Corke's principles, and the even tighter controls set by the parents. She told her of her own wayward nature and her great desire for freedom from restriction of all kinds.

Polly was entranced by it all, her favourite story being the feud between Theresa and Pat Maher the school bus driver. She wondered why such an attractive girl as this should have no romantic attachments and then decided, from what she had heard so far, that a relationship like that would be taboo at such an age, in a small, isolated village.

Theresa made no mention of her relationship with Jack, except to say that he was her special friend.

'It must be like living in a time warp,' Polly remarked, adding hastily, 'No offence meant.'

Once Theresa would have been on the defensive at such a remark, but as the weeks passed she had begun to look back on the last few years with a fondness for the innocence of it all. She had become nostalgic for those times, especially after receiving a letter from Eileen, who wrote that she was now getting used to Dublin, its cosmopolitan atmosphere and its 'air of mild decadence' – Eileen's own words. She wrote also that she had ceased to be shocked at what went on in the city and indeed within the university. It was a different life altogether. She saw Jack occasionally, who had mentioned to her that he had written to Theresa. Eileen wanted to know why the poor fool hadn't received at least a postcard in reply.

Theresa frowned when she'd read the letter. She had forgotten that she hadn't written. She had meant to – Jack was still her friend even if he had broken her heart. The mention of his name brought back feelings she had managed to put out of her mind with the help of the crowded life she now led.

Over here, she was learning that among her contemporaries, relationships came and went with alarming speed. Polly saw her men off with regularity, and was quickly on to the next. It said something for the sophisticated nature of the girl that they never bore her any ill will, and all remained loyal.

She introduced Theresa to the art of surviving on a low income – one of the ploys being to go up to Lyons Corner House at Marble Arch, where they could pile a plate as high as they liked with various salads for two shillings – which Polly did. Once back at the table she would produce an extra plate from under her jacket and they'd share the meal.

Christmas was spent at The Grange. Theresa couldn't face the prospect of going home, and had excused herself on the grounds that she had her first project to complete and was behind with it.

Her mother wrote to say she understood and that she would send her presents over with Richard, who was going to London for Christmas. Theresa wrote to Richard at once and asked if Polly could spend Christmas with them.

He rang her to tell her that it was fine with him. 'Why are you not coming home?' he asked. 'I don't believe that tale you gave your parents.'

'I had a row with Mam before I came away. I don't want to spoil their Christmas by being moody. I'll go over in the summer.'

Richard paused. 'Well! It's between you and your parents, but think about what you are doing to them.'

It was a success. Richard fell for Polly's charm.

'Have you ever done any modelling?' he asked one evening.

'I've done the catwalk – in a small way,' said Polly. 'I needed the money to finance my course.'

'How could you do modelling while still at school?' asked Theresa.

'I'm twenty-two years old,' Polly laughed. 'I'm what is called a mature student.'

'You don't look twenty-two.'

'Twenty-two isn't that old. I'm not approaching my dotage.'

Richard spoke again. 'I mean an artist's model – not the catwalk.'

'I haven't done that – but I wouldn't mind; Theresa and I could do with the money if *she* was willing.'

Richard and Theresa laughed. 'Theresa is an old hand at this,' he said. 'She has already posed for me. My partner will be showing the picture in the spring.'

'What!' Polly listened in astonishment as Theresa recounted the story of her first meeting with Richard – and the outcome.

★ ★ ★

By the end of the spring term, Theresa and Polly were established models. Richard's initial contacts had been followed by other offers, some of which had to be turned down because of their course work. Polly no longer needed an evening job. Theresa was particularly pleased about this because it meant that she had her friend with her when she attended the many parties that someone was always throwing.

It was at one of these parties that she ran into Ross Carling. They caught sight of each other simultaneously.

'God! You are the last person I expected to see here. Are you a friend of Simon Godfrey?' He clasped her firmly to him and hugged her.

'Who is Simon Godfrey?' she laughed. 'I came with my friend, Polly – she's the one who knows everyone. I just go along for the experience.'

'You'll get it here,' he frowned. 'Be very careful what you get up to. Don't smoke a cigarette if it's handed to you.'

Puzzled by his advice, she said, 'I don't smoke – never have.'

'You don't have to be a smoker to use these ones. They have a special function. Look, you innocent. They are doped fags.'

At that moment she looked across at Polly. She didn't smoke either, but she was now taking a puff from her neighbour's cigarette before passing it on.

'Why don't we get out of here and go and have a drink somewhere? I want to know all that's been happening to you.' Ross raised his eyebrows at Theresa.

'I'll get my coat,' she said. She walked over to Polly and explained that she was going out and would see her at the college next day. Polly waved vaguely and smiled.

When they were settled in a quiet corner of a nearby pub, Ross said, 'Tell all. I haven't seen you since your eighteenth birthday bash.'

'I don't know where to start – so much has happened in the last few months. I'm enjoying my course, and especially my freedom.' Her tone became wistful. 'I do miss parts of my life in Tullybra, though. I miss Eileen and my other friends. I miss my cove and the secret swims I used to have there at night. I miss my parents . . . and do you know what?'

Ross smiled. 'What?'

'I sorely miss Father Corke, my old adversary. He was the one who put me right when I set off on one of my capers.'

'Do you need his help over here, then?'

'No! Certainly not. I'm . . .'

'You aren't going to tell me that you're a good girl?'

Theresa glared at him. 'I am a good girl, but it wasn't what I was going to say. I'm trying out various things – like having a gin and tonic without being racked with guilt – and going to dubious parties, and wearing lots of make-up without being made to feel like a harlot.'

He stood up. 'Let me get you another drink.'

'Only one more, I had rather a lot at the party.'

She watched him as he weaved his way through the groups standing around, and thought: he hasn't altered, still the charming rake. She wondered if he still had contact with the poisonous Moira.

'Have you seen much of your friend Moira at all?' she asked, on his return.

'No! I lost contact. Anyway, I wouldn't have stood a chance against Jack Ross. The girl was besotted with him.'

'I wonder if she sees him.' Theresa was surprised at how steady her voice sounded, considering her heart was pumping away at the thought that Moira and Jack were separated only by a few miles of road.

'I imagine Moira would arrange matters if she was still interested.' He paused. 'You were very close to him once, weren't you?'

'We were close friends – very close – but things didn't seem to progress beyond that.'

'Why?'

'I'm not sure,' Theresa said a little sharply. 'Inexperience, I suppose . . . Let's talk about your life for a change.'

She saw a lot of Ross after that evening. She told herself that she was only making use of his local knowledge, but had a sneaking feeling that she found him exciting. He was an experienced man about town, and he took her to the theatre and the opera. Later, as their relationship matured, she asked tentatively if he would take her to visit Soho. He grinned and said he would do better than that – he would take her to his favourite gambling casino and then on to a nightclub, both of which were in Soho.

Theresa revelled in it all, and even Polly began to envy her. She told her so, before adding, 'Actually, I'm glad you are now launched and having a satisfying life. I have some news to break to you.'

Theresa, sitting curled up on Polly's sofa, blanched. 'You are moving away?' Now that she was making more money, Polly had been toying with the idea of moving for some time.

'Worse!' said Polly. 'I'm giving up the course. I want to do modelling full-time.'

'But Polly, we are doing so well . . .'

'No! You are doing well, Theresa. I will never make it in the art world. I will, however, stand a good chance as a model. I have the figure and I have the contacts – thanks to your friend Richard.'

'But why the catwalk?'

'I met Marcel Duprey. he visited the studio when I was posing for Conrad and he offered me a lucrative contract to do a photographic shoot out in Africa—'

'Africa!' Theresa said, aghast.

'Africa. It's only for four weeks, and when I come back we'll get together. I want to buy a flat of my own. I could do with some advice on it.'

Theresa laughed. 'You eejut. You're only trying to make it easier for me to accept your news. You know bloody well you have as much taste in colour and fabric as I have – more.'

'Talking of fabrics,' said Polly. 'Christian Dior is doing a show at the Savoy Hotel. Have you seen his latest look? Apparently, one of his evening dresses has fifty yards of material in it.'

Theresa stared at her. 'And Russia has just got the atom bomb!'

'I refuse to think of atom bombs. I shall dream of one day owning one of those flouncy, gorgeous dresses – or at least wearing one.'

Polly left the college that weekend and flew off to Africa the next week. Theresa was glad that the summer term had started and that she had Ross Carling for companionship most evenings; it stopped her becoming unsociable.

A month later, Theresa had a letter from Tandy telling her that Fliss and he were coming up to London for a day's shopping, and would she meet them for lunch? The letter lifted her spirits. Although she had kept in touch with Fliss and Tandy, actual contact had been scarce because of her course work and their own college commitment. She was hopeful that she would hear news of Jack.

They met at Victoria station. Fliss, her normally rosy cheeks pale with tiredness after the long day, rushed towards her. 'Oh! It's good to see you. I had hoped you could come down when Jack was over, but Tandy said you were probably too busy.'

Tandy was making furious faces at her. Theresa smiled a tiny smile. It smote her that Jack had been over and hadn't bothered to look her up.

'It's OK, Tandy,' she said. 'Jack and I lost contact some time ago – but I expect you know all about it.'

They seated themselves in one of the station eateries before Tandy enlarged upon what Fliss had said.

'Jack came over to do a week's experience at a hospital in Brighton. He spent most of his evenings with us. He would have liked to have met you again, but he mentioned a letter he'd sent which you never answered. He didn't think you would be too bothered about meeting him.'

'It's too late now to worry about it,' Theresa said. 'He has gone back – but you can tell him he was wrong. He means a lot to me. I would have loved to have seen him. I completely forgot to write because I was working very hard at the time. My parents have made the same complaint.'

She turned to the red-faced Fliss and laughed. 'Don't worry, Fliss. You are looking at a grade-one eejut when it comes to saying the wrong thing.'

Fliss smiled back. 'I do tend to jump in with both feet.'

'Anyway! To change the subject,' said Theresa, 'when are you two getting married?'

'Next year, perhaps in the spring. We finish at the college this summer and I'm hoping to get a job.'

'You're not going home this summer for a holiday?'

Tandy looked at Fliss. 'Fliss wanted to. She likes going home to the farm, but I need to get established, so we'll have to give it a miss. Anyway, we were home at Christmas.'

Next day, when Theresa arrived at college, there was a note for her. 'Some young man came past yesterday and left it. He didn't know your home address,' said Mick, the porter.

She opened the envelope. It was from Ross. He was going abroad for two months for his firm. He was sorry, but he would have to cancel their concert date. It had happened suddenly; the chap who was to have gone had been rushed to hospital following a car accident and he'd been given very little option but to fill the gap.

Theresa cursed quietly to herself. This really left her high and dry. Polly wasn't due back for another week from her assignment. Suddenly the anticipation had gone out of life. It had never been dull with Ross around – he was a real fly-by-night, but he was good fun.

She applied herself to the work she was doing on her canvas. She was entering it for the end-of-term cup, and was under some pressure to have it finished in time.

It was some time later, when she was putting her brushes away, that the idea came to her. If Polly was buying her own flat, there was no reason why she shouldn't do likewise. She was now quite used to getting along on her own. Where once she had been very tentative about making journeys around London, she now hopped on and off trams and buses and used the underground as though born and bred to it. She would find a flat somewhere nearer to the college which would cut down on travel time.

She began to feel excitement rise, and on the way home she went into the newsagent's near the college and bought the local paper. There wouldn't be time to set things up for a while, as she was going home for part of her summer holiday, but she could find out about prices and situations.

The greatest disappointment when she arrived home was to find that Night Star had been sold. 'I couldn't find anyone to exercise her,' Richard explained. 'The girl who took over from you has gone to live elsewhere and I can't afford the time to ride. I have a big exhibition coming up early next year. It's hard work.'

The other disappointment was to discover that Colin had been ill and she hadn't been told. He looked thinner and his appetite had all but disappeared. She confronted her mother. 'Why didn't you tell me?' she cried.

Nuala made her sit down. They hadn't been getting along for some time, Theresa and her, but she had to make her realize that her decision had been made with the best intentions. 'There didn't seem any point in worrying you. David thinks it might be a virus of some kind. His blood pressure is raised, but there seems no danger that it will go higher. He must be kept free of stress, so we must always put his health first.'

She looked pleadingly at her daughter. There was no knowing what went through that head of hers. For some reason she couldn't fathom Theresa had distanced herself from them. She desperately wanted to ask her why, but Colin had warned her that Theresa was going through an independent stage in her life. 'She's taking on new responsibilities,' he had said, 'and she wants to prove that she can manage her own life without our parental interference. She still loves us; she just needs her space.'

Theresa went in search of Eileen. She climbed the gentle slope of the hill and felt a kind of peace as she stopped for a moment and looked at the church, standing like a mediaeval sentinel guarding the quiet village. She smiled wryly. Compared to London the village was a haven of tranquillity and peace. Oh! The folly of her imagination; guarding it from what?

'Eileen has not come home yet,' said Mrs O'Rourke, a trifle sourly. 'She is still in Dublin, staying with her aunt Margaret. She'll not be home for another two weeks.'

Theresa was thoughtful as she walked home. If her da was improving she might see if she could pay a visit to Eileen and Aunt Margaret. A few days in Dublin would be just the thing to gently acclimatise her to the relative sleepiness of Tullybra.

213

She travelled to Dublin at the end of the first week. Doctor Owen thought her father had shown some improvement and, indeed, he had been more like his old self in the way that he was teasing her about her love life. He had managed a good meal for the first time yesterday, and when Theresa took the bus to Dublin she felt a lot happier about him.

Eileen's cheery face was the first thing she noticed as the bus pulled into the depot, and when she alighted they fell into each other's arms. 'Aw, it's just great to see you,' Eileen said, adding, 'The new, sophisticated Theresa Brady.'

'Not a bit. I'm putting on an act to live up to what is expected of me.'

'How long are you home for?'

'Two or three weeks. I can't stay for the whole of the summer. I have some work to do.' She omitted to add that she was posing for a couple of artists.

'We'll make the most of it. I told Jack you were coming to stay. He wants to take us for a drink one evening. I'm to phone him and let him know when.'

Theresa picked up her bag. 'That's fine by me. It's been a long time since we saw each other. I'll look forward to it.' Even to her own ears her voice sounded casual, but she was churning inside.

Aunt Margaret made her do a twirl. 'Still built like a rake, I see.' The remark set them off on a tour of nostalgia, particularly about the time when Margaret had dressed her up for Moira's ball.

'I dined off that for ages,' Margaret laughed. 'It was an absolute gas, wasn't it?'

After supper, Eileen went to phone Jack.

'What do you think of our Eileen taking the veil?' asked Margaret.

'If we think about it, there was no question it is what she wanted.' Theresa smiled. 'God knows I tried hard enough to set her on the path to ruin, but He was looking over her and she stood firm.'

'Sure whatever devilment you two got up to would hardly have ruined her.'

'It might have been worse if it hadn't been for the curb she put on us. She always stopped me before I did something really stupid.' Theresa leaned back in her chair. 'How did her mam take it?'

'Not too well at first – Eileen provided her only chance of becoming a grandmother – but there, when she got over it, she was going around acting as if she had given birth to a saint.' They were laughing together as Eileen returned.

214

'We're to meet Jack at Ginty's. He says it's quiet.'

'You aren't telling me you are going to be drinking?'

Eileen suspected Theresa was poking gentle fun, but she answered quite seriously. 'I'm not under the veil yet. A glass of wine won't harm.'

Theresa was glad of Eileen's presence when they met Jack. It helped to alleviate the awkwardness between them. They spent most of the evening talking about their respective careers and what was happening around them. It wasn't till Eileen paid a visit to the cloakroom that Jack rounded on Theresa. 'You never answered my letter,' he said. 'Do you know how much that hurt?'

'Hurt?' She looked at him. 'Did you say hurt?'

'I did. No one meant more to me than you – yet you went across the water with not a sigh of regret and weren't bothered if we lost contact.' He looked round. He didn't want Eileen to come back. He needed time alone with Theresa to try and straighten things out between them. Somewhere, somehow, he had lost her; this could be his only chance to put things right.

Theresa leaned across the table. 'Jack! I had a lot of work to do and I got tied up in my project because I was getting behind. I meant to write, but I just forgot. I'm sorry we lost touch – God knows, I didn't want that to happen – but something happened after you went to university; there is some explaining to do before we can be as we once were.'

'What happened?' Jack whitened. Had it been something to do with Fergal? Surely she hadn't . . . No! He wouldn't believe that of her.

'I – Eileen is on her way back. This is not the time or the place.'

'Meet me again – alone,' he said anxiously. 'We have to sort ourselves out.'

Eileen looked at them. 'I would like to buy my two best friends a drink,' she said. 'I can't go to the bar, Jack – would you get them?'

'I'll go with you,' said Theresa.

While he waited to be served, he turned to her. 'Can you meet me one evening?'

'I'm committed to spending these few days with Eileen, but I could make a trip into Dublin another time.'

They arranged a date. Theresa knew she was going to get uptight about the proposed meeting. Try as she might, she couldn't see them discussing the matter of Pat without a row, and she dreaded the thought that instead of clearing the air it might destroy them altogether – but a confrontation was long overdue.

★ ★ ★

Colin appeared to be improving. Nuala saw him upstairs to bed, then joined Theresa in the kitchen. A chill had crept into the atmosphere now that they were alone together, and this confused her. It was something she had sensed between them since Theresa had gone to England. Somehow the closeness that was between them had gone – it was like living with a polite stranger.

'Your father wants you to go up and sit with him for a while,' she said.

Theresa turned. 'I've just finished the washing up; I'll go up now. Do you think he looks a little better?' She looked anxiously at her mother.

'He hasn't been as well as this for many weeks,' Nuala said softly. 'Seeing you has put new life in him.'

Theresa's only reply was a vague smile as she went upstairs. She knocked and entered. Colin was leaning against his pillow with a book in his hands. He put it down and motioned for her to sit on the bed.

'I wanted to have a word with you, sweetheart,' he said, and covered her hand with his own.

She waited.

'A long time ago – or so it seems now – you promised me that you would try not to let what you had witnessed in Pat McGarry's barn affect your relationship with your mother. You haven't kept that promise.'

'I've never mentioned a word to her,' Theresa murmured.

'That isn't good enough, Theresa. You have withdrawn from her, and she knows it and can't understand why. She loves you more than life. Can't you see that by your politeness you are telling her that you are not her daughter any more – that you are not the girl who was so adored because of her loving nature and her innocence?' Colin stopped, breathless by the effort he had just made.

'Please, Da. You'll have a relapse. I'll try. I really will. I was just so – so hurt, so shocked.'

'I was devastated, too, when I found out that you were not my daughter, but my love for your mother never wavered. I knew that she'd been going out with Pat McGarry – the whole village thought they would marry – but things didn't work out, and they had parted by the time she met me. Pat will always hold your mother's heart, but I have had my place there, and I've been grateful for that. Without Nuala Brady, Colin Brady would not be lying here in this bed at this moment telling his daughter that he has never regretted one moment of his life.'

Theresa's eyes misted. 'I'm sorry!' she cried, and laid her head down by his. 'I haven't the kindness or the understanding that you

216

have. Forgive me too. I have made you unhappy. I never wanted that.'

'Theresa! Theresa! I'm not talking of forgiveness. Don't you see? There's nothing to forgive. What happened did so before I met your mother. The only thing she did wrong was not telling me the truth when she discovered she was expecting you – even then, why should she? We were married before she knew, and telling me might have made things worse.' He stroked the thick hair and raised her head. 'You'll be good to your mother, won't you? She loves us both so much.'

'I promise.' She saw the sudden look of tiredness as he placed his book on the table by the bed. He had aged, and he was still only forty-three years old. This terrible virus that no one could give a name to had knocked him sideways, and it broke her heart to look down on the shell of a man who had once been a force in the community in a kind and gentle way.

Nuala looked up at her daughter entered the room. Theresa walked over and knelt by her. 'Mam! I'm sorry if I've behaved badly. It – it's just me trying to be the independent Theresa Brady who doesn't need anyone now she's grown up. But seeing m'da looking so tired and ill made me realise how much I love you both.'

Nuala stroked her daughter's head. 'We'll say no more. I'm glad to have my girl back.' Theresa would never know just how glad. Seeing the love between Colin and the girl had cut through her, for she had felt left out by Theresa's coolness, and bewildered, though she knew she couldn't confront her because she was never anything but respectful.

'Would you like a cup of tea before we go to bed, Mam?'

'I'd love one.'

Nuala looked in on Colin as she did every night before going to her own room. He was awake still.

She kissed his cheek. 'Are you finding it difficult to get to sleep?'

'Will you go and get your nightdress and climb in beside me where you belong?' he smiled. 'I'll sleep like a log then.'

'But Colin! David thought it would be better to—'

'Away and get your nightdress. I don't want you sleeping in that back room any more. I want you beside me. David can go to the devil.'

A few minutes later she climbed in beside him and kissed him gently as he turned his head on the pillow. 'I love you, Colin Brady.'

'I love you, Nuala.' He felt happy tonight; he could feel the softness of her as her body curved round him and her arm lay

217

lightly along his thigh. Gradually, he felt himself drift off to sleep. His last thought was one of gratitude for his life with her. When his health improved he would take her away on a second honeymoon. They would go to Rome – she'd always wanted to go there. He sighed happily. He'd make the arrangements as soon as he could get into Kilgaven to the Travel Agent.

In the early hours of the morning, Colin Brady passed peacefully away in his sleep.

CHAPTER 16

Theresa ignored the bell, but after the fifth ring gave in to the sheer insistence of it. Climbing from the bath, she draped a towel round her, wound another one round her dripping, freshly washed hair, and stepped into her towelling mules. Whoever the cod was at the door they had better have a good reason for ringing her bell at such an early hour.

She padded across the soft piled carpet of the living room and paused for a moment to check the state of it. The party last night had been a bit wild. She smiled. Her life, since she left Tullybra, had changed, just as she had. Her tastes had become more sophisticated, and as a model posing for well-known artists – thanks to Richard – she earned enough money to pay for her comfortable flat overlooking Peckham Rye park. It was less often, now, that she found herself thinking wistfully of those simple, pleasurable days.

She opened the door, a frown settling on her brow as she faced a broad-shouldered, attractive man leaning against the door frame, a hat rakishly set back on his head and a wide grin on his face.

'I don't know who you are,' she said, glaring, 'but you had better have a good explanation as to why you are ringing my bell at eight o'clock in the morning.'

'Overdressed as usual, Theresa Brady.' The young man grinned.

'Do I know you?'

He looked vaguely familiar, but she would hardly forget having met a man as attractive as this one. His accent was difficult to place. There was a hint – the merest one – of Irish, but the overtones were European.

'Why don't you invite me in? The fella passing by is leering at you.'

'I've no intention of inviting a stranger into my home. I've—'

'Theresa Brady, I'm heartily ashamed of you for forgetting your old enemy so quickly. It's hardly been three years since I left Tullybra.' He moved into the light and Theresa caught sight of the faint marks on his skin.

'Davey? Davey Adams?'

'The very same.'

'God! It's great to see someone from home – even such a shite as you were, Davey.' He looked handsome and well set up, she noticed.

'I've had better welcomes,' Davey remarked. 'I'm a changed man now. I was a silly kitter in those days.'

'Give me a minute to dress,' said Theresa. 'You go and put the kettle on. Have you had breakfast yet?'

'At the hotel, but I'll do you some toast if you like. I'm a dab hand at burnt toast.'

'Never mind the toast, I'll have a cup of coffee. I promise you that by the time I've dressed I'll not be gabbling like an eejut any more. I'm just so excited to see you.'

Davey watched as she went towards the bedroom. He had been worried that she might have given him one of her tongue lashings and thrown him out. God knows, Theresa had nothing to thank him for. He had ruined her chances with Jack. He'd heard that they had parted shortly afterwards. Nora, in one of the few letters she sent him, had mentioned that Jack had started going out with a girl in Dublin who was at the same university – a redhead, glamorous and rich. They came into the pub where Nora worked sometimes.

He had a dire feeling that Jack had found out about Theresa cavorting with the tinker. Although Davey had stopped short of telling him what he'd seen that day, it may have set him wondering.

Theresa came back as Davey poured the coffee into large mugs. She was wearing an expensive suit, and her hair had a designer cut which controlled the wild curls of old.

Even her body – that wonderful body that he had been privileged to see in its entirety – had changed. It looked even better, with its soft curves and tiny waist. She had that subtle air of wealth and good taste that many women would kill for.

Theresa lifted her cup and regarded the young man before her. 'How did you know where to find me?'

'I rang your mother, Jesus, Theresa! I was very sorry to hear about your da.'

She winced. She was still having difficulty with her loss. Colin had only been going into his middle years – sure where was the justice in it?

She'd only seen her mother once since then. She'd spent a week of her term holiday with her but, aware of the slight tension that still existed, she had made an excuse to return to England.

Her mother had been able to stay on at the school as house-keeper to the new Head, who was unmarried, but she now lived in Gran's cottage and cycled into the village daily. Pat McGarry had postponed razing the cottage to the ground as he'd planned. Even that act of kindness made Theresa's lip curl with disgust.

'Thank you!' she said to Davey.

Davey, suspecting that she didn't want to talk about it, fell silent.

'Why did you run away all those years ago?' Theresa asked suddenly.

He looked embarrassed, and didn't answer immediately. She waited.

'I don't know whether he told you or not, but the tinker gave me the hiding of my life for trying to blackmail you,' he said, at last.

'He swore to me that he hadn't laid a finger on you. I'm sorry.'

Davey said drily, 'He didn't lie to you. I suppose, in a way, he never did lay a hand on me. The crafty blirt kept his promise; he belted me about the head and body with a whacking great thorn bush instead. I was takin' thorns out of my arse for weeks afterwards – and before you go blamin' the tinker, I deserved it. He did me a favour. If it wasn't for him telling me to clear off or else, I would be in Tullybra to this day, getting into trouble and gettin' up people's noses.'

Davey explained how he had got a job in Dublin and saved enough money to get to England, where he got work on the building sites, navvying. When he got fed up with being messed around he'd taken the boat across to the continent, where all the big building jobs were going. The war damage over there meant plenty of work. He'd worked like a slave till he got his own group going, then hired them out to jobs all over the country. He became the organizer and the job researcher, who ferried the team around in an old bus he'd picked up cheap.

'I made a lot of money,' he said. 'Eventually I hit the jackpot. I married the boss's daughter.'

'You! Married?' Theresa stared at him.

'Yup! I joined a building firm belonging to a man called Josef Kohl. He reckoned I had potential and he gave me a job as a sales rep. I now go round Europe finding firms that are interested in his development methods. I'll not bore you with the details – but it's why I'm over here.' He showed her a photo of a fairly buxom, pleasantly pretty girl with a large smile and blonde hair. She had a placid, empty face.

221

'She's pretty,' Theresa observed. Davey smiled gratefully.

'Would you come out to dinner with me tonight? I go back Sunday.'

She hesitated. 'I'm going to a wedding tomorrow. I really need to have an early night, especially as I'm doing a long modelling session this afternoon.'

'You're a model?'

'And I paint – I finished my Art course not long ago.'

'Looking around the room, I'd say you were pretty successful,' Davey said, and added, 'Are you sure about dinner?'

'Fraid so.' She hesitated. 'Would you like to come to the wedding? Richard Beck was supposed to come with me but he can't make it. He had to fly to Paris at short notice. It's Tandy's wedding – I could do with some moral support. Jack will be there and I haven't seen or heard from him for a long time.' In fact, it had been at her father's funeral. She remembered that because of the circumstances they hadn't had their meeting in Dublin, and so hadn't resolved their differences.

Davey looked thoughtful. 'Why not? I can't let a friend down, can I? Fancy old Tandy getting married to an English girl. I thought he would end up marrying the brave Eileen.'

'Eileen is going to be someone else's bride,' Theresa said. 'I'm surprised you didn't hear about that when you were home.'

'The subject never came up. Who is she marrying? Anyone I know?'

'She's going to be a bride of Christ.'

'A nun?' Davey was stunned that no one had mentioned such a juicy piece of news. 'Will she be at the wedding?'

'No! She's away on retreat again. When you think about it, Eileen has always been nearer to God than any of us; she was always on her knees praying when the rest of us were rushing out of mass to gather outside.'

When they entered the church, Theresa felt herself begin to tremble as she caught sight of Jack sitting next to Tandy, looking handsome in his dress suit. She noticed with fondness that Tandy was very nervous. No doubt he'd had a stiff drink to bolster his courage. Jack, on the other hand, looked in control.

She sat back in her seat and quietly devoured him with her eyes. Would she never get over this feeling she had for him? She had visited Tandy and Fliss several times since she'd returned and each time Tandy had tried to find out why she and Jack had stopped being friends.

She had become close to Fliss and Tandy. They had stayed overnight with her when she had invited them to Richard's private

222

viewing. His picture, 'My Lady of the Bath', had been acclaimed as his best work yet. She'd shyly told them that she was the figure bending towards the towel, and had been amazed and horrified to find that Tandy was shocked. He had got over it, but for a time it had spoiled things between them. Fliss had sorted him out and told him not to be a damned prude and that if she had a body like that she could earn a fortune and they wouldn't have to work and wait to buy their own farm.

The music changed, jolting her from her reverie, and the congregation rose with a noisy shuffle as the bride arrived. She looked stunning. Her gaze was darting everywhere, and when her eyes met Theresa's she gave a little wink.

Theresa's eyes softened as Tandy turned to his bride and she saw the look of love that passed between them. Why could he not have felt this way about Eileen? Was it because they'd known each other since childhood? She and Jack hadn't made the transition either.

She was grateful for Davey's moral support as he followed her into the reception hall. He looked handsome and distinguished, and she felt a little bubble of satisfaction rise in her as he was ogled by the younger girls. Tandy and Jack could hardly believe that this important looking man could be the same Davey Adams they once knew.

Later, when they were chatting to Fliss, someone bore Davey off for a drink and Theresa found Jack at her side. Fliss excused herself and wandered off to greet another guest. Theresa was aware that there was a space all round them, as though everyone had sensed their desire to be alone.

'Hello, Theresa,' Jack said quietly. 'I was pleased when I heard you were coming. How are things?'

'Things are fine, and you, Jack? Are you still enjoying medicine?' While she was mouthing the words she was thinking: Was this inconsequential chatter all that lay between them? Were things really that bad that she and her old friend had to resort to questions and answers to fill a conversational void?

Jack hesitated before replying. 'Yes. It seems to take forever. Mind you. I haven't much time for socialising these days. I always seem to be studying for yet another exam or major test.' He took her arm. 'Let's go outside. It seems a shame to waste all that lovely sunshine.'

They walked across the lawn towards a bench and sat down. 'I should have got you some food. Wait here.' He strode off, his tall figure disappearing as the mass of guests swallowed him up.

She waited, nervously clasping and unclasping her hands. Food at this moment would surely choke her. Her hands were now sweating and her heart was fluttering in her chest. She had to stop this nonsense. The old Theresa Brady wouldn't be acting like this. The truth was, the sight of Jack had brought all the old memories tumbling back.

She thought she'd got over him. She had a very good social life in London; she was in demand as a model, her circle of friends was widening fast and she had invitations to all sorts of exciting venues and events. So why, seeing Jack looking so confident and smart in his morning suit – but still, endearingly, like the Jack she'd always known – did she have to crumble?

He returned, precariously balancing two plates of food and fresh drinks, and sat down by her side. Folding the napkin across her knee he leaned back. Neither spoke as they ate and surveyed the activity around them. Several children gently ran amok around the standing groups as they played their secret games. In the distance he could see Davey with a group of girls. Who would have thought . . .

'You look successful,' he said at last, eyeing her soft cashmere suit. She had grown even more beautiful. 'Are you still as mad as ever, or has sophistication tamed you?'

Theresa wanted to hold hands and tell him that yes she did still have that reputation, only over here they called it wilfulness; that they didn't always understand her and there were times when she wanted to yell and tell the whole damn lot of them that they were a bunch of stuck-up poseurs, but couldn't because they were her bread and butter.

'I've mellowed,' she said instead.

'Pity!' He smiled. 'I admired that trait in you. You didn't give a damn.'

Davey came looking for her. 'Would you mind if we went? I'm having a great time, but I have another meeting this evening. I tried to cancel it but couldn't. I am sorry. Really!'

She had forgotten that he had to go early. Her face showed her disappointment.

Jack took a deep breath. 'Why don't I come with you both?'

Theresa and Davey looked at him in astonishment.

'Why not? I have a room for the night at a local guest house, but all I have to do is collect my suitcase and pay my bill. Tandy and Fliss will be off shortly. My job is finished.' He turned to Davey. 'Can you delay it for another hour?'

'Certainly!' said Davey, and raised an enquiring eyebrow at Theresa before addressing Jack again. 'And where will you sleep tonight?'

'I'm hoping Theresa can lend me a sofa. I can't go back to Ireland having spent a few paltry hours with my old friend.'

224

Davey gave a little shrug. 'I've room in the car if it all right with Theresa.'

'I don't mind. However, I warn you, it is a small sofa and I have no spare room.' She smiled as she said it.

Jack looked round the elegant room. 'It looks as if you have arrived, Theresa – modelling must pay well.'

'It does. I also do a little fashion modelling; that's where the money is, and I need it to pay the bills.'

'What about your Art and Design course?'

'I finished it. I paint when I can . . . Look! I want to change into something more comfortable. Make yourself at home; the drinks are over there.' She pointed towards a beautiful walnut table on which a silver salver rested, almost hidden beneath bottles and glasses.

Later, following a quickly prepared and slowly consumed meal, they lay back on the settee and relaxed over a second bottle of wine.

'You're sure you don't mind me borrowing your sofa for tonight?' Jack felt mellow and slightly drunk. He didn't know what had come over him in the garden of the hotel, but he had suddenly panicked at the thought that, yet again, Theresa was about to walk out of his life. Somehow this seemed to have been the pattern of things over the years.

'Of course not!' Theresa replied. 'I was surprised when you said you wanted to come, but the idea wasn't repugnant to me. By the way, the settee is actually quite comfortable; it has been tested before.'

'Has it indeed?'

She ignored the innuendo. She was so pleased to have him here. 'My friend Polly often stays the night. She lives over the other side of London.'

By midnight they were both so relaxed they were able to talk – really talk, all tensions gone. Jack spoke of his life at the university and the friends he had made. He told her how he'd been chucked in at the deep end on many occasions and it had only been the friendship of Declan that had kept him from packing it in. Declan was so easygoing by nature he had a way of dealing with every crisis, and some of his calmness in the face of panic situations had rubbed off on Jack to such an extent that now he rarely found anything that fazed him.

It was when he spoke of Pat that Theresa found her relaxed mood begin to wear off – Pat, who had found it difficult to keep up, so had transferred to nursing and was now about to take her final exams.

225

Theresa gripped her glass. How dare he speak of that girl? Had he no sensitivity at all in him?

Jack had stopped speaking and there was silence for a moment, until at last he said softly, 'When did it all go wrong for us – when did we lose it all?'

Theresa's eyes flashed with sudden rage. 'I'll tell you when, Jack Ross! It all went wrong the day I went to visit you – the day I stood by the porter's station and watched you kiss your Pat half-way down the stairs – that's when everything blew up in our faces.' She jumped up and started pacing the carpet. 'And you had the nerve to kiss me as though I meant the world to you, knowing that your Pat was waiting for you. You were testing me out while keeping quiet about your girlfriend.'

Jack stared at her in astonishment. He had seen her angry many times, but never had she been so passionate as this. 'What are you talking about?'

'I'm bloody well talking about our friendship – no, our relation-ship – which meant so little to you you felt able to dally with another girl when you were safe from prying eyes.'

Jack stood up and pulled her down beside him. 'Stop that pacing,' he ordered. 'If you saw this, why didn't you tax me with it? Why didn't you clear the matter up there and then? This isn't like the Theresa I thought I knew. She would have caught me by the throat and demanded an explanation.'

'I never knew for certain where I stood with you, Jack. There were times when I felt we were close to something, and then you would back off. You had no such qualms about Pat though.'

'I never really had anything going with Pat. She was a good friend, and we could have saved ourselves a lot of heartache.'

'Would it have made any difference to us?' Theresa asked with sudden meekness.

'I don't suppose so,' Jack sighed. 'Our emotions were knocking seven bells out of us and we couldn't cope. But at least we would have remained friends.'

She subsided into the sofa cushions. 'That's true. I spent hours worrying about my emotions and feelings angry because of my ignorance. I was always trying to find a way to acquire knowl-edge.'

'I remember,' said Jack acidly. 'I saw you kissing Fergal.'

'I was being tutored.' She started to giggle suddenly. 'How is Pat?'

'Pat is engaged to be married to Declan. They are hoping to get married next year.'

Theresa's heart slipped at the news. She topped up their glasses. 'Declan? The big tall fella who came with you to the dance the night the poisonous Moira was after you?'

'The same. Honest to god Theresa, can you believe those two? Declan must be six foot two inches at least, and Pat only five foot four. That poor girl will have to have a Caesarean every time she has a baby. There won't be a chance in hell of one coming out weighing less than ten pounds.'

The wine was having its effect. They laughed like a pair of drains and rolled on the settee with tears streaming. The idea of the small girl and the tall, angular figure of Declan making love seemed absurd. Somewhere in the recesses of her mind, Theresa realized that her laughter was almost hysterical because part of it was the relief of knowing that Jack was not in the running with Pat any more.

'I'm going to have a bath,' she announced, and reeled slightly as she stood up. 'Does my voice sound a bit slurred to you?' She swayed towards him.

'I'll come with you,' he laughed. 'You aren't too steady.' Lifting her in his arms he staggered towards the bathroom. She is no weight, he thought, no weight at all, and he was as drunk as a frigging stoat.

Once there, now feeling mellow and giddy with joy and the effects of the wine, Theresa slid out of her loose gown and leaned over the bath to turn on the taps.

Jack, his throat constricting at the sight of his wild, lovely girl standing there naked, with not a sign of embarrassment at his presence, followed suit, and they plunged joyously into the bath together, displacing the water so that it shot everywhere.

As the water cooled and they had soaped and rubbed each other till they glowed, Jack suggested that they should have one more glass of wine to warm them up.

Theresa, only just beginning to rouse herself from the effect of the alcohol she had already consumed, shook her head. 'I'm off to bed,' she said huskily, and took his hand.

Jack groaned and pulled her towards him, sliding his arm round her to slip the towelling robe off her shoulders. 'Theresa,' he murmured, 'I want to make love to you.'

'I know you do,' she said softly. 'I've waited a long time for this moment. This is one new experience I'm going to enjoy.' She held her mouth up for his kiss, and as his mouth covered hers she felt that same delicious feeling she had the night they had come back from their walk along the Mile.

That night they made love: Theresa for the first time, and Jack with a gentleness and a need he had never experienced before. The strength in the lovely young body beneath him sent him into paroxysms of ecstasy. Theresa, her mind awash with a desire for

227

him that she could never have realized she was capable of, responded to him with joy and fervour, and when it was over they lay, locked in each other's arms, and drifted into sleep.

Jack was the first to waken. Slowly and fuzzily he realised where he was. Jesus Christ! What had he done? He looked down at the sleeping girl and felt his heart pump. He had never meant to do this. With increasing awareness of the predicament he found himself in, he quietly and speedily removed all traces of his presence and stole out to the living room. Theresa slept on.

Hastily rumpling the settee, he lay down on it and drew the blanket over his body, praying that she wouldn't remember what had happened. They'd been quite tipsy – perhaps she would forget the whole episode.

Hearing her come into the room, he feigned sleep. He sensed she had stopped by him before continuing towards the kitchen. Opening his eyes slowly and carefully, he found to his astonishment that she was still naked. He shut them again.

'Are you awake, Jack?' She held a cup of tea towards him, and groaned.

He opened his eyes and took the cup from her. 'Theresa! Do you think you could put something on?'

She apologised. 'I'm sorry. I didn't think! I always wander around naked; it's one of the pleasures of living alone. I'm surprised it bothers you, you being a doctor.' She went into the bedroom and threw on a silk wrap, then returned to the living room, her face creased by a puzzled frown. 'Jack, why are you lying on the settee?'

He looked embarrassed. 'I hoped you wouldn't remember what happened last night. It was my fault. I should never have stayed.'

'Do you regret it, then?'

'No! Not for one moment – but I wondered if – you . . .'

'Not for one moment!' she teased. 'I don't need protecting. I'm a big girl now. I make my own decisions about my life and work.' She leaned down and kissed him. 'I've come a long way from the girl you knew in Tullybra.'

Jack frowned. He didn't want her to change too much. 'This modelling you do. What kind is it?' he asked.

'Mostly nude, but as I mentioned, I also do clothes. Fashion modelling pays well.' She crossed to the bureau and lifted up a magazine which she gave to him before curling up in an armchair.

He studied it. It was an account of the latest showing at a gallery in Bond Street, and depicted a nude portrait painted by a well-known artist, Van Guysen. It had drawn much favourable criticism, not just for the expertise of the painter, but also for the beauty of the sitter. An electric shock ran through him as he realised that the hauntingly beautiful face and figure belonged to Theresa.

She watched him anxiously.

He frowned. 'Does your mother know that you pose naked?'

Theresa tensed at the censure in his voice. 'I really don't know,' she said coldly. 'If she reads the papers, then she does. We haven't discussed it. It is my life, my decision.' She rose. 'If you have time do go into the George Cartell gallery in Bond Street you will see a couple of paintings of me in there. I am much sought after.' It was not said with pride, more as a statement of fact.

Going into the bedroom she closed the door, angry at the condemnation in Jack's eyes. When she returned later, she was fully dressed, her back ramrod straight. He had tidied the settee and put his cup on the draining board.

'Jack! As I've told you, I have no problem with my nakedness – I never have had.' Her anger now under control, she was able to speak without showing her former irritation.

'Obviously not,' Jack said curtly. 'Anyway, as you say, it's your decision. It's none of my business.'

Theresa desperately held back the tears that were threatening. Last night they had made love with a beautiful, wild passion. Two people who realised at last that they loved each other in an adult way, the embarrassment of their youth forgotten.

'But it *is* your business, Jack. We made love last night and you told me over and over that you loved me. How can you now say that what I do is not any of your business?'

'I'm not your keeper, Theresa. I have no right to ask you to stop doing this – and if I did I don't suppose you would give it up, would you?'

'No! Because I'm not doing anything wrong. If I gave up because you asked me to, then I would be making just such an admission. I would lose respect for myself.'

Jack's eyes flashed with anger. 'I don't want your body being stared at by any bloody man with the excuse of a paintbrush in his hand. Do clothes modelling if you must, but can't you stop this posing for artists?'

'You forget I am one. I learn a lot when I'm posing. I'm good, Jack, and I know that one day I might have some success myself. I love the world of art, and I see nothing wrong in what I am doing.' She lifted her handbag off the table where she had placed it and drew on her gloves. 'I've got to go out. I hope you have a safe journey home. Just make sure you hear the lock click as you go.' She left.

'Damn and blast.' Jack pulled his hand through his hair. He'd done it again. Would he never stop putting his foot into his great mouth? He wouldn't see her again. He suspected she would stay away until he had gone. Angry with himself, he gathered up his things and left a note of apology – for all the good it would do, he thought, bleakly.

When she arrived home later, Theresa read the note, crumpled it up and put it in the bin. It was the end. The Jack who forgave her all her wildness, who once knew her so well, no longer did. Time had happened to both of them. She dropped her key into her handbag next to her missal and, sitting down where he had recently been, stared bleakly into space.

She had taken to going to mass again. Since her da had died she had felt the acres of loneliness get worse. Only in church did she feel that she could come to terms with the suddenness of Colin's death, coming so soon after losing her little gran. Automatic though the responses were, by simply partaking in the chants and intonations she felt nearer to them. Today, though, her mind had kept harking back to the row with Jack. She knew he loved her, but she also realized that he couldn't equate that love with her need to be a free spirit.

Two days later Richard rang. He wanted to know if she could partner him to his latest showing. He also had some important news to impart.

'I'm intrigued. I can't wait to hear it.'

'It's purely personal, but important.'

Theresa enjoyed Richard's exhibitions. It was only at such times that she saw him these days, as the only contact she had with Tullybra was when she wrote an occasional letter to her mother. Although things had improved between her and Nuala of late, she still felt a sense of anger against her for what she had done, but she had to go along with the whole charade of pretending that she didn't know about Pat McGarry because of the promise she had given her da. Richard, unaware of the reason for her attitude, accused her of neglecting her duty towards her mother and told her in no uncertain terms that her actions were inexcusable.

The viewings were always held at the George Cartel gallery, as George was Richard's friend and partner. Theresa wasn't fond of George Cartel. He was a plump, unctuous man who consistently smoked fat Havana cigars with a degree of ostentation. She could never understand how the charismatic Richard had managed to get involved with such a shite as this. There were other gallery owners queueing up for his work who would have been more than pleased to represent him; yet he was also closely involved in other areas of business with the man.

230

George came across to them now, his cigar in one hand, his other held out towards Theresa.

'My dear, dear girl. How simply lovely to see you. I told Richard, did I not?' He turned towards his friend. ' "You must bring the delightful Theresa with you." '

'Seeing as three of the portraits are of myself, I think I deserve an invitation,' Theresa said, smiling cripsly at the little fart.

'Naughty, naughty! I won't have any disagreeable talk today. I am feeling in an expansive mood. Come! We must have a drink of champagne. I think this is going to be your finest hour, my dear Richard.'

As they followed him, Theresa mimed a puking action at Richard, who smiled and shook his head. 'Behave!' he said.

The odious man was right. The show was a great success.

'One of the reasons for my association with George,' whispered Richard at one stage, 'is the fact that he is the most influential man in the art world. If he shows my work, the buyers flock. He is why I can live in a certain style at Castle Donagh.'

Later they dined, just the two of them at a little Italian restaurant just off Oxford Street.

'Now then. Tell me your news. I've been dying to get you alone for ages.' She leaned across the white tablecloth towards him.

'Shouldn't I be saying that to you?' Richard said in amusement. He found it increasingly hard to equate this expensively dressed, beautifully coiffured young woman with the girl he had first met coming out of the sea by Lafferty's Cove. He had grown very fond of her. In fact, he had grown fond of all the Bradys, and had been greatly saddened by Colin's sudden death. He had a high respect for Nuala – a most sensible and sensitive woman.

For some time he had harboured a feeling of guilt that he had, quite without intention, been the cause of Nuala's most recent worry. She had confessed to him when he paid her a visit at the cottage that she sometimes felt Theresa might be in moral danger, and with her being so far away she felt useless.

'You know she is a model – mostly for artists?' he'd said quietly.

'Yes, I know.' She'd fetched a magazine and handed it to him. 'I picked this up in Dublin some weeks ago. Until then I wasn't sure what branch of modelling she was in – she tells me so little of her life now.'

Richard had looked at the picture of Theresa, stretched out on a couch with nothing on, and said anxiously, 'It's all very tasteful. Theresa is highly respected in the profession.'

'I know my daughter,' Nuala had smiled. 'She has never been ashamed of her body and I know she would never do anything wrong. She has a wholesome respect for herself, but the danger

231

and influences are high. Do you know she used to swim at night in the nude? I never let on that I knew.'

'How on earth did you learn about that?'

'I overheard her discussing it with her gran. I knew that if my mother thought there was no wrong in it, then there wasn't.' Nuala had looked sadly at Richard. 'Something happened to destroy the closeness between Theresa and me. I'm not sure when it happened, but it was long before Colin's death. I did think just before he died that things were getting better, but the coolness returned before she went back to England.'

Richard now regarded the eager young face opposite. 'Why do you not go over to see your mother? It must be many months since you paid a visit.'

Theresa leaned back. 'Are you going to lecture me?'

'No! It's your business, but remember just how suddenly you lost your father. Don't let anything come between you and your mother.'

Theresa screwed her napkin tightly, but recovered quickly and said lightly, 'Richard, I'll make a scene if you don't tell me your news.'

He signed. 'I'm selling the house in Dulwich Village.'

'Why? What about Mrs Beatty?' Theresa felt a pang of guilt. She hadn't kept in touch with Mrs Beatty for ages. Time seemed to shift by.

'Mrs Beatty – and if you had kept in touch you would have known this – is getting married to her Alfred, whom she met at her niece's wedding four months ago. They are going to live in Kent, and I felt that as I preferred to live in Ireland there was little point in keeping the place going.'

'But you need it when you come over.'

'I use it twice a year. It isn't worth the upkeep. I shall stay at a hotel. It will work out cheaper.'

The wine waiter arrived. Richard waited till he had gone, then drew a letter from his pocket. 'Your mother asked me to give you this.'

'I'll read it later,' Theresa said carelessly. 'What's the latest news from Tullybra?'

Richard told her what news he had. He didn't have much dealings with the villagers, but Bob kept him up to date with all the goings on. Some of it he dismissed as trivial but the items that might be of interest to Theresa he had stored to relate to her.

'Your friend Fergal is back.'

Theresa nodded. 'It's September, he'll be getting the camp ready. Has he changed much since I came away?'

'He has a wife now. They got married in Kildare. They met at the Curragh. They were "doing" the race meeting and both families got friendly – by the way, you'll be interested to know that Jupiter, under his racing name of George's Boy, won his first race.'

'Isn't that grand?' She was delighted. 'Have you never wanted to get married, Richard?' As soon as she'd said it, Theresa knew she had committed the cardinal sin of prying into his life. He was a very private man.

'No! he said. I never have.' He hesitated. 'Much as I enjoy their company, women have never interested me in that way.' He topped up her glass and began to speak of other things. It was clear that the matter was closed.

Theresa watched him covertly as they ate their meal. He was such an attractive man. She had seen several women glance towards him, but she had a suspicion that they were wasting their time. There was something between him and his partner George. She had known them both long enough to see the rapport between them. She couldn't stand the toad but, there, everyone to his taste. It was a pity, though; Richard would have made a wonderful husband.

Later, in bed, her thoughts turned to Jack. It was now a week since he had gone. Already she was missing him. Did he give any thought to her and their wonderful night together? Although it had ended badly, she hoped he did.

She remembered that she hadn't read her mother's letter and climbed out of bed to get it. It was full of news about the happenings in Tullybra. Her mother mentioned that she was seeing quite a bit of Pat McGarry these days. He'd been a tower of strength since Colin died, she wrote, and went on to tell how he had helped her move to the cottage, and how he made it his business to call in each evening to make certain she was all right.

At this point, Theresa stopped reading and stared into space. Strangely, the news didn't affect her as she thought it would. She supposed, if she was honest, the idea of her mother and Pat getting married in the future had always been a possibility. It wasn't something she wanted, but in a peculiar, disembodied way her mind had adjusted to the idea. She just hadn't let it surface.

Eileen, her mother continued, was still away on Retreat but due back in the next few days. Eileen was disappointed that she had not received a letter from Theresa, so could she redress the situation and send one soon? Eileen had little in her life at the moment but the church and its goings-on. She was rarely seen out when she came home from Dublin.

Life was funny – strange funny, not funny ha ha. She and Eileen had been reared in the same village, under the same conditions

233

and restrictions, and yet they were rapidly going in opposite directions. Whereas Eileen was on her way to sainthood and canonisation, she, Theresa, was travelling along the road to perdition.

She had tried the lot in her aim to be Bad. She'd smoked cigarettes in spite of her resolve never to do so; she'd drunk many types of alcohol and discovered she had a particularly low tolerance to wine; anxious to be one of the crowd, she had once smoked one of the peculiar cigarettes that gave one such a feeling of euphoria – in spite of Ross Carling's warning. Nothing would induce her to try that lark again. she'd spent a lot of the time feeling dizzy and out of control.

Having had a taste of the good life she had to admit to certain addictions. She enjoyed the club scene and being able to dress in stylish clothes, but she'd still kill for a banana split – even the fact that she could now indulge herself hadn't made the novelty wear off. Fortunately, she had not got a weight problem, but she had to be careful. Her lifestyle depended on her body. She lifted the letter and continued to read.

Father Corke was retiring and Father Touhey was taking his place; another young priest would be coming soon. Father Corke was going to move up towards his favourite fishing grounds and Nuala didn't think that they would be seeing him again.

Theresa leaned back on the pillow. She had an aching longing to visit her secret beach; to throw off every stitch and swim a mile's length along the coast; to go into Kilgaven again, with Eileen and Tandy and Jack, to drink Espresso coffee. She wanted to visit Aunt Margaret's shop to try on those dresses that had looked so wonderful then. Tears stung her lids. Change could be hurtful.

She went into the kitchen, made herself a hot drink and took it back to bed with her, feeling lonely and sad.

Jack and Declan walked into Gaffney's bar and ordered their pints. While they waited they scanned the room for a seat. There wasn't one.

'I hate drinkin' standin' up,' Declan moaned. 'Every time we find a pub that looks promising the bloody place starts to become popular.'

That's because everyone else is on the same round trip,' Jack laughed. 'I bet if we went back to the square we first started from, we'd find that everyone had deserted the pub just as we did, and for the same reason.' Having caught sight of a couple leaving a table, he darted off and left Declan to follow.

Declan lowered his long body into the chair. 'Thank God. I'm too worn out to stand. I forgot to ask. How did the wedding and the trip go?'

'All right!' said Jack.

'Don't bore me with too many details, will you, Jack,' said Declan with a wry smile. 'Surely something exciting happened.'

'I met Theresa at the wedding. She looked as great as ever.'

Declan waited. 'And?' he said at last.

'And I went back to London with her. She has a great life, an expensive flat, and wears designer clothes. She has gone beyond me now.'

'You'll not always be a penniless medical student, for God's sake.'

'It isn't that. It's her expectations and her way of life that have come between us. I could never keep up with her.'

'Has she come into money or something?' Declan drank the remains of his beer. 'Drink up. I'll get the next.'

Jack watched him make his way to the bar. He didn't want to discuss with Declan how Theresa earned a living. Seeing that picture of her looking so desirable in her nakedness had shocked him. He'd gone to the gallery in Bond Street as she had coldly suggested he should, and if he had been shocked at seeing her in the magazine, he was stunned into incoherency when he had walked round, under the jaundiced eye of the owner, and saw her in the larger original that left nothing to the imagination.

Her lovely eyes had stared out at him dreamily, and against his will he had found himself focusing on her nakedness, just as he imagined every man who studied it would. No! He didn't want to discuss her with Declan. He couldn't do so with equanimity. it hadn't helped that the oily looking owner had leered at the portrait and said, 'Is she not beautiful? Is not that the perfect body? You, young man, are looking at the most popular model and the most beautiful woman in the world of art. She is much sought after.' Jack had flown.

When Declan returned, Jack tore into a description of the wedding and described the meeting with Davey Adams. He told of the old Davey and his shenanigans, and how he'd marvelled at the change in him. After a time he realised he had battered Declan's ears with his prattle, and could see the poor man was glad when they began to talk medicine until it was time to get back.

'By the way,' said Declan, 'why did you stay an extra day? The prof has marked your absence.'

'I had to pay a visit somewhere,' said Jack dismissively.

He couldn't concentrate on his afternoon work. He could kill Declan for bringing this all up again in his mind. He had been home two weeks now and he had just been getting over his anger and disgust at what Theresa was getting up to, and now it had all started up again.

He remembered that she had, on at least one other occasion, showed that she had no inhibitions about her body; but racketing about on the beach in her underwear with light-hearted abandon was not the same as allowing herself to be seen stark naked by countless men – and he didn't give a damn if the pose was artistic. He wondered what Father Corke would say if he knew what his favourite tearaway was doing for a living. Jack groaned inwardly. He loved her. Why couldn't he accept her as she was; a lovely, sensuous woman with no false modesty? He recalled a remark his mother had made some years before when she had first met Theresa: 'Son! I like that girl very much and I know you do also, but I have to warn you; she will cause you pain. I felt it strongly as I looked at her.'

Had his mother known just how deep the pain would be at times?

CHAPTER 17

For some days now, Theresa had felt generally unwell. She felt, too, that life had suddenly become stale here, in England. She had an overwhelming desire to bathe again at Lafferty's Cove; to sit in Father Corke's study and have one of their famous arguments about religion and god; to see Eileen and hear all about her plans. Most of all, she had a childish desire to have her mother wrap her arms around her as she used to. She tried to shake off the feelings, telling herself that it was due to the fact that Polly was abroad at the moment and she missed her. However, her restlessness persisted.

She came home after a particularly tense modelling session and, throwing her coat over a chair, reached for the telephone and rang the airport to make a reservation for a flight the next day. Having done that, with a slight prickle of apprehension, she phoned her mother at the schoolhouse. She was not there.

She nibbled her lip. She needed to get in touch with her mother. The reservation was for the next day and she couldn't arrive without notice. After all, she hadn't been exactly close with her mam for the past year. There was no telephone at the cottage. She thought hard and gave a sigh. This was not something that she relished, but she felt she had no option. She lifted the receiver again and dialled a number. With a voice shaky with nerves she said, 'Is that Pat McGarry?'

'Yes!'

'It's Theresa Brady here.'

There was a pause at the other end. No doubt Pat was wondering what on earth Theresa Brady was doing phoning him. at last he spoke. 'This is a surprise. What can I do for you, Theresa?'

'I'm coming over tomorrow and I wondered if you could let Mam know. It may not be convenient, you see, and I need to know if it isn't so that I can cancel the reservation.'

'Is she not at the schoolhouse?'

'No!' Did the man not realise that if her mam was at the schoolhouse she would not be phoning him? Theresa hadn't figured Pat for an eejut. He must be as nervous as she was.

'I'll be passing the cottage in an hour. If she's there I'll tell her to phone you as soon as possible, but if she doesn't ring you, then I suggest you ring again later – will that do? Or is there a message?'

Jesus! was there anything that didn't have its complications? 'Will you tell her that I will be arriving at Dublin around six o'clock tomorrow evening and could she meet me? If it isn't a good time to come over, then perhaps she could ring me this evening. I'll still have time to cancel.'

Her mother rang her back. Of course it wasn't inconvenient. She was excited at the prospect of seeing Theresa and asked her how long she was staying.

'I don't know, Mam. I had this urge to come home. I rang the airport on the spur of the moment and managed to get a seat on the plane. Are you sure its all right?'

'I'll be there tomorrow. I can't wait to see you.'

Nuala put down the phone and turned to Pat, who took her in his arms.

'It will be all right,' he said. 'Theresa has got to know sometime.' He stroked the brown hair as she leaned against him. He loved the woman to death – always had. Colin had been dead a while now; they were together at last, and he would defy anyone to take her away from him now. Of course he could understand Nuala's fear that Theresa would turn away from her. Theresa had idolised Colin, and the last person she would want her mam to marry would be himself, for it was common knowledge that he had continued to carry a torch for Nuala since the day she had walked down the aisle. He had hurried from the reception and wasn't seen again for six months, having gone off on an extended holiday in the hope that when he came back he would be in control of his feelings.

When he did arrive back in Tullybra, his father, sorely tried at the way his son had deserted them and the farm, informed him that Nuala Brady was heavily pregnant. He was telling him so that Pat would be prepared and wouldn't go making a cod of himself over her.

Well, he hadn't! But the sickness inside him remained. He wanted to rush to her and tell her he had made a mistake and he wanted her to run away with him. It was a daft thought. There wasn't a devil's chance in hell of such a thing happening – not in Tullybra, and not with Father Corke and the congregation on the side of God, the Pope and Colin Brady.

238

Nuala looked up at him now, her eyes soft with love. She was where she had longed to be for many a year. She had adored Colin for his good nature and his gentle love, but she missed the passion she had experienced with Pat – the passion that the more gentle, passive Colin didn't possess.

His had been a comfortable, safe love that had made her feel secure and happy, but there had been times when she had longed for the heightened desire that had flooded her whole being when Pat held her in his arms when they were young, and kissed her till her very nerves sang.

'Can we leave telling Theresa for a bit?' she asked him.

'Whenever you feel ready,' he said, holding her against him. 'Until then, I will be the soul of discretion. I promise.'

They both met Theresa at the airport. Nuala explained that Pat had offered his services. His car was faster and more comfortable than hers.

Pat silently took her suitcase and put it in the boot of the car in order to allow mother and daughter time to ease into their old way with each other. Theresa, for whatever reason, had shut herself off from them all. Not once, he reflected, had she invited Nuala over to England. She had kept contact mostly by letter and had paid only one visit since Colin's death. Both women joined him now.

'Thanks, Pat,' said Theresa.

'For what? Sure I couldn't let you and your mother drive all the way from Dublin in that little car of hers,' he grinned. 'You'd have spent the rest of the holiday in bed nursing a bad back.'

The journey back to Tullybra was a strained one. It would have been hard for a stranger to recognize that the two women in the back of the car were mother and daughter, in spite of their physical resemblance. They talked together in short, spurty sentences, as though they were saying the lines of a badly rehearsed play.

Pat was relieved when they reached the cottage. 'I'll leave you to it,' he said, when he had deposited them at the door.

'Are you not coming in for a bite and a drink of tea?' Nuala looked at him pleadingly. She needed time before she was alone with Theresa.

'No! I'll see you both tomorrow.' He started up the car and drove off as the two most important women in his life went inside.

When she had unpacked her suitcases in the tiny bedroom next to her mam's, Theresa joined her in the kitchen. 'It's colder here than in England,' she remarked, shivering.

'Well, it is September, and as you know, in Ireland we don't do things by half. Go and sit by the fire and I'll bring the food in. We can eat with it on our knees for a change.'

Theresa gratefully held her hands to the fire. She pulled the boiling kettle away, swinging the kleek gently so as not to spill the water and risk scalding herself, just as her gran had taught her.

She looked around her. It felt strange. The cottage was now a mixture of gran's furniture and some pieces taken over from the schoolhouse. The mixture and the arrangement had, in some way, rendered the cottage neutral. Neither fish nor fowl, she thought, sadly – just like her life at the moment.

Nuala set the small tray in her lap. 'Get that into you. You'll feel more like the thing.'

'Mam?' Theresa hesitated.

Nuala, her fork half-way to her mouth and her heart doing handstands in her chest, waited.

'Are you going to marry Pat?'

How like her daughter. No beating about the bush. She laid her fork down and regarded the girl opposite. 'I – I – How would you feel about it?'

'It isn't a case of how I feel. How do you feel about Pat?'

Nuala sighed. 'I love him – I won't deny it. But you are wrong; it does matter how you feel.' She stretched out her hand and laid it on Theresa's. 'I loved your father dearly – you know that – but I've known and loved Pat for many years, and since Colin died he has been a tower of strength to me. The love I felt for him all those years ago has resurfaced. He has asked me to marry him, but I put him off. I wouldn't hurt you for the world.'

'Marry him! You deserve to. You made Da happy till the day he died. I'd not deny you your own happiness now. Pat is a good man. I can see he loves you.' Theresa didn't look up as she spoke, but concentrated on pushing the food round her plate.

'There is something worrying you,' said Nuala gently. 'I always know when you start punishing the food on your plate that there is something on your mind.'

Theresa took a deep breath. 'There is something I have to tell you. I think now is the time.'

Nuala paled. The serious look on Theresa's face told her that this was of great importance to both of them. 'Go ahead,' she whispered, her throat dry with nerves.

Theresa put down her knife and fork. 'Mam, there is no easy way to start this, so I will tell you straight out that I heard what you and Pat said, the day of my party, in the barn. I know that I am Pat's daughter.'

Nuala gasped. She crossed her arms over her breasts and bent her head to stop herself from fainting. Nothing Theresa could have said would have shocked her more than this. It was too much. She couldn't look at her daughter. She sat there, shame rising in her as she visualised Theresa, there in the barn, listening to the argument between her and Pat.

'My God! I am sorry you had to learn of this in such a way – and on your birthday too.' Nuala began to cry, at last. Now she knew why Theresa had withdrawn from her. She continued to sit there, the meal forgotten, her shoulders heaving with the sobs and the pain of what she had just heard.

Suddenly she felt herself gathered into her daughter's arms and felt the hand stroke her head.

'Shh, Mam. I've grown up a lot since that day in the barn. I told you, I know you loved Da and were a wonderful wife to him. Sure it wasn't your fault that fate dealt you such a blow. You made the best of it and, as I said, I know for a fact that you made my father a happy man. The evening before he died – you remember he asked that I should go up to see him – he told me how happy his life had been with you.'

Nuala lifted tear-stained eyes. 'He did? Oh Theresa, I can't tell you what that means to me – hearing that. sometimes I felt suicidal with the guilt of it all, but I made a vow that I would never let Colin suffer for the wrong I had done him. To know that I succeeded eases my heart.'

'Do you think he knew he was going to die that night?' Theresa asked, tears thick in her own throat.

'I think he did. He insisted that I sleep with him – for the first time in weeks. I'm glad I was with him when he died.'

Nuala put her arms round her daughter and held her close. Suddenly, all the tensions that had been between them were disappearing like wraiths of smoke.

'You don't think . . .' Nuala found it difficult to voice what she was thinking. 'Do you think your father ever suspected? I don't think I could bear that.'

'I don't think he did – not for a minute,' Theresa said gently, and added, 'I would prefer it if you didn't tell Pat that I know he is my father. I don't think either of us could deal with that, not just yet.'

Her mother nodded and Theresa returned her hug. Things would work out for them, she thought, and aloud she said, 'I'm starving. Let's tuck in. We can talk again in the morning.'

Eileen had been home two days before she met Theresa in the street. She was coming out of the chemist's when she caught sight of her. She ran the short distance between them and said breathlessly, 'Theresa. I heard you were back. Why didn't you let me know you were home?'

241

Theresa laughed. 'How could I, you eejut? Sure you weren't here to tell. University isn't doing a tap for your thinking, is it?'

Eileen reddened. 'Right, right,' she said. 'What I meant to say was, why didn't you write and tell me you were coming over?'

'I didn't know myself till the evening before I arrived. My poor mam must have had a fit when she got the news that I was coming over the next day.'

'Well! Isn't that just like you, Theresa – always impetuous.'

She has changed, thought Theresa. She has lost weight. It suits her. The once plump rosy cheeks had fined down and the eyes looked larger now that they were not pushed up in a crease by the cheeks. She looked trim and, somehow, tinier.

'You've lost weight,' Theresa remarked, and watched Eileen blush. That hadn't altered. Eileen blushed at the drop of a hat.

'Have you time for a cup of tea? I'm sure my mam would like to see you again.'

Theresa glanced at her watch. 'Why not? I have an hour to pass before Mam picks me up. I was going to pay a visit to the church—'

'It's locked up now,' Eileen interrupted. 'During the summer it got broken into and some silver and a lot of money was stolen.' Poor Father Corke nearly had a nervous breakdown.

Theresa was appalled. In all her years living in Tullybra, the church had been a haven of coolness on a hot, crowded day. Even she, the least likely of them all, had crept in quietly on occasion for a chat with Himself up there to ask for a blessing, or to have a row with him because he hadn't answered a prayer sent up in dire distress.

'That's awful.' The world is changing, she thought, and the waves of change are lapping at the gates of Tullybra.

Eileen's mother didn't seem as overjoyed as Eileen had predicted. 'Are you home for good then, young Theresa?' she said, eyeing her with one of her famous sideways looks.

Theresa was aware that Eileen's mother had never entirely approved of her. She had kept a keen eye on what happened when Theresa and Eileen had gone off on 'one of their jaunts', as she referred to their excursions into Kilgaven, Theresa said quickly, 'No! No. You'll be pleased to know I'm only over for a short break.'

'Why should I be pleased to know that?' said Kathleen O'Rourke, giving her daughter an embarrassed look. 'Sure you are always welcome. This is your home, after all.'

'I know fine well you disapproved of what Eileen and I sometimes got up to.' Theresa showed no mercy. She knew just what was going through the other woman's mind. 'Eileen was not

242

so easily led as all that, in spite of what everyone thought. Eileen is stronger than she is given credit for. She kept me under control.'

Kathleen O'Rourke looked sceptical. The idea of her quiet daughter being able to control the actions of the more forcibly natured Theresa Brady was laughable.

'I did wonder if she would like to come out with me tonight. I understand there is a good film on in Kilgaven,' Theresa said.

'Eileen never goes to the pictures these days – do you, Eileen?'

Eileen, feeling that she was missing something that was going on between the two of them, said, 'That's right – but only because I had no one to go with. Do you mind if Theresa and I go upstairs for a cup of tea and a chat?'

'Not at all. You are welcome, but make sure you put everything away when you have finished.'

Some things never change, thought Theresa, as she followed Eileen up to the rooms above the shop.

'What's been happening lately?' she asked, as Eileen busied herself with kettle and teapot.

Eileen brought her up to date with the latest events, some of which Theresa knew about from her mother's last letter.

'I think the burglaries that have taken place lately have been the reason why Father Corke, the blessed man, has decided to retire,' Eileen said with some bitterness. The thought of Father Corke not being around saddened her. He had been the one who had steered her right, after all, when she had agonized about taking up the religious life. It was he who advised her to go to university and use the experience to help her see the way forward.

'By the time you're done you'll know one way or the other whether you want freedom or the restrictions of life in God's service,' he'd said.

Theresa was surprised to hear that Nora Adams had married one of the barmen in the pub she worked in and had settled in Dublin to a life of respectability; and she was amused to learn that Biddy Devlin no longer wore her garish dresses and had taken to wearing a lot of black since her husband had lost his job and gone off to England to look for work.

'What about Moira Kennedy?' she asked, her curiosity getting the better of her.

'I understand she's in England now. I think she has gone over to be with Ross Carling.'

'She may be in England, but she isn't with Ross. I see him frequently at parties and he's playing the field.'

'What doe that mean?'

'It means he goes out with anyone who looks any way half-decent and wears a dress. That fella has no notion of settling down with any one girl. He lives for parties, nightclubs and, strange as it always seems to me, the opera.'

'What have you been up to? I bet you have the grand life over there with all those film people and artists running round begging for your time.' Eileen had nearly burst with excitement when Theresa had told her in one of her infrequent letters that there was not one, but three portraits of her hanging in an important gallery.

Theresa told the wide-eyed Eileen about her life in England, omitting anything that would shock her old friend. She smiled at the excitement in her friend's face as she listened to tales of what now seemed to Theresa a perfectly ordinary lifestyle.

'I'd love to go over there. Is it as decadent as we thought?'

'No! Life over in England is more sophisticated, but the family unit works the same over there as here.' She laughed at the disappointment on Eileen's face. Her own suppositions had been just as naive until she made the great escape and found that she'd had the wrong idea altogether.

In fact, she had exchanged one kind of prison for another, she thought, wryly. Sure she had more money and more geographical freedom, and she wore chic clothes and mingled with people who had seen and done things that the folk of Tullybra would consider the devil's own work, but she had shipped her values along with her luggage and was still bound by them. Freedom, she discovered, could be found anywhere – even in Tullybra. All that was needed was courage to be your own person.

She put her cup on the table. 'I've got to rush,' she apologised. 'I'm late for Mam and she'll be ranting on.'

Eileen said, 'That's fine. Are we going into Kilgaven, then?'

'Of course. *Ivanhoe* is on – with Robert Taylor. We'll have a banana split afterwards. I'm still mad about them.'

'Followed by the antidote, of course.' smiled Eileen.

Theresa laughed. 'Followed by the antidote.'

'It won't be quite the same,' said Eileen. 'I love coffee now. I got the taste for it since I started at the university.'

'You must tell me how you are getting on there.' Theresa went down the steep stairs and out of the shop. Kathleen O'Rourke was busy, but gave a tiny wave and an even tinier smile.

After mass on Sunday, Theresa was hailed by Father Corke. 'They haven't arrested you then?' He looked at the slight figure before him and added, 'Are you being starved, or what? Sure there's nothing of you.'

'I eat like a pig; I always have. I lead a busy life and I burn the lot off,' Theresa laughed. Out of the corner of her eye she saw Pat

McGarry walk across to her mother, who was chatting to Kathleen O'Rourke.

'I hear tell you are throwin' in the towel,' she said, raising her eyebrows.

'I am, I am. Sure there was no challenge in the job after you went off. The group that followed you are all good-livin'. My work had dried up. I haven't given a decent tongue lashing since you left.'

He'd aged, this old adversary of hers. He was more bent now, and his white hair was more sparse.

'How's your arthritis?' she enquired softly. She watched him try and hide his misshapen hands beneath his cassock, but the effort caused him to wince.

'It's bad enough,' he confessed, 'but there, it's a damn sight better than having nails through my hands and feet any day – and I can still hold a rod.'

'Do you know, when I was younger, you scared the devil out of me at times?'

'I had success of a kind, then. I didn't think you took a blind bit of notice. You were a right hoity article. I'll die a happy man knowing that I managed it.'

'You did better than you thought.' Theresa grinned. 'Even now I can't commit a decent sin, for that voice of yours keeps popping up in my subconscious.'

He gave a hearty laugh. 'I'll tell you something funny. Sister Anunciata told me one day that you would make an excellent nun.'

Her laugh rang out across the churchyard, causing many to stare at them. 'Good God – I mean – Dear me!'

'Good God will do.' Father Corke patted her shoulder. 'Away over to your mother. She's getting a bit impatient. I expect the lunch is about to burn. Take care of yourself, Theresa Brady, and say a prayer for me.'

'I'll do that. I understand Himself up there listens more to sinners.' They smiled at each other.

He watched her walk away towards her mother and Pat McGarry. He had seen her potential the day he poured water over her head at her baptism, when those blue eyes had opened wide with the shock of the water and looked at him in fury before she took the place apart with the noise of the yell she let out.

'What on earth was Father Corke saying to you?' asked Nuala.

'He misses me,' said Theresa, and smiled to herself as her Mam, only half listening, hurried her to the car.

She was glad to be back in England. She needed to get back to work to help her rid herself of the depression that had set in towards the end of her holiday. She had begun to feel restless and vaguely unhappy because she seemed to be the only one who had not got a set goal. Her mam had made up her mind that she and Pat were going to marry before Christmas. Jack was well on the way to becoming a doctor and was obviously content with his social life. Eileen was on the way to sainthood and was quietly happy about her vocation, and Tandy and Fliss were deliriously happy in wedlock. There was only herself – the one with all the plans for a great life – still searching for fulfilment. Jesus! Even Davey Adams had made it.

She threw herself into her work, and when not working she filled her social calendar to bursting point. She was so busy she didn't realise how tired and vaguely unwell she felt until she almost fainted. Even then she thought she was going down with a cold. It wasn't till she woke up one morning feeling so ill that the sight of food made her retch, that she realised it was serious. She had to cancel a session with Paul Nottingham, who was painting her as part of his new exhibition, and make an appointment to see her doctor.

On the evening she went, she knew she looked awful. She'd had yet another day of dragging herself to the bathroom to be sick, and the thought of food was out of the question. The most she could manage was a bowl of thin vegetable soup and a slice of bread.

Polly took one look at her and insisted on coming with her. She said that she was extremely worried about her, and if she didn't agree to stay home, she would cancel a very important session she was doing abroad and hold her in bed by force.

The doctor, when he had finished examining her, returned to his desk and waited for her to dress.

'Have I got a virus?' Theresa asked anxiously.

He looked at her. 'I think not,' he said, hesitantly. 'I'm afraid I have to tell you – you are about eight weeks pregnant – perhaps longer. It's hard to tell at this . . . Are you all right?' Any vestige of colour she'd had before had gone.

Theresa looked at him in horror. 'I can't possibly be pregnant,' she whispered.

'I'm afraid you are.' Doctor Meade shuffled his stethoscope around in front of him. He never liked breaking this kind of news, even to those who had come to him with a vague suspicion already formed. This girl had clearly no idea.

'Didn't you realize you had missed your period?'

'But I didn't!' Theresa gasped. 'Although, come to think of it – it wasn't a lot.'

246

Polly, idly thumbing through a magazine, looked up as Theresa walked across the waiting room. 'What's the matter?'

'I'm pregnant!' Theresa gave a distracted look around.

'You? Never,' Polly said in disbelief, adding, 'Let's get out of here. We'll go straight home.'

Once there, Polly sat Theresa down and took the chair opposite.

'I can't be!' Theresa cried, holding her arms round her body.

'Oh my God!' said Polly. 'You must know who the father is?'

Theresa didn't answer. She was remembering the night that Jack and she had made love.

'I do know who the father is,' she said at last, her eyes closed. 'You have never met him. It – it's someone I was once in love with and he went off to university and met someone else. Just recently I met him again and I'm afraid we celebrated our renewed acquaintance with copious amounts of wine. In short,' Theresa said bitterly, 'we were as drunk as two stoats.'

'It isn't the end of the world,' Polly said. 'You aren't short of money and you'll cope. I'll be around.' She crossed to Theresa and put her arm round her shoulder. 'Unless, of course, you are going to tell him?'

Theresa smiled sadly. 'It isn't that easy,' she said. 'You don't know what it would be like. Respectable Irish girls don't get pregnant. I couldn't face the disgrace – and besides, the man concerned is just starting his fourth year of medical studies, so I can't burden him with this terrible problem.'

They sat in silence for a long time, till Polly rose and went into the tiny kitchen to make a strong cup of black coffee. She hadn't wanted to alarm Theresa, God knows she'd had a big enough shock as it was, but the months and years ahead could prove to be pretty rough.

She returned to the sitting room and sat down beside her friend. 'Have you thought about what you are going to do?'

'Yes!' Theresa replied, her voice firm, her eyes staring straight ahead. 'I'm going to have an abortion. There is no other way.' With a cry of anguish, she buried her head in Polly's shoulder and sobbed her heart out.

Polly held her while she got the worst of the shock out of her system before saying, gently, 'Are you sure about this? I mean, with your religious and cultural background, you could cause yourself more stress than if you went through with the pregnancy.'

'I've got to! There are too many things against me having the baby. My mother is just getting married; the father of the baby is right in the middle of his medical studies; and I couldn't cope with the population of Tullybra if it ever came out.' Also, she couldn't

247

bear losing the respect of Father Corke, she thought wearily.

Polly made her drink the coffee, remaining silent as Theresa managed to get the liquid down between sobs.

'I can help you,' she said at last, with a sigh. 'I know of a very discreet clinic which deals with "gynaecological problems". All you need is money. You will be invited for an examination and then a letter will be sent to you telling you that you need an "operation".'

'Wouldn't my doctor . . .?'

'Don't be naive, Theresa. Abortion is not on the list of "can dos" yet. Legally this is not allowed – but eyes are closed because the alternative is back-street jobs sometimes resulting in catastrophe.'

Polly fumbled in her handbag. 'This is the address, but before you make the final decision – think it over. After a good night's sleep things might seem less awful.'

'Will you stay with me tonight, Polly? I don't think I could bear being on my own.'

'I'll stay with you if you promise to eat the meal I'm going to make us. First, I have to telephone to break my date.'

'Oh, Polly! I'm sorry. I didn't realise—'

'I'm only going to postpone it. I've had to do it before.' Polly felt that this was a crisis. Somehow, she had to make Theresa change her mind. She didn't know what she would be letting herself in for – losing a baby this way left terrible scars.

CHAPTER 18

Having made the decision to have the abortion, Theresa saw no point in delaying things. 'I've already made the arrangements,' she told Polly. 'My mind is made up.'

'Take more time to consider,' Polly pleaded. 'Talk to someone. It is such a big step.'

'The fewer who know about this the better, and I don't want to prolong the agony. I will have guilt lying on my conscience for the rest of my life and I will have to live with it – I don't need anyone to tell me that.' Her voice broke. 'I'm not the first one to conceive a child and despatch it to Limbo,' she added in a whisper. 'I know I will have to answer to a higher authority for my actions.'

'I'll be here for you,' Polly promised. 'But be sure about this, Theresa.'

Theresa nodded her head. From where they were walking in Peckham Rye she could see the windows of her flat. They seemed to stare at her balefully. Maybe if she hadn't moved out of The Grange she wouldn't be in this mess now.

'Let's go back and have some tea.' She took Polly's arm. She didn't know how she would have managed without her friend. She had kept her sane, for in spite of her air of bravado, Theresa was quaking inwardly with fright. She could hardly believe she had got herself in such a situation. Mad as she was, she had always stopped short of sheer lunacy – yet here she was, discussing abortion as she would discuss the best way to dispose of the remains of the Christmas turkey. It was only now that she was about to face the prospect of signing into the clinic that the full force of what she was doing hit her.

Polly was going abroad in a week's time. By the time she came back it would all be over. A tear escaped. She brushed it away hastily. Wasn't it just Theresa Brady's luck that her first and only sexual experience had led to pregnancy? Sure not one of them back home, knowing of her wild reputation, would ever believe that she hadn't been living it up all the time.

The bold Theresa Brady had finally met her come-uppance, and she had not the courage to face her mother or Father Corke – or indeed the judgemental inhabitants of Tullybra, many of whom would say that she got what she deserved for the way she had behaved.

Later, when Polly rose to leave, Theresa smiled and said, 'I'll be fine. Don't worry about me. Give me a ring when you get back.'

That evening, having had another bout of sickness, she went to bed early. Her doctor had told her that it was more usual for sickness to start in the third month, but sometimes it occurred earlier and only in rare cases did it become a major problem. She hoped to God she didn't become one of the rare ones. Things were bad enough.

The phone rang. At the sound of her mother's voice she wanted to cry, but she held back, and when her mother asked if she was all right as she sounded a bit hoarse, she assured her she was and that she was just getting over a cold.

'Are you ringing for a reason, Mam, or just a chat?' Her mam had taken to ringing her more often now that they had sorted things out.

'I rang to tell you that Pat and I have set a date for the wedding. It will be the Saturday before Christmas. I hope you don't have any important work on at that time.'

'No, Mam. I'll keep that date clear. Are you having a big do?'

'Indeed I am not – at my age? Besides, it's my second marriage.'

'Sure what difference does that make? It's Pat's first and he's entitled to have a big splash.'

Nuala laughed. Her voice sounded loud and crackly over the phone, as though she was laughing in a cave with a storm outside.

She spoke again but Theresa couldn't catch the drift. 'What?' she yelled down the phone.

'In the name of God, Theresa, my ears have gone.'

'Sorry, Mam. There was crackling. What did you say?'

'I said, if Pat had his way he'd go over to England and have it done on the quiet. You know what he's like. He's become more sedate in his middle years.'

'He's done no such thing. He still has a reputation for haring about.'

'That isn't in the same line as dressing up and walking down the aisle in front of everybody. No! We are having a few people and I'm wearing a grey cashmere suit with a cyclamen-coloured pillbox hat and veil, and I'm wearing a pair of colour-matched sling-backs.'

'Sounds decadent! Do you want me over a couple of days beforehand, or will the night before suit?'

'I'd like you over before, if you can make it. I'll be gettin' every nervous. I could do with the company.'

Theresa put down the phone and lay back against the pillows. If she had not decided to have the abortion she would be four months gone at the wedding. Would she have been able to hide the fact? She wasn't certain how big she would be at that stage. This was just one more reason why she had to have it done. A great one she'd look, waddling down the aisle with her own mother looking rake-thin.

Unable to face the prospect of going by tube to the clinic, Theresa had ordered a taxi. When it arrived, she gathered up the large carpet bag she used for her modelling trips and, with a last look round, she closed the door and walked towards the black cab. She hadn't taken much with her, just a change of underwear and some make-up, a book to read, and her nightdress.

The clinic was situated in a quiet, tree-lined avenue. She dismissed the taxi two streets away and walked the rest. No sense in advertising the fact that she had achieved what she set out to be – Bad. The idea, which had been so attractive to a young girl in a country village in Ireland, at this moment had lost its appeal. In its place was a desire to put the clocks back and find again the innocence that she'd had then. Just lately she had been finding that the high life had not the same to offer as a swim at her beloved secret beach or a carefree trip into Kilgaven with the promise of adventure. She smiled. Having a drink in a pub had seemed such a decadent thing to do; the wearing of make-up so risqué for a young girl of seventeen.

She entered the clinic and was surprised at the opulence of the reception area; it looked more like the foyer of a hotel, with the heavy carpets and the comfortable furniture. The place was bedecked with professionally arranged flowers. Even the desk where a soft-spoken girl greeted her was surrounded by blooms in expensive vases. They must have cost a fortune at this time of year.

A nurse in a pale pink uniform showed her to her room. Theresa looked round. Here, the clinical aspect had been retained. It was neatly furnished with a bed, an armchair, a dressing table under the window, and a small wardrobe in the corner. There was a shower room with toilet to the right of the rather firm looking bed.

The nurse quietly explained that she would give her time to settle in and then she would come again to take her blood pressure. Theresa was only vaguely listening. Her whole being felt suddenly as cold and clinical as the room. Only now was the

251

significance of what was about to happen really taking hold. She nodded absent-mindedly and sat down on the bed, too busy with her thoughts to notice that the nurse had left.

Nurse Fordham made her way down to the reception desk where Tanya, the receptionist, was idly twirling her pen in her slim, long-nailed fingers. She raised her eyebrows in silent query.

'Don't know about this one,' said Celia Fordham, shaking her head as she leaned on the desk. 'She's deep. Not a tear; not a question asked or answered. She just nodded and sat on the bed. The eyes looked dead. I think she could do a runner – I'm not sure.'

'I think she's done this before,' said Tanya. 'She was too cool about it all. I reckon she leads a high life.' She turned the book towards Nurse Fordham. 'See? Model.' There was satisfaction in her voice. 'You're not telling me she's not experienced. These girls have a gay old time. I know that face from somewhere. She's a high flyer in the modelling world, I'm sure of it.'

'We'll see,' said Nurse Fordham, and made her way to the clinic rooms at the end of the hall to pick up her equipment.

A young doctor visited after supper. Theresa listened carefully this time, as he explained about the importance of the operation and possible after-effects. 'You will need help,' he said quietly. 'This is an important decision you've made. I'm sure you have thought things out carefully, but sometimes after the event emotions change. You may feel guilty and depressed. Have you made any provisions for counselling, or would you like me to arrange it for you?'

She just nodded.

He looked at her chart. 'I see your blood pressure is fine. I'll just run my stethoscope over your chest and then I'll write up your pre-med.'

When he had finished he sat down on the bed again. He was puzzled by her attitude. Most of the young women who came to the clinic felt depressed about the whole thing, but this young girl seemed to be in an even deeper, darker world of her own. He was very concerned about her.

'Would you like something to help you sleep?' he asked gently.

'No!' Theresa said. 'I deserve to suffer a night without sleep. It is a small penance for what I'm about to do.'

'If you change your mind, tell a nurse. I've written you up for a sleeping tablet. You will need all your mental and physical strength, and a good night's sleep is essential.'

252

'No! I'll be all right. Will I see you again before the op?' Her voice told him she didn't care one way or the other.

'If you need a visit, I will come, but normally I don't see the patient till the time of the operation when I give the anaesthetic,' he said.

'That's fine. I just wondered,' said Theresa dully.

As expected, she spent the night tossing and turning. Her dreams were weird. Her gran and her da were there. Unsmiling and stern, they seemed to be delving into her very soul. She tried to explain. They didn't answer. They just looked and looked and looked, their eyes filled with condemnation. She pleaded with them. Still they stared, silent, and then they disappeared.

She woke the next morning with a raging headache, her mouth dry and foul tasting. She struggled to the shower room. She always felt better after a good splash. It didn't help. There was an ache in her heart that no amount of cleansing could eradicate. The truth was, she would not feel good about herself for a very long time. She knew that with certainty.

Nurse Fordham entered. 'How are you this morning? Did you sleep well?'

Theresa looked at the smiling face and wanted to punch it for the insensitivity of the question. She felt her temper rise as she watched the girl shake the thermometer. 'Would you have a good night's sleep under the circumstances?' she replied sourly.

'I'm sorry. That was crass of me.'

Theresa sighed. 'Not at all, not at all. I'm being moody and thoughtless. You are doing your job. Please forgive me.' She tried to smile but her mouth didn't get the message. She lay back on the bed and waited for the thermometer to be placed under her tongue.

'I'll be up in ten minutes with the pre-med. You are the first on the list.' Nurse Fordham waited for it to register.

Theresa felt stricken; her hands plucked the sheet. She said nothing, however, merely watched as the girl left the room.

'The odds have shortened,' Celia Fordham whispered as she passed Tanya. 'The signs are all there now.' She made her way to the clinic room to prepare the medication.

When she returned with the covered dish which held the syringe, she found Theresa sitting fully dressed on the bed.

'I'll let the team know,' she said gently. 'I had a feeling you wouldn't go through with it.' She uncovered the dish to show an empty syringe. 'No point in wasting good medication,' she smiled.

'Will they be cross?'

'Certainly not. It happens. It's your decision. It wasn't an easy one to make and we understand. We are here to help.'

'Thank you.'

★ ★ ★

Theresa climbed into bed that night exhausted. For the first time since she had discovered her condition, she felt quietly happy. She knew with calm certainty that she had made the right decision at last. Sitting on the bed, waiting for that premedication, she had realised that she actually wanted this baby. The feeling of shame and the fear of condemnation was still there, and there was a rocky time ahead, but this was Jack's and her baby, and it had a right to be born.

She smiled as she remembered the nurse with the empty syringe. The woman had read the signs quicker than she herself had done. She wondered what Polly would say when she came back. Polly hadn't once tried to influence her either way. She was a good and wise friend.

There had been a letter from Fliss saying that she had interesting news and she hoped that Theresa could come to stay. She hadn't seen her since she had come back from her honeymoon.

There was also a letter from Polly, hoping everything had gone well. She would be home sometime next week and would contact her.

She rang Fliss and made arrangements. She would be collected at Hassocks station.

'I could take the bus into Ditchling,' Theresa said. 'At least you wouldn't have to come so far.'

'It isn't worth it for a few miles.' Fliss explained. 'Besides, I don't get to use the car that often. I'll use any excuse for a ride out.'

'What's the interesting news?' asked Theresa.

'I'll tell you when you get here.'

She had to be content with that. Fliss was a great girl. She would make Tandy very happy. Theresa wondered idly if Eileen had chosen the religious life before Tandy made his announcement, or had his defection influenced her?

Fliss was waving frantically as the train pulled into the station.

'Good trip?' she asked.

'Not bad. I got a fast train from Victoria. The scenery was pretty so I didn't get bored.' Fliss looked positively glowing, she thought. They chatted as they drove along, until Theresa became engrossed again in the countryside. It really was very lovely, the Downs running along the skyline to their right.

Fliss and Tandy had rented a small cottage by the roadside, intending to move into their own house as soon as they could manage a down-payment on a mortgage. Tandy was working for a local sheep farmer.

254

'He's mad keen on sheep farming,' Fliss told Theresa. 'He fell in love with the Southdown sheep as soon as he started at college.'

'Weren't you going to set up on your own once?'

'Fliss, busy with the boiling kettle, didn't answer until she had set the heavy tray on the small table and started to pour. 'We still mean to. My parents are going to put some money into the scheme and Tandy's father has promised to give it some thought. It was he who suggested that we wait a year or two till Tandy has gained some experience, which is why he's working for Ted Hawkins. Ted knows more about sheep than many farmers could learn in a lifetime.'

Theresa sipped her tea gratefully. She was beginning to warm up after the chilly journey down in the unheated carriage. The heating had gone wrong. Her feet had suffered most. It was nearly the end of October and already there had been a couple of mild frosts. The cold didn't seem to worry Fliss who looked rosy cheeked and healthy. She was pretty in a robust, country-girl kind of way, Theresa thought.

'What is this interesting news?'

'Brace yourself.' Almost bouncing with excitement, Fliss said, 'I'm pregnant.'

'But you've only just . . .'

'On our honeymoon.' She blushed. 'We were so in love and so excited we forgot to – to . . .'

'Well! Congratulations!' Theresa stared into the hot embers. The fire had begun to die. She felt her eyes begin to fill with tears. 'It's the hot embers,' she said, with a sniffle.

Fliss looked curiously at her. 'They're dying down,' she said softly. 'Tell me what's wrong.'

'Look, I'm not going to spoil your lovely news with my tale of woe. It isn't anything – I'm just so happy for you.'

'I don't believe you, Theresa. Something is wrong. I would like to help. I may not be able to do anything constructive but I can listen.'

'You can't. Help, I mean. It's something I have to cope with by myself.'

'You aren't leaving things there. Nothing can spoil my happiness. Now tell me why you look so sad so suddenly.'

'You won't mention it to anyone? Not even Tandy – especially not Tandy. He mustn't suspect.'

'Will you stop it? I wouldn't tell a soul.' Fliss crossed over and sat beside her.

'I'm also pregnant,' Theresa said at last, her voice muffled.

There was thick silence. The big clock on the wall appeared to have developed a loud tick.

'Who – I mean – dare I ask . . .?'

'Jack!'

'But you hadn't seen Jack until the wedding,' Fliss gasped.

'We got together afterwards.' Theresa told Fliss about the reception, and how Jack had come up to London with Davey Adams and had stayed the night. 'We had rather a lot to drink,' she said guiltily. 'I shouldn't have drunk so much wine. I know I have an intolerance for it – it's the one drink that really hits me fast.'

'I thought you and Jack . . . I mean, you were . . .'

'We made it up during the reception. Even then I thought that I would go home and that would be the end of it. But Jack suddenly decided to come to London with Davey and me,' she said slowly. 'I have never slept with anyone else – never.'

'But I can't understand how—'

'We had a lovely evening, reminiscing about our days in Tullybra,' Theresa explained ruefully, 'and we polished off two bottles of wine. The truth is we were as drunk as a pair of stoats. Jack, having woken up beside me, got out of bed and hived off into the living room – in the hope that I wouldn't remember anything, I suppose.'

'Are you going to tell him?' Fliss held Theresa's cold hand in her own plump, warm one. She rubbed it gently and waited.

'No!'

'But Theresa, he would want to know. I'm certain of it. You must tell him.'

'Not a word. I'll handle this alone. You promised, Fliss. Jack has still some time to go before he is qualified. The last thing he needs is a problem like this hanging over his head.'

'Why should you do it alone? How will you manage?'

'I have a trust fund due to open up next year and I've saved a lot of money from my earnings. I may not have been in the top one hundred highly-paid models, but I was a high earner.' Theresa paused. 'Perhaps it's just as well I didn't become famous – think what the papers would have done with this bit of information.'

She decided there was little point in telling Fliss about the abortion episode. God knows, the girl looked shocked enough already. 'Just think,' she said with a wry smile, 'we may have conceived on the same night.'

When Tandy arrived home, they were busy in the kitchen. He gave Fliss a resounding kiss and Theresa a hug that nearly took the breath from her. He held her away from him. 'You've put on a bit of weight, Theresa Brady. It suits you. I've never seen you look so glowing.'

Fliss and Theresa dared not look at each other.

'You, on the other hand, have lost a few pounds,' Theresa said. 'Is Fliss not feeding you?' She punched him playfully and eyed him up and down.

'I'm still trying to get my stomach round this English food. I haven't had a good bowl of broth that you could stand a spoon up in since I left home, and I'd kill for a soda farl and salty country butter with a mug of buttermilk. Everything is refined to death over here.' Tandy laughed. 'Have you heard our news?' He twirled his wife round, a beaming smile on his face.

'I have indeed. I'm very pleased for you.'

Tandy enquired about her mother while they were having their meal. 'I hear tell she's marrying Pat McGarry.'

'You heard right.'

'How do you feel about it?'

'I was the one who told them to get on with it.' Theresa put down her fork. 'Mam made m'da very happy when he was alive. I don't think he'd begrudge her marrying again for a bit of company and happiness.'

'I didn't mean to be nosy,' Tandy said. 'It's just – well – I wondered if you would be hurt.'

'I like Pat. I don't mind a bit – besides, I'll have somewhere nice to stay when I go over on holiday, and a lovely swimming pool at my disposal.'

'Mercenary article,' laughed Tandy. 'To think I once fancied you.'

'Hey!' said Fliss.

'I'm going over for the wedding. I'll give them your blessing,' said Theresa. 'Any word for your da? I think he has been invited.'

'I suppose he would be. M'da and Pat were great friends over the years. I think m'da found it hard to settle down for a long time.' He grinned. 'Mind you, he kept himself busy begetting ten children. He had no time to stray.'

'Have you told your parents about the baby?'

'Not yet! We haven't told Fliss's either. We wanted to enjoy the news ourselves. We'll tell them soon.'

'I'm honoured that I'm the first to know.' Theresa smiled.

'There is a reason for that.' Tandy looked over at Fliss. 'You see – we want you to be godmother.'

Theresa stared at him. 'That – that's wonderful,' she said. 'I hope I'm not off somewhere at the time.'

'We'll give you plenty of notice, don't worry.' Tandy, feeling in expansive mood, suggested they should pop down to the local for a drink.

'Best not,' said Fliss, glancing at Theresa. 'Pregnant women shouldn't take alcohol.'

257

'A load of tarradiddle. Anyway, you needn't drink. We'll set you off on the orange juice, and Theresa and I can attack the hard stuff. I'll not take no for an answer.'

The pub was packed but they managed to find a corner and Tandy took their orders.

'I'd like a Pimms,' Theresa said.

When he'd gone, Fliss said, 'Was that wise? You really shouldn't take alcohol.'

'It'll not do me a button of harm. Sure nothing has proved that it's dangerous. I'll only have the one and then I'll go on to the orange juice.'

'He'll still wonder why you aren't drinking.'

'I'll tell him I've had something in my stomach and the Pimms is not doing it any good, and I'd better go on to the orange juice to settle it.'

They giggled together at the near truth. When Tandy came back with the drinks they were still laughing.

'Tell me the joke,' he said.

'There was no joke. It's only Fliss's heightened joy coming out because of her condition. We just felt like a laugh.' The lie rolled smoothly off Theresa's tongue. I haven't lost the touch, she thought, her eyes growing soft as she remembered the many times Eileen had ticked her off for the ease with which she could lie. She missed Eileen so much it hurt. God knows what she would think of the situation Theresa had got herself into now. 'Can I not let you out of my sight?' she used to say, when Theresa did something foolish and she wasn't there. If only she had been at the wedding, how different things might have been.

'You're looking sad,' said Tandy. 'Drink up and enjoy yourself.'

Next morning, while Fliss cooked lunch, Theresa took her sketch pad and went off to capture the beauty of the late autumn landscape. It had been Fliss's suggestion. 'I think it will be good for you to be by yourself for a while.' Theresa had smiled gratefully. She hadn't done much painting and sketching just lately and she realized she had missed the concentration and the resulting peace of mind that it brought to her in the midst of a busy life.

Two days after she got back to the flat there was a phone call from Richard. He was over to set up a new exhibition at the galleries and wondered if she would have dinner with him at his hotel.

'Are you staying at the Sheraton again?'

'Yes. It's comfortable and the prices are fairly reasonable. They set a good table so it seems a better option to eat here rather than

258

go out into the cold. It's all right for you youngsters, but at my age my bones feel it more.' He chuckled, and added, 'However, take a taxi – my treat.'

'If you think I'm going to be proud and turn that offer down, you have another thing coming, my lad.' Theresa laughed. 'Getting up to Victoria is trouble enough.'

'I'm serious,' said Richard.

'So am I.' She laughed again. 'I'll be in the foyer around eight o'clock so don't leave me there too long.'

He was already there when she arrived. He rose and walked towards her, smiling broadly.

She was well wrapped in a loose-fitting coat, but she felt herself redden. Removing her coat, she handed it to the young attendant who had silently joined them. 'I'm starving,' she said brightly. 'Lead me to the food.'

Richard had been right. The food was delicious, and served quietly and discreetly by the waiters. They had been shown to one of the tables in a secluded corner and Theresa was thankful for the mellow, subdued lighting. She had agonised over what to wear lest her condition be obvious, and had chosen a black dress with a full skirt. Perhaps she was being over-sensitive – even the plumper Fliss wasn't showing signs of her pregnancy yet – but she was concerned about the odd look Richard had given her as she arrived, and she toyed nervously with her wine during the meal, taking small sips now and again.

'Isn't the wine to your taste?' Richard asked.

'It's fine. I – I've had a bug just lately and I find that if I drink wine these days I feel slightly giddy. I seem to have developed an even quicker reaction to it than usual. I wonder if I've not quite recovered from the bug.' Theresa knew she was rambling on too much but she was desperate. This man was no fool.

'Or you could be pregnant,' Richard said softly – so softly that Theresa wondered if she could have been mistaken. Her heart began to pump, her first instinct being to deny it hotly and start with the Theresa-Brady-in-a-temper bit, tossing the head and glaring; but she knew fine well that it wouldn't work with this man. She slumped. 'I had hoped it wasn't obvious,' she said tremulously.

'It isn't,' he reassured her. 'But you forget: I am an artist and I have studied your body closely while painting you. I knew as soon as you walked to me that there was something different, but it was when you refused the wine that I was certain my suspicions were correct.' He took her hand in his. 'I promise you, no one else would notice.'

'I'm not going to name the father,' Theresa said, with a touch of

259

defiance. 'I don't want him to know.'

'I wasn't going to ask,' said Richard. 'Have you made any plans?'

She shook her head. 'Only that I'm going to cope by myself.'

'Your mother will surely have to know.'

'Not till she and Pat come back from their honeymoon. I'll not spoil their day. Besides, I'm living over here, so it will be easy to keep the whole thing quiet.'

'You will have to think things out more seriously than that, young Theresa,' said Richard, shaking his head. 'It might be better to come into the open. The hard fact is that you are having a baby and it can't be hidden for ever. What about when the child is growing up? Are you never going to be able to visit your home in Ireland? People forgive. You must swallow the pill of pride and live with the fact that, in the eyes of that narrow little community, you slipped up. Time will mellow their attitudes, I'm certain.'

'You don't understand. The people of Tullybra would look on me as being a right bad article and a disgrace to my mam and da.' She didn't add that they would be smirking behind her back because the bold Theresa Brady had pushed her own face in the muck and disgraced herself. She couldn't stand that. If she was guilty of the sin of pride, then so be it. There was no way that she was going to go around in sackcloth and ashes for the narrow-minded lot that made up the population of Tullybra.

She relaxed. It was a relief that Richard knew and was not unduly shocked. If only her mam would take it as well.

'I hope Mam takes it as well as you.'

'Did you know that I'm giving her away?'

'No, I did not – but I'm pleased.'

Half-way through the meal, Richard touched on the subject again. 'You don't have to live in Tullybra, you know. Dublin is far enough away to leave you in splendid isolation, but near enough for your mother and Pat to visit.'

Theresa looked thoughtful.

'An artist can work anywhere,' Richard continued. 'I take it you are going to paint? You have a great deal of talent and I would hope you are going to make use of it.'

'Of course I am,' Theresa said. 'I've been posing and modelling to build up a bank balance, but when my money is released, sometime soon, I shall give it up – I just don't know if I want to return home.'

Later, in bed, her thoughts were troubled. Three people now knew of her condition. How long before others did? She made frantic calculations to find out how far along she would be when she went over for the wedding. She'd be four months. She hoped it was true that some women didn't show much till the fifth month. With very careful dressing she just might hide it. Sleepily, she wondered if she could prevail upon Polly to help her choose the right clothes.

Polly was delighted to learn that she hadn't gone through with the abortion. She too had been through the same experience a year before she had met Theresa, and she had gone through with it. It had been hell; but once she had come out of counselling she had set her sights on making a success of her career. As the months passed, the knot of sadness inside her had finally dissolved and now, at the top of a very high-profile career, she had finally overcome it. She hadn't mentioned anything to Theresa as she hadn't wanted to influence her decision.

Modelling, once only a reasonably paid profession, had taken off in the past two years, and Polly was now very nicely set up. She had a wealthy boyfriend whom she loved, and plenty of work. If, once in a while, she shed a tear for the action she had taken, she felt it was a price she had to pay.

They were in Theresa's sitting room. Polly, having returned the previous evening from an assignment abroad, was regaling Theresa with all the incidents that had occurred during the photography sessions. It was an exciting new side of modelling – going out on location.

'I need to go shopping for an outfit for Mam's wedding,' Theresa said to Polly later. 'Could you come with me? I'd really appreciate your help.'

Polly was delighted. 'Of course I'll come. You know it's my favourite form of exercise.'

The shopping trip was arranged for three days hence. Polly said she knew just what was needed. Theresa was thankful. She had lost confidence in her ability to choose for herself.

'We'll go to Bon Marché's in Brixton. I saw Diana Dors shopping there once, and if it's good enough for her then why go all the way up to the West End?'

As Polly got up to go, Theresa laughed and said, 'I hope you aren't thinking of dressing me in the style of Diana Dors – not in my state.'

That evening she phoned her mother. She was irked at the wait, but all the long-distance lines were taken up. She poured herself a glass of sherry. Pregnant or not, she needed it.

At last she got through. 'How are things going with the wedding preparations?' she enquired.

Nuala said things were going well. It was going to be a small affair and the caterers were doing a nice spread at Pat's place.

261

'Who is going to be your bridesmaid?'

Nuala gave a merry little laugh. 'I had to ask Kathleen O'Rourke. Honest to God, Theresa, I was holding my breath hoping she would say no.'

'Why in the name of God did you ask her if you didn't want her?'

'Sure what else could I do? She has been my friend over the years. I'd not pass her over just because she's twittery and soft-witted and has no dress sense. Anyway she didn't feel she could work up the courage, but thanked me for thinking of her and said she was aware of the honour . . .'

'That sounds like her. Who have you asked, then?'

'I've asked Margaret, and she said she'd be glad to, seeing as her sister hadn't got the nerve. Of course I felt obliged to buy my outfit there – did I not tell you this?'

'You did not, Mam. I expect you're running around like a cat on a hot griddle now.'

'Will you come over early, so?'

'I will. I want to spend a few days with Nuala Brady before she becomes the stranger Nuala McGarry.'

Nuala caught the slight sadness in the voice. 'Are you sure you don't mind me marrying Pat? I thought you sounded a bit odd just then.'

'I'm delighted for you,' Theresa said.

'I can't tell you how happy that makes me,' said Nuala softly. 'I know how much you loved your father and I wondered if you might . . .'

'Mam! I mean it. I've always liked Pat and I've suspected for some time that you and he would end up driving each other mad in the end.'

'Cheeky article.' Nuala's laugh rattled down the phone.

Theresa smiled. She had made her mother's day.

CHAPTER 19

There were two weeks left before the wedding. Theresa became more nervous as the time passed. She studied herself in the cheval mirror, turning this way and that to observe any changes in contour. She couldn't detect any. Her complacency didn't last long, however. She woke up two days later and felt distinct movement. Filled with alarm she rung Polly who laughed at her fears.

'It's perfectly normal. You didn't think the baby would just grow quietly and then pop out at the last minute with all its bits intact, did you? Have a bit of sense.'

'What's going on in there, Polly? I get worried, sometimes – and I'm sure I'm starting to show.'

'I saw you only yesterday. I know you are exaggerating. Get yourself down to the surgery and book yourself in for some lessons, you daft nugget. Find out what the old bod is likely to do. Meantime stop going on about your size. The clothes we choose will hide any extra weight just brilliantly – besides, your mam won't be seeing anything but stars in her own eyes on the day.'

'The witches of Tullybra will, though.'

'I'm putting this phone down. I'm not wasting my time on your suppositions. I'll see you when you get back. You're off home in a few days time, aren't you?'

'God! I wish you were coming with me. I'll lose my nerve.'

Polly was right. She was behaving like a real eejut. This was not the old Theresa Brady. The effect of easy living and no real challenges to keep her up to scratch had rendered her as soft as treacle. Here, no one batted an eyelid at anything she did, so she had lost all her defiance. One thing Polly had said made sense. She should get into whatever scheme was going to help her find out more about her condition and what was best for her baby.

There was another tickle of movement, but this time a little thrill swept through her. She sat down on the sofa and cupped her hands round her belly. Whatever you are in there, she thought, with a sudden glow of happiness, I'm your mam and I'll not stand any nonsense from anyone. I promise you that I will protect you from the world.

By the time she was due to fly to Ireland, Theresa had got herself under control. She carefully packed the outfit she was to wear at the wedding. She and Polly had chosen a high-necked blue woollen dress which was softly fastened with a loose-woven belt of the same material. Her coat, a navy blue duster with large, deep pockets, was made of heavy taffeta – even she had been satisfied when she saw herself in it. Her hat was palette shaped with a long feather, and her shoes were navy blue court. Altogether, she looked the height of fashion. She'd turn a few heads among the congregation, she thought in satisfaction.

Her great worry was that Jack might be one of the guests. She hadn't liked to ask Mam, but he had always been a great favourite of hers and there was always the chance that she might invite him because of past associations. Her heart raced. She would just have to meet the situation if it arose. That night she went to bed early, determined to be at her best when she arrived at Dublin airport the following morning.

Jack Ross was bored. He didn't much care for Opthalmics and the days seemed to pass in a dreary succession of eyes and ops. A surgeon he would never be, he decided – certainly not an eye surgeon.

Declan entered the room, his tall, stick-like figure a welcome sight. 'Shouldn't you be doing a round with Mr Kerridge?'

'It's been cancelled – thank God. I hate Opthalmics.'

'Once you realize it's only part of your course and it isn't carved in stone that you should love it, it isn't so bad – anyway, I don't think that's the problem. You've been off-course ever since you came back from England.' Declan poured himself a cup of coffee before continuing. 'The old spark only shows itself on the odd occasion. Why don't you get it off your chest? I'll give a listen and do my counselling bit. It will be good practice.' He grinned and put on what he considered was the special look that counsellors wore, settling his face into a simpering look with creased eyebrows and his hand under his chin.

'You look like a constipated bull,' Jack laughed. 'Go counsel your arse, Declan; I'd end up committing suicide. You are the worst listener I know. You'd send me up no end.'

'No I wouldn't. Pat would disagree with that statement. She says I'm a great listener. She empties her mind to me on many occasions when she has problems.'

'And what do you do?'

'I give her a good kiss and she feels better.'

'You're not givin' me a bloody kiss to make me feel better,' Jack grinned. 'I'd rather eat poisoned meat than kiss those blubbery lips. I don't know how Pat can abide you.'

'Pat is more discerning than you, you culshie. That's why she left you for me.' Declan hurriedly slurped his coffee and slapped Jack on the back. 'I think you're in love but you won't give in. My advice to you, my friend, is to take the big step and get things straightened out with the delectable Theresa. Change your mind and go to the wedding tomorrow.'

Jack sighed heavily. Declan had hit the nail right on the head. He was madly, deeply, in love, and he'd blown it. He had been wrong to get worked up about Theresa and her chosen profession. Dammit! He'd always known that she had no problem with her body. It was what had attracted him to her for the whole of their teenage years, when she had entranced him with her naturalness.

He frowned. He was surprised that he had been invited to her mother's wedding. He wondered if Theresa had had a say in that. Shifting his position he looked despairingly at the clock. He'd better get cracking. He had to attend an op session in ten minutes. He bloody hated eye ops.

That evening, as he entered his room, the phone rang. He wondered, tiredly, if he should ignore it. The last thing he needed was someone trying to get him out for a night's carousing. All he wanted at this moment was a hot bath and a period of quiet study.

The phone continued to ring; wearily he picked up the receiver. It was Tandy. Jack listened carefully to what he had to say, his face going white with shock at the news imparted. He didn't say much in answer – what was there to say? One thing was certain: his hope of a warm bath followed by a quiet study period had just gone out of the window.

Theresa watched her mother walk slowly down the aisle and felt her eyes sting: her mam looked so lovely and so happy. The outfit she had chosen emphasized her trim figure, and the little hat sitting jauntily on her head allowed the thick hair curling round her ears to catch the light from the stained glass windows as the winter sun shone through.

Pat took Nuala's hand in his as she smiled radiantly at him, Theresa realized that her mother, after so many years, was with the man she loved. To her surprise, she found she didn't resent this fact any longer. She had a feeling that her da wouldn't mind a bit either.

Her thoughts flew back to that evening in the big barn, when her father had stopped her from rushing out to confront the two lovers. His love had been so entire that he had lived all those years a happy man, with the woman he adored.

The reception was being held at Pat's farm. Officially only thirty people had been invited to the wedding, but the church was crowded with villagers anxious to wish the couple well.

'So much for a quiet wedding,' Pat whispered as they came out of the vestry after signing the register.

Nuala beamed happily. 'I never thought we'd get away with it,' she whispered back, 'so I made plans.'

He stopped suddenly, causing those behind him to stumble. 'What d'you mean?'

'I told the caterers to lay on a bigger spread. All you need to do is announce from the altar that any who wish to come are welcome at the reception.'

Pat grinned. 'You're a great girl, Nuala Brady.'

'You mean Nuala McGarry,' she admonished shyly.

Pat hugged her there and then in front of the altar, before announcing to the congregation that anyone who could make it was invited back for food and drink and, as the party would no doubt go on until sunrise, those who couldn't could make their way along in the evening. He smiled at Nuala as the murmurs of acceptance began.

It was just as a good Irish wedding should be, he thought, giving his new bride a hug as they walked out into the winter sunshine for the photo call.

Theresa hooked her arm in Eileen's. 'I was a bit worried about all this,' she whispered, 'but it has turned out all right in the end.'

Eileen smiled. 'I never had a moment's doubt, you eejut. They look right together.'

'I wish my gran could have been here; she loved Pat McGarry as much as she did m'da. Once, a long time ago, she thought that Pat would be her son-in-law.'

Eileen's eyebrows rose in surprise. She was about to reply when Theresa was directed to her mother's side for a family photograph. Sometimes that girl had the oddest ideas – she hadn't changed.

They stuck together at the reception like a pair of Siamese twins. There was a lot to catch up on.

'Are you still set on becoming a nun?' asked Theresa, as they sat together on an upturned hay bale in the big barn. The reception had been transferred there, at Nuala's instigation, when she decided that it was going to roll out of control.

Eileen turned and looked at her in surprise. 'Are you mad or what, Theresa Brady? For why should I change my mind? You know I don't make hasty decisions. You might – I don't. And

266

speaking of decisions: have you decided what your future is going to be?'

'My future is all set,' said Theresa firmly.

'Your future is anything but.' Eileen's face was serious. 'Your future should include Jack, and well you know it.'

'It does not,' said Theresa flatly.

'And how is your career going?' Eileen continued, ignoring the tone of Theresa's voice. She decided not to press the issue of Jack: she had hopes that one day the pair of them would come to their senses and realize that, metaphorically speaking, they were joined at the hip.

'I'm doing all right. I now do more fashion work. It's less arduous and more lucrative, although I still prefer modelling for artists.'

'You've changed.'

'How so?' Theresa's chin lifted. The one thing she cherished was her Irish background and her upbringing. Just because she wanted the freedom to do the things that other girls in other countries took for granted, didn't mean she had denounced her background. She waited for Eileen's reply with some trepidation.

'You seem more sophisticated; you dress very fashionably, and you seem to have risen above us all now.'

'Eileen! I have not in this world done any such thing. I am the same person I always was. I wouldn't go thinking that I was better than anyone else.'

'Calm down.' Eileen laid her hand on her arm. 'I didn't mean that it was intentional or that I thought you looked down on us all. I only meant that you have been places and done things that sets you on a plane above us.'

Richard Beck hove into view and walked over to them. Eileen rose. 'I'll go over and wish your mother and Pat all the best,' she said. 'I'll see you later. we still have a lot to talk about.'

'Did I interrupt?' Richard smiled.

'Not at all. Not at all.' Theresa patted the bale. 'Sit down here, Richard.'

'How did I do, giving the bride away?' he smiled.

'You did just great.'

He hesitated. 'I hope you don't mind, but I actually came over to have a word with you about the baby.' He looked around to make certain they were not overheard.

'I somehow guessed you had something like that in mind.' Theresa put her plate on the ground. 'Before you ask – I haven't mentioned it to Mam.'

He nodded. 'I didn't think you would tell her on her wedding day; you have too much sense. I just wondered if you intended to tell her at all – only last time we met, you seemed to have this insane idea that you could live in England and no one would find out about the baby.'

'I was off my head – anyway, I did mention that I would tell Mam and Pat as soon as they come back from Dublin. You can't have been listening. I hear you are spending Christmas Day with us.'

'Yes. It was kind of your mother and Pat. I would have thought they would have preferred to have a quiet family day.'

I expect you are invited to keep me out of their hair so that they can canoodle a bit on the quiet,' Theresa laughed. 'How do I look? No one seems to have noticed I've put on weight.'

'I'd say you look just about right. You were too thin anyway.' He took her hand. 'Stop worrying so much.'

'I'm a bit scared about telling Mam and Pat about the baby,' she confessed in a small voice. 'It's bound to come as a terrible shock to them.' She looked imploringly at him. 'This is the first time in my life that I have felt so scared about facing up to something I've done.'

'Don't be. You should know your mother well enough to know that she might be shocked, but she'll take it in her stride, as she does most things, and will support you to the hilt.'

'There is one consolation,' mused Theresa. 'I'll be over in England when I have the baby. No one over there gives a tinker's curse so long as they don't have to pay for its keep.'

'You have Polly, I know,' Richard said, 'but don't you think you would be better to come back here? Your family is here. I am here. We will be with you all the way.'

'Not if you begged me.' She was aghast at the thought. 'You haven't seen what happens to the "fallen" in Tullybra. No quarter is expected, and none is given.'

'If you change your mind you only have to lift the telephone,' Richard said gently.

Theresa was dead on her feet. The party that followed the reception had gone on into the early hours. Pat and his new bride had set off on their mini honeymoon, leaving the revellers to carry on under the supervision of a small group of his friends.

When, at last, they had all gone, Theresa and Grace McCarthy, Pat's housekeeper, had taken one look at the mess in the barn and, shutting the doors on it, made their way to the house.

'I wonder how many of the lot that helped to make this mess will be along to clean it up tomorrow?' said Grace.

'You mean it will be left to us?' Theresa was appalled. She had intended to go into Kilgaven to do some Christmas shopping.

Grace McCarthy smiled. 'I'll get the farmhands to do most of it. You can be off into Kilgaven.'

With much relief, she climbed into her bed. The house seemed cold after the warmth of the big heaters in the barn, but she was asleep within minutes. Her mind had started to work on the problem of telling her mother about the baby, but the last matter she remembered considering was how she could hide the fact that Jack was the father. She would have to be strong about not disclosing the name, no matter how much pressure was put on her.

She awoke feeling refreshed and more optimistic. Grace McCarthy had set out a good breakfast, and Theresa managed to put some of it away so as not to upset her. She had passed her driving test shortly before she had become pregnant, which meant she was able to use her mother's little Morris Minor to get to Kilgaven, where she spent a pleasant morning and afternoon trawling round the shops. Eileen had been unable to come with her, which was a pity. She would have enjoyed the day even more.

When she arrived back at the farm, she found a note from the housekeeper telling her that young Jack Ross had called and would be back at six o'clock. Grace was going over to visit her daughter and wouldn't be back till tomorrow. She hoped Theresa didn't mind, only it was the only chance she had to get the grandchildren's presents to them, as she was spending Christmas with her daughter in Dublin this year.

Theresa's heart did a dive. The baby shot round in her stomach in protest, causing her to give a yip as a cramp-like sensation shot through her side. She sat down and looked at the clock on the kitchen mantelpiece. She had an hour to prepare herself.

She ran a bath and laid out some fresh clothes, nervously wondering if the dress she had chosen would hide her burgeoning bump. So far she had been very lucky. She eyed herself in the bathroom mirror and was convinced that she was protruding quite noticeably. It had only been the clever cut of the clothes that Polly had helped her choose that hid her condition. Jack, starting his fourth year at med school, might not be easily duped. She just hoped to God he hadn't done his obstetrics yet.

He arrived on time. She jumped as she heard the positive knock on the door. Taking a deep breath she opened it.

'Hello Jack,' she said, nerves making her voice tremble.

He brushed past her, his face dark with anger, and stood in the middle of the room awaiting her like a god of retribution.

'Make yourself at home, Jack,' she said, her lips curling. She might be nervous, but she was as sure as hell not going to be treated with such discourtesy. ' "Hello Theresa" would have been acceptable,' she added.

'I hear you're pregnant,' he said grimly, ignoring her words and the tone of her voice.

She gasped. 'Fliss told you?'

'I've not spoken to Fliss. Tandy rang me the night before the wedding. Fliss let it slip when they were discussing the possibility of you and me being godparents.'

'Well! I suppose I can be grateful that you didn't dash down the aisle in the middle of my mother's big day to have it out with me.'

'Don't be so bloody facetious.' Jack began to pace. 'I tell you this, Theresa: of all the times that I have been annoyed with you over the years, this is the first time I've been this angry.'

'Why? What business is it of yours?' she asked, her voice cold and deadly calm. She knew the inference he would cull from her words, but it was the only way she could stop him from having to accept any responsibility. She dropped her gaze before his look of stunned surprise. 'You mean . . .? No! I'll not believe that you – No! This is my baby you are carrying.'

'I am carrying *my* baby. You can get that into your head, Jack.' Still she kept her eyes averted.

'Are you telling me that the Theresa I've known all my life has slept with another man?' The hurt in his voice drilled through her.

She laughed bitterly. 'I slept with you, Jack. Does that make it any more right?'

He shook his head slowly. 'I thought – I . . .'

'One more experience under my belt, Jack. She felt her throat constrict as she uttered the words that would damn her in his eyes. 'Would you like a drink of tea?' she asked, her anger suddenly diffused by the sight of his slumped figure. He nodded.

As they sipped the tea, Jack broke the silence. 'What went wrong between us, Theresa?'

The look in his melting eyes struck hard at her heart. She watched him as he turned to stare into the roaring fire, that lick of hair she loved flopping over his eyes as he drank the remainder of his tea in one great gulp.

She wanted to reach out and draw him into her arms, but she had to be strong. He had no need of such a responsibility and, further, she still wasn't certain that he loved her. She couldn't bear the thought that he would ask her to marry him just because she was carrying his baby. Not once, even at the height of their passion, had he said, 'I love you. Marry me.' She couldn't be sure that their passion had been anything more to him than the urges of a virile young man.

'Why did Tandy think it was my baby you were carrying?'

'He misunderstood.' Her voice was steady.

'I'd better go. I've a long drive back,' he said suddenly.

She looked at the clock. 'You'll never go back tonight, surely? You're welcome to stay – there's plenty of room.'

Jack smiled wryly. 'Look what happened last time we did that.'

'Nothing happened that I didn't consent to.' Theresa's nerves were becoming more taut the longer they were together, but she was determined that he was not going to break her resolve.

Christmas was something that she had to get through. Her mam and Pat did their best to help them all enjoy themselves and, indeed, to a certain degree, their efforts bore some fruit. Theresa managed to hide her unhappiness under a thin veneer of jollity. Richard, however, was not deceived.

'Theresa, you'll have to try harder,' he muttered once. 'It's only the fact that your mother and Pat are wrapped up in each other that stops them from noticing that you are like a wet week.'

'I'm doing my best,' she scowled. 'Short of dancing the fandango on the table I don't see what else I can do – and as you have already noticed I'd be wasting my time anyway; they can't see further than their own noses.'

Nuala looked towards them. 'What are you two whispering about?' she asked, smiling at them.

'Richard was just asking me if I'd like to go for a short walk to air the brain.' Theresa smirked at Richard as he gave her a killing look.

'Wrap up well, then, I should think it's really freezing outside.'

They rose and left the room. 'You little minx,' Richard said. 'I hate the frost and, believe me, there is enough out there to freeze—'

'I had to get out. I'm stifling,' she pleaded.

He dragged his scarf and hat off the stand and waited while Theresa ran upstairs to get a coat and some heavy footwear. He wondered idly if Nuala had, in fact, noticed that the normally ebullient Theresa was subdued. She had toyed with her food and taken little part in the conversation at lunch, and although she had tried to put some effort into playing the board games, it was obvious that she didn't care whether she won or lost. Once, Richard had seen Nuala look at her, but she had been distracted by a yell of triumph from Pat as he won.

The freezing air was exhilarating. He had to confess that he felt better for being out of the slightly overheated room.

'There, you see?' said Theresa, holding his arm close to her side. 'I knew you would enjoy it. I know I felt as though I'd melt in there, and besides,' she added, 'I wanted to have a word with you.'

'I know what you're going to say.' Richard stopped. 'You're

going to tell me that you want to put off telling your mother about your pregnancy.'

She looked at him. 'How did you guess?'

'I would have suggested it myself,' he sighed. 'How can you tell your mother such news when she is happier than I've seen her since your father died? It would be too cruel.'

Theresa breathed a sigh of relief. 'I was so afraid you wouldn't see it that way. I watched the pair of them and I knew the time wasn't right. I will tell them soon, I promise.'

'You go back to England shortly, don't you?'

'I have a sitting next week. I'm doing it for a friend. He was at art college with me.'

'Have you got much work on after that?'

'A little, but soon I'm going to have to stop. I'm beginning to show more when I have no clothes on.'

'Would you do some work for Jacques? I told him I'd ask you. He already knows of your condition – I thought it better to be honest.'

'Does he still want me?'

'Of course, you idiot. Why do you think I'm asking you?'

'That's great! I had visions of me sitting in the flat with nothing to do but watch my bump grow, and the thought depressed me.'

'Have you seen Jack?'

Theresa hesitated. 'He came to visit me the evening after Mam's wedding.'

'He must suspect.'

'He knows! He had a phone call from Tandy, but I think I've managed to convince him that the baby isn't his.'

'I don't believe it. He is too intelligent. He will soon realize you were lying.'

'I've always been able to convince Jack of anything,' Theresa said.

'You mean you've always been able to twist him round your little finger. I think he'll go back to his hospital, give the idea more thought, and then realise that two and two makes four. I suspect you haven't seen the last of young Mr Ross.'

She shivered. The moon, with its frost ring surrounding it, was briefly obscured by a cloud, so her face was hidden by shadows. She was worried that Richard could be right; but she had to make Jack think that he was mistaken. She wouldn't put his career in jeopardy – not for anything.

'Jack has never actually said he loves me,' she said miserably. 'If he had, it might have gone some way to making me feel less sad about how things have turned out.'

'If you can't see that your young man is head over heels in love

272

then you lack insight.' Richard pulled away from the fence they were leaning on and turned for home.

Polly, who had been abroad for some time, came round to see her as soon as she got back.

Theresa had been looking forward to having a long chat with her. She craved the solace that she was certain she would find when she told her of the latest events. But when she told her of Jack's visit and their discussion, she was shocked when Polly echoed Richard's words.

'I can't believe that when he has time to really think things out he won't realise for certain that the baby is his – anyway, I don't know why you are so set on keeping him in the dark about it.'

'Polly, I told you. Jack has still some way to go before he qualifies. I will not let anything get in his way, besides, he has always disapproved of my wildness. This has proved he was right – I won't have him try to change me.'

'Has he ever indicated that he wants to?'

Theresa sighed. 'Many times when we were younger. He was always saying in despair, "Theresa, one day you will go too far".'

'Well! This time he helped.'

'Polly! Even if he did love me and wanted to take me on – I wouldn't let him do it. He can't afford a family.'

'You have an inheritance due when you are twenty-one – where is the problem?'

'Jack wouldn't let me use my money.'

'Then you and the baby can live on it and Jack can visit. You really shouldn't keep him away.'

'I'd go mad if I was living in Tullybra under those circumstances. You don't have any idea what my life would be like. I don't want to discuss it any more. I know what I'm doing, Polly.'

'Just when are you going to tell your mother? She might have some ideas about things.'

Theresa winced. 'I know I've got to tell her soon, but even so, I will make my own arrangements about my life and my baby's future,' she said, defiantly.

'I'll bet you were a difficult child,' Polly observed mildly.

'I was even more difficult when I reached my teens. Poor Eileen was sorely tried by me. I got the poor girl into some scrapes that were very near the knuckle.'

'I've always liked the sound of your friend Eileen. What does she have to say about all this? God! You haven't told her. She's going to be upset that you didn't confide in her,' said Polly, aghast.

'I couldn't tell her. She's going to be a nun. Can you imagine what she would think?'

'Sometimes I wonder what makes you tick. I would imagine Eileen has enough charity in her to circumvent any feelings of shock. She wouldn't become a nun if she hadn't. You do your friend a terrible injustice.'

The following day, as she posed, Theresa thought over what Polly had said and realised that she was right. Eileen was the one person who knew just how strongly she cared for Jack, and she *would* be discreet. She would write to her, and at the same time she would write to her mother and explain all – and then wait for the phone call that would surely come. Her pulse stepped up its beat and a vein in her temple throbbed as she sat under the hot lights. That evening she penned two letters and posted them off on her way to the studio the next day.

Two weeks had gone by since she had written her letters. She'd had the expected phone call from her mother. It had been a very emotional conversation and they'd both cried.

'I'll come over. I hate to think of you being there all on your own with this hanging over your head,' said Nuala. 'Oh, Theresa, my poor child. You should have told us sooner. I wish I was with you.'

'Mam, will you quit rangeing on there? I've had time to get over the shock. I'm fine. I wanted to tell you really badly, but I couldn't spoil your big day and then, when you got back, I couldn't either, because you and Pat were so happy.'

'I wish you had. Sure what are mothers for if not to comfort and cherish their young?'

'Mam! You're gettin' maudlin.' Theresa giggled, and Nuala's trembly laugh echoed down the line.

'I am, I am. I don't know whether to laugh or cry. I'm very excited about the idea of being a grandmother, but I'm concerned for you.'

'You're young enough to be a mother again yourself. Have you thought that one over? We could be wheeling our prams together.'

'Merciful God you're right there.' The line went quiet.

'Are you still there?' Theresa asked.

'I am. I'm in shock – Theresa! I don't think you did right to let poor Jack think the baby isn't his. He has his rights.'

'Mam, I don't want him to know and that's that. I explained all in my letter. Leave things as they are – and Mam?'

'Yes?'

'Thank you for not castigating me for what I've done.'

274

She and her mam would be all right. There was now only Eileen.

Eileen's letter arrived a few days later. That evening she took it out of her pocket and settled down by the fire with her cup of coffee.

Dear Theresa

Didn't I always say that I couldn't let you out of my sight? I'm happy that you are having Jack's baby, though. You two were always meant for each other. I always felt sad when you were at each other's throats, although it was more you at Jack's. I sometimes wondered how he put up with your wild outbursts. The man is a saint.

I think you are doing the wrong thing by not letting him become involved with you and the baby. He should be given a chance to make up his own mind. I suspect the bold Theresa Brady is more afraid of being turned down than she is about whether or not Jack will manage to finish his studies. Something should be invented to turn your brain around and set it to rights. At the moment you are thinking back to front – but then, hasn't it always been that way?

Your sorely tried and trusted friend,
Eileen

P.S. Before I take the veil I hope you will ask me to be godmother.

Eileen's letter made Theresa smile. Eileen had always seen through her. She had been the one, more than anybody, who had been able to prick the arrogance that she had sometimes shown. She realised just how much she missed her. Eileen was wrong, though – they all were. She loved Jack too much to see him tied down with a wife and a baby he hadn't bargained for.

Theresa had long finished her last assignment. A blind man on a galloping horse couldn't have missed her bump, and at six months she was finding it difficult to rise from chairs.

Polly was her salvation, although by now most of her friends were aware of her condition and were trying to help in their various ways. The place was coming down with white coats, bootees and dresses for the baby. The same reason for the colour was given by all. 'As I don't know whether it is going to be a boy or a girl I/we thought white would be a good choice.' Polly bought a yellow outfit: 'Just in case it's born jaundiced,' she laughed.

275

Every week she went to her ante-natal classes, and every two weeks she saw the midwife, who was pleased with her progress. She found the days were busy but the evenings dragged. Her mother had paid a flying visit and pronounced her looking fitter than she'd ever seen her. She stated that she was relishing the fact that Theresa was like some enormous great balloon, and not the proud, slim kitter she had once been, who'd made her look fat by comparison.

'Mam, never in a month of Sundays have you been fat. I was just too skinny and rangy. I'm eatin' like a pig at the moment.'

'Well!' said Nuala. 'There you haven't changed. You always did.'

Her visit had been a joy. They had gone shopping and recalled the time they went on the rampage without Colin.

'Then we were like two green cabbages trying to pretend we were the great sophisticates,' Nuala laughed. 'Now look at you. There isn't an area you don't know or a restaurant or store you haven't been in. You would find Tullybra very dull now.'

Theresa was sorry when her mother went back home; they'd had a great time together and she was back to spending her evenings alone. Sometimes a friend would drop in with a bottle of wine, but those times were becoming more rare.

The fortnight following her mam's departure had been a particularly barren one where evenings were concerned, so it was with a sense of relief that she answered a ring at the door. Polly was abroad on a 'shoot' for a fashion magazine, so she wondered idly who it could be. Shock streaked through her nervous system when she opened it and saw the tall figure standing there.

'Jack! What are you doing over here?'

'Are you going to invite me in?' he asked.

Seeing the firmness of his jaw, and judging the tone of his voice, she suspected that he was going to give her a hard time. She stood back so that he could enter, and stood waiting in silence for him to speak.

'Not much of a welcome, is it Theresa?'

'I thought we had said all we had to say over in Tullybra.'

'Not quite!' he said. It was obvious he was trying to keep control of his emotions.

'By which you mean . . .?'

He removed his coat. 'May I sit down?'

'Jack! Will you stop behaving like the hero in a bad film. Of course you may sit down. I'm just in a state of shock. I – I – you are the last person I expected to see. I thought we had said our final goodbye at Christmas.' Nerves were making her voice tremble. She stood by the fireside because she knew that if she sat down and had to get up again she would be like a beached whale, and she was damned if she was going to lose her dignity.

'You look—'

'Fat?' she interrupted.

'Blooming,' said Jack, and added, 'Stop being so defensive, Theresa – I'm just as nervous as you are. Could we have a cup of tea? By the time you've made it we'll both be calmer – we have some talking to do.'

'Yes, I will make a cup of tea, and I am not feeling nervous. I'm just taken aback by your visit,' she answered.

When she'd brought the tea and set it down on the small table, she poured for both of them and then removed herself to the fireplace again.

'Are you going to stand while we talk?' Jack asked in amusement.

'I've been sitting all evening.'

He rose and crossed to her. 'Then I'll join you. I can't sit there while you stand in your own house.'

'Jesus, Jack! Will you tell me why you are here and quit chuntering on about my manners?'

He took her hand and pulled her over to the settee. 'Sit down beside me,' he ordered.

To her dismay she fell heavily, losing all her balance.

Jack sat down beside her and helped her to right herself. 'You lied to me back in Tullybra,' he said, and calmly sipped his tea as he waited for her reply.

'I did not.'

'Oh! You didn't actually tell me that the baby you are carrying was not mine, but you put it so negatively that the inference was there – so, by inference, you lied.'

'I said the baby was my baby, and that is true. I shall decide what happens to us.'

'I know that the baby is mine. I know that for certain now, and the reason why I've taken the trouble to come over here is to ensure that you know I mean business,' Jack said firmly.

'Who told you that you are the father – apart from the misguided Tandy, that is?' Theresa's lips had set stubbornly, but Jack was having none of it.

'My information came from a reliable source. Nothing you say – or don't say, for that matter – will convince me otherwise. Furthermore, you are going to come back to Ireland; we are going to get married; and we are going to live happily ever after.'

Theresa froze. 'What – what?'

'Do I have to repeat everything, Theresa Brady?'

'You can't come into my house – flat – and make a statement like that, Jack Ross. How dare you! And not a mention of love – not ever – not in all the time I've known you.'

'I never knew how to tell you. I suppose I just hoped that you would know somehow.' He stroked her wrist.

'What a cod you are, Jack. Sure how could I read the signs? You were blowin' like the wind. The tide never came in and went out again more often than you did.'

'You never gave me much sign that you could love me, either, so.'

She sighed. 'I never knew how, any more than you did. That's why you caught me kissing Fergal. I wanted to know if I could tell you with a kiss, and then the one time that I came near it – when we took the walk along the Mile – I later discovered you kissing Pat and it kicked the heart out of me. I couldn't trust you after that.'

'In the end it took a gallon of drink to get us together.' Jack shook his head at the folly of them both.

Theresa hesitated before she spoke again. 'You are trying to tell me that you love me?'

'I always have. Ever since the day on the banks by the Tullybra bridge, when you leaned over me like the knell of doom and stared at me with those eyes and I felt your body nudge mine. I was lost from that moment.'

'But I thought . . .'

'You thought what?'

'Never mind,' said Theresa. 'Now what?'

'Tell me first that the little baby in there is mine.'

'It's an insult for you to think otherwise, Jack Ross.'

He put his arms round her, drawing her close, and tried to kiss her. 'I can't reach you for the size of your bump,' he laughed.

'Isn't it ever the way with us? We're useless at this. We'll have to put in a lot of practice.' She turned on her side and raised her face to his.

'Why were you so anxious to let me think the baby wasn't mine?'

'I didn't want you to have the responsibility in the middle of your studies, and I was frightened that you would reject me for going so far beyond the pale. You were always telling me that one day I would go too far.'

Jack murmured against her hair, 'I would never want to tame the wild, bold, Theresa Brady. It was why I fell in love with you in the first place. My problem was that I was too immature at the time to cope with my feelings.'

Theresa sighed with happiness. Dublin was near enough for

visits to the parents, and not so quiet that they wouldn't have some life about them – and when the time was right, Mam would tell Pat that Theresa knew she was his daughter. The trickiest thing would be convincing Jack that they could use her inheritance to live on till he qualified, but she was sure that she could manage to convince him. The great thing was that she was where she belonged, with the man she loved.